The Followers

Merlin Cullinan

"I hold it that a little rebellion now and then is a good thing"

(Letter to James Madison, Paris, 1797, by Thomas Jefferson)

"Riches are like Dung, which stink in an Heap; but being spread abroad, make the Earth fruitful."

(A New Guide to the English Tongue, 1740, Thomas Dilworth)

Part I

In The Beginning

"By constant feints and excursions, we may produce on the enemy an impression of intangibility...."

Sun Tzu, *The Art of War*

Where we first hear about the plan for a new Message to go out to the world ~ we encounter the first headlines and the stories behind them ~ the first of J's invisible diary entries is revealed, leaving us to wonder about the identity and methods of its creator ~ the value of religion as a tool for conversion and as a disguise for action is considered ~ we are introduced to the voice of a commentator and chronicler of events~ we meet some of J's elusive enforcers, and follow their action.

Who would get the Message?

He didn't care about who exactly would receive the Message. Its meaning would be assessed, dissected, interpreted, debated, and discussed for decades, so its content didn't have to be precise. Imagination and intelligence would furnish the message with plenty of meanings. Meanings could take care of themselves. The point was to provide the stimulus, the charge, the source.

At the corner of the Avenue Montaigne and the Rue Francois I is a set of traffic lights. On the south east corner stands an established Parisian fashion house, its sparsely dressed windows a sign of the riches inside, where two black-clad security guards peered through the reinforced glass of the locked front door. Diagonally across the street from the designer store is a small bistro where local workers began their days, taking small drinks and trading gossip. It was a good place to watch the comings and goings of pedestrians and cars, of hotel guests and residents walking their dogs. It was quieter than the river of sightseers on the Champs Elysees, two hundred metres north.

Cars here were parked bumper to bumper. It was considered impolite to leave any space between them for manoeuvrability without contact, as if every car needed to caress at least one other before coming to rest or departing. They lined up right up to the traffic lights, and to the very edges of every street corner, reducing visibility, and pushing pedestrians out into the traffic to attempt to cross anywhere. Between the two Peugeots parked on Rue Francois I immediately outside the store, a BMW Mini appeared to have found its way into a space few other cars could contemplate. It had been sitting there since six am, when it looked like its driver had been rewarded for vigilance by the departure of another early riser heading off, and before the parking restrictions kicked in. The departing Renault driver had ensured there would be no chance of the Mini being unable to park by spending a long time securing and maintaining the space against anyone else who decided for whatever reason that they were going to try and get in there.

The driver and the modest Renault set off towards the périphérique, never to be seen again. Soon after the Mini had nestled alongside the kerb and in front of the first Peugeot, the second Peugeot was reversed up even tighter in front of the new arrival, its snout now just sticking out over the edge of the corner, well within the tolerances of Paris's traffic wardens. Its driver then wandered off along the Avenue Montaigne towards the river. The Mini had been stolen during the night from a quiet street in Levallois where even France's most CCTV'd area had the occasional blind spot. The car's owner, a single woman of twenty five, had gone to her apartment for an early night after a long day working in the marketing department of a multinational food company with one of its offices in La Défense. The habits and movements of the driver had been monitored. Sandrine knew she wouldn't be using her car again until after the weekend, because Friday meant she would be having a meeting in the middle of Paris, and it was easier and cheaper to get to that office by metro.

Sandrine was 5'5'', with the dark hair and olive complexion of the Moroccan family background she had. She was pretty but not striking, not a traffic-stopper, which was ideal. The woman who stole her car looked similar enough for neighbours not to notice a difference from their apartment windows, had they been looking down along the street at the time the car was driven off.

The Mini was driven across the Rue du President Wilson and towards one of the buildings that had formerly numbered among the scores of Levallois' *garagistes*, those who had made their living for decades from repairing Paris's growing population of cars, before property developers had decided more could be made from people than metal. Again, and out of sight of cameras, the Mini had pulled up between two planted Renault vans, the discouraging space between them protected further by the positioning of what looked like a pair of heavy oil drums. The driver stopped, slipped out of the car, and climbed up through the small opening offered by one of the Renault's doors, moving up onto the passenger seat and sitting down, silently, staring now through the van's window and at the back wall of a grimy building. No looks or words were exchanged between the man in the driver's seat, and the new arrival. From the other Renault, a man in a one-piece dark blue overall stepped out and squeezed into the passenger side of the Mini, which offered more room than the driver's side. Five minutes later he was back in his van. The engine started up, the van reversed out of the space, turned, and set off towards the river and the roads out towards the suburbs. The dirty white cargo carrier was on its way back to the second-hand dealership in the north where its original number plates would be restored, and where its re-spray and valeting would ensure it was spruced up for a quick sale to some self-employed bargain seeker.

The Mini driver got out of the other van, silently returned to the car, got in it and set off towards Paris, and the parking spot in the 8th arrondissement. When she got out of the Mini, she went straight up Rue Francois 1, turned right into Rue Marignan, and then walked on towards the Champs Elysees, still giving up little of value for the street cameras, her clothes all part of a large-run major fashion chain's seasonal selection, the kind Sandrine selected, her walk imitative, her body language relaxed. All she had to do was walk along the main road, head up and right into the Rue Boetie, and, two hundred metres along, drift into the narrower streets, where she would find her regular café, her regular coffee and croissant, and her regular banter with the early morning crowd, who knew her well.

At eleven am, the new Rolls Royce Phantom drew up quietly in the Rue Francois 1 by the fashion house's side. The limited edition answer to conspicuous luxury glinted in its two-tone colours as it caught the September sun, tinted rear windows covering its contents from prying eyes. It could not park by the kerbside, so it drew up alongside the Peugeots and the Mini, a dark blue ML Mercedes pulling up behind it. Two men stepped out of the ML, its warning lights flashing. One of them called the store on his mobile, and nodded at the security guards inside. The other looked up and down the street, eventually positioning himself by the nearside rear door of the Phantom. These were two of the six-man private security detail on duty that morning. They were dressed in de rigueur black, their head-set microphones cueing their importance before the purring saloon car, ready to spring forward at the first sign of trouble, real or imaginary. The driver remained at the wheel, impassive. Small gestures punctuated the dialogue going on between the security men outside and the store's own security, as little time as possible passing by. Then the rear door of the car opened. The large 32 year old woman in the unique silk dress, shoes, jewellery and perfume stepped out onto the road, two of the security detail looking up and around the whole area. There were no other people in sight within ten metres of the car. The woman was led from it, the first security man trying to get her high-heeled bulk to move swiftly towards the store's door and its coutured interior. They were right by the little Mini.

At this point the green *Send* button on another mobile phone was pressed, and the Mini bomb exploded. Designed specifically for the place and occasion, its force was directed principally sideways but with a raking angle of fifteen degrees, making the most of the car's own metal and plastic as weaponry, and ensuring the destruction of the passenger cabin. The lead security man and the female passenger were blended with the burgundy element of the two-toned Rolls Royce. People some distance away reacted to the sound and pressure of the explosion, intuitively knowing something was wrong, shocked, trying to avoid shards of glass that had shattered and rained down. In the panic, people moved at different rates and in different directions, just trying to go somewhere, anywhere, away from the root of the problem. The button presser fitted in with those in flight. It wouldn't be long before he too was in a small bar, his iPod disguised protective ear plugs removed, taking a coffee and a cognac, listening to the speculation about the event as the grapevine began to replace the shockwaves in the area.

It had been easy. Following the Rolls Royce and its entourage for days had revealed the flawed approach. It was the same in other cities, in other countries, the bad habits of impatient egos. The pattern of places visited had been captured, the time appointments were made had been monitored, the varying of routes had been analysed. The fashion house was the weakest link in a circuit of shops visited, restaurants posed in, and favourite haunts re-selected. The security chief tried to get the woman to vary her choice of places to entertain and be entertained. After all, he was the brother of her husband. He got her to vary times, to the continued grievance of guests, but their curiosity guaranteed they still remained eager to meet her anywhere. She had weaknesses too, like the stubbornness she called her independence. She had particularly favourite things, and the fashion house's offerings were very high on that list. No amount of silk or chiffon could cover the chink of materialistic petulance. She was only an incidental target. Actually, Mrs Bannon was a part of the Message.

Headline: *"Paris Bomb Kills Hedge Fund Boss's Wife"*
Cue: *"You Can't Always Get What You Want"*

* * *

J's Invisible Diary. Entry.

It is never going to be easy. You have to make a mark and leave misleading traces of how you do it. There have to be signs that theorists can capitalise on in papers, books and magazines, blogs, blockbusters and merchandise. You have to resist the temptation, ever, to tell anyone outside the circle what you are doing, or record it on tangible material, at least while you plan on being alive on Earth. And of the circle? Well, as the old saying goes, three can keep a secret as long as two of them are dead already. But there are still material things, objects, items that have identities, significance, connections to other objects, to people, to sellers, buyers, places and times. Anything that is done, after The First Event, The Big Bang, has to be done in advance, so the discovery of process would take time, people producing histories to explain circumstances and circumspections, theories guiding the gullible to a convenient point of singularity, an explanation, faith in what truly happened, before. There can be no use for technologies lending themselves to easily discoverable forensics, those things that identify themselves and their links to you, their location, and yours, their ability to pick pieces of you up and hold them, nurture them so forensic lovers can fondle them and undress their secrets.

What can be done about the intrusive devices, the satellites, the

10

microphones, the other invasive penetrative probes? What about bugs, interceptors, electronic tags and digital photographic blankets smothering societies in encoded smog? It will in future be critical to avoid the use of words alerting remote ears to trouble, of pattern-revealing travel, of purchases revealing provenance. The internet has become a spore-ridden entity, like the post before it. In the 19th century the Postmaster General was also the Chief Spy, mail a gift for steamers and cypher fetishists. Co-ordination has to work at a distance, in undetectable or falsely-trailed ways. No-one could be seen in attention-raising places, doing attention-raising things. No-one could stand out. As long as there is nothing to trigger alarms immediately, nothing to suggest anything is other than to be expected, everything would look A-OK, normal predictable bad stuff as seen through reporters' eyes.

No, more will be needed because even the normal can look suspect to trained and nervous eyes. With meticulous planning there should be no reason to suppose any tracking devices will reveal what is really happening at first. People would be looking at other things, for other things, tidily within their own circumference of good and evil, of threats and risks. The complacency of the increasingly known will be setting in, and until the next surprise comes along to shake up the system, everybody will be busy doing the newly narrowly defined, and ignoring the freaks that bring in fresh voices and channels of doom-mongering.

We will use religious cover for some of the early actions. It will usually generate attention in short-hand ways, because the boys in the driving seat of the selected religion have already made a powerful investment in ways of getting attention, and they don't like to see variations in their tales being set up. They're also good for knocking the sometimes different ethical values of other religions, with their assumptive gold passes to the *ONE TRUTH* of their own persuasion. We can continue to build on a religion as a launch pad or as a powerful weapon in its own right. We'll speed things up this way, in certain quarters, using Faith in support of acts, our messenger. The time for a moral backlash has returned, bigotry in new guises. The Americans should understand this bit rather well, though they'll think it's the Devil that's delivering the message. What happens, ironically, will drive them towards a fanaticism of their own – the fight against All Evil. That will mean more laws and restrictions, the continuing dilution of long and hard fought-for freedoms in the name of liberty and security. But somewhere along the line someone is eventually going to start to get the real Message. Who owns the truth will only be a part of the scene.

11

Who owns what, and how much it is worth, and what is its real value, will be harder questions we will be spotlighting, for which there is as yet no legislation, but watch this space.

***

Years ago, before The Mission, there were stories about what could be done, what could be known. You heard the tourists tell tales that the parking ticket you once didn't pay in Sausalito would reach the ears of Immigration and you'd be refused entry to the USA. One day some group of government faithful clerics or clerks would let the parking violation officers scan the number of your rented car and the fine would be deducted from your mobile phone without them ever knowing who you really were, the GPS video time-encoded receipt being mailed to you and filed on the car's electronic user profile, both. Any problem, call the authorities. But not, just, yet. Personal RFID tags were not compulsory everywhere, nor embedded chips (outside the inside of pets). But the demand from the higher-ups would come. Security – defending personal freedom and liberty. Human Rights. Everyone in a half-mile radius of a crime at a specific time being automatically logged had not yet come to pass. But it would. And a thinker would be forced to update the view to read "Man is free, but is everywhere in electronic chains", and newspapers or social network sites, whatever form they took as the means of delivery changed, would have whole sections on who was close to whom when the what happened, whether they knew it or not, and how close an encounter to the celebrity or the crook or both you had come.

***

Some golf courses are more deceptive than others. The old Scottish links look open and inviting, and on calm days can even display their own version of kindness. When you throw in disturbed elements they are wild, and few tame them. Then there are the ones that look daunting, with great hills and valleys, man-made obstacles, huge distances, narrow greens and devilishly placed pins. There are the stunning, beautiful settings, where even getting to play requires ritual, patience, and impeccable timing. But whatever the location, there is always one thing they have in common. Whatever kinds of bunkers had been devised, whatever trees had been planted, whatever the grass, the birds, the wind, the salt, the sun, they all had space, and long spells

12

when players waited for others to play at a distance, waiting for a hole to clear, or taking time to select a club, ponder a putt, mark their cards, and eventually move on. They all shared rules, and within the rules were parameters about time and slow play. These were supplemented with statements about tee-off times and fair play. It all meant you could be reasonably sure where players would be on a course if you knew them and it well. If you really knew the players you would also know about their rituals, the way they made a practice swing, the way they addressed the ball, the time they took to set up the shot, the way and the place they would stand and wait for a partner to play, little patterns and dances in the game, the way some shots were pulled, the tendency for one to always take two shots to the green on a particular hole when others would try for one.

You also knew that, outside major tournaments, the crowds wouldn't be there, leaving players to contemplate the pressures of competition without being under the scrutiny of outside broadcast cameras, but still a tense challenge in a world-class sculpted landscape. Golf is the pursuit of power through peaceful means, the gladiatorial no-contact sport with its green blazers and its high-tech weapons. It was a different form of truth.

That had first struck Winton in 1990, waiting for things to develop on the edge of an enormous sand-trap, sitting in hotels, trying to pick up news, waiting for something to happen. Looking outside through the tinted windows, you saw the muted white of buildings, the hot glass, the pale bleached rocks, flatness and heat conspiring to shape a 50 degree mask you didn't want to put on. And what was man's testament to his conquest of the toughest types of nature he could tolerate? Golf courses. On television, a local tournament was pushing its physical tranquillity, its greenness, into the bedrooms of the hotel, languid voices making sporadic comments on clubs, scores, and clothes, a narrative underpinning the mental war going on in the minds of the sponsor-clad warriors, branded caps keeping the rough edges of the sun out of their eyes as they lined up for the long 17th. Satellite TV beamed down an earthly paradise some fifty miles from where earlier versions of Eden had claims to roots. For some of those close to the sets, who often also spent much time in the desert, in the heat, worshipping water, they struggled to applaud the greens and the endless water features of these Western-designed Edens. What did they think of the winner-designed course in their neighbourhood, pampered and nourished with their water, to keep the visitors feeling familiar and comfortable within the challenging surroundings? Even if they could, would they be

13

allowed to play? Even if they were allowed to, would they want to? Were there other things to do with time? It was not a set of questions many of them had time for. Maybe one day there would be a great Kuwaiti golfer, but he wouldn't be starting from where these people were, and when he got near the top he'd spend more and more time in America, which seemed to have golf courses everywhere you turned. This is what civilisation was supposed to bring you, the great dream, the great outdoors, the chance to demonstrate your integration in the great classless society that was the West. Is that what all the fighting was for? Victory summarised by the awarding of contracts to American golf-course constructors with some politician driving for democracy? The rhetoric would claim significantly more than that but this is what it was supposed to look like on the ground. Heaven on Earth. Despite the gap between the arid and the ripe, the struggle for survival and the struggle for status, Winton had indulged as well, knew his way round a few places, traded stories, heard the tips from a thousand amateurs, laughed at Lee Trevino's lines, the Gary Player routines, the ones he used for his own dealings, "The more you practice, the luckier you get."

He decided to try this advice in an area he had not had time to invest in before. The call of the grape, the soil, the terroir, and versions of civilisation those could bring, whether you drank wine or not.

This, after all the other missions, took him eventually to owning the speciality wine-store in Carmel Valley, California, about as far away from Bahrain and Basra and Baghdad you could get. He had become an oenologist, and then a dealer in all the Californian manifestations from bulk producers to tiny wineries tended by fanatical devotees. Carmel, The Valley, Monterey, the Ocean, Route 1 pointing south to Big Sur, San Simeon, providing a playground for business and 'W', the letter that signified his enterprise as well as his name.

When he took time off, that private time also now took in fishing, and keeping his hand in with his shooting skills. He had never married, feeling his formative years had not put him in the best of light to offer someone any real notion of long-term stability, or extended cosiness. There weren't many women who were prepared to take silence as the answer to questions about what he might have done, where, and to whom. So he formed fleeting affairs, working their swifter way from attraction to decay. Apart from the middle periods when occasionally the prospect of going where so many had boldly gone before had arisen, this life choice had left him free to respond to occasional new challenges as they came along, from those who he still knew and trusted. The ones who understood.

After training, he had only ever missed one target, but it still got to him, because it was beyond his control. That's why he continued to practice, to keep working to the highest level he wanted to believe he could still deliver from. After the Special Forces had tried, and been unlucky, W had been given a crack. It was the same venue, Tikrit, in Northern Iraq. It had only been billed as a slim chance, with agendas and itineraries shifting as usual at the last minute, friends and relatives of the target being let down, by non-appearances, sudden changes in details, diversions, and times. There was occasionally a ruse to sift out some other weak cousin who might have succumbed to the temptation of moneyed Satans offering dollars for co-ordinates and times.

But it was still worth a chance. The revenge of the disaffected Kurds, merely a tribal act of re-positioning, balancing, bringing justice in a way mountain men understood. Saddam would die with none of the pain of many of his adversaries, no consciousness, no prolongation of suffering, nothing stretched out on a long road to a tortured death. One bullet would take his unsurprised brain through the blender, a cocktail carrying traces of the fear and terror of generations.

The information suggested the leader would be there to share support on his birthday with some members of his extended family, for honouring the Baathist path which had kept him and most of his closest supplied with loyalty. He would be making a short walk from a car across to the door to a garden, where celebrations of his presence were to take place. Even with bodyguards, there was a good chance of securing the headshot, even at close to a thousand yards. The sightings, the angles, the wind, the temperature, the pressure, had all been meticulously factored. Winton had watched the mental version several times, the virtual projection of Saddam taking the short walk. The simulation all showed it was possible, at least for someone as skilful as him.

The car drew up, the guards got out, followed by the Man. Then, suddenly, he got back in the vehicle in the driver's seat. The guards stood back, and he launched off, dust enveloping the bemused onlookers, some worrying instantly about the lack of protection, others not daring to propose any thoughts on the ensuing action. But Saddam clearly thought he was among friends. He hadn't raced a car in the sand and the dust like this for a long time. Some of the guards followed instructions and hastily trailed the dust cloud in their back-up vehicles, taking care not to overtake the wild racer ahead of them. There was no way they could beat the driver and live to tell the tale. All Winton could do was watch the car recede, finally executing a hand-brake slide, turning and stopping, a laughing Saddam getting out of the car, his body language saying beat that if you dare. The back-ups slowed and stopped well before the Man's car, the head guard emerging to praise his master's handling. The Leader took his place again in the more customary back seat, and they all drove back to the village, stopping this time on the other side of the walled garden. The chance was gone. It hadn't even been a deliberate change of plan, the kind Saddam effected in more hostile environments, like the City he was less relaxed in. He was at home. There would be no shot that day. The Kurds eventually led Winton away, after his slow and stealthy withdrawal, their patience to be tested another time, maybe in another place. The job was debriefed, filed in the secret box, and never mentioned again.

Setting himself up in the woods facing the Pebble Beach course was much easier. He had been able to recce positions without fear, and had been able to monitor the patterns or incidence of walkers, joggers, curious dogs, lovers, and any others who decided to meander on and off the woodland paths near the fairways. He had two chances here, one coming towards him, and one going away. He preferred the first option.

From his place in Carmel Valley he drove up to Monterey, through the town, out past the old cannery row and the aquarium, past the cries of seals in the harbour, past the cheaper lodgings, the motels, coming up to the peninsula as it narrowed. He parked by his regular place where he could have coffee before setting out into 17-Mile Drive, where the local owners knew he liked to exercise around the woods and the rocks, close to the sea. He was like many early visitors, ready for brisk walking or jogging, the little back-pack with its knick-knacks, the water bottle. Why would they ever think about the parts of the rifle he was carefully transporting on the trips, assembling and then caching the device deeper in the woods, waiting for the moment? He was just another regular visitor, drawn to the beauty spot, but not so close he'd ever want to really live there, where the gawkers would be rolling by, trying to see what they could glean about the rich residents of the woods, taking in Lone Cypress Point, the photo-opportunity, moving on, past the golf courses and the Clubhouse, right on through, out, and into Carmel for the compulsory stop and wander round the arts shops, an altar to natural lifestyles at unnaturally elevated prices. Carmel was a souk for alternative pursuits and solutions to life's challenges, to reaching new levels of spiritual height and richness, in the belief that there didn't have to be anything ugly in life, if only you had the time, the money, the energy, or life-force to pursue and then capture the natural calmness and superiority that this trail had to confer on its disciples.

The course today was typical of the season. There was the usual moisture in the air, but none of the sea-fog that signed late spring along this coast. The sun was climbing, but weaker than in high summer, and the light was soft enough not to cause unwanted flashes off reflective surfaces. Checks at the clubhouse had revealed the tee-off time for the regular members' foursome, a group that preferred an early start, not wanting to mix with the cigar-chomping visitors whose every posture was designed to show they could afford to be playing rounds here, even if their handicaps would never trouble any pros.

Of the four female players, the woman in her late forties was the best, combining God's gift of a natural swing with a small fortune in top-flight lessons, and many hours on famous courses, especially this one, her preferred venue. The clothes were tailored to her own desire and colour choices, no brands being able to capitalise on her patronage, although she was careful to follow her favourite coach's recommendations on clubs and balls. She could have become a professional player, but had far too many other interests to keep her focused on one pathway.

The year before, she had had an accident pursuing her first love, horse-riding, in a fall on one of her husband's family ranches. Fortunately she wasn't alone, and the doctors had managed to relieve the pressure on her brain without causing her any long-lasting damage. Horse-riding might have claimed her life for itself, striving to stay way up there in the statistical table of causing most frequent deaths from sporting injuries, but it wasn't to be. Another horse-riding incident would have been too much to handle, and would contain far too many unpredictable elements, so research had moved on to other things.

The leisure time came from being the wife of one of the four children of a major grocery-chain founder, and with the three other brothers all in the business, the wife of son number three had been allowed to live a life of relative luxury once the old man and his abstemious ways had parted to meet the great Buyer in the sky. He would have choked at his children's growing collection of corporate jets and pretences to humbleness. That she was indulged was in stark contrast to the way other women were treated by the new ruling clan of the continuing dynasty. It emerged that female workers' were consistently and continually suppressed in the retail empire. Objectors were ruthlessly sought out and terminated, and harassed beyond their severance from the enterprise. The benevolent corporation was revealed as following practices and holding attitudes about its workforce that would have made nineteenth century mill owners proud. Thousands of women tried to hold down survival jobs in low-employment areas, and many were cast out for opening their mouths to speak about conditions while the Family's wealth soared.

The golfer's attitude was modelled on Marie Antoinette's, and the peasants were to be encouraged to eat cake, as long as it was bought from her husband's family chain.

Winton knew the form of the foursome, and how long it would take them to reach the selected hole, setting parameters for previous tee-offs or the off chance of others being allowed to play through. This would make his morning routine look normal and natural, and he ensured the usual people on his route said a hello, or waved, or passed the time of day as he took the first coffee, and as he would for the days and weeks to come. When they reached the tee for the drive, the grocer's wife would be going first. He knew from observation that she always used the same set-up. There would be the positioning of the feet, the look up the fairway, the minor adjustment of position and angle for the shot, the checking of the grip. There would also be the two practice swings, always the two, the slow-motion version of part of the drive, helping the relaxing and the breathing to come into harmony before the power would be brought into play and with the consistency of the well-trained and well-practiced, her head followed precisely the same actions. Winton knew the precise distance from his vantage point to the tee-off area, and her repetitive actions gave him a bigger opportunity to perfect his own shot. Just before she settled for the big drive, he squeezed the trigger, and the bullet's trajectory corresponded minutely to his calculations. She never managed the shot.

The gun was a totally customised long-range sniper rifle, the ammunition recognisable and traceable only up to a point where it suddenly would have had to have been somewhere quite different to exist, and the confusion would only leave intrigue. None of the package's parts, other than bullet fragments in and around the target's head, would ever be found again, scattered on a spread of sports fishing trips in the deep trench that came close to the shore. A waste of a fine weapon, but it was a weapon that could trigger no past. The golfing four were instantly surprised and then shocked, and others reacted to the sound or reverberation of the shot, un-silenced to enhance accuracy, and totally considered in the planning cycle. By the time anyone had begun to do anything practical, like try and get out of the way, or call for help, the gun was already disassembled, elements in separate disposable containers, waiting to begin their seaward journey. Winton

18

looked around from his forested point, and set off back on his normal route, his reactions to any other listeners or observers of the golfers honed to reveal a shared surprise and fear at the source of the commotion. By the time the emergency services and the police had locked down the peninsula, he was already back in Carmel Valley, and only the coffee-shop owner wondered if his early-morning customer had by any chance been near the incident at the time it happened.

After two months of professionally counselled grieving, the only tolling bells were the ones that signed someone at the supermarket check-out needed a price to be found that hadn't scanned in properly.

Headline: *"Supermarket Heiress in Golf Course Killing"*

Cue: *"Round Round Get Around..."*

***

We join the debate about privacy and security, and the apparently different rights of the rich and the poor ~ the notion of one powerful enough to create a new religion and change the world's behaviour, is laid out ~ concepts of revenge and the restoration of primal values are laid out ~ the occupations and attitudes of principal protagonists are captured ~ the weaknesses of wrongful protection are uncovered.

J's Invisible Diary. Entry.

See the lawyers marching in again, the double-sided prosecutors and protectors of privacy for gain. No, you only have everyone looking at you if you are poor. Let's look at all the sides. If you are rich, sure, you can't stop law enforcement agencies from working at knowing where you are, but if you pay enough you could have certain peekers and pokers scrambled out of the mix, encoded traces only being made available to the highest authorities as evidence in dire emergencies (which come with a separate premium rate for absolution).

The abolition of electronic slavery will become encapsulated in the Freedom of Movement Act (FOMA), which will be a brilliantly worded rationale for the absolute necessity to know where your criminally-minded citizens are at all times, whatever strata they claim they belonged to. An entire society under suss. But not their guns. No-one is going to make you put an electronic identifier on your gun, or its bullets, in the Fountainhead of Democracy. That would be too easy. God Bless America. Land of the Free.

But if you are, actually, you know, poor, you want the same things as the 'others', even if your ways of getting them seem intolerable.

19

These ones piss on people because it's the only way to get attention. The only time you look at the drunk on the subway is when she calls everyone a cunt. In this world, in what some call the concept of communitarianism, individuals just become examples of selfishness. This allows the Superior Beings to justify repressive laws for the sake of the common good. That's why things have to change.

No, the only way to fight is to use the accumulated wisdom of the past, a past which is often denied by the technologists, who believe all secrets can be revealed in the runes of their modern circuits and chips, capabilities and intentions both, despite being repeatedly shown that this is far from the case.

But let's return to the real question. The real question is what are all these people and machines protecting the voiceless citizen from? There always has to be some kind of manifestation. It was easy in the old days. Threats, they said in America, came from the colours of King George in The Old Country, or later from the rednecks of the south, or from those who thought the unruly blacks had forgotten their sense of place, from the red commies who were trying to nuke them out of the comforting world of 'Give us this day our daily bagel', from the yellow Chinese who were trying to take over the world with cheapness and chopsticks, from the white-robed Arabs, whoever they were, with their fanaticisms and their fundamentals and their unpronounceable names and claims, wherever they are.

The Devil takes many forms. One of the hardest to recognise is the one within. The one at home. There can surely be no devils in this camp when there are so many others dancing abroad? Better the devil you know, eh? The one you can see on TV, raised to the form of an evil deity, or the representative of an idealised evil concept, Terror, some 'thing' the government talks about, attacks, fights, the one the protesters demonstrate against, the ones whose gods cannot be, obviously. And you wonder if the One True God ever gets the creeps with all these politicians making out they are shaking his hand with their clammy claims and justifications.

One way forward is through the successes of the past. The Whisperers. The Navajos, the whistlers and callers creating no end of confusion for listeners trying to fathom a meaning from these living Enigmas in the Pacific, during The Second World War, the ones whose languages the Japanese couldn't fathom, passing messages for the advancing US army. But the problem always comes back to the basic question. If others are involved, what if they are caught? What if they can't resist sharing what they've done? Plenty of holders of secrets

20

cannot go beyond life without some form of confessional catharsis. What if they are discovered, or uncovered, by accident, by luck, by stealth, by design? Like the problems that have faced encoders for years, with all their Alices and Bobs and encryption keys, as soon as you give something away, you risk being exposed, and although quantum encryption promises un-crackability for now, there are probably lots of tomorrows left over to rewrite the history books of discovery.

What are the best ways to send the Message, to carry a signal? What is the best way to get a message across? Old questions needing old answers. Whatever it takes will be done to get the Message through, to get the right level of exposure, of notoriety, of a series of Warhol's fifteen minutes of world-changing fame, to set in train consequences that will stir actions and perceptions for years. A collection of messages. Seminal moments can only be seminal if they are noticeable and serious, so there are also potential issues of scale, of time and probability, of power law distribution curves. A new Moment is required, and a consequent momentum, its name to be decided retrospectively, the way it would be responded to after it has all been fully conceived.

***

Did all change-masters know how it would be, for a great part of the time? How long did it take the world to get used to one man's idea of change, how long before they realised they didn't want to dance any longer to one person's beat, flagging heart, settling mood? Could The Mission be accomplished alone? Did anyone else need to be involved at all? It would take longer, be a marathon not a sprint, but why not? J continued to assemble the questions. Preparation and patience were good things. After all, no-one else had commissioned this task. No group of paying malcontents was seeking his services. They preferred other methods. Even terrorism had fashion trends, elements which caught the imagination for a while until fatigue kicked in, and the next level of incomprehensible action came onstage, waiting its turn to be rationalised, to be put in perspective, to be feared but managed, contained without quite being tamed, an inconvenience like cold germs or warm cola. One thing for sure, the world would change, and only a few people would ever even remotely think he had something to do with it.

21

***

J's Invisible Diary. Entry.

People make claims they never fulfil. They have ambitions they abandon. They make threats they never execute. 'Getting their own back', it's sometimes called, or teaching people lessons. Revenge, an eye for an eye, a game of dare, a basic view of status, crime and punishment. The Message will begin as just a series of Acts. Maybe eventually it will lead to a new set of commandments, breed a new way of being, but all that will come later, and not solely from here. Scribes would say there would have to be new ways. And for those who don't follow, reminders that The Events, the Acts, could be repeated, on another scale again. Disobedience cannot be tolerated without a price. We all live in relative conditions. Who would want to pay that kind of price, willingly? It couldn't all be settled with money. Money has much to do with the whole problem in the first place, just like most of the time.

***

Alice was bored. The quaint house in Laurel Canyon was large enough to lose a part of you in, and in her view was less showy than the other house they had further to the west. Oh, and less vulgar, not so much celebrity trash in the neighbourhood. The views over the trees were soothing, the pool tranquil and mostly still except when the cleaner came round. The kitchen fought with the pool to be prince of calm, rarely bothered with action and only disturbed when Alice made middle of the night raids on vodka and chocolate. Oh - and when the two maids sometimes hung out there, except when you wanted them to do something useful, like bring more drinks and ice. Even the principal salon was almost always empty, keeping company silently with several recognisable pieces of modern art, which she tolerated as assets rather than aesthetically.

Her main directory stored enough contacts to keep most star gazers in lunches and dinners for months, at parties for as long as you could stay awake, and in supply from everything her exclusive emporia could muster, the ones you couldn't totally rely on the staff and the concierge services to find themselves – not to her level of nuanced satisfaction. In the early days, only two years ago, the new levels of service and attention had been sampled like trinkets from the smaller packages under the Happy Holiday tree. Surfeit quickly dulled use. So many things were taken for granted now, or abandoned around the house like out of favour teddies, distractions tossed aside or put in cupboards. They couldn't scratch the itch of the tawdry boredom of Wednesday afternoons, Thursdays, or most any days. Before she had married Fyodor, the man twenty years older, she had wanted all that had been spread out in front of her. It wasn't her main interest, but it helped she had found a short cut to an additional fountain of money she would have had to work for ever to find on her own, even though she wasn't exactly destitute. A Provider had materialised. The twenty year gap had seemed like nothing at the euphoric time of seduction and capture. The future was way beyond worrying about. Now was the place to be. In the light of Hatfield's restaurant that day in October, he'd looked like the attractive grown-up version of most of the talent she'd been spotting.

He was with two male friends, she with a female friend. He had been spied, and she wanted to know more. It turned out the man was available, meaning the divorce had been put behind him a long time ago, before it was too expensive, and he hadn't gotten around to changing his status again. He was something very successful in software, according to her aide the maître d', who had chosen to share some of his knowing confidences with his safe female friend. For a short period after they were formally bonded she would escort him occasionally to those dull but sometimes necessary parties where heterosexual couples were the preferred mix – it was still like that in some parts of the city. Most defence contractors weren't renowned for gay soirees, certainly not where media coverage was guaranteed.

So, he was big in software and he didn't want to talk about it, which was great by her. As long as his jet had a bathroom and cold Krug, she wasn't interested in anything electronic or digital. Later on, the nearest she ever got to having her attention caught in the plane by something electrifying was by the blond hair of one of the regular pilots. It turned out he was also a frequent user of the restaurant, but on most nights when she wasn't. It had been a girlfriend's birthday that had got her to the place on a Tuesday, a night she'd normally be in her apartment conducting damage limitation after a protracted weekend of challenging new encounters. The official celebration of Naomi's birthday had been up in Malibu on the weekend. Now, on the date that was indicated on the birth certificate, it was time for the girls to share the things that couldn't be covered at the main event. They'd known each other for about eight years, when they'd met at UCLA, where Alice studied law fitfully, and they had become confidantes about their respective conquests in the world, comparing and contrasting life's challenges and adventures as regularly as their different schedules allowed. Naomi was in television, working in a sea of lawyers on contracts with clients and prospects, especially the Disney Corporation. She was making a killing for someone on merchandising and product placement deals. She wasn't doing so badly.

Alice had taken a different path. She had a small, by her measure, private income from the family trust her great grandfather had established. This kept her in a certain sort of style, but not the most exciting it could be. It was certainly a style that was significantly grander than could be sustained by what the local law practice paid her in LA. Instead of following Naomi's way, or that of many others of her college peers, a slide into a cosy profession, a sacrificial laying down at the altar of a major law firm, or a hitch up with one of the hedge fund boys back east, she had deliberately chosen not to fulfil her mother's dreams, and had gone for a different kind of lifestyle. Under the cloak of 'making a difference', there was always a part of her that needed a fix, a twisted kind of thrill, to remind her that she was alive underneath the collection of two-piece suits. Dipping into some of LA's less salubrious streets was one of the ways she fed the need. It hadn't been a cinch, but she had managed to persuade the recruiters that she had a planned career route and desire, and that her actions were not a deluded attempt to be some kind of self-righteous armed social worker, or twisted rejecter of her privileged past, a dangerous seeker of penance among the dispossessed of Compton. Of course, deep inside there was a piece of rebelliousness against the siblings and the relatives who had graced the past and the present with their acquisitions and their success, but what got her the job was the way she was able to connect herself to a different form of reality, convincingly. Her motivations were assessed as soundly based. At first she was treated as a weirdo by some of those who recognised the name and the connection, but most of the sarcasm and the jokes slipped away once those close to working with her felt she was working out fine on the real job. It was only like the movies in the sense that she still lived in a large apartment that her regular pay wouldn't cover for the rental of the hallway, and she tended to keep quiet about some of the social scene she was connected to. Her closest friends too wanted to know about her 'street life', but many stayed clear, thinking they might catch something nasty from the high society dabbler in low life. For acquaintances it was either a cheap source for smutty jokes or just too dull to mention. There was nothing trendy to note about her company, its location, or its co-workers. Her life was compartmentalised, and that suited her just fine. Being an almost anonymous lawyer had brought its own, surprising, rewards, but it couldn't deliver the whole pizza. She still needed something else. That's why she remained a huntress.

She never wanted to give up everything at 22 to be arm candy for a perfectly dentured rich kid. The someone, if anyone, would have to respect what she did, who she was, the time she needed for herself. Or the deal was off. This excluded a big bunch of contenders. A lot of career builders wanted to share their almost total absence of free time with equally minded career partners, at least until the first millions were working to build the next millions, and we're not talking options here. The chosen one would have to be different from those just looking to tick the next box in life's grand agenda. It would have to be someone, like her, who didn't depend on one thing.

Relationships with her had usually been more about take than give, but here was someone that had caused her to lapse. She wanted to give. She thought she had become a victim of that chemical process called falling in love. She had returned to the restaurant the following Tuesday, and there was Fyodor with two different male friends. Maybe it was the routine, like hers, to get together and run through things, the weekend, the business. She got the maître'd to arrange for the sommelier to deliver another bottle of the pinot noir their table was drinking, having checked that two bottles was normally OK for the party. Fyodor looked around, saw her, smiled and mouthed thank you, returning to the meal with his companions, three rib-eyes signalling there was not a lot of vegetarianism going around. He came over to her table towards the end of the meal.

Whatever that was for, thank you very much anyway.

He didn't introduce himself, knowing she must have figured at least that part about him from the staff.

That's fine. Perhaps one time you might like to share one of those with me, as opposed to with those charming men you are with tonight?

She gave him her personal card, and a confident smile.

Well, Ms Remmer, we might just try a little tasting sometime.

He smiled too, and turned smoothly away, returning to his table and inquiring friends, her card already settled in the left hand pocket of his chinos.

And that was their first face to face encounter.

She was used to that. Talking to strangers, asking questions, assessing people, judging reactions. Except here she didn't really feel she was talking to a total stranger. There was something she felt she already knew about the man she had decided to meet, including the fact she thought he would say yes to a rendezvous. The phone call came

25

three days later. Fyodor had been busy, out of town, whatever, but anyone who was prepared to pay $250 for a pinot noir just to say hello was worth returning the complement for and she agreed to dinner some two weeks later when they both had a space that looked like it wasn't rushed but they might still care.

She told him what she did, what she'd done, and then some more about what she'd done, and why, and where. He'd passed the first test, the listening test. Then he delivered the media-friendly autobiography – school, Stanford, PhD in electronic engineering, a spell with the government, and then the establishment of SoftWorks. Despite her obvious intelligence she made it clear that the only technology that interested her was the stuff she needed to be on top of for her job. He told her that one day what he was doing would probably feature in many people's lives too, but for now it was taboo to talk about, and they parked it there. There was the usual laying down of markers, about the brief early marriage that hadn't worked out when he had got involved in government projects he wasn't able to discuss at home. They tested each other briefly on families, leisure, travel, tentative explorations about places, issues, perspectives, the food, the brilliance of the now white wine. The evening folded, they pecked and made polite touches, and then they both faded into the night, agreeing in principle to a second encounter, which would probably include all the trimmings. That's what she had decided. That's the way it happened. She would take the next step.

She got him from the restaurant and took him home to bed for the conversion, when he would have to take a decision that she was more than a good dining companion and wine connoisseur. She liked the smell of his skin, he liked the taste of hers. By breakfast they were planning another encounter, a little closer than the second one, somewhere else, somewhere almost neutral where there was no baggage. They opted for Las Vegas, where memories could be shed like skins. They were ready to take chances, to gamble. They were on a roll. She wasn't inquisitive about his work, but she clearly liked its rewards. Even she was getting a little tired of the rebellious role she had taken. He was surprised about Alice's line of work but at the same time he liked that she was headstrong, that she had specifically chosen this path. He also liked the way she couldn't avoid her past completely, and played the role of sophisticated society partner when it suited her. They enjoyed the space and freedom they both felt was at the right level in each other's company.

It seemed like Alice might have netted a rich admirer, lover, and friend, and Fyodor had the woman he had never come closer to, who judged him for who he was, he thought, not just for what he had, who kept him vibrant and alive. But he never stopped working, and she made him feel even more energetic in his work.

That was the beginning of the troubles.

Going in deeper she knew he worked obsessively. She thought that might change, just enough, when they were together properly, to make her a little more than a solo soul rattling round the houses in California and Colorado, and the hotel suites on the occasional business trips. But whatever he said, something always came up. It could be a glitch with a program, a client with a concern, an investor deal to be closed, a new angle to be thought of and produced. The excuses were always the same. Just a little more time today honey, and then we can be free together. But the debits began massively to outweigh the credits. There'd never be time. All the catching up in the world wouldn't count towards anything. He was set up in a life of events and deadlines of his own after all. Although he loved Alice in his own way, he lived for his work, though he couldn't confess this, not understanding it. He was driven by virtual things, by intangibles, by trying to predict mid-term futures out of present chaos. He wasn't rooted in today. He thought Alice was a spirit who would wait around to share some kind of end-game. He lived for a world of tomorrows. Ignoring many of the potential rewards of the future, Alice lived for the present, and increasingly dismissed the future as not worth waiting for. Her day job was OK, it still satisfied a portion of her needs, although Fyodor would say it was about diminishing returns. Fyodor, when he was still around, could occasionally make her feel that wonderfulness of their earlier encounters, but it wasn't enough. Ultimately, despite her claims she wanted to stay, she was already letting a part of herself start to run away. She wasn't going to martyr herself to a relationship in which she was only a fleeting presence. What was wrong with Fyodor was that he wasn't really there for her on her terms, and he couldn't be. Whatever he said or thought, he couldn't really conceive that part of her nature. She was twenty years younger than him, and she was missing out on now. Fyodor was regular and reliable. That was the problem. He was like clockwork. No, he was like his super accurate software, a great piece of dependable software. On Tuesdays he was back with the boys. She had a full diary of events she was increasingly a loner at. She got more out of the other law practice guys than at home. It was exactly not the way it was supposed to be.

That was when Alice decided to have some fun again that wasn't love, to restore the game of life to a part pre-Fyodor era, just to give her the kind of company she craved. Fyodor wouldn't notice, and Alice believed whatever she did would not touch the esoteric relationship they now had. It was about reclaiming a part of the state of herself. She noticed increasingly that the free time with Fyodor was having less emotional meaning, that her smiles were imperceptibly fading, her laughter not quite resonating in the air so much, her sense of excitement, of daring, becoming an old ghost. She wasn't lonely but she was more alone, and the gap wasn't being filled with girlfriends or gay friends. She wanted some fun, the kind that only came with certain kinds of men. Not relationships, just brief encounters, no further questions, no return calls, no e-mails, no see you agains, no backgrounds to tar the moment. With a twist.

She would have to play this game in different places, as different people. She wouldn't play the game anywhere near where she worked. So she began with three areas outside her Alice domains, two across the city and one up the coast, where no-one she knew would likely be surprising her with a Hey Alice shout across a bar or restaurant. She had plenty of choices for times. Fyodor kept up his endless pace on discovery and experiment. She knew how to balance her looks between seductive and distant, knew how her techniques worked in most restaurants. Dinner, make the move, never go beyond the first date, play out a story, figure a new identity, listen to some guy do the easy bit, talk about himself, and then take the initiative again, somewhere else. She would lead them to whatever hotel she was staying in 'on business', just passing through, and then have playtime. Some went home late, some stayed, but by morning it was all over, whether she was working or not. She was careful not to leave ID information for the really curious, the bag rummagers, those who might want another ride. Her hire cars were parked in another place, there were no incriminating credit cards, licenses, un-coded mobiles, stray messages, or talkative hotel receptionists. She was just another Diane Keaton looking for Mr Goodbar, only this time her name was Stephanie, or Stella, or Susan, with surnames she'd pick from the day's paper, and a diversity of consulting jobs that were vague enough to talk about without betraying any professional shortcomings, based on the jobs and lives of friends she knew well enough to give her plenty of scope to create believable anecdotes, and certainly enough for first encounters of the none too serious kind.

Sometimes she closed out before the evening's approaches had really kicked in – a vibe, a style, something in the look, the language, that made her decide to pick up the tab and say she was just feeling generous that day, nice dinner, and that was all. She would say goodbye, a tiny piece of her hoping the target wasn't too upset at her discontinuing largesse. Once or twice at bars the tables were turned, bottles returned with polite no thank you's from guys who were too attached, or from those whose companies wouldn't accept what might be considered bribes, or from those who thought the CCTV might catch them in a moment of transgression. But generally she was a good chooser and didn't make too many mistakes. Certainly there hadn't been any real surprises in the bedroom, no sudden personality shifts or behaviour. Both parties appeared to enjoy the show.

She kept an on-line diary under yet another name, noting a few bio details she'd picked up from her ephemeral admirers, her little comments and ratings part of her fanzine for herself, able to be adopted for different personas, capturing the frailties of the heterosexual cowboys and angels she stole and converted from George Michael's song. To those few who ever got pushy about contact details, she gave them fictitious business cards with a tame mobile number and e-mail address, a little indulgence before she shed them, the detritus of the modern digitally-aided affair. She could read the shy ones, the self-styled studs, the strong boys, the ones who thought they were the Fabulous Foreplayers, the ones who got up in the night and combed their hair in the vanity mirror – you got it. Her survey of men gave her confidence and cynicism in equal measure. She'd always liked the early soft romanticism of Fyodor, but he didn't respond to calls for more. She was continually chasing something else, some further clues to her own self, to where she might be.

That was both the problem and the opportunity.

The problem was that she was good in her variety role. She was never tempted to tell even her closest friends about it. Her lawyer's 'street-life' was as far as they got, her intimacies only covering the part of her life she played as Alice. These were her other lives, after work and Fyodor and their barely tangential circles. It was planned but sporadic. She thought none of the players would really suffer any real lasting damage. If Fyodor called when she was away, she always had a response quickly, and he trusted what she said. But he was really only calling to remind himself she was there, she thought.

Fyodor was, in a way, working in software, and it was a good cover for his real work. Software was useful – there were always sensitivities about new ideas and intellectual property rights, talk about non-disclosure and lawsuits. What he was really working on was the development of intelligent radio frequency identification dust. He was working on micro technology, on better means of tracking things, including people, wherever they might be. This dust had to be robust enough to stand up to vastly changing conditions, be difficult to detect, and be smart enough to be active only when prompted by external triggers. For the government, he was big in a world of tiny spies, the kind that first might be deployed in the 'war on terror', but which just might then find themselves being deployed on everyone, for their personal security. Following his first fortune, which really had come out of creating some intriguing insights into algorhythms, and consequent products, he had been lured by the world of real-time mass-interconnectivity, of mapping crowds at the level of the individual, and some with darker agendas and even deeper pockets had found ways to encourage him to look at yet more adventurous solutions, as the government described the more distasteful elements of its defence agenda.

Alice wondered how many of her catches were doing the same kind of thing, not secret projects of the government kind, but the people portfolio, and how many of the other women she saw were building their own Other World in her vicinity, the world built on lies and deception, just like the real world, or all those dream spaces everyone creates for themselves, where you live and write your story, occasionally observed, occasionally visited by others, maybe abducting you and taking you off to their own worlds to be part of some other narrative. Sometimes people really did live on other planets.

The opportunity in this wasn't all hers. It was also that of one of those who was observing her. She hadn't got to the idea herself that anyone else could possibly have noticed what she was doing, and she was unaware of the systematic steps that had been taken to map her new private world, the world that was still connected to the observable universe that was Fyodor's. It would have been difficult to do what had been decided if she had been working harder in her job. It would have been harder and potentially more dangerous to have tried to see her in the big houses Fyodor owned, where there was always a chance of someone appearing on the scene at just the wrong moment, or the security system actually being efficient enough to withstand some professional tampering.

Death through the accidental over-reaction of opportunist burglars wasn't a big story, and wouldn't carry any lasting weight. Now perseverance was paying off. Timing was working.

One of security's principal weaknesses is that in what is supposed to be considered by those living in it to be a civilised society it still doesn't know, today, everything about everyone at the same time. It's a kind of security uncertainty principle. There is still an attempt at balance between control and discretion, observation and freedom, protection and privacy. Almost all intrusive actions are positioned under the clichéd umbrella of protecting personal freedom for the greater good of society. Outside the military it often turns out to be frustrating for those supposed to deliver security, both to do it without upsetting the protected too much, and to manage their own feelings about the average person's total inability to respect the need for certain behaviour to get the best out of it. The closer you get to people the more they resist it, unless they get addicted to it like some pop stars and politicians. It is an invisible juggling act except where the presence of beef gives the wrong impression that protection is all around.

The time-scarce wealthy were often the hardest to manage, wanting the garage gates open long before they arrived at the house, the doors left open, unchanged codes and keys, cursory ID examinations. Yet they demanded Protection as a right, and thought that the more money they forked out the thicker and deeper and smarter it all would be, as long as you didn't have to take it too seriously of course. That was for the security detail to worry about. If you weren't that week's rap star it didn't necessarily look good to be surrounded by heavy flesh. It drew too much attention, or put out the wrong message – you're a gangster, a drug dealer, the wrong kind of big shot, or just paranoid.

It was these kinds of attitudes that had made it so difficult to conduct realistic checks at airports, and why many opted for the increased expense of going into private aviation to avoid the public gauntlet of the official frisk. There was also the bonus of patronising those who only flew 'commercial'. There were machines around that could see exactly what you were and weren't wearing and carrying, from weapons to prosthetics. But some folks would clearly rather be blown up than have some $10 dollar an hour security guard see what shape you were in as you walked through the scanner. These were the attitudes that made this kind of security expensive and slow, gave it a contemptible reputation, and pushed yet more costs and time lost onto the fare-paying passengers.

The vanity of regular ordinary people was a drawback for the very same folks, and not many people got blown up twice after the first lesson. This was precisely the good news that those who wanted to breach security could explore. It was less the systems and processes, but the inevitable lapses in de-motivated security operatives that rewarded the keen-minded vigilant. Here was the gap where you could often exploit attitudes driven by events and circumstances – the ones who should know better but can't help themselves in wanting to be a little different, sticking to rules and regulations in some areas and breaking them to suit in others, chasing the little frissons that made life marginally more exciting.

Alice was like that. It made her one of the ideal candidates.

***

As usual, research produced the short-list of prospects. More detailed field work then took place. Where did these people spend their time, their money? Who did they spend time with? When, if ever, were they alone? What was their security like, at home, and elsewhere? Where were the weak points, where were the holes, the windows of opportunity? It was during this phase that Alice was identified as a most likely prospect, as another player, with a usefully secret life. Observation and tracking made it clear there were two agendas, and no other proper surveillance. She had a predilection for late thirties to early forties males, unlike her choice of husband, and selected ones who were out dining with male friends, those who had self-confidence without dominating events. She didn't check them out in any depth, like with her future husband, because she didn't want to become known by other maître d's in unfamiliar restaurants, and it lessened the thrill. The photographs showed patterns in the selection. With careful management she could be the caught not the catcher. She picked a high-end portfolio of places where she could make a play – nothing like weekly appearances, too obvious, more of a loose cycle that could harmonise with the business trips the executives she was portraying might make. You could follow the form. It helped the planning.

***

She took the phone call from Sam, three days after the wine sting at Bouchon's. Not too fast, not too slow.

Hey. Thanks again for the wine, it's Sam here.

Oh, hi. Just a moment.

She took her mobile, mouthed to her work colleague and pointed to the door that she was just stepping out to field the call. Her colleague thought it could have been a client not wanting to have a confidentiality broken, who knows, so it was no problem to see she took the call in the reception area, where no-one else would be paying too much attention, the receptionist busy on other calls.

Sorry, just had to step out of a meeting for a moment. So, you liked the Margaux. And your friends too? It's a good year.

Why'd you do it? It's not as if you know us, and it's not exactly cheap.

Why do you think?

Because you want something?

Well, maybe. Maybe because it's a way of saying hello without the pain of instant rejection. You know. Face to face. That hurts.

She was balancing between the seductive and the shy. She knew that if she pushed too hard these guys would pull back, so the shyness played well against the surprise attack.

Well it's certainly a change from being offered a Bud. Thanks again.

Look. No problem.

Maybe you'd like us to return the compliment sometime?

Maybe *you* can. Any suggestions?

Well, there's another good restaurant not far from where we met. It's called Opal's. Maybe you know it, and perhaps there could be something to surprise you with there. How about next week?

Can't do. But the 24th, two weeks from now, Thursday, would be good.

There was a pause. There often was, and she could sense his mind riffling through dates and commitments, apologies and excuses.

Look, the agenda looks pretty good around then. Let's meet at, say, 7.30, after the first groups have gone, and we'll pick something tasty.

OK. See you there.

Look forward to it.

She knew the next potential fix was lined up. The familiar tension of excitement and doubt pushed down from her stomach, and she thought about how the evening would play out, from the compliments about the wine to the closing of her hotel bedroom door, with Sam sliding into bed, and her.

After one and a half bottles of wine, water, and lobster tails, and the run through the background stories, it was after eleven, time flying while two life stories were compressed in the spinning perfume of pheromones they were now trading. He paid the bill, another rite of passage, and they walked out into the autumn evening.

Don't know about you, but there's no way of thinking about driving now. Share a cab? You must be staying somewhere round here, and wherever that is it can drive on home.

As a matter of fact it's El Encanto, and passing on the driving sounds like a good idea.

They got in the cab, and as it set off they both looked out of their windows, taking a break from the story-telling. Their hands found each other and held on as the evening asked permission to enter the next stage. As they pulled up to her hotel, she turned to him.

Look, you're not driving anywhere, and there's always another cab. It's been a lovely evening. Why don't you come into the hotel, we can have a drink, or a coffee, whatever, and say goodnight there? It's better than here, or the sidewalk.

Are you sure?

Really sure.

Well OK then. Just the one.

She was in.

They both settled on another cocktail, and a low sofa under the dimmed lights, some chill-out music lounging in the background. They'd found a couple of themes, travel and art, and were swapping stories about European cities they'd found romantic and cultural in an intertwined way. Paris. Venice. Florence. Carrying them off to savoured moments, the fact that they had both been there with other people was not worth mentioning in the flush of fresh discovery. As another hour passed she decided it was time to stop the sport fishing and go for the trophy photograph.

You could probably do with a nightcap, somewhere quiet. Let's go.

With that she signalled the bartender to add the drinks to her room number, and had Sam on his feet and moving towards the exit faster than he could compose an objection, even if by then he'd been disposed to form one. He was getting happier to see where this lady was leading, and if it was anything like the far-ranging conversation they had had, it could be a great place to be taken to.

Suite 105 was one of the grander addresses at the hotel. Her seduction ritual included securing rooms with spacious balconies or private gardens and verandas, somewhere to watch the stars, or somewhere to relax in after the night's performance, her own post-coupling peaceful space. She never chose the absolute best for these plays, because it didn't seem right for her character to be there, even though she could easily afford it. It was still expensive enough to make her new partner feel he hadn't made a mistake by not saying goodbye earlier.

So your corporation isn't too tight on travel expenses?

Well. It comes with the level, so don't feel too uncomfortable about it.

It was too late to stop drinking, and while Sam helped himself to champagne, Alice under the name of Andrea disappeared, returning in a bathrobe, barefoot, holding a glass of Meursault up to the air. They chinked glasses, looked at the stars, and looked at each other as the slow jazz played itself to sleep in the bedroom. When he'd finished the drink, she took the glass from his hand, put it slowly down on the glass table on the balcony, took his middle finger, and led him inside. By the time they reached the bed she had shed the bathrobe, and as she let go of his finger, it all began.

By 7am it was history. She was awake, making sure Prince Charming was responding to the early morning light. He would be showered and gone in fifteen minutes, a relatively discreet departure, the short walk out of the hotel grounds, past the houses, and on down towards the centre of Santa Barbara, time to find the kick-start coffee, call a cab, and retrieve his car before going to work and freshening up in its always open spa, another incentive to encourage people to stay on the work campus where they could keep fuelling the company's future fortunes and fame. She opened the doors to the veranda, smiling at the half-drunk Meursault still sitting on the table-top in its ice-bucket, and let the curtains flutter in the morning breeze, freshening up the room from its night-time aromas. As usual, her breakfast order was delivered, a combination of a desire for privacy, and a wish to not be noticed in the hotel's open restaurant, even though the layout of good food there was very tempting. After the fruit and the water, it would be time for the shower, and the relaxed leaving routine. There would be no-one dashing into the law office at eight this morning.

The observer was pleased to note Alice's consistency with her playground routine – structured play, wasn't that how the child psychologists would describe it? He looked like a local businessman, open-necked button-down shirt, chinos and loafers, the small shoulder bag for an iPad or odd paper, someone on his way to meet a colleague, to share thoughts about a conference or the way the day's agenda was shaping up. He walked with the quiet anonymous confidence of a person knowing well the one he was visiting, the Californian middle-class conservative uniform causing no concerns in this environment that a T-shirt and flip-flops just might, even though that was often the mark of a Palo Alto visitor trying to keep his multi-millions discreet – the inverted snobbery that caused many a traditionally-trained salesperson to miss a beat when they wondered what the scruffy-looking dude was doing eyeing up the Ferrari.

The veranda looked across the slopes of the hotel towards the sea, and each room was designed to keep guests' eyes on the panoramas, and not on each other's neighbours. Alice emerged once more from the interior, showered and again in her bathrobe, which she unconsciously pulled a little tighter around her as she noticed the man in the blue shirt ambling towards the rooms in her direction. She saw him go to one of the other rooms, out of sight for a minute, and presumed he had found who was looking for. She decided it was time for the small indulgent coffee she allowed herself each morning, and sat down to pour it. The guy who didn't make her head turn appeared again and made his way toward her, beginning to sign that maybe he wanted to ask her a question. She watched him make his approach.

Excuse me, the numbering around here's funny. Do you have any idea where 101 might be – it doesn't look like they described it at reception?

Well, he wasn't asking for her room.

Dunno.

She summoned up as much lack of interest as she could without appearing to be totally objectionable.

He turned left to peer along the walkway, stepping slightly nearer to her own balcony, all the better to see whether any stray room service people were, for whatever reason, about to walk into or out from the surrounding rooms he knew were supposed to be vacant. He paused and looked at her, face on, and then he opened his bag, looking like he was about to start scrabbling for a note or confirmation of a room number. She raised her left arm languidly and pointed in the other direction, up and further back on the slope.

Maybe it's up around back where the other gardens are.

The sentence was long enough for him to make the move. He jabbed the needle into her left forearm, uncovered from the elbow down by the bathrobe. She began to form a loud objecting surprised expletive, but his other hand had already covered her mouth, and he had begun to manoeuvre her back into her room. She tried to fight, but her visitor knocked her out. He wasn't interested in what her body had to offer. Once inside, he put Alice on the bed, went out and retrieved the ice-bucket and breakfast leftovers, not wanting to tempt any room service people too quickly to get too close, and closed the doors. He put the Do Not Disturb sign on the main door, and knew the staff would respect that at least until check-out time passed. The dose of tetrodotoxin, sourced from the Gulf of California, was plenty concentrated enough to accelerate its predictable effects on Alice's body, and initially it would look like she had had some kind of respiratory failure. The true cause of death would emerge later.

The mysterious businessman left the room, and walked his casual way back up to the hotel entrance and out, and any descriptions or security camera footage from the entrance revealed only a clichéd guy in clichéd clothes, a Spanish descendant going about his work on an autumnal coastal morning, as Santa Barbara got on with its seductive life. The former Ms Remmer and all her other Alices in Wonderland were gone.

Fyodor fretted about the mystery for a few weeks, and then re-buried himself in the business of finding ways to keep tabs on everybody, everywhere, all the time.

Headline: *"SoftWorks founder's wife found dead in hotel"*
Cue: *"Needle of Death*

***

More autumn activity is shared as the action spreads out ~ the key issue of honour and respect is presented ~ a challenge on Western values from other perspectives is put in play ~ the first deception campaign is tested to gauge reactions and response ~ puzzles are constructed for people to work out meaningful links.

When he'd taken the brief, it had been a humid afternoon, September, and the pool at the hotel on Margarita Island was full of kids, animators encouraging them to play games, their voices booming through loud-hailers, celebrations of their fondness for the human voice, their own, rising above the rest of the shouting around the poolside. Locals seemed impervious to the noise, and carried on spreading sun tan liquids and creams across their bodies, and each other, adjusting silver reflectors to get the rays behind their ears, sipping coffees and beers, reading magazines, chatting, and all smoking in a tryst to keep tobacco companies' shareholders happy. It was a typical Venezuelan setting, and the newcomer looked like any other regional visitor catching the sun at the resort. He had flown in the day before from Caracas, on the short hopping route that went via Cumana. With a Venezuelan identity he had passed easily through customs and immigration. He took the short walk out of the airport and chose a taxi with a lazy looking driver, who agreed to take him through the lively town and across the island to one of the popular tourist areas. The town was typical. Several modern half empty office blocks, shops that looked closed from the outside because they used almost no lighting, shops that sold whatever they had come across that week, shops like travel agents that advertised how they could get you to anywhere but usually displayed a sign saying back in twenty minutes, which meant nothing.

The one he was rendezvousing with had sailed into the island and used the identity of a just dead local to smooth the passage, no details yet having made it onto files and records. After the next embarkation the ID card would be cut up and fed to the barbecue grill at the stern of the boat, the ashes gifted to the ocean once chunks of fresh tuna had been grilled and the charcoal reduced to tepid dust. The dead local served a brief but useful reincarnation. He had come to life again that morning, and would be gone twenty four hours later, having signed in to the marina to make a lay-over for some minor boat repairs, taken care of by another crew member. To any onlookers this looked like a common stop on the chartering runs from Trinidad and Tobago west, across the northern coastline, some easy ocean sailing out of harm's reach of much seasonal serious weather. To the more than mildly curious, the story was that the vessel was being returned from some wealthy one-way cruisers who would by now have flown on, the local crew sailing back without the loud partying guests.

Towards the end of the afternoon, around seven, and certainly before dinner, the re-born man had taken a bus to the Hilton Hotel. He took a table near the bar, busy with happy hour tipplers, and ordered a deeply unoriginal Cuba Libre. At ten past seven his appointment came into the bar, ordered a local beer and sat down on one of the three remaining stools, opening his local traveller guide and searching for restaurants, the regular tourist, maybe a businessman taking a break after a successful meeting. He sipped the beer and looked idly about him, using the mirror behind the bar to extend his view of the customers and guests. He saw the sailor, and, turning, pointed a finger in his direction, the sign that said, hey amigo, what are you doing here? Nothing too ostentatious, not the long lost buddy routine, just the sign of two people somehow connected in the process of beginning to acknowledge a link. Beer man came over and sat down next to Cuba Libra man, and they began to talk like two friends catching up on people and places, blending in with the holiday crowd, the local with the traveller, the old working chums who might have gone sailing or fishing together. The barmen would have nothing useful to remember, if ever asked about the two drinkers. Knowing the noise of the other tourists provided the beginnings of a reasonable sound barrier, the banter moved on to another topic. The Whisperers were at work.

Do you remember the last time we caught up with our American friends? It's probably time for a visit. What do you think about California?

Sounds great. Anywhere particular, or do you want to do a whole tour?

Maybe a bit of wine country in the north, and then drift down towards LA, you know the scene. A night in Jenner, up the Russian River, the quick spurt down the freeway and then lunch in Sausalito.

Don't tell me, then it's down to Carmel and the roll on to Santa Barbara.

Nothing like consistency to refine the good times. But if you can't make it?

Well it depends on the timing, but it'll be fine. Whenever.

Yeah. A nice inconspicuous convertible and a stash of stuff old boys like us shouldn't be resurrecting.

Speak for yourself Big Boy.

The 'old friends' routine continued for ten more minutes, and then came to a conclusion.

Great to see you again. You could come over to the boat but there's still a lot to do. Hey, you've probably got a much better deal going anyways. Here's the new local guide. There's probably nothing you don't know about round here, but you'll see marks for a couple of spots for you anyway.

Cuba Libre man handed over the new guide book he'd marked, got up, did his own finger sign, said goodbye, and moved on. It had been a useful time. The second visitor left the bar and lobby and took a taxi again, waking up the driver with a strong Spanish accent from the heart of the old Empire. In the back of the car he ran over the conversation one more time. It had been very promising, full of confirmations and fresh news. Once in town he got out, tipping the driver unexceptionally, and walked off into the night, the driver having no idea who his stingy Old World visitor had been. He took a mental note to listen carefully for that accent again. He wasn't too keen on spending his nights shuffling miserly Europeans around, Spanish or not. The visitor was soon forgotten.

***

39

The black-hulled yacht turned heads. She was almost new, and after the late September crossing from the Canaries, and a short spell in Antigua's English Harbour to return her to her pristine condition, she had set off for the Windward Islands to prepare again for a slow return journey northwards, cruising first between Grenada and St Vincent, sampling the rums, the different styles of hospitality, the different attitudes towards travellers, smugglers, and anyone in between, and then on up. The boat's owner was in Europe that week, but his wife had taken their plane into Grenada, and joined the boat off Lance aux Epines. The live-aboard crew had set the boat up perfectly, and she had been provisioned with fresh local ingredients, from mangoes to lobsters.

Inna could have eaten well at the restaurant in the nearby Calabash hotel, but on the first night she didn't have the energy for its formal old clientele, even though the food then was about the best on that part of the island. No, she would sit in her jet-lagged haze and be quiet in the air-conditioned saloon, while the chef presented her with something fresh and light, discreetly. It was cool enough to discourage any tempted mosquitoes, and she was happy not to acclimatise immediately to the evening and its fast sunset. Turning one of the large flat screens to a channel showing old movies, she put her bare feet on the leather sofa and nibbled the small sweet lobster, softening it with chilled Chablis that had survived the journey well. The first thing she had done when she boarded, as the captain had anticipated, was to demand the closing down of all communication systems except the one for the movies, from the lap-tops to the satellite phones, the faxes and the mobiles. There were to be no intrusions, no disturbances, and she knew her isolation always irritated her husband. But unless he specifically wanted something he could always get her through the captain, eventually, really knowing he would be bound to keep at least one channel secretly on in case the Boss wanted to speak to him, so what the hell. She needed the break. She needed to get away from the growing bustle of New York, the cold, the planning, the never diminishing rounds of parties, smiles and asides, demands on the wardrobe, the shoe designers, the hairdressers, the jewellers, the personal assistants, and all the other advisors in the entourage who were essential for survival between the Hamptons and Central Park South. By New Year the boat would be near St. Barts, and the whole crowd would be close by again. She'd be back in the throng as everyone checked out who was still in, who had fallen off the rock of favour, and who new was trying to muscle in. But well before that there was the sail, the slide along Grenada's west coast, the choppy crossing to Carriacou, the push past Canouan and its New Yorker-crowded resort hotel with its tiny scary aircraft connections. There'd be a time to say hello to a couple of friends at Palm Island, a push round the Tobago Keys, a quick visit to Basil's and the mwah mwah moment with another pair of Mustique autumn escapees, a night in Bequia where another friend's sister would be lolling about on their showy vulgar chartered motor boat, and she'd be expected to coo at the scope of it all, her own yacht looking modest in the shadow of the 60 metre gin palace. Then it would be up to St Vincent and the return jet to New York. You couldn't be away for too long, whatever kind of break you wanted, because fame faded faster than fashion. Inna squirmed at the thought of yet another Gulfstream V trip back down for the New Year link with the boat, drying her skin with its awful dehydrating air-conditioning and pressurised cabin. But she wouldn't swap any of it for one second.

The following day she began to catch up on her chosen trashy book reading, the titles and racy plots keeping her brain ticking over as the boat tackled the mid-day sun and the swells. For once the captain and crew were sailing calmly on, not being pestered too much by the constant flow of demands from the often bored mistress of the vessel. They were well compensated for their tolerance, but were always reminded that the reality of their owners' presence was always much worse than the glow of memories, when they would have the boat to themselves and the Boss Woman would have gone away again, the kerosene vapour trail of the dearly departed the last perfume to linger over the boat, as the jet took off from an island runway.

The main man was considered to be easier to handle, though why he bothered with the boat at all occasionally passed through the minds of some of the crew. When he bothered to show he spent almost all of his time on the computers and telephones, dealing with everyone, everywhere. For him it was just a floating office, another place to keep the deals alive, the mines and the new opportunities to accumulate money from his portfolio of extractive industries in tough places around the globe. He saw the boat as a kind of liquid asset, he regularly joked. But at least he let the crew get on with their job, unlike several of his friends, who had to be the in-charge know-alls as soon as they embarked on their own vessels. He never wanted to work on the boat himself, to sail. He was only really interested in the electronics, in the display technology. He never showed much interest in where they were going, as long as he was in touch with his whirling outside world. In many ways he was the ideal owner. The boat was just another big boy's badge, something he spent maybe a total of two weeks a year on. The rest of the time she was permanently minded by dedicated professionals, who were allowed to attract a specially selected coterie of charterers, keeping the boat immaculate all along. If they got to sail, they were happy. Boats weren't meant to sit at anchor all the time. He didn't need to charter, costs at this level didn't concern him, but it was something he felt some of his possessions had to do. They had to do something, not always sit idly by, just like him, and like all his other working assets. Cars were for driving, not for cocooning. No interest in collectors for whom every extra mile on the clock represented a loss in value. What was the point in having the car if it wasn't able to be driven? He cared less about the cars than his wife, who collected them like handbags. Whatever was cool had to pass through her hands. Over just a few short years she had acquired and discarded cars as accessories, enough to keep a Fort Lauderdale forecourt-finish dealership in highly profitable happiness. What she was good at were displays, of fashion, of fickle friends, of must haves and can't do's. It was a demanding preoccupation, full of detail, having to know how last season's handbag strap was so not on because of its width. To be in fading Manolos when the Choo or Louboutin star was rising would have been a major faux pas, but no-one would ever say anything straight to your reconstructed face. There was so much to know, to be in charge of, from diets to detox, skin care to stimulants, new age revelations to rehab, fitness to feng shui, an endless pool of talent to spot, to promote, to reject, to counsel against. Steering through the minefield of gaffes and slips, embarrassments and potential outrages was a full time occupation. If it could be played on-line it would be very difficult to reach the higher levels, there were so many subtleties to crush the weak and complacent. Remember, fashion is only now, but style must be eternal.

The benefit of the worship of the moment was that it made you highly visible. You couldn't open a fashion-leading magazine without being referenced, commented on, observed and photographed. A major party without her presence would be written down. An opening, a ceremony, an award, all would jostle for position according to her presence, her timing, her outfit, her unspoken judgement. Not because she was the richest, the most successful, the most insightful, but because she worked harder than most to be the Barometer of Best, and to ensure her close circle of conspirators controlled her election, each and every day, until one day they themselves would be elevated closer to the throne, beyond the constraints of daily fashion and into the mature world of transcendent style, into an endless future of being forever en vogue without having to slip back down into the quagmire of this Tuesday's titillation. That was the reward for years of devotion to the now, the accurate anticipation of the next now, the next moment, setting the next sign and measure of success, of writing the book on how to read the situation. Witness the ascent into the timelessness of being an icon, and staying alive at the same time. This was the way it should have been, without the disruption.

Keeping tabs on the woman was as easy as reading the weekly magazines she dominated, going to social websites, watching the news. Almost every move was detailed in the diaries and blogs of the celebrity watchers and chasers, the paparazzi, the strings of hangers-on and copycats, refuelling the value of The Queen of Gleam. So surveillance was not exactly a major challenge for the one who had been briefed, who could find out where she was at almost any point in a day, or night. All that was needed was the patience to wait until even she took a step out of the spotlight. And that time was now.

Checking where boats of this size were going was easy. They had trackers, transponders like aircraft, and voyages were filed with customs and immigration, as well as with harbour masters, all the time. In addition, local suppliers always seemed to know when the next large boat was coming in, so they were primed with their local delicacies to offer after the mobile call came in. The days of sailing up to the vessels in small boats with even smaller outboards, and an attempt to sell fresh catches over the rail, were over.

Bequia was ideal. Port Elizabeth allowed plenty of space for vessels of varied dimensions, and the principal action point was busy, visitors and locals mixing around the bars and the scrimshaw shops, the art boutiques and the bookshops selling maritime memorabilia. There were plenty of day trippers and wanderers, and arrivals and departures were relaxed, boats being checked in by well-known local skippers without the actual boat guests having to present themselves in person to the authorities. There were the usual diversions on offer, more local boat trips, to snorkel or fish, and the diving schools competing to offer beginners to experts whatever experiences they sought.

He had arrived two days before on a well-travelled boat from the north, whose crew were looking to spend a few months taking winter-warmer tourists on little day and sunset cruises out of the more southerly islands, people who wouldn't be too fussy about the boat's newness, but more intrigued by stories of her made-up past, and suitable amounts of weak rum-based cocktails to wash them all down with as the sun dipped below the western horizon. As a qualified ocean yacht-master, he hid his experience from the local captains, who were content to find him an able crewman on their leisurely voyages, and he used his judgement to ensure he still got to a destination at an appropriate time, without having to resort to the island-hopping airways and their enhanced fondness for checking identities and tracking routes.

After a couple of days of further recceing, and getting re-acquainted with the island's attractions, he knew which of the dive schools would rent him additional working gear to that he had brought on the boat, and who would be relaxed about his high level of credentials and number of dives, as the falsely identified credentials, but his real experience, showed. The tide tables and moon phase were perfect, the water warm, unlike on many of his assignments, where cold and darkness permeated the sea as well as the sky.

He took the small rental dinghy, and the diving kit, across the water to the north side, and tied up alongside a boat he knew was empty, wasn't being given any attention, and wouldn't be for days to come. He climbed aboard and settled himself in the cockpit, filling in time and getting himself into his familiar state of relaxation, watching the stars, keeping an eye out for meandering strangers, either lost looking for their recently moored boat and trying to return from the shore without the best of memories for how things looked different in the dark, especially when you had forgotten to put the masthead lights on, or simply the curious, motoring slowly around to see what kinds of boats or people might be in the safe haven, as close as they dared get. Occasionally he looked across the water to see the conveniently black-hulled yacht nestling on the water, and logged the time passing when the crew decided to go below, and Inna was left to her customary desired peace in the large open entertaining area towards the rear of the boat.

At 23.30, he slipped into the water, and set off for the quiet submerged swim, the lightest of tanks and equipment to carry. After five minutes he was close enough to surface and note the continuing absence of anyone other than Inna on the deck. He knew that at 23.45 latest she would extinguish the indulgent small Cohiba, and go below herself, the routine rebel following her own private rebellious timetable. He also knew she always preferred to return to the stern master cabin by the dedicated owner's entrance, allowing for total seclusion from the crew, cabined forward, beyond the galley and saloon.

He reached the transom and its step-ladder, left in the water to make the clamber onto the bathing platform easier from the sea. Quick-releasing his tank, which he tied to the bottom of the ladder, he climbed silently and stealthily on board, completely familiar with the layout of the boat's deck, and able to avoid any tell-tale stumbling over cleats or winches. He was a black shadow on a dark teak deck. He moved behind Inna, and then rapidly covered her mouth with his left hand, and pushed the long needle into her stomach. Holding her tightly, she quickly succumbed to the dose of sux, or succinylcholine. He lifted her 53kg body and carried her two metres back to the stern, lowering her into the water with customary stillness. Unable to exercise any form of muscle control, to shout or to swim, she quickly went under the blackness. She would be discovered at dawn, apparently drowned, perhaps after slipping off the bathing platform before going to bed, and hitting her head as she tumbled down. No-one was ordered to check if the boat's mistress had gone to sleep.

Inna had returned to the strong water she was named after.

The Beer man who had last traded messages in Margarita Island recovered his tank, swam back to the anchored yacht, and went to sleep in the cockpit. He returned the dinghy the next morning, together with his rented kit, and some exciting story about exploring a wreck, logging the dive onto his on-line record. The commotion wouldn't begin for two hours at the earliest, and then he would be on another boat dribbling down to a night in Mayreau, the trip he'd organised on his arrival those two days before.

Inna's husband mourned the latest extraction from his life briefly, and shortly afterwards began the swift search for a cheaper, younger model.

Headline: *"Mining Magnate's Wife in Drowning Tragedy"*
Cue: *"In the Air Tonight"*

***

The point was simple. In one way. The point was about honour. It's just that it looks different depending on where you're standing. J had taken time to choose his teams carefully. He knew why they would respond to the call to honour and respect their dead or mistreated colleagues. He knew he could appeal to codes that had been sealed in the closeness of mutual dependency, both insulated from the safety zones of civilian playgrounds, and in other cases entirely nurtured there. He knew they would be interested in the need for things to change, some still cynical about the chances of achieving any lasting differences, knowing the limitations of their efforts, but as prime charges, essential.

45

Words always echoed 'They did not die in vain,' or 'We shall always remember their contribution,' It was time to get some desired attention, as he had planned it, not for themselves, but for the issues, against corrupted selfishness, and about the famous lack of respect. In the analysis, in the projections, those close to the ground and those whose skills could be counted on to deliver a range of productions of the fruits of his imagination had come together.

These first versions of the Message, updated, had found their source a long time ago, the seeds appearing when J had read a book about life for women in Saudi Arabia, which magazines picked up on big time. At first it was just a curiosity factor. Many people thought that if you swapped a backwoods life for that of a desert princess, then accepting the lifestyle change was all part of the deal, so why complain so loudly? The way women were treated was handled by women's groups and other political or charitable agencies. It wasn't for long on the main agenda. And then it began to trickle through again. Once the invasion of Iraq had ended, and it had turned into a convenient insurgency, when deaths and their methodology began to be reported as monotonously and blithely as weather forecasts, some of those still in country who weren't just aid workers began to rail against what they saw as the increased shackling of women. A journalist wrote about how "It is amazing how many ways Iraqi men control their women with their obsessions about reputation, honour and that all-purpose baton 'proper Muslim behaviour'." This guy wanted women to be free of what he saw as vicious Islamic prejudice. He went on, "Once more you are reminded that the real agents of Iraq's fate are not media-friendly issues like fighting, the occupation or even constitutional convention, but subtle non-documentable social norms that regulate the lives of nearly every person in the country – especially females." For his troubles this writer was found dead at 11.30pm on Tuesday August 2nd 2005 just three miles outside Basra, shot three times in the chest. The British Army boys knew all about it, but it wasn't their policy to suggest how Iraq's version of democracy should work.

Others helped build the case. Western women's brains have been colonized by men, say some Middle Eastern women. They have sex without marriage. They are an obscenity. They try to belong to the oppressor class of Harvard-educated ruling families that control so many countries in the world, embezzling money, drinking wine with white people, engaging in Freemasonry and planning wars on the innocent. Westerners presume they themselves are intellectually and ethically superior to Middle Easterners. But for better or for worse,

46

Easterners vent their aggression at the criminals of their own society, instead of venting their aggression at competing ethnic groups or by bombing other countries like liberal westerners do.

It was just conceivable that this dormant interest could be used again to spark something more useful, a tool that would rekindle a version of the war on terror in a way that would keep the agenda burning brightly for a while longer. A research team was set up to look at ways of constructing the case for a new way to hit both the capitalists and the fundamentalists. It was clear that more work would be needed to help foment this part of the plan, and execute it, but the rewards could be most useful, most useful indeed. A verbal 'expedite' was issued to the deniable teams to begin preparations for the first chapter in the fight for respect.

***

J's Invisible Diary. Entry.

There is great potential to recruit people to this version of the cause. An official UK analysis said that 'a small number of young British Muslims are known to have committed or participate in terrorism abroad... a number of extremists operate here...it is less than 1% of the country's Muslim population'. That's still 16000 people. And many of them are clean skins, meaning they have no criminal records. They can be recruited through a single contact, outside the traditional environments, like mosques, and they can be encouraged to maintain a low profile. Also, they don't develop the networks of associates or political doctrines common to many other extremist Islamists. Those who go abroad to fight provide an interesting demonstration of Brits killing Brits, or Americans, like Abu Hareth, who was killed in Fallujah in April 2004. Behind those seeking martyrdom are a host of quieter ones who don't even get onto the suspect radar. Intelligence tied up in identifying and following suspects for months won't come close to the real new players. They would provide a layer of extra cover. It will be awkward for the chasers, because the old familiar handles, the collective group-branding exercise of the old Al-Qaeda kind, will no longer be there to offer almost tangible targets. The future will not be so simple as to hold up a leader on video screens, or a mass produced manifesto.

The eventual response from the spinners and chasers will be to say that the perpetrators of the actions are cowardly and will be beaten because they have no vision, no stated aims to change things for good, positively, but the old approach of setting up public pariahs was no longer the way it was going to be. It is all about values, ideas, intangibles brought to life through silent punishment, the embracing of death as the true acknowledgement of its power to renew life. There will be a shift. The deaths will be of others. In the old days Muslim fighters knew how to die, but not how to live. This will change. The positions held by the attacked are identical. Both sides will say, 'Anyone targeting this society is our enemy. They are targeting you personally as much as anyone else, no matter who they are…but injustices must be dealt with by scholars and politicians, not by hotheads.' We shall see.

***

Marina was one of the contenders for the Prime Consumer title. She was the core model for what had brought Inna into the spotlight. She didn't seek the unwitting fame of Imelda Marcos and her thousands of pairs of shoes, but she was fair game for other counting feats. There were things you absolutely had to have, and others that could be easily dismissed. There were fads, things that had to be monitored, tested, talked about, managed and filed, and above all, acquired. There was just so much to do, so much to know, and so little time to keep ahead. It took hours every day, a constant stream of others' money. It was a perfect virtuous circle of conspicuous consumption. It was about things, about ways of doing things and not doing them. Doing things the wrong way made you look such a fool, so it could only ever be that others had to do the wrong things, and be fools for you. Wearing things on, over, under, creased, folded, in combinations of materials, colours, patterns - it was a constant challenge requiring constant checking. It had always been so, and it had always been that so few had the grace and panache to carry off excellence constantly and consistently. She had voted herself into the Club of One when it came to assessing her abilities to combine all for the benefit of her admirers, and to the detriment of those who just couldn't cut it and keep up. Marina devoted herself to being a focal point in the world of consumption. She was La Princesse du Jour, as she chuckled to herself in one of the 360 degree mirrors in her dressing suite. She couldn't stand the sight and presence of Inna, one of the few who might deflect the radiance away from her in her monde, and the loathing was entirely mutual. They didn't like their mental doppelgangers, even though one was a provider, and the other was a taker. But physically they were kilograms apart.

Some things just wouldn't do. She had her own illogical dos and don'ts. She remembered the story that the Sultan of Brunei only ever wore a shirt once. How strange he would never feel the softness of mature washed cotton. She had many things she had never worn at all, except maybe fleetingly in couturier's fitting rooms. They were things she had to have, not necessarily connected to wearing. They were possibilities, options, ideas. They were in cupboards, wardrobes, in rows, on shelves, by length, by shade, by designer, and knowing she could be *that* size whenever she willed it, she held these items up against her body and reminisced about some party or place where the piece had featured once. She hadn't been born for the 'perpendicularity' of fashion in her prime, so she had gone the other way, exaggerating and dancing with curves, form, shapeliness, and there were no artificial servants supporting or compressing her contours. The raw material on which she draped couturiers' fantasies was the true pure source, untainted by scaffolding and scalpels, simply toned by spas and soothing hands. Her hair was always the colour and length it needed to be to presage the next phase of coveted styles, her eyes retouched in photographs to reflect the preferred shade for a season, something violet or iced-blue, her nails familiar with the wavelengths of colour, her lips the carriers of peach to passion, cherries to celebration. There were advisors. Stylists, hairdressers, like the others had, all with their different teams and favourites. Each eyed the competition, rushing to copy and jump ahead a fraction, to express individuality, being first, while subtly acknowledging all along that you just might be the keystone founder member of the exclusive club, the rest merely temporary members whose subscription required that particular bag, belt, scarf or ring this week. And behind it she knew, really, that for all the counsel, all the sycophantic smiles and nods, she took every decision, every time. Counsel was something you sought but never took. That was the secret. Of course she knew everything she had was copied, and thousands of people would be wearing the signature items she first displayed in cities, high street value meeting the fashion queens, but for her value was no substitute for authenticity. Copies were like forgeries, good enough to capture the flavour of something, but not the essence. Her fashion collections were her own portfolio of art, pieces that would be snapped up by collectors in the future. This rationale, this analogy with the world of paintings, she had worked on, crafted carefully, as the supreme statement of her beliefs about her taste and acquisitions. Since her husband spent more on his personal fetish, an addiction to emerging modern art which he traded in the same way as everything else in his life, she felt she had no need to defend her passion, and she used his own arguments to justify her investments, something in the order of $4 million a year, excluding the body care and the personal help. It was barely the price of one of his pieces, which he would move on in three years anyway. Look at the return on investment he got from her. She made him look everything he wasn't, and he ought to be grateful for that.

Looking this good, when it counted, required back-up, a team whose members had to be changed sometimes, or whose emphases and roles had to be adjusted. No one in the cosmetic court could be allowed to get too powerful, or share all the secrets, and for those who thought of selling out on the back of the insights, the employment contracts were generous up front and punitive in the breech. Those contemplating detraction would only be heading for a road littered with lawyers and litigation, not exactly a freeway to riches. Wasn't it the same with anything worth having? She would have talked the way her husband did, about how you needed the best to take care of the worst. Nothing came without expertise, human hands and brains, the fuel to keep it all firing, money. And where did the money come from? From deals. The whole world was about deals and dealers. And the deals her husband pulled off were spectacular. It helped that he had a Swiss-based drug company and a number of governments behind him, an endless source of ravenous investors, and spiralling prices for the goods and services to be delivered, enough to keep the dynasty alive and well for at least two generations, and after that, who gives a damn? She didn't much care about anybody, and she didn't crave fame beyond the grave. She just wanted to be ahead of today.

There was a tight schedule of appearances to make and maintain. There was a season to be designed, of places to grace, people to be with, events to perfume with one's presence, to dignify, and things to avoid at all costs. The back-up team also had to be flexible enough to handle accidental last minute changes, hiccoughs, and the temperament that changed its mind for changes sake. It came with the ticket. Don't you recognise this icon? It could only ever be a rhetorical question. If she wanted her hair done in Hamburg there was a jet ready to bring her hairdresser to the golden locks. If she needed a fix of Japanese fish there was a fish, and a qualified chef, already winging their way to St Moritz or St Tropez. And if the order was unfulfilled there was an army of replacements waiting to prove they could master the just-in-time caprices of the world's finest Marina for an appropriate premium. She was a concierge service's dream. Once Marina knew what money was, what it felt like, what all those little '0's meant after the numbers, she settled into her element like a dealer in digital dealing heaven, where points and fractions, nanoseconds, altered the balance big time, and usually in her favour.

She only knew the actual price of something if it looked threatening that it might be taken away. Then she not only knew its cost, but could calculate its perceived worth to others as well. That for her was real value. Otherwise everything was clumped together under the title 'Mine'. Her husband's chief accountant sometimes made the point that if his wife had been one of his operating companies he would by now have divested himself of the 'revenue opportunity' she represented. But he simply nodded. Her expenditure was always passed. It was easier to tolerate the excesses than to deal with the sulky consequences of curbing them. That could mean she might divert some of the money into having him trailed, or looking for some sympathetic country to move to for ten minutes so she could file for the biggest divorce seen in history. It was a small price to pay for her form of loyalty, which was occasionally useful on the circuit when trying to sweeten a deal or connection.

Within the schedule, in the back-up team, you were supposed to know which things were unmoveable, even for weeks on end. When her movements had been tracked and monitored over two or three years it emerged that there were sacrosanct periods, those between major public events and appearances, and those for reconstruction, rebalancing. These were the times when she was vulnerable, where she was in the untested hands, in unfamiliar spaces, and where the prying eyes of publicists could be distracted by other events.

In this offstage period, wherever Marina was, she always took a body massage at 1600. She chose the providers and they had to pass her own kind of interview before she would let them near here, but that was usually only to reinforce her dominance and stature over the chosen service provider. Once in there she would begin to relax with new hands and faces and would tolerate small differences in the sequencing of the content of the sessions. She wanted ninety minutes of consistent attention, with her chosen music, her chosen setting, and her newly chosen adorer. With her eye protectors on, and the sounds doing their heartbeat steadying work, she was relaxed in her controlled domain, the meditations only punctuated quietly by the timely return of the masseuse, who would have re-entered the treatment space after Marina had got herself ready and positioned, making calm noises, ready with newly heated oils, therapies and water, breathing slowly, readjusting the atmosphere to the presence of a submissive otherness again. She thought these people were being treated to an immaculate specimen of what self-devotion could bring, and was prepared to share a tiny piece of her outer self for a brief spell. So much more rewarding than the feeble creatures they had had to deal with for much of the rest of their therapeutic days. The pattern never shifted, the masseuse always took the break. It was the crucial five minutes, the gift of a parcel of time. It was enough.

This time she had decided to stay in a Kasbah near Marrakesh. The decision triggered action as soon as the flight plans had been filed. The summer heat had dissipated, and in the southern mountains some 1000 feet above the desert plain that carpeted the spaces between the cooler foothills and the city, the former designer's home was a good place to relax before the demands of the autumn gallery and exhibition openings. The Challenger 300 jet was nestling at Marrakesh-Menara airport, its crew sunning themselves at the Hotel Mamounia in the city, and Marina was in the attentive hands of one of the team she had selected from the Kasbah's spa staff. As a guest of the hotel's owner, the spa team was used to the demands of high-expectation guests. It looked like most people were functioning well, and there was going to be a period of peace.

Another guest was staying there with his girlfriend. They had come up from the south by road, having spent two nights at the Gazelle D'Or outside Taroudant, making their way slowly over the Tiz 'n' Test pass for a couple more nights in the mountains before returning to London and the rush of work that preceded Christmas. That was the storyline. It had apparently been a last minute choice, a few days they both found they could spare after a summer of extra work they had elected to do when everyone else was away playing, and before January, which would be the next time they could seriously consider doing anything. The man was a freelance journalist with a reputation for getting gritty stories from the world's hotspots. Digital radio was a favourite of his, and it also gave him freedom to engage his listeners' imagination in ways television couldn't. He had little time for the shallow voyeurism of what many people had come to know as reality television. That was like watching the world through CCTV. No, there was still a place for people to conjure up a setting in their minds, and he played to that. His girlfriend was a commercial property consultant, and on the back of a major success secured that September with the revitalised Middle East investment programmes, she had decided it was time to join the journalist for a really long weekend.

They had taken one of the rooftop suites, knowing they would be more likely to guarantee a room at the edge of the season by pitching high and not asking for discounts. A full hotel would have forced a postponement, but the time had come. The suite was in the main building of the hotel itself, with access to the rest of the hotel via three separate routes. It was an ideal location to continue a wind-down before picking up the pace again in Marrakesh. The outdoor pool was still warm enough, the evenings beginning to take on the edge of coolness, but calm enough for most to enjoy the restaurant terrace. The spa was doing its quiet business in beauty treatments. He had already got to know one of the spa staff, and had succumbed to the encouragement to have a Hammam bath on the second day.

He had had plenty of time to look around the place that had been converted to an exclusive hotel, with its tranquil indoor pool, its three treatment areas, and, best of all, the four ways in and out of the spa area. He had been asked to double check his appointments by the spa supervisor, in case any times or treatments had to be moved, which gave him more time to assess how busy the team was, and just how much business really was being generated. His girlfriend had also made appointments for three sessions which they had negotiated around their desire to be together at certain times of the day, and this had created a busy demand on spa staff attention around the 1600 slot Marina scheduled for her extended massage. He had noticed that the spa girls tended to begin their sessions slightly late, dawdle over their time-outs, and finish sessions slightly early. No strain on their part then.

The couple had champagne on their terrace and watched the sun make its descent towards the tops of the western peaks, the first of the brightest stars winking at their attention. The staff were getting used to their tips, and they took time to pass pleasantries with them, asking about their lives beyond the hotel, the effect this new version of the old place was having on the local community, the state of the business, the little adventures and episodes that made raconteurs of them all, an aggregation of little experiences that would help form positive memories, positive recommendations for other prospects. Whenever he walked across the hotel grounds, from the pool to the bar, from reception through the courtyard, from the restaurant to the terraces, he made a point of acknowledging the staff, so they would remember him, the Anglicised Arab, Wafi.

On the second day, at 1630, he was in their suite, having walked from the pool bar, finishing a Pina Colada and leaving the tab open, saying he had to take a call he was expecting on the land-line. It came

53

through, he spoke a greeting, and then said he was ready to hear the newsroom draft that was being prepared for his return, and for which they wanted his feedback. Five minutes into the call he put the receiver down on the table by the telephone cradle, the voice electronically bumbling along in the background. He closed the curtains, put the red Moroccan slipper on the door to signal Do Not Disturb, took a long look through the windows around the upper area of the hotel, and left the room.

He had only ever seen staff on the top floor before 11am, cleaning, or between 6 and 7 pm when they put cushions out and lit the candles for the rooftop bar, which didn't really come to life until after dinner. That meant his route to the spa took him through the now empty small reception area of the restaurant, and down the short staircase to one of the courtyards, where a sharp left turn allowed him to make the shortest passage. Reception was west of the courtyard, and faced north from behind a large wall, so unless any guests were specifically being introduced to the hotel on the get-to-know walk around, and he had listened for any sign of cars arriving at the gates, he was virtually guaranteed no attention from that area.

He slipped into the corridor that held the spa office and the smaller treatment routes on either side, the indoor pool area just a few paces further on, where one of the masseuses was treating another female guest to an aromatherapy treatment behind a screen in the peaceful atmosphere of the indoor pool area. In the Hammam, he knew the local Moroccan girl was two thirds the way through her mud and water routine with another guest who had been volunteered for this invigorating experience which in other countries would have had lawyers reaching for their abuse of human rights reference works. The other treatment room was empty, and he went into it, waiting to hear Marina's personal therapist leave for the customary break and head to the office. He left the door ajar, so if she did decide to go into that room for some reason he was ready with his Hey just trying to find my partner, and you're here routine. But having listened to the woman during her first session he didn't think she'd be doing much. He also thought she just might have caught a bit of the regulars' fondness for compressing time, and stretch the five minutes to seven, before returning to the supine contours of Marina's body. She did come out, pretty much on time, and went straight into the office. He slipped by, and after three minutes he entered Marina's treatment room. She was on her back, asleep or doing a good impression, her eyes covered with some sort of soothing cucumber complex, her arms by her side, relaxed on top of the massage table, a thick but light cotton towel covering her body from shoulder to foot, her arms resting on top of the towel at her sides, the new age music counting its flutey way through another seventy two minutes CD length of peace and serenity.

He moved towards her and raised her left arm by her wrist. His right arm then introduced the small needle quickly into her skin and deeper into a vein. She pulled up sharply, reaching for her arm. She also made the kind of 'what the fuck?' exclamation that comes with total unwanted surprise, and that would draw the masseuse back to the room. It was long enough for the wrong masseur to leave the room and spa before the resting masseuse came back. The little gift of batrachotoxin, care of the neatly named Phyllobates terribilis, a Central American tree-frog, had been delivered. Marina wouldn't be strutting her stuff, or jousting with Inna, any time soon. Initially, it would look like paralysis from some kind of major body malfunction, something that had been dormant and had decided to come out to play today.

Wafi and his girlfriend stayed at the hotel for dinner, as the mystery of Marina was handled with quiet discretion by the hotel staff, whose first priority was not to distress other guests, or put out the impression Inna's condition had anything to do with them, and the masseuse was initially questioned by the local doctor about anything that had been put on the disclaimer form, or said, that might indicate the possibility of this unfortunate event occurring on theses premises. They would only preserve the privacy for a day.

The vacationing couple left at 3.30 am, being met twenty kilometres away in the middle of a small village by the Frenchman who was going to take them ballooning on the desert floor that morning. After the spectacular burn and rise to meet the climbing sun, and before the thermals kicked in, they drank the champagne the balloonist traditionally produced from the hamper, and looked around at the beautiful unfriendly landscape. By mid-morning they would be back in their off-roader, and driving north, the long slow meander up towards Tangier, and the easy crossing to Tarifa. The long weekend would be stretching out a lot further.

The press did retrospectives for a while, until Marina's place was taken by a new presence. The Swiss husband used all of that country's desire for privacy to remain quietly in the background, complictly approving the testing of new drugs on thousands of people who lived outside the regulatory frameworks of the markets where he expected to sell refined patented solutions to rich folks with cravings for high-cost extended lives.

Headline: *"Swiss Pharma Chief's wife in luxury hotel accident"*
Cue: *"The Drugs Don't Work"*

***

J's Invisible Diary. Entry
One of the great skills of a successful force on a mission is the practice and pull of deception – making the enemy think your plans and actions are all being directed somewhere else, wrong-footing them, tying up their resource in wild goose-chases and rippling circles expanding out to horizons of emptiness. Getting people to look in the wrong places is priceless, and there are so many wrong places to look. Thousands will be tied up looking at the wrong dissidents, at violent gangs, at Latino, Black, Asian, Arabic, Caucasian clusters, at internet trails and telecommunication traces, at religious fanatics and disaffected drug groups, green earthers and animal rights activists. A number of these will be happy to claim a slice of the action, a contribution to it, as much as others will publicly state their denial of responsibility. The noise will provide interference, chaff, a form of cloaking you elect to pick threads of your stories from. It is from the pool of decoys that much of the attention will be focused on, reinforcing stereotypes about aggressors, about outsiders with no respect for homeland securities, morals, values, and rights, missing out on insiders who are the deepest threat to social stability, those whose activities in the shadow of the masking flags do the most harm while the stereotypes take the rap – the fanatics, the evil ones, the flawed. Only the righteous will prevail.

***

The forgotten idea of giving, of putting things back into the society from which you have extracted personal material wealth, is out ~ another target is taken out of the equation ~ the process of introducing and directing meaningful change is discussed ~ the response of the initially threatened and outraged is logged ~ the need for constant novelty to capture the imagination is established ~ here endeth the First Lesson.

So far, the deaths had occurred over the concentrated time period of a couple of months, a triumph of organisation and operational efficiency. An autumnal season. The early news stories appeared around the world, and at first it looked like a bizarre sequence of chance events, accidental deaths apart from Paris. It would take a little

56

longer for people to begin to see links. Seeing them would be part of the process of getting The Message going. There was no point in keeping the nature of the deaths a secret, only the identities of the deliverers of them. There was no desire to keep methods suppressed from experienced investigators' eyes. No, the point was only to buy a little time through tricks any fiction writer could pick up off the internet, except here they were coupled to the ability to make them work in reality. If the targets changed plans suddenly, or made unpredictable moves that could truly compromise action, then missions would be stopped until more favourable circumstances and conditions arose, although it would be disappointing to have the plan stretched out over too long a timeframe. All the research had revealed that the targets had strong routines and habits, which had led to their selection in the first place.

There was also the point that the victims were not the ultimate targets.

There would be another option if people needed a little extra help in understanding this angle. But people were going to have to work a little harder first. There was, after all, another reason for not getting straight to the point.

That was why the website had been prepared. It had been prepared in Dari in a style that paid homage to some of Afghanistan's greatest poets, speaking of heroic deeds. It would be routed around the world, and anyone clever enough to track it back would see its source in a now empty and closed internet café in Toronto. One or two suitable people would be aided in getting to discover its content at the right moment, even before the global internet trawlers picked up signs and alerted the screen-bound terrorist watchers. The story, that would then find its way into other mass media and discussion forums, would be simple.

There was a growing number of mega-rich men who made their money from practices that were particularly disrespectful of others, while claiming to be virtuous. They utilised technology to scale operations up to levels that had not been possible before, and were able to accumulate wealth at unprecedented levels. Many hardly put anything back into the societies they exploited. Those that demonstrably did would be treated honourably. Those that didn't would be Indexed, and encouraged to change their behaviour. In the first place, their wives and girlfriends, who epitomised all that was decadent about so-called Western values, would be taken away from them. This would be the first level of payback for their selfishness, and would demonstrate the preferable and virtuous ways of following another

Path. It would set the moral rollerball off, set a conceptual cat among the fluttering pigeons.

It would all be music to J's ears, another piece of harmony in his collection of suitably cued mnemonic songs.

***

The day would begin with six presentations in three cities in the Netherlands over a period of just eight hours. Then it would be on to Frankfurt, in the confines of a Falcon 50 chartered business jet. The 42 year old was on a roll. She was the youngest of three children, and grew up in the summers mostly on Long Island. She went to Princeton, and then, after the required spell at Harvard, did time with the Procter & Gamble company, Bain, and a Venture Capital company. In those early days she had tried to be close to her husband, a cosmetic surgeon, and his own burgeoning career and practice. In those days too she wasn't a celebrity star, simply an exceedingly bright and rising one. She had two sons, three years apart, starting when she was 29. It wasn't until she was 37 that the rapid change began, and she was headhunted into an ailing household name in electronics. She had now become the Silicon Valley celebrity known by her shortened Christian name, still trying to be the neighbourly mom, putting out that she believes people are all basically good, and that what she does reaffirms her faith in humanity. She says it without sounding fake or sappy. She means it. She's made it. And then she claims it will all be over in two or three years. After that it will be philanthropy, teaching, going to Colorado to ride horses. With $1.2 billion in stock, that's some way to ride off into the sunset.

But for all the community visionary idealism, the wonderful boundary-free company has a questionable attitude to acceptable corporate behaviour, high-level fraud and moral challenges in a loosely regulated space. It's the digital version of the kind of market you could go to in Kandahar, where anything can be bought, sold, or obtained by tomorrow, at an interesting price. It's about minimising the irritants of regulation in the face of the warmth of profits. Fine. This backcloth supported her selection.

Her husband was growing richer by the minute, and living on the borrowed insight that he was selling dreams. What he was actually selling were fabrications, man-made, that would come back to taunt him in unforeseen ways. Giving women the looks they craved, or those their alleged beloved ones craved, was a literally booming business, with millions wanting differently shaped breasts, noses, lips, contours,

58

and anything else that transformed them into something they believed was more desirable, or more sustainable against the deniable process of ageing. The problem with Buford was that he saw so much opportunity, and was in such a hurry, that he wasn't prepared to test his suppliers with enough rigour to ensure their products could deliver, every day, until death us do part. His research robustness and due diligence was also suspect through the elaborate networks he had had created that gave him profit shares from these very same companies, and then from the other companies that were providing supplementary support products from creams to pills, all offering endorsed routes to immortality, or at least an extended healthy beautiful life, as seen through the eyes of the beholders. His Emperor's New Clothes did indeed look splendid.

He was planting seeds of destruction in women's bodies. As well as getting well up the monitoring lists of the nouveau riche, and becoming a byword for transformation in fashion and healthy lifestyle magazines, he was beginning to come under the scrutiny of one or two news outlets that still practised a form of investigative journalism, and the consequences of the beginning of implant malfunctions was starting to emerge. The fact that women were prepared to spend so much on alterations played beautifully into the hands of one or two other storylines against the deathly worship of capitalist decadence that were being disseminated.

In the Netherlands, for those with strong feelings but little knowledge in depth, the background had a usefully Islamic air to it. *Die Welt*, the newspaper, noted that "a crusade is under way by fanatic Muslims, focused on civilians, directed against our free, open Western societies, that is set upon the utter destruction of Western civilisation. The enemy is spurred by tolerance and accommodation which are taken as signs of weakness. Ethnic minorities will soon be the majority in Holland."

***

J's Invisible Diary. Entry
   There is nothing wrong with using religion as a decoy – tried and tested. There always has to be some trigger with an emotional element, some detonator that is easier to place in the intensively conditioned. That and extreme social conditions. Tools can be found in the Netherlands, in Colombia, in the US, in England, in Germany, in Japan. It would be foolish to think that action will only be taken by the wild.

Behind those who make sacrifices, who seek martyrdoms, are cooler intelligences that have their own reasons for making a mark through others.

***

Holland, the Netherlands, the Dutch, whatever the collective descriptor, had been a natural target. The place had prided itself on being the most tolerant and welcoming country in Europe for immigrants and asylum seekers. In Amsterdam, Rotterdam and The Hague, new arrivals outnumbered the under 20 year old Dutch natives. Policy had been to create a multicultural society where difference was accepted and appreciated. Turks and Moroccans had no strong historic links. Mosques, schools, language teaching, housing, all were provided to all. Issues of immigration, culture, identity and crime were rarely discussed by the political elite. A Dutch Member of Parliament, Geert Wilders, was threatened with beheading by radical Islamists as he pronounced that Moroccan troublemakers should be expelled, including a young street terrorist who had been run over by the woman he had just stolen a handbag from. He died. They should, he said, "be detained, de-naturalised, and deported." And the right kind of background grew from there. No more Muslims to import spouses through arranged marriages. The immigrants hadn't integrated. The cheers in Rotterdam as 9/11 happened were an interesting sign. Assimilation was on the agenda. It got higher after Pim Fortuyn was shot dead in 2002, the country's first political assassination since the seventeenth century, committed by a white Dutch animal rights activist. This was a stage with appropriate scenery already in place.

Then it spread to others, like Theo van Gogh, who was pushing Holland's defence of free speech through a provocative film about the treatment of women in Islam, a nice throwback. He was shot dead too. The killer called for a jihad, and the authorities woke up to the fact they had a jihadist group, locally born and recruited, living amongst them. The alleged assassin was a twenty six year old Moroccan Dutch who spoke and wrote excellent Dutch and had gone to a good local lyceum. But he also spent time at Al-Tawhid mosque in Amsterdam, and he had joined a militant Islamic group, Hofstad. He had grown up in a reasonable district of West Amsterdam, and when he was arrested he was living in good accommodation.

Politicians who had views about all this had to go and live on secure military bases surrounded by bodyguards. This was what J envisaged as extending to other figures that stood out for the wrong reasons. The Dutch liberal attitude played directly into the hands of imams with a political agenda and money. Debates on Islamic issues were seen by home grown Muslims as an attack on their identity. They worried the decadence of Christianity would rub off on them. The clash was about the culture at home and the one at school and the one on the street. Democracy is Satanic. And the Dutch came at it from the other side. The essentials of Islam are not compatible with liberal democracy. Even moderates were on death lists.

***

J's Invisible Diary. Entry.

There is a need to find new touchstones across groups. Can it be possible to work across religions against the same goal, or can that only work within the walls of a specific religious practice? Can an end goal triumph over the demands of creed? Maybe not. But there are still opportunities for co-ordination, for creativity within confusion and its resultant chaos.

***

The spiritual vacuity of Dutch society left them open to a cultural Islamic takeover. Political leaders asked whether the Muslims could accept their values. Gay marriage. Euthanasia. It was good for providing further distraction.

Amsterdam was easy. People were aware. They were used to strange sights. Cities created visible extremes. You could walk from the soft light and the international flavour of Freddie's small cocktail bar in the Hotel de l' Europe, and in two minutes be fingering your way through DVDs and magazines in the all-tastes-catered-for sex shops of the red light district, passing the museum of cannabis on the way, the tiny old bars, the university, the loft apartments, the second hand bookshops, the 'original' coffee shop and the smoking accoutrements' specialist. Gay couples would hold hands and window shop. Someone would guess which language you spoke from your dress and body demeanour, asking in your tongue which drug you might want to try today. Police would wander through the parade protecting the normality of it all, while partly dressed girls and women posed and played with the curtains at the neon lit windows of their canal side aquariums. Shy men peered furtively from behind their beards and anoraks looking to see if

61

they could fumble their way to another frustrated fuck, while other groups of men and women rolled by, laughing aloud in feigned confidence at the wonder of it all, the men who would later masturbate alone to the memory of the girl they wouldn't have, the women comparing the sizes of the sex toys they'd bought to take home to Prudeville. It was just another night in old Amsterdam.

Further out from the centre were smaller places with their mini versions of the sex and drugs souks, the stripped down red-light zones, the more intermittent cafes with their drug-dulled moths, young ones trying to see what the point of the light was anymore, older ones making wider arcs as they moved to avoid what they saw as danger signs. Graffiti changed the appearance, and its messages shifted too, anger and hatred taking on different hues. As you moved towards more traditional places, surrounded by roads that kept the travellers out, and rural areas that protected the past in quaint displays of Protestantism, the visible faded. The gaps between the old and the established, the new and the different were less public. Segregation took place without overt signs. You had to look further for where the two types of society were creating fresh tectonics. It was precisely in these places where the best raw material emerged. It wasn't where everyone was looking. People had suspicions, but they preferred predictions from within their own ways of seeing things. They couldn't create new scenarios outside their wide open windows. They encouraged people to look in, to see how they had nothing to hide, so they wouldn't have to look out, to acknowledge the ways things were moving, creeping up on them, seeping into those areas they had worked on which they called 'respect'. It was clear some of these people would need saving from themselves. J was in a position to help the agents of change. God couldn't be on all sides. And the Devil, he'd be fine as long as he kept on getting his supply of the bad ones. He wasn't so choosy. He didn't get jealous any more when he wasn't cited, when he got blamed. That was all a long time ago. These days he'd take who he could get. The thing was, he didn't have to go underground any more. It was all out there on the streets.

Sil was the name that stuck when she had first moved to the Valley. Christened Priscilla, it lent itself to that American habit of shortening names as a sign of familiarity and approval, and the press loved the endless wordplay with all things silicon. Now she was watched as a bell-wether for the shifting fortunes of companies that made a living from playing with sand, she had a regular press following, and usually an entourage of media pundits. With her husband's career, she was also a regular media feature on the arm of Buford, or as a commentator on her husband's work, technology literally shaping the future. If nothing else, she provided a starting-point for debates, since she had no visible signs of having taken on any of Buford's product offers with her own body. All this meant that most of her agenda was published in advance, and media flocks could be on location, hoping to capture early worms about new products or launches, acquisitions or takeovers that had just been signed into the public domain, and any other sound and vision bites they felt had a waiting audience across multiple channels. The desire to spread the word of Sil was a gift.

The Pulitzer wasn't the swankiest of hotels for corporate meetings, but it combined relaxed elegance with a location that wasn't surrounded by car parks or the lingering smell of kerosene at the edge of airports. Sil had had the best rooms secured, and the select investor meetings had all been set up to offer a customary illusion of intimacy and professional respect. Seeking interest to back the discovery and potential roll-out of a host of products and services based on patents owned and not exploited was the theme of the day. The response had been as positive as it usually was when people were reviewing whether to put significant sums of other people's money into untried technologies.

It was time to step out into the narrow canal-side hotel entrance, where the car to Schiphol's general aviation terminal was waiting to go. There was a space of around four metres from hotel doors to the car, and the entrance area was surrounded by cameramen and interviewers eager to hear Sil's latest pronouncement.

The good thing about contemporary cameras is that they have a great number of lenses that can easily be attached, and pictures or film can be transmitted, with GPS co-ordinates, as they are captured. The other benefit is that the long lenses have plenty of space in them. There are further benefits. With this kind of subject and action, there is never a lone photographer, never the patient individual in the hide, tripod adjusted, waiting for the elusive bird to make an appearance. It was all action, and now. The potential danger was only from jostling and shoving, as cameramen tried to get the best position and shots of the Valley darling.

For one cameraman the quality of the picture was irrelevant, and he was more than happy to be at the very edge of the photographic throng, right by the doors. Other professionals, if they had noticed, might have regarded him as an amateur, since he had minimised the time for getting a face-on shot, and would probably only manage a blurred profile before he was actually behind Sil. Their professionalism played into his. The Canon EF Supertelephoto lens looked the part. The Middle-Eastern looking cameraman had other cameras, the pro jacket, the signs he was one of the pack. He raised the camera again as Sil threw a few comments in the general direction of the eager feeders. She had already passed him, and the back of her head was the principle feature he saw, as the others knew it would be. He pressed the capture image button.

Sil felt a small prick on the back of her neck, like a mosquito had just been attracted to her in all of these male aromas, and dismissed it as she maintained her rapid news delivery, still moving towards the car. In another two minutes, she would be moving down the narrow road, and on towards the airport. The mass media men were winding up their customary swarming and chest-beating behaviour, already looking to despatch their latest nuggets of digital gold. The photographer with the poor position had already lowered his camera, and began to move away slowly, looking preoccupied with what appeared to be the concern of the one who had missed the profitable picture. He turned left, walked around the side of the hotel, past its restaurant in the collection of houses the hotel had joined together, and moved towards the centre of the city, where a short relaxed walk would take him to Centraal Station, and the Thalys train to Paris. The camera had provided an excellent cover for the high-speed needle gun. The noise and shouting of the media made great sound cover, and no-one was looking to see what, if anything, had found Sil's neck.

Hours later she was succumbing to the needle's poison, and didn't make it to the next photo-opportunity. It was, depending on your perspective, a death by natural causes. After all, what could be more natural than aconite. Only its concentration had been enhanced by a little human help, just like Buford's business of prematurely killing people. What a shot.

The surviving children's names were added to The Index.

Headline: *"Queen of Silicon Valley Dead"*

Cue: *"She's a Killer Queen"*

***

J's Invisible Diary. Entry.

Looked again at forms of expression, at ways of making a point, and drew up maps and matrices to co-ordinate thinking. What's best? There is so much choice. Reviewed some of the options.

You can try the academic route. The creation of an argument, a position, deep research, the dissemination of papers, lectures, books, the response from peer groups, the discreet and learned articles, letters, e-mails, chats and forums, with the occasional break out onto a national or international stage. It could be years before any decisive action ensued.

There is the celebrity route. Get known for something and then be invited to share your views on everything. You could be a journalist, a politician, a religious leader, a pop star, or any combination, and you could induce inflammatory responses quickly. You could lobby, you could legislate, you could dictate, bend ears with your influence and money, your controlling interests and networks, leaving trails and setting precedents that others could pore over or follow.

There is both public and private war, ways to stir up interest through poking a sharp stick in the entrails of established religions, territories, creeds, and colours, a palette of excuses for propagating change.

There are quiet ways, and noisy, spectacular ways, named ways and anonymous ways, respected ways and reviled ways. There is a need for something to keep it all going that might then take years to inflate from small seeds. A Universal Expansion. There is a need for something to change forward, not to change back.

There have to be more causes these days. Things have to have reasons. Accidents can't happen anymore. Whatever happens has to be someone else's fault, somebody you can point to and blame. So, there will also have to be causes spread around to give people something to speculate on. Why did this happen? Who did it? There goes that blame thing again. There is no story in the toiler working totally silently on a long and unspoken goal, goes the thinking.

Plenty of other reasons will be found to give different profilers something to chew on. "We are looking for people who do not share our values of freedom and integrity, who do not believe in the sanctity of family and personal freedom, who do not accept that everyone has an equal opportunity to contribute to our society and to enjoy the rewards of that level of contribution".

"We will not accept these attacks. We will not tolerate acts like this in our society".

The same old songs about more rights and protection, coming from the mouths of those who spent their lives asking for protection, getting it, and then moaning about it not being enough – where will the spiral end?. They are no longer soft targets, the game has moved on. Everyone doesn't get equal protection. They never did. How far do you

65

have to go to protect someone before they are themselves in a permanent prison of protection? Under the banner of freedom, how far do you have to be insulated from the world before you can say you are safe? How much obsession and caution and habit and neurosis are you prepared to adopt for your freedom, moving every night, maybe more than once, living like leaders in cages of conflict, refugees from others' ideas? Why should you have to run? There's no place to hide. Why should you try and hide? Because you have too much of what the others want, and little means of keeping away from them, even if you can hide most of what they say they want.

If one person has more than the next, that's normal isn't it? As long as the one with more helps and the one with less is grateful and tries hard. That's the way of the old world isn't it? Or is it just the mythology? Don't religions buy into that stuff, the long running ones? But how much more is OK, and on whose terms? Science, the subject that religion beds or rejects when it suits, stepped in to offer its own view that, if people behave like a number of non-equilibrium systems, like earthquakes and stock markets and the distribution of cities, then there's always going to be a tiny few with most of the goodies. Hey, that's science, so knuckle down. Don't fight nature. But even science doesn't say exactly how big the biggest should be, or exactly when the next biggest big is going to come along. It seems to stack up doesn't it? For every place and generation you can name a few who have most of it all, and no-one who has most of the rest, which doesn't amount to much. A few self-made billionaires, a few families, a few dynasties, never was so much owned by so few – but wasn't it really that way all along? Most of the time there's an attempt to clean up the acts of families like some Mafia way of trying to launder a way to legitimacy. What, slaves, tobacco and cotton trading as one enterprise? No, no, surely we passed beyond that generations ago, and after all didn't our cousins set up the anti-slavery society? Poor deals for the workers? That was only because in the early models we were still ironing out the paths to more enlightened working practices. Any funny blood in your veins? Only if it helps our current causes, and if it does, we can get some. What do you suggest? Still so many questions.

There is no mystery, which is why it is harder to capture the imagination. There will be a need to keep creating new events, to keep people thinking there might be a different expression of reality out there, momentarily glimpsed, a different kind of universe. What will the new work show? It will be like the greater works in the medieval churches. It will be the new way to depict human suffering. The history of pain will have a new chapter.

Cue: *"Started Off With Nothing, and Still Got Most of It Left"*

***

It was time for another point of view, another disembodied voice following J's pathway to the future. J saw places so afraid of their human nature that they were putting enormous amounts of energy and money into processes of denial. No-one could be dirty, smelly, or politically incorrect. Fatness was an illusion, or a right, not a condition. Universities who dared to have people with points of view, or attempted to practice freedom of speech, were attacked by primed predators lurking in the intellectual bushes, on the fringes of campuses, stirring up vapours about attitudes and gender. There were so many strait jackets being put in place that more countries looked like places run by fundamentalists but with a genetic error that welcomed garishly lit shopping malls. There should be no diversity of viewpoint, chanted the nay-sayers. Intimidation was being practiced on more and more fronts. Alleged dissenters in the US were being found in numbers not seen since McCarthyism. People were discouraged from showing differentiating traits, shortcomings for whatever reason. Non-compliance was rewarded with being ostracised. For the more stubborn, this easily shifted into criminalisation, removal from civilisation, and the long-term erosion of identity that came to all but the most self-collected. Freedom was becoming more constrained, even for those who thought they were above such restrictions. That suited J. The people being targeted needed to feel like that – more constrained. He couldn't change everything at once, but changing one thing might affect a lot more later. They needed to understand what they had to do to earn their freedom back, or at least a version of it. Money can buy you privacy and security up to a point. The point is where it gets crazy, and you end up killing members of your own family for alleged breaches of trust. It was back to the land of tragedies, kings and tribes, tyrants and tantrums, again.

***

J could have these thoughts. They came in without interruptions. One of the advantages of working his way was that there were no phone calls, no electronic messages. He was passed by in a world of otherwise mutual digital dependency. It worked beautifully. Apart from anything else those things took up so much time, so many resources, yet here he was simply looking at an enormous expanse of sky, time, territory ignored by others, like a hard to remember numbered galaxy someone had once registered and no-one cared to point their observation devices at anymore.

Then he remembered the conversation that time way back, over the bottle of wine with an old friend. He said he was rehearsing a story for a book, and described its beginning.

She said at first that it sounded OK in the plot if you were to take out the wives and girlfriends and mistresses of powerful guys who only cared about themselves.

Why?

Because they're just as bad, and they're easier to get to. Isn't it interesting that whenever you see the big guys going down the women never get it do they? Apart from some maybe, like Mrs Ceausescu that Christmas Day, or the old Russian Tsarist Tsarina lot. Generally the women just get away with it. They may well say they knew absolutely nothing about their partner's activities, professional or otherwise, but they never have any problems with the lifestyle do they? So there they are, on their big show me yachts, in their big private jets, buying the bags and the jewels, the houses and the art, and to them it's just all straight. It's legit. They never say is this for real, where does all the money come from? They're complicit. Yet when The Big Man goes down, no-one takes the old lady down too do they? She's the victim. What could she have known, having supported the man selflessly through his long and until that moment illustrious life? There just don't appear to be too many Lady Macbeths getting outed these days. So why not take a few of them out in a different style? After all they're much less protected than their husbands.

J thought this was an interesting perspective, that maybe the women could dramatize better the way to get the Message across, some kind of leverage against the Great Egos of the world.

Then she stopped the flow and went quiet for quite some time. On reflection, on pausing, after another long sip and the refocusing of the distant eyes which eventually returned to look at him, do you know what she said then?

She said there was no point doing any of that because after all, who gives a fuck about the women? They're easily forgotten, easily replaceable, they don't count for much, they're not worth the effort long term, and they won't get the same media coverage as the guys would if they were taken out.

He pushed deeper. What about equality, stature, rights, what about the mere thought of taking out a dozen of these creatures?

And she persisted.

It's just not something anyone will care about for more than five minutes.

He thought about it. For maybe four minutes.

They finished the wine and moved on to other topics, catching up on life and its tittle-tattle. She'd never take him seriously about it, or connect him to the reality of the action. If something ever really happened like that it would just be a coincidence, like saying that someday someone might fly two jet planes into iconic towers, or that there might be suicide bombers in Western cities, truth stranger than fiction.

But for J it was better than that. Beginning to send out the Message this way would be a really good way to test the delivery system, and team loyalty. It would allow for the tougher parts of the Message to be despatched later behind greater levels of security, stronger decoys and deceptions, and with consequences that just might finally begin to be regarded with a mind to taking corrective measures.

***

How governments generally react to change ~ we meet Kashif, a rare truth seeker, burdened by pressure to protect the status quo ~ we begin to see things in a different light ~ why a more robust version of the Message will be put out ~ the compilation and management of invisible Lists and agendas ~ the relativity of morals in building a new religion ~ the tantalising questions about purpose and beginnings.

Wherever there is a human element in play, actions and directions can change. There is a different response to fresh stimuli, plans become more sophisticated, and backgrounds harder to trace and fathom. The safety of a woman's logic was very useful where terrorist hunters remained primarily men. And so, the Message, the First Lesson, went out into the world.

"We need new prophets, false or not, narrowing down the infinity of plausible futures".

"They infiltrate the undiscovered country of the future, stealing over the border to bring back reconnaissance maps of the world to come."

***

69

There are two basic problems for those who are supposed to keep the world safe from crazy attacks and behaviour. The first is that to thwart them requires a 100% success rate for the future, indefinitely, where the attackers only need to be lucky once. The second is that to even begin to approach a level of acceptable success, there is not enough time or resource available to find the gold in the seams of data eavesdroppers supply all day and every day.

Once the website condemning the decadence of rich Western men's women had kicked in, there was too much material within days. For every agency and electronic monitoring network, unless there was a specific search request or high prioritised file, there was a decade's worth of what someone thought was relevant background data coming for each assigned analyst to allegedly try and turn it into something useful while it still mattered, and even that was far away from being able to produce actionable intelligence of a preventative kind. It was like working on the SETI project. Additionally, for every remote crumb on the table that looked like it would rocket an agency into the higher firmament, there were at least twenty claimants. Most data only became intelligence after the fact. Pictures became clear after the exhibition had closed, retrospectively, and so were only useful to those whose job was to conduct post mortems and ask, 'How did you ever miss that?' The frustration was that the form of intelligence as pathology was accounting for an enormous part of the hidden budget each year, and steadily rising cynicism about the defenders of democracy could be heard in the streets, chanting that the contribution of such investments to the un-declarable prevention of attacks was unjustifiably significant. So shut up and put up. Even if you thought you knew something, some competing agency grappling for a survival budget would rubbish the input, some other would fail to pass it on, yet some other would fail to spot it had incremental input that could make a real difference because its file called a potential conspirator Jose not Joe, and those human scanners dismissed the connection. Hundreds of troubling people were out there because of variant name-spelling, and others were hassled all the time simply because their name was spelt the same as someone on a suspect list. So if you weren't already on the radar, you might enjoy that status for a long time. Even if you were, you could do a lot before the file grew to being so high a mountain it just might get noticed. Even then, the mountain might just get driven around, and so become part of the background scenery.

Generally speaking, you got promoted by being noticed positively, not by being a real uncontrollable pain in the ass. So human nature kicked in. People used their eyes and ears and experience and intuition to sift towards the favourable and the comfortable and get fond of it. It was much easier to rise up through the predictably uncertain than by jumping out of some cake and yelling 'surprise' about some unknown uncertain. Few like unpalatable truths until someone has stopped ridiculing them and they become the new normal. Schopenhauer spotted that one and no-one liked him for it either. That was the history of science in a sentence, just another form of unwanted revolution. Radicals, unless they put up 'Welcome' posters, were hard to spot, and even harder to pin down. Inciting people to improve things – a crime? Wasn't that what governments in enlightened places were supposed to do? There was more and more fodder for lawyers everywhere, and all those other pretenders to harmony usually acting under some banner containing the words 'Organisation', 'United', or 'Group', all helping each other to help themselves. You just had to laugh – off-site of course, when you noticed that some countries had been elected co-hosts of parties brought together to discuss human rights, although bias might suggest the agenda would be easier to satisfy if it was about ideas for the continuing suppression of the populace, for their own health and safety. Teams of top-grade mathematicians, linguists, classical studies graduates, and international politics PhD's lined up to join the fight against yesterday's enemies, having failed or forsaken careers in financial services and new social networking operations. That was how Kashif came to be in an arcane assembly of decoders called Pattern Resolutionists. Just a different kind of PR Group.

For a government salary, a far off pension promise, and the privilege of signing your life away to a one-way set of official secrets acts, you got the chance to bring your freshly honed analytics skills to a mound of jigsaw puzzle pieces you, and others you didn't know, were supposed to shape together to form some giant comprehensible picture of manifest evil that the armed good guys could go after, so you and all your relatives and friends could sleep soundly, paying taxes to keep this version of the world Free, and God Bless US All.

Here was a group that wasn't short on data. It had tons of that. The material came wrapped up in all kinds of perspectives and caveats. Whatever else it was, it was politically hot because every case and project that came in had been only partly solved, or not at all, and plenty of people who had been expected to produce results and hadn't, had plenty of reasons why that was not the case, usually blaming others, their arrogance, or their ignorance. Sometimes there were files that highlighted the gaps between people and departments and agencies that were supposed to be co-operating for some ill-defined greater good. Sometimes the files just revealed trails that had dried up, because it took too long to build cases. Sometimes the files simply showed that crime as defined by them still paid, especially where it could exploit systems with multiple fail-safe mechanisms. The killings' files remained open, no statutes of limitations there, but memories and emotions faded or softened as time went by, generations began to die, and the meanings of guilt and crime and punishment took on new shades and clothes, relative all.

Unsolved cases remained on the files of all the agencies that had become involved, but resources, even with huge budget increases, always appeared to be constrained, and besides, few could afford to have a bunch of lateral-minded geeks to fantasize about possibilities and probabilities every day, clearances given or not. Once a list of likely perpetrators had been compiled, combed, and exhausted, it was time to move on, and leave others to nose through the stuff, trying to sniff out scents or pieces like some wonder dog, or dropped pieces that might have been lying un-noticed on the table or on the carpet or at the bottom of the box of other jigsaw puzzle builders around the globe. That was how people like Osama bin Laden were first picked up on. Retrospectively, the identifiers were given some credit, but it had been far too late to prevent the acts we all came to see under the headline billing 'Al Qaeda' and its worldwide tour, merchandise available on-line.

Like many things in organisations, styles of operation ran in fashion cycles, like centralisation followed by decentralisation, and back again. New generations of aspiring managers sought innovation through change. In that way, electronic signals intelligence, through satellites and other eavesdropping networks, started to enjoy a reputation as safe objective information gatherers, as opposed to the rather old-fashioned, get your hands dirty surveillance called 'feet on the ground', or as the jargon compilers called it, 'humint'. This had been deemed too subjective, too much like old black and white movies, with shadowy figures and innumerable changes of transport, dead letter boxes and strangers passing in the night, a slow unreliable world of second-guessing and subjectivity. Even signals intelligence still required the application of interpretation, but hey, it was the real deal, and quantified. Mind you, as some of the sigint devotees pointed out, what real choice had there been? Politicians were tired of reporting the deaths in suspicious circumstances of their boys and girls in dodgy places, or endless negotiating dramas that inevitably unravelled and unveiled other embarrassing layers of nation-state activity in support of God's favourite earthly domains. Arrogance played its part too. The glorious United States' own Central Intelligence Agency had one of its biggest operations in the Middle East based out of Beirut, in the days when it was still a jet-set city of fun and intrigue. Some three hundred operatives were there, and only one person, the station chief, spoke Arabic. At least with sigint you got to pick up the original speakers' words, and it was easier to get a grip on capabilities, if not intentions.

The PR Group was treated like the PARC Group had been in Palo Alto when Xerox was flush with government cash for research projects. Here was the group left to itself to come up with extraordinary ideas, some of which worked. Like the Xerox poets and musicians and other apparently savant and mad caps, they sought solutions to challenges others didn't know existed, and which couldn't be derived through logical deduction and due process alone. They took leaps of uncertainty on purpose. For this reason they were avoided by many like some un-cool virus, in case they tainted the career-builders in other environments where progress was up regular ladders and through clearly delineated boxes on widely circulated job family trees. They were called shit sniffers by the regular cynics, and granted only reluctant grunts of approval if they actually came up with a result. It was another benign demonstration of corporate co-operation and excellence in the face of adversity. Kashif liked it just the way it was.

He had been the team leader on an earlier case, where one of the smart high-ups, listening to his own team, had reached a different point of view about a certain development, but hadn't shared it with them at the time, precisely because he liked to back up his hunches with evidence, and not just sound off, or pull rank. The team had been caught up in a little piece of back-slapping, not to be discouraged occasionally, when it emerged that George W Bush, through Homeland Security, had delivered a result through his efforts. There had been no fulfilled 9/11-type follow-up on American home soil since precisely then. Apart from folks with bombs in their shoes, or those trying to herd a fleet of airliners and blow them all up simultaneously on the edge of the Atlantic, another intelligence-foiled plot, there had, it appeared, been fewer incidents of enemies trying to destroy planes and their warm-bodied passengers. The detractors of democracy seemed to be on the wane in this regard. The high-up had smiled as his team enjoyed the brief moment of exultation, and, one day later, after calling the head of the PR Group, he had had a set of data despatched. He didn't believe

73

the enemy had stopped. It wasn't in their nature while the Stars and Stripes continued to fly. The question was if they had reduced or stopped this form of headline building, what were they planning to do in its place, because you could be sure they would be planning to do something. He didn't know, but he sure as hell wanted to, and he reckoned he had nothing to lose by letting the loonies loose on the case. It was a tactical decision that might yield a strategic advantage. Kashif's reputation would be growing, infinitesimally.

He looked through the files, made requests for recordings of messages, updated himself on groups and cells, opinion formers and influencers, and, using the authority of his sponsor, accessed more information without having to provide lengthy rationales. A picture began to emerge.

Just like for him, those pursuing asymmetric warfare sometimes needed insights and breaks to see the way forward, to see a new form of light, opening new doors. In the pantheon of heroes from the old days, it had been the hijackers who had got all the headlines. Then it was the bombs, in cars, in trucks, in boats. Then it was the turn of the suicide bombers, and ever more stealthy elements in bomb-making that refused to disclose their identity easily to scanners and other monitoring machines. Even if disruption through increased security, and the cost and inconvenience of that for millions of regular citizens was good support material, every so often there was the need for a piece of spectacle, a reminder that God was still on the side of the just, though since 9/11 it hadn't been quite so easy, and every year there were new impositions and checks, shifts in policy to detect one-way cash-paid ticket holders with only carry-on or no luggage, closed access ramps to terminals, locked cockpit doors, movement restrictions for passengers after take-off and before landing, all retrospective defences.

But goods came in all shapes and sizes and materials. They weren't just passengers and pets and cases. The US alone had millions of tons of goods coming across its borders every year, by road, by ship, as well as by plane. On the sea, maritime security now forced ships to reveal which five to seven ports they had been in before setting sail for the US, and overall security clearances had to be filed well in advance of approaching home waters, with records of cargoes and containers and their movements as well being submitted to scrutiny. Airplane cargo was something else again. Flowers, Medicare, drugs, fruit, fish, other foods were all being flown around the world for customers who didn't give a hoot about carbon footprints and sustainable sourcing. Old converted passenger planes and dedicated cargo planes alike were still plying the skies when commercial passenger flights and aircraft had been upgraded and moved on, whole generations of pilots flying un-social hours to deliver premium goods to demanding markets while the consumers slept. Planes followed merchant maritime patterns, itineraries being matched to maximise loads and market opportunities, hours flown, crew rosters, servicing needs, profitability and satisfied punters. Some profits were so high it was still worth flying aged fuel-inefficient craft, and re-liveried veterans of the skies could still be spotted lumbering around the aprons at obscure international airfields around the world.

Kashif had spent time looking at routes and tracker maps. He looked at previously targeted high profile carriers and airports, types of aircraft and performance characteristics, countries where security was less literal than others. He learned how many operators were banned from even approaching others' airspace, how many were more likely to kill crew and cargo through poor maintenance activity, as opposed to any dedicated terrorist input. He got into more detail about multi-routeing, as owners tried to keep planes flying as long as possible, with fewer, more profitable landings. Supply chain management was a dull descriptor for the behemoth business.

He was surprised how many orchids were in the sky, or tulips, just one of a series of surprises as he looked at manifests and customs clearances. This wasn't a business he had experienced before, and that was why he was approaching it with freshness, without bias, without prejudice, or the blind-spots of regular acquaintance. He did what he was supposed to do, looking for links and connections in otherwise impenetrable data, looking for patterns. He looked for notes, for the music in what for many would be unfathomable notations, and turned them into something tangible. He had let the data gestate for days – that was how it worked. Sometimes those who used the PR Group service beyond his immediate employers got bugged by what they considered to be inaction. Where was this guy, he's nowhere to be seen? He was easily put down as not working like them. That was the point. He wasn't working like them. As usual, the data didn't give up its secrets easily. It was a matter of perception, of interpretation.

$60 + 40 = 100$. $40 + 60 = 100$. Same answer, different order. Commercial planes, passenger planes, cargo planes, private planes. Different ratios landing at different places, flying established corridors in established patterns to established timetables. Many routines. Public information. There were no mysterious rendition flights here, no Special Forces ops, flitting in and out of questionable places on questionable assignments. Journeys looked regular from major hubs, and anyway, he wasn't tasked with trying to identify planeloads of drugs flying to and from private strips out of Columbia to Canada – that was not the call. He had to look more closely to see the emerging solution, if there was one.

Like chaos theory, big changes occur when you alter minutely the initial starting conditions for a set of actions. Bombay – London – New York. Indians on international routes. Similar patterns as with airlines exploring communities' desires and airplane profit demands and capabilities around the world. Hubs and spokes, spare capacity, cabin-fillers. Competitive established routes and emerging alternatives, emerging nations, and emerging revenue potential. Sana'a – Frankfurt – New York.

That was the beginning.

Yemen wasn't exactly full of people who wanted to go clubbing in New York, or getting residency even if they got that far, and anyway, wasn't this a cargo route? In a modern cargo plane, flagged in a legitimate European country, plying a Yemen/Europe route, brief stop-over, and then a Germany/US route, with different cargoes, making money down the whole line, and keeping the aircraft doing what it did best – flying.

That was it. The intercontinental routes were the same, but the way-back points of origination were not. The flight plan for aircraft going to New York was from Frankfurt to New York. Planes would then be given similar pathways to Newark International in New Jersey. But cargo planes weren't full of people. That was when Kashif asked for more files, for more transcripts, for more messages. Now he was looking for answers within a more tightly defined set of questions, less general knowledge and more a speciality subject, a quiz word, not a cryptic crossword. Some of the conversational banter began to take on more than a literal meaning. It was the moment to tell his sponsor what the situation was. Pass the parcel time.

They've noticed what we haven't.

So far it's all been about high profile airliners full of passengers and babies and toys, sacrificed for the jihad. Cargoes get screened, sure, but the planes themselves? These guys are looking at softer ways in. They can get bombs on planes at the start of their multi-routes under less controlled conditions, and no-one's doing a thorough check at the interim destinations. Checked cargo gets loaded on and off. It's not the cargo that's the bomb, it's the plane itself. Get in on a final descent or approach to New York, and then watch your flying bomb go Bang. So far, no-one's paid that kind of attention to the cargo planes. It's not the contents, it's the container.

They began to listen harder, to search deeper, to push their scant on-the-ground sources, and piece together the new jigsaw. It would turn out to be a pretty picture. Kashif was right, and so was the high-up. It was what the terrorists had stopped doing that opened up the search into what they might be doing. If they had continued with decoy chatter about passenger planes, no-one might have noticed in time.

They weren't always so fortunate. Sometimes cases came along that had other kinds of blank walls. He got to look at some of those too. Jigsaw puzzles never used to be this engaging.

The Paris bombing was almost tossed his way as a teaser, after the French and national investigatory powers of the victim and her husband had drawn a blank on the case. Their basic attitude was that since the guy had so many enemies, and his wife even more, getting to him somehow was only ever going to be about when, not if. They had it coming was not the judgement of the official coroner, but it was the common view of the guys on the ground. Justice must prevail. But the website launch got him thinking again, and asking for more information.

***

Elements of the precedents were good. Jesus got thirty three years (allegedly), but it took a while longer for his message to be taken up and spread around. The idea here was to enjoy a, shall we say, full term, and sow the seeds for a steady dissemination, nurturing growth for after that, through scriptures that captured his ideas. He would be sending out a more robust version of the Message soon. The beauty of the system, the process, was to be flexible enough to allow others to take up your ideas for their own ends, so the message would be internalised, and so filled with higher levels of commitment and purpose than some kind of lowly third party, fire and theft type endorsement. J wanted latter-day saints to decide the cause was true, the one true way, for the sake of the greater good, and all of us. The price of entry was not salvation, but satisfaction in the here and now for those carrying out the obligations of the past.

There had been churches, corps, corporations, bodies devoted to causes, and now they would be joined by Choosers, people who could see and make choices. No choice was still a choice. Choosing had consequences. If you made the right choice you could belong. If you

77

made the wrong choice you could be dead. All that was required was the following of simple unholy orders. In the emerging social code and its accompanying moral platitudes, life would be more conditional, but choices would be clearer. God would still forgive sinners. It's just that during their time on earth, they may not come to a happy mortal end.

***

J's Invisible Diary. Entry.

The practice runs have been useful. As Jennifer had said, no-one cared about the women. After a few days or weeks no-one talks about them any more outside of close friends, family occasionally, and police and other investigatory forces. But then how long does anybody figure these days? The prescient like Jimi Hendrix recognised you would often be more famous when you were dead, but there were other reasons for the fame to linger. If the start point was to be young and pretty, so much the better. So for Dean and Munro, Cobain and Phoenix, Kennedy and The King, you're on to a winner. If you're languishing in jail for some corporate crime, who cares to remember? But that's it you see. If you take out the famous, you get remembered for that too, but differently – Lennon, Marvin Gaye, and if you have a promising crazy bit you get even more notoriety, think Manson or Oswald. Taking out some rich invisible wives really isn't going to stir up memories for long is it? But what are we talking about here? Are we talking about remembering things because of people, or because of actions?

Maybe there are two kinds of things we remember. People, and Principles. Connected or not. So everyone thinks about Samuel Adams and John Hancock and Paul Revere, and then everyone thinks about No Taxation without Representation, or Feed the World, or Greed is Good, or In Space No-one Can Hear You Scream. So what are you really trying to get people to remember? The person or the principle, or can you get the two really connected? The preference is for the notion of getting the principle remembered, and staying alive rather than dying for the cause, famous or not. But could a principle be taken seriously without a major sacrifice? Jesus, it's hard sometimes.

***

J's Invisible Diary. Entry.

78

Who is this all for? Is it for the Big Chiefs who need to remind themselves of something they pay others to do? Is it for those who have forgotten, or those who never knew? Is it for those who are downtrodden, abused? How can anyone who elects to do something be considered to be abused? All over the world there are people who simply want more. What is wrong in showing them what the best of the best could have? Nothing, unless all they do is carry on taking and never giving. It isn't about heredity, or privilege, it's about application, perseverance. Everyone has opted in. So you think that by committing a crime you're going to be listened to? You think that by trying to take away what anyone can have they're going to say, sure – that's fair? That for the first time for ages, in some countries, when the second someone gets ahead, are you going to say – now hold it there? Enough is enough.

Don't you usually have to go to prison for a while if you have a point of view, if you're trying to change things, to make things different? Lenin, Hitler. If you stand for something, don't you have the right to defend your position? Nations go to war for the sake of the nation's dignity, so it goes. But they don't get to go to jail if they kill for their beliefs. If they don't agree with killing it's called murder, or terrorism. Evil are the things that mess with your agenda. If you are in a minority you are both a danger and a threat. If you are alone you are either an evil genius or a madman. Labels of convenience. If you haven't actually killed anyone yet, you are a dangerous thinker. In some places you will be seriously curbed from letting your thoughts lead to anyone else's action, unless you make it to the top, when what you do will be called defending the values of the people. If you go too far your reputation, historically, will be to confine you to the rogues' gallery, but between initiation and infamy there's one hell of a ride.

Of the things that can be kept, and the things that can be discarded, it all depends on who you show the lists to, doesn't it?

***

J had spent a lot of time drawing up lists. Each list was compiled, considered, and discarded. It was a tidy way to work towards a target, or a methodology, or a set of game rules. Keeping lists, and records of them, was not practical. What was needed was a process of producing and remembering them that needed no tangible records.

Different lists produced different reactions. There'd been the pet dogs' names list, celebrity dog deaths, but that only affected those who read *BARK*, those who thought animals should be more entitled to welfare and wills than people. What a laugh. Statesmen and politicians were listed, but were too replaceable or poor in most places, though they obviously thought themselves not so. There was the time when Russell Crowe got mentioned on a list. It seemed some of the global terrorist honchos had brainstormed that eradicating a few celebrities would have a major impact on moral values and well-being. Oh yes, those hard-faced Arnies who refused to leave the US at the first sign of a threat off-shore, or was it simply that their Gulfstream insurers made unseemly demands on their cover premiums?

But if that Hollywood list had ever been published in full there would have been at least one or two artiste management gurus out rehearsing the speech to their fading stars saying, Hey, you know, if you were killed by Al Qaeda you'd just be so much, you know, a martyred star. Back catalogues were being reappraised for the early re-release of material as the news hit the net.

***

J's Invisible Diary. Entry.

The lists are just another way of playing with issues. If you can't have a laugh along the way, what's the point? It is always said that fanatics are flawed by their condition. It leads to weak spots, chinks in the armour that could make you vulnerable. What is your fantasy football team? What is your greatest ever gig, with any musicians together, doing any songs you like, your ten greatest movies, your twenty favourite remixes, your eight greatest black and white movies, your five favourite Arnold Wesker plays – stop. Just a moment.

Where are the issues? The issues of Judgement. At The End of the Day, whose books balance? Who's got the best accounts? Who signs off on these, and what's buried in the notes? Should we pick people randomly, or should they be picked for a reason? The reason may be arbitrary as well.

One reason might be you work for a company that's connected to another company by virtue of size. Wow. Not by virtue of numbers of employees, or charitable donations, or good place to work surveys, but because this year, or last year, or next year, you feature in the list of BIGNESS. Not everyone is going to make the connection immediately. So we'll have to give any future connections another little push, and point it out to the media so they can create even more humungous statistics. This year you're just going to be a victim of size. Will the

80

successors want to downsize rapidly? Well. It all depends on what it means to stay on the bigness list, if that's the criterion of choice for next year.

That's the other thing about lists, another reason you don't have to write them down anymore. It's a whole industry – books, magazines, web compilations, charts, TV programmes, everything that can be reconfigured and sold. All you have to do is reference them. In the 'olden' days in England, a *Sunday Times* writer had the idea of compiling a list of the richest people in the land. There were three kinds of reaction. Those who wanted to be in on it come what may, those who thought to be on it was infra dig, and those who thought the very mention of it would lead to outrageous intrusion, and a subsequent security problem of enormous magnitude. A great idea needs a time and a place as well, and the last group were only missing out on the time. Now you can find things out you can do something about them. You can say to people on one kind of list, Hey, if you don't change your ways we'll come at you with a small screwdriver and make your glasses really wobbly, or you can say, Look, see this dead person. If you don't do something, you're next, which is usually when society kicks in and does its dance. As the old Prof said, where should the state erect guardrails in a mobile and fragmented world?

But in a civilised society, you're supposed to recover from a bruising aren't you? That's what's civilised isn't it? You recover from the knockdown, from the bully, from the corporate attack, the collapsed company, and with your friends and family, your network and your skills, you go back out and start again if you can.

That's what the movies and the books say. So you don't need to get all vengeful about the people who did you wrong, do you, because there's all kinds of professional help out there to ease the pain. It's not the Wild West any more. You can't just go out there and shoot someone who's done you wrong. Well, unless they're trespassing on your property. At least, in the USA. We've got laws for that kinda stuff.

"Permission is tacitly granted for acts of violence, plunder, even for murder, if they are carried out in the name of higher interests, according to established rules, and against a limited number of men of a particular type and belief". The whole of a society could be transformed in a single day.

Eventually someone's going to decide all this is of a higher interest, but it just needs a bigger trigger first. So let's say we are now going to create the bigger threat that will temporarily change behaviour. Maybe it takes more than a threat, but let's just see. Folks don't change when you tell them there is a better option. They only change when they work out they have no other option. What kind of life is that? For those we want to make a point to – look at your near future.

You can't go out without wondering about your personal security, rich dude. That's normal – sensible even. You can't go anywhere without planning, without protection. You can't really be spontaneous. You have to be surrounded by protectors. Your food has to be checked. You can't shop alone. You can only fly by private plane. You can only go to restaurants that have been pre-screened, even closed just for you. You have to have protection for your kids and relatives, your houses, boats, offices. Well, Mr President, what's so tough about all that? It's no different for the movie star, or Ms Pop Singer, minus the astrologer and the third hairdresser. This is the turf. Welcome to freedom, be as paranoid as the money will let you. Live in cosseted isolation or in controlled public sightings, with others taking care of all the potential downsides of unprotected exposure. Welcome to the new world of riches, divided only from other people by walls of cash and restrictions you redefine as the privileges of success.

Fame, or wealth, or both, segregation from the ordinary, isn't that what it's all been for? Not having to mess with all the little ones who collectively gave the means for you to get where you are, but who you can't tolerate being close to unless it's at some official sponsored gathering where the smiles and the autographs and the words of hope and encouragement can be occasionally doled out before returning to the cocoon of freedom you bought yourself. Once you're in the cocoon, maybe you don't need too many reminders of what it's like beyond the wall. So putting you in that position doesn't constitute a threat at all does it? The cocoon is actually what it's all about, and if you have a professional enough support team you forget about the cocoon altogether. It's everyone else who's trapped. You're the only one who is really free. Forcing you to have more reinforces your justification for it. A Golden Circle. The cloak of freedom.

Anyway, when those circles touch what do you get? You get a community. Let's call it the West. It's those who seem to have tacitly agreed that the way of the world is all about worshipping the freedom of individuality – granted that takes a huge support crew, democracy, and a free market economy. That being said, the price of individual freedom comes high, and for those whose expressions of it don't coincide with the authorities you end up with more people in prison per 100,000 head of population than almost anywhere else. See, the authorities only like rich people as well. All this effort comes down to the same mantra. Most want recognition. So anyone fighting for individuality and freedom and democracy is also a terrorist, unless they're already rich. The authorities that aspire to the circle of freedom hate those who can't get inside their own golden circle. When you're labelled a Poor Terrorist you're in a lot of trouble, or going to be. Who is in a state of freedom; who is in a state of incarceration? Who is in a state of loss?

No-one wants to kill people necessarily, but there are fewer objections if it occurs in a moral framework that gives it a justification, like a war declared by a state. Try telling that to a court though. It's like *The Secret Agent* ... to have any influence on public opinion now you must go beyond the invention of vengeance or terrorism. It must be purely destructive ... a blow fit to open the first crack in the imposing front of the great edifice of legal conceptions sheltering the atrocious injustice of society.

Like Conrad's agent, you need to be a moral agent. And like Laurence of Arabia, be a man of the shadows, an armed idealist, committing atrocities in the service of an idea of your own, an idea driven by what had happened to those around you. It is a balancing act. It is important to give yourself up to a belief, regardless of whether it embraces truth or error. What is important is whether action borne out of the idea has a profound effect.

***

J found it interesting. Different angles. Different perspectives. He was, despite a sharp cynicism about many aspects of the Human Condition, naïve and gullible in certain others, as observed. Not only deeply affected by values like honour, he also felt a basic condition of existence was good works for others, not necessarily passionate, but a kind of graceful virtue. He also knew in his system of beliefs that wrongdoing would lead to bad outcomes – he had never been able to reconcile himself to simply turning the other cheek. Wrongdoing for him was also a relative concept – not an absolute one. He had got to a place where he felt wrongdoers of his defined kind deserved to be punished. He had first based his Message at the point where he thought some wrongdoers might, just might feel a call to corrective action if their Partners were punished, if they had something taken away from them, so they felt a pain that came from something outside themselves. He realised he had made the mistake of projecting his own feelings too closely onto others, like a flawed Old Testament figure. He had been

83

missing part of the point.

Hurting partners to get to perpetrators wasn't going to work in this case. Partners were just baubles and bangles, shiny shiny, to be discarded or lost or disposed of, and not worth fretting over much. They were just part of The Deal, another element in lives dedicated to winning over everything and everyone, in that order. Getting rid of a few partners wasn't going to dent centuries of machismo in overcharged beings whose mission was material acquisition at all costs, or being top of the pile, top of the heap, whether that involved hiding behind embroideries of the spiritual, or purely masked behind bejewelled statements of diamonds, sapphires and gold.

He also realised there was another aspect of himself that, despite his occasional lapses in thinking, meant he was closer to many of those he was dealing with than he had thought. He hadn't exactly shown any tears or remorse at the recent partings of dearly unloved partners. Perhaps he was some kind of brother to the Big Swinging Dicks, the Masters of the Universe, the Head Honchos, the Numero Unos, the Big Cheeses and the rest of the slices of God these characters believed they resembled, or were. He was their missing moral consciousness.

***

The world was full of museums and monuments, roads and bridges, airports and convention centres, named after patrons in search of false memory preservation, who had bullied and beaten their paths to the tops of steaming dunghills, and now felt they could hide behind the stone facades and blessings of passive galleries, nodding retrospectively at their acquired benevolence and aesthetic qualities, these great donors of beauty in the service of power and acquisition. But nearly all of them had weaknesses too. Somehow, through social conditioning or biological drive, they had been unable to resist the pull of short term immortality, and had found means to reproduce half-versions of themselves through partners. Legitimate and otherwise their blood and genes would carry out their purpose as carriers and replicators of their definition of success into a new near future, and beyond that be damned. Partners themselves were never truly ideal. They were separate, distant, impure, but sadly necessary at particular points in personal history, helpful to bring to fruition some form of continuity. They might carry only a proportion of the genes, but that would have to do.

J smiled at the elegance of the idea that he would be sowing seeds of

84

a different kind soon enough. He had read that out in nature, there were seeds that sat patiently in soils, under ice, buried, dormant for decades, longer, waiting for a confluence of events and times to trigger a moment of creation, of blossoming again, of celebrating a brief but spectacular notoriety of colour, driven by the power to produce refined versions, shaping timetables towards perfections, the soulless mission of improved replication.

He would appear to be sowing seeds to blossom in a world of replicas, at a special time along an invisible line. It was a neat equation, and oh so natural. There was also something elegant about the refined Message which would take longer than a moment to fathom, and so would be more fulfilling in its eventual comprehension. Those like Kashif who found themselves on the side of looking for clues and unravelling mysteries would again find it a challenge to discover motives swiftly, and would be equally perplexed at the extent and scope of the actions taking place. Many would still be chasing old chimaeras, non-existent Islamic warriors, months and years down the tracks, when all had moved on.

After a second period of testing techniques, and refining the targeting, it was going to be even harder to spot the final breakout early, the final form of the Message. New searchers would effectively be looking at something that looked like the mutation of a virus, for which there seemed to be little immediate apparent cure, yet for which future prophylactic action could be immensely expensive, and without guarantees. What's more, the murderous virus could only ultimately be contained by a moral shift that just might prove to be beyond human capabilities. It wasn't just a physical threat, it was mimetic. Here would be a form of death that stifled the past through a highly focused present. It was the kind of virus nature occasionally designed to remind humans of their distinct fragility, and, like those, sought out a particular strain of human hosts.

But where did the roots of this form of viral warfare originate? This would be a question that dominated all the discoverers' drive for answers.

Part II

Before the Big Bang

"War is a thing of pretence"

Sun Tzu, *The Art of War*

"Never take a person's dignity: it is worth everything to them, and nothing to you."

Frank Barron

1

Where we search for the origins of the Message ~ we look deeper at the subject of Respect ~ we examine shifting values, and follow the lives of people who have earned respect, lost it, had it taken away, or been deserted because of it ~ we wander through Fredo's life, one complete story of elusive Respect, and we open the album on others' tales.

We need to go back to help us understand the future. Time to go back, to visit old times and triggers, the long-since sown seeds of later actions. Time to get closer to understanding what caused the itch it would be so hard to scratch away later.

Respect.

Not a long word, but deep as the deepest mines. You were supposed to know it, see it, recognise it, respond to it, give it, earn it, show it and understand it. But no-one ever shared its secrets. It was like school rules you were never shown. Osmosis, whoever he was when he was at home, was supposed to intervene and whisper in your ear how it was all supposed to be done, how you had to wear your cap at just that angle, how you were expected to grow your fringe long and then flick it over one side of your face, how you had to have one side of your shirt outside your trousers, and one sock higher than the other, and if you didn't tie your laces this way then you were a clighty, whatever that was. That big old cold book the dictionary didn't help, and there was nothing with pictures to reveal what they all meant, the ones demanding it, those whose eyebrows were raised, who looked at each other and sighed collectively, nodding to say you just don't show any respect. You couldn't buy it, and even if you could, you wouldn't ever have enough money to get even a slice of it. Fredo couldn't even afford one cigarette's worth of respect, even if that contained any. Respect was one of those fluid adult words that could be used to cover an encyclopaedia of hidden, transitory, ever-shifting rules and examples, interpretations of behaviour, expectations, judgements, and verdicts. How could any self-respecting individual ever do that, they would chorus, united in the absoluteness of their observation? Yet for each, their set of references, their examples, were different, and respect and self-respect, fluttering before them like a pair of courting butterflies, were as elusive, something you could only watch as they moved on and away from you, busy with their own self-interest.

What was there to respect? Do this. Don't do that. Did you do that?

Your brother and sister say you did. Smack. Don't lie. That makes it worse. Don't do that again, do you hear? No way to appeal. No way to let truth have its way, trying to protect itself from onslaughts like a tired matador who had sweated away his pride. You were supposed to take the blame for others, to bite your tongue, to save those who were supposed to be weaker than you who had sinned, even though you didn't know what had happened until the reason had been spelled out to you through arrhythmic beating. Didn't-we-tell-you-not-to-go-near-that-oven-and-those-pans and so on until the tormentor got tired of the monotonous hyphenated language and decided to respond to another distraction. So if you take the blame does that mean you get respect? Is that what those unsmiling people meant when they said Jesus makes you respectful, at those cold halls with the cold floors that smell of something they have decided defines clean but makes you feel grubby anyway, under those cold lights, and by those radiators that only warm themselves, the lay preachers pushing out their frost-embalmed words in borrowed styles of doom and devilment, the Methodists, whatever that meant. In later rebellious years he could have tittered at the Methodism in their madness as his tongue tasted suppressed streaks of the acerbity he used defensively to win acquaintances and woo women. Then it was all held down by his teeth, as he concentrated on how hard he could bite his tongue without any really nasty long-lasting effects, a challenge that made a tiny contribution to eking the time out through the interminable sermonising of the darkly dressed miserabilists standing at the front of the cheaply built chapel, whose heating had been donated by someone who really no longer needed it. Words floated through the hoary air like icebergs, hitting the ears of the dulled and reluctantly dutiful congregation, helping them all sink into compliance, the assembly of believers and hopers, sitting in their leaking holy lifeboat. They were all heavy and hard, like a new housewife's cake. What was all this stuff about Samaritans and tax collectors and water and wine and weddings? The only use this church had was that when all the whining stuff was over, and the last hymn had been warbled from the back by the feeble old ladies, matching the tiny organ's vibrato with their weakly breathy throats, when someone had collected all those bags fresh from the furtive pressing of coins into their dark velvet openings, the amens releasing a flurry of coughs and shoe-shuffling, of coats and scarves being thinly pulled over cold shoulders, when the last of the leavers had muttered goodbyes to the preacher and the neighbours and Uncle and Auntie Jo and Eileen, who weren't really, then the wall at the back, outside, made a great goal for

90

the boys to kick the heavy old leather football against as they returned to the dreams of the real stuff, at least until the caretaker eventually got bored with the banging and shooed them away, the church's curtain of charity closing as he locked the doors and gates of God for the night.

Fredo was close to his immediate elder brother, and his immediately younger sister, but there were five others in the family, three elder and two younger, stretching out over eleven years, distant in both directions, a mass of growth, of demands, of basic needs from bed to food to warmth, the daily fight to survive in the tiny terraced house. The father had been invalided, his lungs slowly losing out to the gases of the trenches he'd enjoyed at His Majesty's Pleasure in northern France, the legacy to the barely living. Not that that had deprived him of the drive to sire eight children, but there was nothing left for that other attention-demanding monster, work, so he sat around convincing himself through the bottle and the consoling effects of cigarettes, while he watched his wife wear out from the ceaseless strife of life. She obviously lost a sense of respect, because she decided to die when Fredo was eight, leaving the surviving family mass to fend for itself around the defeated father. Fredo wondered why the only person he was truly close to had decided to go just then, and he hoped, nervously, that if he stayed close to his two nearest siblings, and always stood up for them, they might do him the small favour of staying around long enough to show him what this still elusive respect thing was all about. Behind the never-locked front door, it was hard to fathom. Surely there was more to it than sneaking home the right bottles of beer from the shop without the owner being troubled to inform the Authorities? Surely it was about more than making sure the front step was washed and scrubbed weekly? There must be more to life than sweeping away the fag-ends, removing the dried footprints from the carpet football field, the coal dust, and the long-running disease of fatigue setting up cobwebs in every corner. He never had the courage to ask if you could get respect in a Lucky Bag if you bought one, legitimising it. He didn't want to get the Look.

School was like a lingering cold. It was no fun beyond the playground, and served no purpose other than to present an alternative series of threats and challenges from those on offer at home. Ritual rote learning in an atmosphere of intimidation made the short days seem like centuries, and most of the teachers were preoccupied with other things in other places, especially that place they thought they'd said goodbye to once. Germany was Trouble, and in this neighbourhood, any teachers harbouring ideas that the Germans were on to a good thing were careful to keep their idealism to themselves, or move to cosier quarters where intellectual debates about intentions and capabilities were more likely to be tolerated, at least for another year, and before some started talking about having a piece of paper in their hand, which seemed to have about as much effect as writing to Father Christmas. No sooner had people started to forget about The War, then talk returned like a killer disease and all those who had spent years signalling impending doom were dusting down their sabres and smiling at the inevitable fulfilment of their prophesies. The only thing Fredo knew was that he wouldn't be there much longer, because as his elder brothers got closer to facing the need to work, he knew his turn wouldn't be far behind. After all, someone would have to look after the family, feed them, be responsible, and unless school was going to pay him to turn up, education this way didn't look like an option, not that it was an education anyway, and hunger wasn't particular. He was interested in history and sums, but if the brown ale ran out his Dad would make sure he wouldn't be fit enough to go to school, and home wouldn't be worth calling that either. Economics was not a theoretical pursuit in that part of the world.

Unsurprisingly, to him, the Germans didn't seem to know much about respect either, because there was an awful lot of talk going on about showing them what it meant, and Fredo felt faintly curious that perhaps he should try and meet one of these creatures, since he and they were very much in the same boat when it came to being unable to unravel the mysteries of the key word. Just how they were going to be given a demonstration also remained a mystery, because for what seemed like a very long time, nothing appeared to be happening at all. There was a lot of talk, and a lot of stodgy black and white newspapers, and huddling round the radio, forms to be filled in and queues to be practiced standing in, but no Germans. It was nearly another year, a whole new birthday, before things took off, and then nothing much happened either. Fredo was left wondering why people took so long before doing anything. Intuition made him feel a kind of undefined fear in some, a nervousness, a cockiness in others, an arrogance, a tiredness in the prematurely old, the rising of the sap in those still proud of their former role as saviours and defenders of the vaguely defined faith, the smiles of the opportunists and the dealers, the smirks of the philanderers, the fretting of fiancées, the slow accumulation of things being saved for rainy days, the nurturing of alliances, the banking of credits with those who would hold the keys to supplies in the dark times ahead, the quiet distancing from those held to be of whatever wrong persuasion, the weak, the foreign, the overly frightened. For Fredo war was the only disruption he knew. Perhaps it was this that would reveal some of respect's secrets to him.

And what did he think of the deprivation? He had nothing to compass it with. What of the spirit of the defenders who would eventually be ready to "fight them on the beaches", the grittiness of Londoners, the Blitzers, some of whom were starting to show up with their funny voices and their funny ways, the playfulness of performers, the little actors in their Paths of Glory? It was going to be just more of the same, five years more, the most conscious third of his life, when you grew up quickly to copy the men, finally getting an occasional chance to smoke one of their cigarettes, trying to cadge chocolate from fit men with strange accents they called Americans, trying to snatch kisses and misunderstandings from girls who had no real eyes for them, preferring the feel of more Western hands above their new nylon stocking tops. Other, tired men, pale men, limped by, or crossed the street with distant eyes, looking for some sign of stability in a past that had itself left them behind, impatient with absence and grieving, seeking solace in snatches of daylight. Checking out the ARP's was only a momentary diversion. Trying to get exciting titbits about the Germans from those who didn't look like ghosts occasionally led to rewards that were far greater than the frowns and formal clichés from those who stayed behind, the essential workers, those who tried to make life go on to new rules, bending less and less into more and more, so you were meant to feel grateful and full of what they claimed was fresh air, and that everything was so much better than it would be if the Germans ever managed to get their feet on the shores, which of course they wouldn't, thanks to Winnie. Fredo missed the idea of his mother. But he didn't miss other distractions much, like books. There were none of those things at home. And the summer was great, because even the blackout couldn't take the summer sun away, and you could see the endless unrepeated patterns of contrails turning slowly pink as the sun wandered over the eastern sky to wake the Germans up even earlier, and the pilots would have to rub pretend sleep from their eyes as the next day began overlapping the last one. By the time the birthday came around on 6 September there still didn't seem to be much evidence of the Germans having learnt any respect, so Fredo was just going to have to wait a little longer to discover how they might decide to reveal one of its facets. Two weeks later, they stopped coming over in droves, and everyone was suspicious about why. No-one had gone back to school, and it was the end of their holidays. The Germans hadn't run out of

93

petrol, or planes, or pilots, but the skies returned to an untainted September blue, and contrails stopped knitting clouds together, aerodromes were quiet, the occasional engine firing up briefly on test, like the sporadic snores of exhausted men asleep in the sun, restless and turning their dreams away from the glare, seeking solace in private shadows until the next whenever siren would return them to this particular game of reality.

But there was no call. Things were in suspense. Beliefs, nightmares, support crews, girlfriends, radar watchers, command centres. The only sound was the old leather ball still cheekily slapping against the church wall, and the distant peal of Catholic bells on the other side of town, signalling that perhaps it was safe again for their Jesus to walk the streets, and not be sprayed by some straying fighter. His chariot could descend unharmed. You'd think he'd probably have something more modern these days.

***

There was no "after the war". Other than the time everyone went crazy and said for a day it was all over, things carried on as before. Maybe things got even worse. There were no treats, the rules and the hangover carried on, biting into every exposed area of life, from food to clothes, heating to entertainment. The apparent victors were as wounded as the adversaries, bloodied, exhausted, hanging onto the ropes only inches above the other prone contestants, the slimmest of victories on moral points, except for that word 'pride', which dominated an ubiquitous spirit. It was closely followed by that other word again, 'respect', which everyone talked about as if you could cut a slice of it from somewhere, sit down round a table and eat it, so all would be well. That was it then? You were supposed to have won the right to claim conceptual victories about freedom, values, reason, goodness, integrity, rich inner landscapes which were meant to act as alms for a disrupted reality, displaced persons, broken relationships, disconnections. But all these are comparative.

For Fredo there was no 'thing' to compare the experience with; it was the way it was. It was absolute. A lot of people began to wake up and look around and say, well what are we going to do next? There were the few who spotted, as they always do, opportunities to make hay from even this weak summer sunshine, but many too felt pangs for something else lost, ended, a phantom amputation, the ceasing of the flow of adrenalin after the curtain came down the last time on the long theatrical run, when the entire crew would be splintered, seeking succour elsewhere. The Director of The Big Production, Great Britain, had seen the show and its audiences reaching the end as well. As the impresario GB-diluted would come to create a new production, or find others who could stage a new spectacle, keeping the players and their applauders together for another long run. He sowed these seeds well. Having uprooted one huge and creeping weed, he was able to point out to the English world of little gardeners that weeding is a constant process, and that in other parts of the big garden, long hidden roots were about to shoot, and couldn't be ignored for much longer. At least, that's what Fredo heard from some of those returning from their tiny vegetable patches, their allotments, to compare their thoughts about what the future might hold. Keep it simple, keep it in terms we could all grasp, and then it'll all be manageable. A rotten apple, that Hitler chappie, and now we're being told there's a rottener one, a Russkie, who was supposed to be on the same side as us. Just goes to show. Even in the most cultivated garden lurk enemies. Remain ever vigilant. There's a new strain waiting to wage war among the flowers, waiting to slide tendrils around weaker stems, and crush the flowering life out of them, leaving the garden monotonously green and hostile. It was going to be the Russians' turn to take on the lead role as Enemy Number One, and in their train, anyone else who elected to pursue their own version of living which wasn't what the Western winners wanted. War carried on by other means, which gave many people a good reason to believe they could still put up a fight, all they knew how to do, even if they didn't really understand quite what the new enemy and his intentions added up to. The threat was enough. There was still going to be a lot of stuff going on, bad stuff, and people behind it who weren't showing any respect. The threats were big enough. Sure they were.

There would be a need to keep the Armed Forces topped up, to keep Our Boys on top of their game, to keep saving the rest of the world from itself, like an ageing fussy aunt, unaware of her own creeping decrepitude. New enemies, new shadows, new fears to be instilled, new causes to espouse, old eternal values to defend, and the paying of huge reparations into the diminishing Empire's respect deposit box. The convenience of the continuity of war by other means meant it was much easier to rationalise the achingly slow time it was taking to re-build the home nation from its depleted resources, and capitalising on the population's conditioned response to deprivation. You may be hungry but you can hold your head high. Britain's finest hour. Whatever the young thought, those who had passed their formative years under the threat and then the reality of war, many were about to be obliged to support the country's holding aloft of the flame of freedom themselves, and National Service was the way to honour those who had laid down their lives to keep the flickering flame alight. In spite of the dubious rite of passage, from civvy street to passing out parade, for many, the chance to escape the dead ends of towns, the no-hoper or none jobs, was the only thing worth thinking about. Maybe you could be a winner among winners, maybe that way Respect would lay

If you happened to be young and German, you were simply and suddenly denied history, and silently punished for a past that was unexplained. You were guilty before you were innocent, and you were instructed to be thankful for the present and its extended deprivations.

There you were then Fredo, able to march in harmony with others, to pass muster with a gun, to look passable under inspection, to be fit, to be away from the smoke and the damp and the dark of the dingy industrial heartland, ready to swap all that for the fresh smoke of some other distant battleground. Welcome to The Posting abroad, where, apart from teaching the still rebellious a thing or two, you were supposed to help the occupied understand why they must be professional penitents for all time, and then some.

There you were, your uniform a blue serge, an RAF boy now, proud as punch, and ready to uphold the victor's pledge anywhere out there in that still hostile world. You used all the time there was to build friendships, to be a team player, and all the photographs showed you there, in all those teams, hockey, football, cricket, pitching yourself against others, boxing, bringing together all the defences of home with good trainers, a focused fighting machine, a talent in the ring, a talent in the teams, ready to represent The Force from Kirkness to Korea, and all points between. The unit held together, found links and squeezed out weaknesses, ready to tackle whatever the wrongdoers wrought. You weren't briefed on the finer points of the enemies' ideologies, or the wider political and cultural contexts of the new theatres of war, but you were well set up to recognise the heinous deeds and potential of those threatening the friends of the still cosmetically made-up Great Britain. As well as the novel Cold War, there were plenty of skirmishes and uprisings and emergencies to add to the tray of offerings for young men to reach out for and put right.

You had plenty of time to wonder just what all those people who had a grudge looked like, what they'd really be like, as it were, in the flesh, as you nursed your sea-sickness through six weeks of sea and ocean sailing, that first time properly away from home, sitting roasting underneath the deck of the aircraft carrier, occasionally being tossed tools and being told to join the paint duty, battleship grey endlessly applied to the ship's sides, the Med pushing past the bow beneath the nets as the carrier cared for itself en route to the East, a relay from Portsmouth to Gibraltar, Malta to Cyprus and on, the Red Sea, Aden, Singapore, the flags of victory flying over tattered towns, all holding on to each other in the comfort of connectedness, a team spirit displaying bruises like bronzed medals. It looked like it was going to be Malaysia that was going to be the place that needed sorting out this time, and the tales of what was going on would be embroidered and evaluated in between dances at the Raffles Hotel in Singapore, between beers and swaps for the tickets for dancing girls. Some kind of 'insurrectionists', live monkey-brain eating fighters who didn't know their place, who raided the single narrow-gauge railway train in the jungle and did unspeakable things to innocent passengers. They were the ones who needed sorting out. Worse than the Japs they said, which must have been quite something, Fredo felt, from what he'd heard. Soon he would be put in a position to check this out directly for himself. He was due to meet the troublemakers the Brits had largely trained in the first place, and his dreams were going to be filled with the sights of what happened to those the enemy deemed to be unsuitable trespassers on their planned-for new ruled-by-them homeland. He was part of the support team, on the ground, back at base, keeping the machinery of the new conflict oiled and functioning, ready to serve the democratic freedom defenders in whatever configuration the planners dreamed up. He had swapped the damp of Ilkeston, Derby, for the humidity of the Malaysian jungle. Singapore occasionally found him conveniently locked in a bar as it ran into its compulsory closing hour around the time of the mid-afternoon rain, sipping Tiger beer until opening time clicked round again, and the doors opened to greet the freshly rinsed humidity. It made a change from the rheumatic seasonality of the Derbyshire latitudes, but you still had home-sick reliefs in the NAAFI. It was another form of reality he stepped in from time to time, and he took to bar stools when soldiers and pilots failed to return, or when he visited the base hospital to see others he knew nursing wounds and traumas, wondering what the fuck they were doing there and what did it matter to anyone anywhere else. But it was better than Korea, where the stories told of much worse things and imagination took over the task of decorating scenes with deeper strokes of gore and occasional glory. In many ways the fighting, the engagement, the struggle, was in time a tiny part of the remote background that was the maddening routine and

97

orderliness that pervaded daily life away from the action, the preservation of homeliness abroad that had fuelled generations of Empire builders. Behaviour continued as if it were simply an exceptionally hot English summer's day, the fixtures of football, hockey, cricket, the same as before, the need never to relinquish that English soil so far away, the need to know that England was captured in every invitation, in every encounter, in every discussion, held together through food and drink, through the radio, through the endless comings and goings of those fresh from home or returning, tales of friends and football clubs fighting against a background of sweat and cicadas, against the epileptic strobing of the ceiling fans, against the crunch of peanut shells on the bar floor, the creeping effect of Singapore Slings slaking equatorial thirst.

But he had learned one thing out there. It had crept up on him over the weeks and months. Lack of respect was what happened when people died if they didn't take the trouble to get to know each other, to work with each other, to be together. Real respect was about being bothered, about caring beyond yourself, it wasn't something you could see on a uniform, or in an order. Sure, there were fights, bickering, cock of the rock strutting, sarcasm, back-biting, jokers, weak links, sadists, smart arses, dumbos, the whole clichéd lot, but with one or two exceptions, what bonded them after all the posing and the posturing, was the insight that produced respect, and you couldn't bottle it. Once you'd seen it, felt it, experienced it for real, you knew it anywhere. The dangerous learning was that you also recognised its absence anywhere, and that this was far more conspicuous than its presence. 'Lack of respect' was dangerous words making an ever more potent meaning-laden phrase that would have graver consequences again, later, for everyone.

So, in a world of fading Empire and a shifting idea of Britishness, he'd signed up for ten years, a lifetime commitment for an eighteen year old. A catapult into the big world with a large amount of red bits still coloured in on maps. Basic training and a posting to carry on doing the same stuff as legions before, only somewhere fifteen degrees warmer, on the other side of the world. Back in England, having done one's bit to quell the bad boys, having gone through the wringer of re-discovering the seasickness that wouldn't go away, cooling down in the ship as it returned from the tropics to the Atlantic, a progress actually modified only by the switch in the professional sailors' uniforms, matching the darkening of the sea and sky, it was all about waiting again, waiting for the next order, waiting to serve, waiting for the next threat, the next new enemy. In between there were the short leave periods, the forays from camp, the frantic fit bicycle rides from base and its surrounding arc lights to the other bright lights, the swapping of Singapore sweat for cold northern seas and sand, the ever irritated wind blowing along the promenade and against the piers, trying to dislodge trams from their rumbling tracks, and the lights and laughter of the magic vortex, the Tower Ballroom. That place Blackpool had had seventy years practice in separating people from their money and had honed its techniques, its baits, on generations of fun-blinded millworkers, suspicious Scots, extravagant billeted Americans, and all the wild-eyed innocents in between. It was a machine for transforming money into soluble madness, the laughter of those who for a few days had escaped the rigour and monotony of mill work and mines, the constant supervision of jobs in the dwindling heartland of the depleted Empire's industrial capacity. Despite the draconian efforts of a forest of stiff-backed landladies, no-one was going to stop these momentarily carefree people from enjoying themselves after they'd been thrown out onto rainy streets by the sergeant-major seen-it-all women who forbade a return to the digs until five o'clock, tea-time, tornado or not. There were tensions, the predictable onset of fights over forgettable causes fuelled by flirts and too many schooners of draught sherry, gaggles of lads and lasses making nervous come-ons as the docile donkeys looked on. Every yard another distraction, the tiny tented spaces promising to reveal the future, Petulengros putting out prescriptions for a carefully crafted progression towards success and satisfaction, the seduction of sugar, rock as long as your arms, waiting to challenge your teeth as you tried to prove whether the stick really did say Blackpool all the way through, the two-headed babies, the shoot and win every time stalls, the clash of vinegar and hot-dogs between food fuel stops, the interruptions of Players' cigarette smoke and horse dung behind the clattering landaus, horses blinkered from the distractions save for the voice of the coachman and his whoa's and clicks. There were the shouts, always the shouts, come along on the ride, on the motorboat, a trip in a large bareboat to the middle of nowhere and back, three miles out in the brown Irish Sea, bobbing about and looking back at the Tower, wondering if you'd make it back to the beach before parting company with your fish and chips, the come on have-a-go's, the special offers, the deals on sea-shell souvenirs and sniggering signs, saucy postcards, empty deckchairs, the challenge of cockles and whelks, forlorn children glimpsed inside the Lost Children bus and its beige sadness, signs for the shows, the twice nightly parades of singers and dancers, jugglers

99

and headlining comedians, two and a half thousand souls a session, rolling out of the Opera House, mad for more. And in the Tower Ballroom, beneath the spinning mirror ball, on the sprung floor soaking up the heels and the live sounds of the band, uniforms clashed as they danced the girls around, each weighing up the potential of the ones they were jiving with, those who had already decided they preferred the boys in blue, who could spot a rank in an instant, assessing the prospects of young men with clean nails and clean haircuts, blue eyes and blue shirts, money to parade with, laughter that defined the pressure of time before the next departure to God knows where. Only some things get left behind, and on this occasion it was the boy in the belly of Fredo's recent catch from the sirens of the ballroom.

***

Common enough, the surprise of how did that happen, the scrabbling around to make it 'alright', the ritual shock and horror and the shame of it all, the dash to legitimise a moment's passion in the name of love and forever-ness, the cool stately progression and planning for the natural timely official coupling the wedding signified, the hot 6 June, another D-day, and the lump barely showing. The shame was officially buried under confetti, and true love emerged, gold-banded, photographs capturing the celebration of innocent love, legitimised lust. Reality returned with a new posting, leaving Mrs Fredo behind to nurture the bump at her parents' house, as the husband went off to defend Her Majesty now from yet more ungrateful aggressors. It was a year of highs, literally in the case of Sherpa and Tensing, the orange pride of Blackpool's FA Cup victory, old man Matthews making his immortal mark, the regal joy of the newly established Queen, a new Elizabethan Age, the happy reunion of tradition and progress, the retention of The Ashes, the media telling its subjects to Be Proud of Britain.

Respect had reached its pinnacle. Fredo was twenty three. In five months he would be a father. Amen. In this new beginning was an end that would stretch on and on, a slow wasting disease, an aimless drifting, a space getting darker and darker, further and further from that sunlight that had been labelled Respect.

***

In which Fredo's search for respect continues to prove elusive ~ how the world overtakes the searcher ~ Other places reveal similar stories ~

the world in general yields to equal passions – blood and family, faith and creed, endless feuds, hard wired ~ the past and present remain irreconcilable ~ apparent home truths are the same whatever the uniform, corps or corporate.

Fredo still didn't really understand the detail. He still had the same bad dreams from Malaya. He received the new messages, but aside from stories about how the Russians were just waiting to bomb the West to bits and inflict their version of the way the world must be upon us, no-one outside the Force seemed to care too much. Even though everyone by now had seen the pictures, the mushrooms, none of it related to home. What was happening in that filtering out was the loss of appropriate words. They only got used in the past tense. There were new words now, television and Teddy Boys, there were programmes from America showing how life could really be, even in comedies, every day, beamed into terraces still without inside toilets. They took up present time and space, they providing distractions from the dullness of doomsters and politicians. There were things to buy you might want, to choose, to talk about, Ideal Homes and time-saving products, a world receding from chores, dancing towards new levels of excitement and comfort, nuclear radiation just some kind of background sizzle, like fried bacon.

There were plenty still out there, the ones now building Britain's new aggressive deterrent, testing it to death in Maralinga, selling the Australians a tale on damage limitation.

Not quite how you saw it later, as you tended the V-Bombers with their enormous doors and tiny windows, checking dials and wires, the smell of professional oil and metal the signature of serious business behind the pilots' seats, the no-escape space where the support team sits, waking to set off the Armageddon Alarm. These birds break down while they rest, ever fussing to be fuelled and caressed, delta wings drooping, waiting for the two-minute scramble to take flight above the clouds and on, beyond the reach of misleading radio clatter, counter-productive propaganda, jamming and futile defences. There was a job to be done, and you were there to do it. Britain's nuclear rattle, defence of the realm, the all-weather birds primed to return to an empty nest, empty, an empire of emptiness, and what kind of victory was that?

Away from the runways, the ever-present perimeter lights, the fences, the hangars and their fledglings, a sort-of life went on in the identical married-quarters houses. Vans brought food, fish, meat, books, and new arrivals baked jam tarts to say hello to the established,

101

little sweet red badges of acceptance, tokens of neighbourliness. The cinema, with its Mantovani and its orange ruched curtains playing the part of maintaining the peace, showed *Snow White* and scared the little ones with witches and apples, keeping animated links to the land of opportunity. The games went on, the matches, the visits to and from the base, the trips to nearby towns and villages, steamy branch lines and sleepy tank engines, leather straps holding the windows open to the air in the second class compartments, coaches tap-tapping along in a relentless Morse code, smoke settling on the undulating staves of the telephone lines, white noise. Bicycle rides and picnics, sandwiches and the smell of May-cut grass, the thrill of parcels in the post, the strange goings-on in the kitchen of those television cooks Fanny and Johnny, exotic dinners, wine, and children's television, the four-syllabled announcer's word, *Picture Book,* and the *Woodentops* so like the world of the camp. Buses and trains, always having to keep moving, to go somewhere, because here was only ever temporary, except for the few days around Open Day, when everything held its breath in anticipation of the thrill of the show, the display, the noise of the power of protection, sowing its cover across the skies, showing you that somehow there was always a comfort blanket there to make sure the Reds wouldn't be able to steal your scones just like that.

Then it's decision time. Ten years is up. What choices do you have then? You can sign up for another dose and if you get fed up this time you can try and counter your misplaced commitment through the discouraging penalty of buying yourself out, or you can quit now, service over. You have given. You can go out into that other version of the world again, and let some-one else worry about Suez and submarines and being a world power, Eden and his merry men and all the rest.

Fredo could go to the pub now, play a different game, be in an un-mined garden, and when the kettle boils he could drink tea without worrying if he would get the blame when the plane he had worked on smoked its sick way home, landing with its nuclear warheads primed and stuck. In many areas there were jobs. It seemed high wages beckoned those with professional skills, the lights in civvy street looking brighter than they had for a long time, less of the cold shoulder cruelty of camp lights discouraging closeness and questions. It was time to make and maybe even spend money, to be part of the bigger group, families, to pursue pleasure, affluence, and to win that measure of success, that dream you kept trying to turn into reality with civilians, respectability. That was the new idea now, respectability, subtly

102

different from respect. The way to do it was through the little house with the bathroom and dining area, the wireless and the TV, modern lighting and gas, the nostalgia of a coal fire but no longer the heart of warmth for the whole house. Tinned salmon on Sunday, tea-time treats, time to fill in Football Pools coupons, time to tinker with an old BSA motorbike in the back yard, time for a pint or two. Being quids in. Paying to keep up with the Joneses. It was a life being bought on hire-purchase, a life in new instalments, great until you became a defaulter, a ghost in Never Never Land.

The week was turning into a round of experimentation, with new-fangled foods like fish fingers, a weekend look from Burton's tailors' window, the knick-knack hunt in Woolworths, performances to watch by Lonnie Donegan or Tommy Steele, the erosion of the fixed Monday-Sunday menu, the ubiquity of sliced bread, the emergence on the grey and white screen of talks about the darker side of life behind the curtains, angry young men whose anger so many couldn't fathom. To escape from the suburbanisation you stepped into a different cinema each week to watch Charlton Heston perform new miracles, and John Wayne win against evil in all its forms. The tension between the quietly deteriorating traditions of Great Britain, its romanticised music hall legacy, and today, were tightened weekly by the yet more incursive fruits of Americana, the uptake of vocabulary and habits, people now ecstatic at the sight of Elvis or a Burger, the beckoning light of a juke-box, tombstone for many small-town live musicians, and good riddance to many, they thought. That was the way style and modernity and sophistication were being delivered to Fredo's doorstep. No-one went abroad, away, overseas, unless there was going to be another war, not at this level of society. Inflows from Europe were another thing altogether. Resistance still applied when it came to foods like pasta, or cappuccino. The cook, Elizabeth David, was not the answer to the kitchen's needs round these parts. She was the enemy. Olive oil, langoustines, garlic, were all the work of the devil, except in the minds of those snooty buggers who tried to call themselves middle-class. There's nowt better than what you get here, they chorused. Dissent wasn't respectable. It was safer to stick to British innovations, and American aspirations. Break away, no, stay, push, no, be still.

Coming out of the Force meant being reminded of all those things that had been in suspended animation for so long. The return to the streets of old brands of cigarettes, penny Woodbines, the dangerous smell of town gas-works, the smoke of engine sheds, the dark shiny damp of rain on cobbles, fending for yourself, the slow creeping shock of realising that, well, after all, people were less proud of you than they once were as you returned from uniform. It wasn't quite so easy to be garnered with a job and consistent comforts from a grateful citizenry. There was little sophisticated machinery to work on, no interest in time unless it was called overtime, grabbing all while it was fleetingly there. At 27 it was time to grind, grubbing around as a mechanic in the day, frying chips until midnight, saving halfpennies to escape the increasing grudge of being harnessed to in-laws in their house, a four-year old to feed, and a non-working wife wanting to 'own our own home'. It was boring and frustrating both, and when it wasn't those just induced feelings of confinement and rejection, there was a general resistance to what appeared to be the return of bureaucratic officialdom and attitudes, a feeling that you were now being tainted by a past you had not been able to choose, rejected for being saddled with a set of values that were under the microscope, being put under caution to put up or shut up. The anger was internalised. It wasn't the wear on your sleeve rebellion of a Dean or a Brando, a Teddy Boy or a Beatnik, it was a slow growing wasting borne of a discovery of loneliness, insecurity, incomprehension, a stifling brought on by the new, stoked by the conformity of resignation.

The only ones you felt you could talk to about it were either still in the Force or far away. You couldn't tell anyone else. It wasn't done. If you had a problem with authority now you followed the union, but if you didn't you stayed in the shadowy corner and kept your head down. If you'd tried to better yourself at night school you failed because you were too tired from the two or three jobs you were spinning to pay attention, to graft mentally any more, and all that had to be someone else's fault didn't it, but there was no-one to understand that, the old working class ball and chain stiffness stifling ambition and self, darkening the lights of aspiration and mobility, of breaking out of the pull of the dirty finger-nailed world, orbiting freely in a space where people didn't play by the same interminable rules of incarceration and the leashing of imagination. But he couldn't shake off the feeling that he deserved a better chance, that he had served, and a credit was now somehow due back to him, that if he'd only known the word there was some rightful meritocracy that would help him achieve his place. But no-one around him had heard of this either. In fact, you were really only worth knowing if you knew your place, and you should be bloody grateful for that too sonny. If only he had realised he was being held in check by a snobbishness of all-enveloping proportions, which claimed honesty and straightforwardness as its vanguards, and practised

104

hypocrisy and petty vengefulness like gossips and playground bullies, strutting in the shadows of the Infant School toilets, he might have been in a better position to plan and effect an escape.

***

Then there were the women. The ones he decided he wanted, other than his wife, and knew he could never have. Toys in the toyshop you craved and coveted sinfully. The wife who allegedly doted on him, or his weekly pay packet, was the New Consumer. Always wanting something, the new detergent, the medicine, the toothpaste, the frozen food, the magazine, as if it wasn't enough that everyone else wanted a piece of what he brought home as well. Then it was sofas, records, holidays, treats, clothes, drinks, cigarettes, sometimes it would just be a lot easier if the Bomb dropped after all. Just do your best. But no-one wanted what he was best at. He didn't like too many folks, suspicious of many, so many threats to the peace he craved at twenty eight. He began to hide, behind the sleep of the overworked, in front of the fire, before and after tea, beside the radio and all his special programs and their arcane Goon jokes only he found funny, behind boxing matches and the sport on TV's *Grandstand*, long-lasting cricket, a pretend depth of thought behind some escapist novel where he had to be summoned from his concentration by repeated coaxing, the envied distance of his level of involvement, the growing hide and seek behind the variety and number of drinks, glasses chiming an interlude between snoozing and sleep, protracted distracted silences, the oppressive weight of the misunderstanding filling his overheated ironic living room, cloaked in the glow of the gas fire, and the ritual removal from the wall of all electric plugs as a sign it might finally be time for bed. All that changed was the time the curtains were pulled closed against the show of the outside world and its indifference, according to the season.

He'd already had to endure death and bereavement too soon, and then the nuclear threat joining these two as the third witch. It all kept him tossing and turning at night, a gnawing fear about further abandonment, of being let down, of letting down others who hadn't made it this far. No-one out there cared, they were complacent, they had what they thought were better things to do, as advertised, and he couldn't shake off the feelings that no-one else had a clue about the way the world really was, the way he saw it, caring less. The poxy meddling shop-stewards nagging, looking for ways to slow things down, make demands, nurture grumbles, thieving ideas of dissent from

105

their comrades and brothers, protecting their own petty interests and short sightedness. Not a one of them would ever be on *This Is Your Life*, him neither. He couldn't wait to find Radio Luxembourg, to find some scratchy jazz fleeting across the airwaves, a break from the daily doldrums, a link with the past through dance and bands, the Ellington Basie Bechet line. It was his private way of avoiding being regimented again, that schizophrenia between the pull of discipline and the push of escape, the tiredness of being told what to do blown out by saxophones and drums. What had the fifties done for him, eh, apart from make him ten years older? He was trapped in a new house, surrounded by brands and brashness, temptations and demands on time and money and energy, fading energy. Some called it freedom, choice. Of course, like others, he was supposed to smile and be grateful he'd never had it so good. Live now, pay later.

He felt like Anthony Sampson who he'd never heard of and would never meet, but was the one who voiced where his intuition had taken him to, that Britain was a place that didn't believe in anything and was confused about its direction. There seemed to be no time for his kind of proficiency, his hard-earned form of expertise. Everyone was rushing past with contempt and wads of hire purchase agreements, chasing rainbows. He turned to drink as his best secret friend, and for a further thirty years tried to turn an addiction into a characteristic. He became a professional Entropist. Meanwhile the other shadow grew.

He returned to the military, after a fashion, by managing to secure a place with a major developer of military aircraft. He was there as the experimental planes and their variants were put together and tested. He was there when, occasionally, a test pilot wouldn't complete a flight, and was lost under the banner of progress in defence. Designs were tried and modified, materials were introduced for lightness and flexibility, strength and endurance, and any combination of ways to improve killing potential and manoeuvrability. In those days, safety requirements for experiments were written up as arse-covering let outs, and people were exposed to all kinds of dangerous materials and levels of toxicity. It was a time when official government films advised children to get under their school desk in the unfortunate circumstance of an atom bomb detonating five miles away from them, and of military men being given sunglasses to watch mushroom clouds within easy eyesight of ground zeros. Working inside and outside of a stream of fast jets and bombers, leaking all manner of fluids and test mixtures, Fredo's body absorbed a cocktail of dangerous microbes, which lay dormant for years in their host's body.

Encouraged to take early retirement through unexplained sickness, he was pensioned off, and began to spend yet more time in the company of his secret friend. That was when the cancers kicked in. Fredo died in a hospice, leaving a grieving wife and a son to keep the memory of him alive. No-one had the inclination or the money to find out who else might have suffered similarly, and what the great corporation and its protective government were hiding from the world, the loss of so many in service to ever more effective ways of killing. There was no roll-call, no wall of remembrance. In the last days, Fredo finally got what he needed from the hospice. Respect.

***

The flags flew. American units were coming home to small town America. When the buses' doors opened and the men came out into the cheers, most had frozen faces and wary eyes, stepping forward to give silent hugs which muffled the cheers. The collective reunion was brief, parties dispersing to their own private cocoons as though something like teargas was clinging to the public spaces.

They were home. Except they weren't. Physically they were in a place they had once been, but otherwise it was a distant mental landscape, what they saw, what they heard, what they felt.

Butler County had given up 381 souls to defend God's country since 1942, and here were more dead soldiers, except they were still on active duty. The new generation of National Guards had thought they were going to be peacekeepers if ever they were called up to the frontlines. Two of them went to Iraq because they were friends, and friends go with each other to face challenges. But when they got there they were put in teams thirty miles apart. One of them was killed by a suicide bomber. The one who came home kept going mentally back to the dead zone, his eyes distant and fixed. Back in the world he'd first lived in, he kept the alternative he'd physically left behind through a vague set of generalised references, mixed with resistance to crowds and busy places, jumpiness, the constant lookout for danger in what was supposed now to be peaceful territory.

He had post-traumatic stress disorder, like others who'd come back, and they weren't talking to each other. There could be more than a third of them like that, living in their own dead zone with a community that had no idea what they'd been through. On their own - surrounded. Things were missing from the recent past, missing friends, missing power, now they were back in Boringville. Then they closed down

107

some more – not answering the phone, not opening the door, not talking to their own family, not being able to concentrate on anything. It's hard to let it go, to let what has happened be acceptable, to say good-bye. Especially when you convince yourself a lot of the bad stuff can't have happened anyway. And you have nothing in the bank to save you from the past.

***

Northern Ireland had been easy. Tough, disciplined, pressured. The patrols had experience, knowledge was tacit, shared, the enemy was understood. Eighteen years after Bloody Sunday all sides knew where they stood. It was dangerous, nervous, tense living, but the experience of urban strife had been enormous, and the British soldiers and ex-soldiers became valuable in other places where civil unrest, as they called it, required some form of armed response, legitimised by the ruling authority of the day. Wet streets and terraced houses, thin shivering glass that shattered in old peeling window frames, the singing coming from inside the bars, taunting the unwary, checks, patrols, checks, debriefs, harassment, testing, more checks. These were the memories, the features of the tours for the rotating regiments. For others it was the smell of wet vegetation, the long long rains, the hours of close-up surveillance, watching suspects, waiting for drops, for caches to be tapped, for meetings to take place, to be interpreted, added to the intelligence files. The world of surveillance had two manifestations, the ever-so-public demonstration of presence and control, and the ever-so-surreptitious world of spies and swoopers conducting their own war in the green land. Whatever the politics, these were trying places to be, and dangerous people to be with. And all the soldiers conducting the public face of peace-keeping knew that they were despised, and that whatever they did they would be in the wrong, in the eyes of the disaffected citizens, and the critical perceptions of the media.

Most of the time it all added up to a quiet confidence within the forces, handling their mistakes and losses with their own grieving, responses and reflections. The successes they reserved for celebration on their own turf, the private places beyond the scrutiny of the critics. It was a collective experience that was supposed to serve them well for other operations. Buildings might change shape, there would be no glass in the windows, the rain would be swapped for heat and dust in the summer, gritty ubiquitous sand, and cold winter nights would

108

replace the relative comfort of the softer vegetation, faces would alter, attitudes would shift, but underneath it all there appeared to be some constancy about how to handle conflicts in urban environments. There was *A WAY*, not the same way or style that other forces might use, or feel happy with, but a way nevertheless, and it was a variation on the long-drawn history of what was now called hearts and minds approaches. It was with this experience and conditioning that the smaller group found itself in Basra, trying to get the locals to see what good the removal of Saddam had brought, without much success. There was invasion, then there was insurrection, insurgency, an attempt to put an end-by date on hostilities. As usual, in the 21st century, the locals' attitudes were not primed for flower-giving and kissing of the form filmed by the propaganda units of former liberating armies. When you were being liberated into a world of extended chaos and factionalism, where old sores still festered beneath the band-aids and bandages of dictatorship, there was little to celebrate as a newly liberated citizen, even if you could find anything to celebrate with. Democracy didn't always dance in ball-gowns.

The moving patrol was routine in their sector, covering a market, its surrounding houses, and a mosque. There was the usual need for careful vigilance, and the danger of complacency creeping into the familiar. There was always action around the market, even if there weren't always things to be bustling for. There were opportunities for people to be concealing unclear behaviour and action behind counters, behind clothes, in mounds of diverse materials. You had to be very careful, try not to mess with innocent actions like the simple tidying away of utensils or metal objects that had a dull sheen in the bright sun, yet weren't weapons. You had to repeat what you had been lectured on, trained for about habits, customs, preferences, careful not to insult the citizens in their expectations and interactions. The outside of the mosque was the place where you kept the keenest eye on the faces and the gestures of the men gathered there, in different sized groups, some always provoking responses, others huddling in tighter, quieter formations, discussing whatever they felt in their own dialect. Whatever you remembered about the Irish, at least you could understand most of them, yet here there were only a few who could hear and understand what was going on. Few who had any knowledge of English volunteered it, and communication often consisted of a fractious series of mimes and shouts signifying action – stop, come here, turn around, go away. Searching people you could only speak a dozen sentences to didn't soften up the quality of the relationships very well. Older men

109

looked on or through you, living out their days in their own different world. The younger ones still had fire in their eyes, or fear. It was important to try and establish which variety you were dealing with quickly. The real troublemakers learned not to be demonstrative, not to push their voices and faces too far, not to provoke aggression publicly. They too knew that not every soldier came with the same levels of experience, and fear could trigger fatal results from strung-out soldiers and a switched on gun, especially in the middle of a series of tense confusing squabbles.

The patrol had stopped at the edge of the square in front of the mosque, and was eyeing up the crowds to spot the regulars or the unfamiliar, deciding whether to check out a pair or to let it go, spits of contempt landing on the floor around them. Their colleagues in a separate patrol were now on the opposite side of the square, to the right of them, and behind. Three remained in the rooftops of the shops looking over the place, keeping a higher watch over trouble. In ten minutes they would be handing over to the next patrol, and it would be time to report anything out of the ordinary to the hungry waiting to devour the morsels of observation that would be fed into the men and machines that were compiling The Big Picture.

Sadeed had been standing in the square with three friends. They were like other small groups, talking animatedly about whatever it was that excited them out there – football, women, soldiers, pay-back, the predictable banter of young men in an occupied territory. The bravado saw two of them looking pointedly over at the first patrol, making cheeky gestures, laughing together at their toughness towards the soldiers. It looked like the teenagers were having a good laugh at it all. Wayne thought he'd probably do the same if he had been in their place. It was just like pushing it with the police and the soldiers in Belfast, or at the football game when he'd been up close with the coterie of fans dedicated to their club and braying for the blood of the un-speakables who had come to challenge them that week, that Saturday of extreme excitement or despair, when ninety minutes would make or break the whole weekend, and no-one else would understand what it was all about. He nodded to Barry, and they both looked at the cocky kids, still being brave at a distance. It was Sunday. It was getting hot, and the rising temperature was driving aggression into the voices of some of the less mature men near the mosque. The theme was familiar from the tone alone, and although the deep meaning was lost to them, they recognised the universal rejection soldiers all over the world faced. Wayne still couldn't fathom why these people weren't remotely happy

110

about what had been done for them. He was seeing it all the wrong way round.

A van drew up in the square, a tired white Toyota that kept things moving around the villages, patient with the endless stream of drivers that punished it day after day. The first patrol group gave it the fast check they had been trained to. It wasn't accelerating, there were two quiet people in it, there were signs of recognition from people in the square, and acknowledgements back – no signs of panic, unusual fear, or ill intent. But since the soldiers themselves had never seen this particular vehicle or its occupants before, they intuitively knew they would check it again. Wayne approached the driver, Barry covered the vehicle, and Carl continued his sweep of the square, taking in the other patrol members, and methodically covering the area.

Wayne was now at the driver's door, and the driver, while looking irritated, knew what was coming. He was used to this, and carefully, slowly, indicated that he had all his papers for the enquiring soldiers. It didn't do to make hasty moves in front of these men.

Sadeed and his friends appeared to be splitting up. They high-fived each other in the mocking style of young Americans, and after a final laugh, went their separate ways across the square. Sadeed approached Carl and Denzil, the smiles from the last words with their friends still on their faces, some lingering joke still playing across the memory. That was the last thing Carl and Denzil saw as Sadeed detonated himself a yard in front of them. Wayne, in the lee of the van, was saved from some of the blast and residue of the bomb. It was only two soldiers who were totally taken out. What level of martyrdom would that bring the smiling boy?

Whatever else it was, it was like Ireland on drugs, and all the experience added up to nothing for Wayne, who at 10.50am had lost two of his friends and colleagues to a smiling kid. If he hadn't been the one to go and check if the melons on the van were legitimate, he would have joined them. It was a typical market day. Just another Bloody Sunday.

***

The apartments had the universal style of deprivation, some broken windows, forlorn washing hanging itself out in the dampness, broken rails, the kicking tin loitering of bored kids, the rise and fall of couples, arguing over whatever it was that kept the tension in their unremitting lives alive. Rain had played its part in dulling the concrete and seeping

111

under the paint the sun had started to peel off months ago. There were satellite dishes for show, connecting nobody to nothing, and a couple of tired old cars parked on the tired road by the tired grass. We are peacekeepers, Jurgen thought. We are here to keep this lot safe from others, though it looked like they really needed saving from themselves. In this town in Herzegova were people who had honed their differences over at least a millennium, waiting in turn for the scale to tip momentarily in their favour, so they'd have a chance to clear out a few of the infidels before it shifted again to the other side, feuds fuelled by blood, soil, and beliefs no-one could untangle. It had been decided that in the eyes of the so-called civilised West things had got out of hand, and when the phrase had been publicised to capture the action, ethnic cleansing, it was time for other grown-ups to step in, only they weren't allowed to say stop, put your toys down, kiss and make up, have some coffee. No, these grown-ups could only hang around looking like they might be able to do something but actually were able to do very little. Peace keeping meant don't touch, don't interfere, don't mess. Interference brought even more hassle from your own side, flooding the fields with political correctness, and coming up with ever more elaborate excuses about why it wasn't right to become involved, and how you should manage that – armed social work with no responsibility attached for doing nothing. You were only in trouble for trying. It was a frustrating winter, to say the least, while four hundred miles away the Christmas markets were drowning out the sounds of sadness with carols and gluwein, tinsel and fur.

The Land Rover, the ironically christened Defender, painted out in the colours of peace, had come to the spot where a foot patrol had decided the noise levels had risen a little too high in the apartment block, and another two breaking windows suggested it was a touch more aggressive than the usual Saturday night domestic scene. When they went up the stairs they simply followed the noise. Five men in clothes that mixed military surplus with civilian shirts and scarves were in the apartments, four of them hanging around, watching the leader shouting at what was presumably one of the tenants, a thin, bearded male of around 27 or 28. Also in the room was a woman, about the same age, a young baby in one arm, and two other children, maybe three and five, sticking close by her. What could have been the parents of either of the adults were in another corner, on a battered sofa, trying to be invisible in the face of the argument going on before them, though you could see the anger in their eyes towards the casually aggressive men who had knocked their way into the space. The arrival of the soldiers did nothing to interrupt the flow of the leader for another minute, and then, turning to face the patrol, he took a cigarette and lit it, blowing the smoke back into the face of the silent seated man. One of the patrol asked the leader of the pack what the problem was.

The problem is that this lazy non-working scum only makes one contribution to this place, and that's to make sure his whore wife keeps dropping more scum kids to soak up our time, our place, our money, our rights.

And your point is….

Our point is that we don't want any more of this kind around here, and if he can't keep his dick out of that bitch we'll make sure they won't be living round here abusing our hospitality for much longer.

The message was translated for the patrol leader. He thought about it, and came back through the interpreter.

We understand what you are saying. We think you've made your point. It's time to go now.

It came back, another re-cycling.

You know nothing. You come here and mess with things you don't understand. You are not invited. You are not welcome. You are simply getting in the way of our destiny. You will regret coming here.

With that, he spat out, threw his cigarette onto the carpet, and looked around at his silent companions. He nodded, left the room, and the four followed in support, each giving the eye to the intruding patrol.

The bearded man looked tired and depressed. It wasn't a new routine for him. His wife trembled and wept, the children trying to make themselves smaller in the room, the baby sensing fear and producing its own line in the chorus. The older couple clung to each other, the man now swearing at the departed, the frustration of years of intimidation coming out in well-practiced phrases and gestures.

The translator asked a couple of questions. Who were the men? Did they need anything? Knowing the men made no difference to anybody, and if they needed anything at all it wasn't going to be coming from this patrol in any form of long term safety.

When the shock had subsided and the anger returned to the level that only pricked the skin, the patrol made its polite farewell and returned to the Land Rover. It was now another ordinary Saturday night. It was time to return to base.

These people lived in a different space, that was too hot in summer, too cold in winter, the seams of time holding the blood of ancestors in their houses, their burnt wood or rubbed stones, in layers, as each family and faction claimed its brief foothold on the topsoil, and was consequently crushed. The only fertile thing was the collective memory which drove them all to repeat themselves endlessly, an homage to a dim past fuelled by a burning present. The land yielded little. It was the idea of occupation, of ownership, of dominance, that kept the light on in their eyes.

Just before the end of the patrol, when they were about to make the last circuit of their route before handing over to the next team, the radio had summoned them back to the apartment block. Apparently there had been more noise, more disturbances, but it was all quiet now. Not a living soul to be seen outside. As they got close to the cold concrete, Jurgen noticed a freshly broken window, and another open one. On the ground, two floors below the place they had been in an hour before was a bundle. A still mound. Getting closer, the flashlight picked out the arm, the awkward angle and the small fingers pointing towards a silent star. It was the body of a baby.

The patrol rushed into the building, up the stairs, and along to the apartment. Inside, the two old folks were still sitting on the sofa, staring out forwards, stiffly, the holes in their foreheads the next immediate sign. The mother lay on the floor in a pool of blood, her breast severed and clear signs of mutilation below the waist. The two children lay side by side before her, their throats cut like goats for a feast. The bearded man was across the room, the last of his blood darkly staining the thin rug on the floor. On the wall, the blood read, "The seed of the Beast spills no more". The only question was the order in which they had been made to watch each other die. The patrol had to wonder if their presence had accelerated the family's death, and whether peace-keeping was the best strategy the office-bound civilian masters could produce for the soldiers to pursue as they compiled their statistics for Christmas.

***

Steve had come out after the second tour. By that stage he'd seen too many limbs detached from their owners, as roadside bombs played cat to under-protected mice, and vehicles lay twisted and dead, part-rusting tombstones to what were seen as temporary difficulties. Instead of making unpredictable swoops from helicopters, which were anyway rarely available, it had been decided that patrols must continue as a core element in the strategy the chiefs had decided was expedient. It was like The First World War again. It was endless short advances, gains, losses, re-possessions, slogging it out yard for yard, metre for metre, through seasons of heat and ice, in unsympathetic air, ashes to ashes. You'd

114

think they'd brought back the old generals, believing it should all be done through strength of character, with the magnificence of cavalry. Bombs still had scant respect for this form of chivalry.

When he got home he'd felt lucky to survive. Then he felt guilty. It didn't seem right to share with people what he'd seen. They thought a dangerous night out was about getting shit-faced and being cautioned by the police for pissing on the sides of cars after midnight. How could they get it anyway? He'd heard it from other mates, one or two, but they were either still behind, in the action again, or they'd started to slip away to their own other worlds, and they didn't have the time, or the money to meet up and hold on to what had bonded them. The Bosses, and some of the big Society, had now actually paid the shilling, and they wanted no more reminders about it. What had a bunch of nutters living in the Middle Ages got to do with anything they really wanted? He'd heard about the lack of respect, seen it even before he joined up, but thought it might be different now, in his case. He was becoming a commodity, an embarrassment, this unwanted Hero, and he began to slide into silence instead of answering the question, what have you been up to lately?

He followed the pattern. After a few weeks back home this time he grew quieter in the day, and his girlfriend asked him why he was so moody. He couldn't find much to say to his two kids, who were killing cartoons on the latest games, unaware what the smell of blood and cordite did to your memory. Night time was customarily the worst time, when the dreams and the sweats and the shouting came, and after another month he was banished to the downstairs sofa, told to get a grip, and left alone with the memories of the smiles and anguish on his comrades' faces, caught in the melting metal, or obliterated in vapour mists of blood and skin cells.

He'd leave early in the morning, before the kids were readied for school, and he'd run a few miles round the edge of the small town. Running in town itself upset the police – you weren't supposed to be running around the place – the CCTV cameras didn't like it. You must be up to no good, unless you were on a designated running path, and wearing the signs, the trainers, the pants, carrying a half-drunk bottle of over-claiming water. When he came back he slunk down more, affecting the gait of a hooded teenager, slow and defiant, saying come on if you dare, as he went to the one tired café that wasn't part of some chain, and sat down with a mug of tea, four sugars, and a greasy sandwich, while the owner traded half-English insults with the day-glo vested immigrant workers from the vans and the council, yellow safety helmets in piles on the floor, like Easter eggs from an overgrown Disney chicken. This was the freedom he was defending. The scores of matches played at the weekend drifted through the air with groans of derision, and sides with no national players fought each other with oligarchs' money. He'd sit around for a while, turning the pages of tabloid papers, occasionally nodding slowly as someone looked over his shoulder and said something profound like "look at the tits on that". It was the same tableau every day, except Sunday, when the frying fat took a rest day.

His girlfriend had a part-time job during school hours, so he'd wander back 'home' and dick around watching TV, or spend ten minutes watching a film one of the kids had downloaded. Then he'd frig around some more on the internet, and eventually drift back into the trap of his own thoughts as it got towards noon. He'd done well so far, but every day noon was starting to stretch away, and coming back from the café it became easier to hit the booze earlier to ease the time travel, so he got closer to the Special Brews as their pain relief removed the piercing reminder of his girlfriend's heirloom clock banging out the first twelve hours of the mid-week morning.

The major problem was he'd had to leave the last guy on the roadside, it was just too hot to get them and they'd been ordered out, threateningly. He'd pulled the three others free. One died on the roadside, one made it with no physical scars but hardly a mind worth having. The last one lost an arm and a leg, and was making do. But Steve wondered whether the guy hated him or was grateful, and he couldn't decide how he'd feel himself if he'd been 'saved' this way. He nurtured the guilt alone, masticated it, re-shaped it, pushed it around, but he couldn't bring himself to spit it out. He just let it stay there, building the cloying taste in his mouth.

Someone said he'd been cited for a medal, going in to rescue his comrades under intense enemy fire. He wasn't even aware anyone was shooting at him at the time. He just wanted to get his mates out of the mess and into safety. He didn't notice the lucky graze as a bullet passed along his arm, a Taleban trinket he called the scar, but he never wore short-sleeves back home now.

Friday was really bad. Everyone was busy, everyone was going out, including his girlfriend. She was off with the girls, she said, instead of staying with Captain Gloom, and the kids were just fine with the take-away Pizza and the new rented release –"Kill Everyone and Be A Hero", or some variation on that. Wasn't that what he'd done? There was no level seven where he was coming from.

He waved a 'Bye, see ya' hand as he walked out of the house. Tonight was lucky night. Mac was suddenly in town and did he want a beer or ten, his shout? They'd agreed a bar in town, not so far away then. At least there was a promise of a few laughs. Even though Mac said he'd stand the beers, he'd still managed to save a few quid for something like this, and he bothered to shave, because he didn't want Mac to think he'd turned into a lazy twat.

They met at The Eagle, the start of what they thought might be a plan, a recce of some six or seven old dives, swearing they'd each be standing up long after the other one fell over

Mac said he'd been lucky. He'd been trained in Signals, knew a thing or two about technology and communications, enough to blag a job working in a computer store, good enough for now, and he was after getting tickets to work on Apple. He was together, knew he'd have a life after the Army, and he seemed able to 'let go'. After the initial debate about paying for rounds, Mac bought two for every one of Steve's, 'cos if you've got the means, it's all said and done, boy. Steve was embarrassed and grateful all at once. Said he was still weighing up the options when pressed about his plans. Mac was wise enough not to push it further, and they got round to visiting some old adventures together, mocking the place they'd returned to, with its tossers and slags, its fatsters and its mobility machines, its fatter taxes and its falling-over kids, its million pound a week foul-faking sports heroes and its one-hit wonder stars. Whatever happened to....? It's all worth fucking fighting for, mate, they agreed, high-fiving the air and laughing through another glass, darkly. It was after midnight when they said goodbye, each swaying off in different directions.

It was only two minutes later that Steve decided he really needed to get rid of some of the beer, and there being nothing like a public convenience in the country any more, found an alley at the side of a nightclub that, from the smell on entering, had played out the role he expected of it before. The bliss of the ever-rolling stream hazily crossed his well-cooked mind, and, zipping up, he told himself he was now ready for the tab home. Coming back out onto the street, eight or nine guys in reflective suits and sprayed hair suddenly surrounded him. He paused. What looked like that moment's leader spoke to the pack.

'Ere, this geezer comes and pisses on the side of our club. What the fuck is that about?

Steve decided to stay quiet – no point trying to take on this kind of bunch. He just swayed in the breeze, trying to look dumb.

Can't even stand up for 'imself.

Steve dimly felt the blow behind his head. It was a fire extinguisher from the club side-door exits. Tumbling, he hit his forehead on the curb, and slipped into the gutter. He heard the shouts of the Taleban, confused voices, English somewhere in the background. Once he was down, it was easy. They rolled in, boots ready, and kicked him under a chorus of chants about a football referee. Pisser, wanker, and on. He drifted into the blackness a large part of him now coveted. Unsure of whether this was a feint, or some other devious trick, and knowing they could be recognised in the light, they kicked him back into the alley, and after two minutes, he lay there, crumpled and unmoving in the dribbles of his own piss.

The gang, adrenalin now fading, looked to follow fight with flight, and as they slipped away into the night, the one who set it off said,

Relax. We can't have fuckers like that round our way. They fuckin' well need to learn some fuckin' respect. The laughter echoed under the lights.

The inquest concluded it was death by misadventure.

At least, before tonight, Steve had known where he stood.

***

All Killian meant was well. That was his role. Just to help everyone have a better time, and he would take a little pleasure out of that for himself too, at the end. Killian wore everything on his sleeve, his heart, his emotions, his friendship, all coming at you through the firm handshake, the direct look into your eyes, and the endless self-deprecating patter which he felt defended his need to be direct, forthright, open. That was Killian's style. Well. You know, Killian wanted everybody to be happy. He could never understand why people would try to be destructive about this, and if only he'd known it, he would have agreed with Aristotle's logic that happiness must be the ultimate goal in life. Unfortunately, he had chosen to spend a significant part of his life in a place where people were professionally misanthropic, and used a spectrum of devices to curtail reaching a state of well-being that Killian considered to be everyone's right. These devices included the use of local government laws, lawyers, the police, and the people themselves, who regarded Killian's form of hedonism as intrusive at best, and the work of a maligned spirit a close second. Why shouldn't people be allowed to make noise, laugh, get drunk, play games, tease each other, dress up, stay out all night, pay a lot of money to be entertained, given facilities, treated? Unfortunately, the place where he found himself was one where, aside from youth's rightful rebelliousness, a large slice of the people weren't taken with the drink and the noise, public displays of conspicuous pleasure, or forking out for anything they considered to be poor value, or poor taste. It was not, perhaps, the most encouraging match.

Killian had arrived circuitously. He had had a spell serving the unwanted country's interests, soldier to a Queen, a traitor in a traitor's land, as seen through the eyes of the disaffected. He wasn't welcome, or safe, on his own soil. He had left his native country, having sold his interest in the family business, and, determined to see if other parts of the world had attitudes closer to his own, had set out in his twenties to sail his new boat beyond the local coastline. He got as far as a small British island and decided it was time for a rest. There was an old boat moored near his, needing some care and attention, a boat he liked. He watched and waited, eventually being lucky to see someone who looked like they might have more than a passing interest in the vessel appear and step aboard her. Killian had at least a drop of Irish luck left in his blood. True enough, the visitor turned out to be the owner and, though cautious of most strangers, took a liking to the open-faced traveller on his new boat. He shared his fondness for the old boat with his admission that, yes, she needed care and attention, and Killian, pursuing his intuition, volunteered to restore her beauty, bit by bit. He loved the boat too. It was the love of the boat that bonded them. He soon discovered the boat's owner was a significant local operator, and offered to ease Killian into some useful introductions to help keep him interested while he worked on the restoration project. So he stayed longer. He chartered his own boat to wealthy guests at top hotels, treating them to champagne service as they cruised the local waters. Feedback was always positive, and as the old boat regained her glory, the local businessman and the traveller became closer. Killian had few rules, and close to number one was don't bite the hand that feeds you. Killian became his sponsor's biggest supporter, most loyal and dedicated follower, trusty, and willing hand. He wasn't overtly sycophantic, he wasn't toady, but he delivered the goods, and the businessman felt comfortable with someone he didn't have to play complicated games with, someone outside the crazy family, someone who made him happy, someone who was so far different he didn't have to worry. It was the beginning of a long friendship. The businessman was cautious, wary of parasites and politicians trying to win favour in his court. Killian knew happiness lay in keeping the boss contented, and while he had few professional skills or qualifications outside what the

119

army had taught him, he tackled every new enterprise with streetwise cunning, dusting himself down, picking up the pieces when they broke, and learning more about the fickle ways people made their money. He was on a lead, but it was a long one. Killian had one new idea in ten, but ten ideas a week, and the businessman nurtured the good ones, fed them, financed them, occasionally pulled on the lead, sometimes broke the news about Killian's naiveté without poisoning his drive, and a number of people began to enjoy the fruits of their efforts, some despite themselves.

It wasn't always a champagne and angels ride. Killian took too many hits of a certain kind of invisibility cloak himself, alcohol being the major one. Sometimes the ghosts from Belfast's streets got too close to him again, and gnawed away at his carefully honed happy-go-lucky persona. So that took care of the first marriage. His insistence that he was only providing pleasure to those that wanted it found him repeatedly hassled and hounded by grumpies, objectors, and all those who sought to preserve the status quo through suits and the courts, through political persuasion and commercial obstruction, through smiles masquerading as commitments, and all the other tools people select to keep things unchanged when it suits them.

But he kept going. He caught a little of the litigious disease himself, and a dose of paranoia about who was conspiring against him and his boss's greater good. He fought off those who continued to try to tap The Big Man for money. He looked for those who could help him steer a path through the obstacles of local laws and interpretations. He continued to work with strays, with lame ducks, giving them a chance and then letting them quietly go. The woman who tamed him saved his life once, and he felt he had found a new direction. He realised that all along he'd been trying to sell a brand of happiness to people who only wanted their own-label version of it. He'd promoted, he'd pushed, he'd negotiated, he'd discounted, and all the people wanted was for his version to be taken off the shelves, de-listed, banned from distribution, and prevented from being manufactured.

He fought back through the personal form of happiness he called attitude, and no-one was going to take that away now. But not everyone wants to be happy. He decided he had to get away one more time. Many of the people who heard he was going were glad. Finally, he'd got the message. He was out of their lives and going to be bothering some other folks. The islanders he left were happy again in their own way, extending their own life sentences. The Boss got on with running the other 99.9% of his empire. But Killian couldn't get away from himself.

***

J's Invisible Diary. Entry.

Respect – continued. So what do we mean here? Give us an example. Let's go to El Distrito. That's Cali. Let's take a Columbian diversion. Let's get down to that word again, the one that is responsible for so much death and destruction, physically and mentally, the one that keeps powering up the anger and the action: our old amigo.

No-one there fights over drugs – that's too easy. It's about space, distance, all the displaced have to hold onto, dimensions that can be bounded with a 50 cent bullet, the price of a life. What we need then, are a few boys to deliver one of the messages. They're all cheap, fearless, easily riled, not yet all cripples, abundant, and best of all, totally indifferent, unreachably indifferent. They just want to be dared. Only it's not a playground game. Life is for living now, it's so cheap. This is the place where you get shot for not wanting to keep on playing football, for insisting the loser in a game buys the beers. For them, society is simple. Raise your eyebrow at the wrong moment and you sign your death warrant, unless you're quicker, better, more ready than the other one who's been dissed.

It's more complex in the so-called developed places, where you're not a soldier of the streets, but someone who signed up to a different life. One thing keeps coming back – many people can't move on from where they'd been when they were in that old-timer place called civilisation the first time around. There's a problem for some of them accepting society, or society accepting them, when they return from the other side, some other place where they have served. Quite a number are full of self-loathing, low self-worth, and they drag themselves through the uniformity of others' lives with the props of booze, drugs, mental breakdowns, and irrational violence. They don't trust what they find any more, they feel alone, as if they don't belong, as if no-one understands. Some of them never get a grip again. We can't do as much as we'd like for them, but there are others who will respond to a call, a call to restore a sense of camaraderie again, of honour, to follow what they will subscribe to as a just cause, a chance to put something into a different perspective. But remember, it's just a point of view. Many of them have more in common with those they have fought against than those they are fighting for, more in common with their counterparts in Bosnia, or Kosovo.

It is necessary to have those that have been disillusioned but still

121

have spirit, ones who know the outside world couldn't care less about what they did before, even less when they were antipathetic to the causes in the first place, like with Nam or Iraq. The First Gulf War, maybe, but second time around, no way. Notions of honour and duty have changed big time, except no-one bothers to explain that.

It's not just regular soldiers. Look at Todd Cunliffe, twenty two years with the Paras and the territorials, called up with a week's notice before being sent to Iraq in 2003. After all that time, that service, that pride, he got injured. We don't know whether he was lucky or not. His best friend was killed, but then he wasn't ignored afterwards. Coming home to see he'd been sent out to fight for a lie was more painful than the injury.

There's no voice for these boys. The Ministry of Defence refuses requests by a national newspaper to interview war casualties. Todd Cunliffe was back home in the UK before his wife knew, and he had to hitch-hike home, carrying 45 kilos of kit, with a major knee injury. Just one case, and there are plenty more out there, from several engagements. All we have to do is find the right set, and give them a powerful, special voice. Whatever that voice is, it won't be being driven by a religion, except where good cover may still lie, as we tested it.

Pete Schultz, all time US military hero and American football star with the Arizona Cardinals, was shot dead by his own comrades in 2004, but the army didn't like that version, so they made a hero out of him and his death, lied to his parents, and got the Administration to back up their story, all the way up to the President. He had been mistaken for the enemy, and killed as he tried to scramble for safety behind a rock, but he was billed as one killed by enemy fire while attacking a hillside full of Bin Laden supporters. This was high-profile stuff. They literally blew up the poster boy. So what was the conclusion? Maybe lying is no big deal any more, concluded PS's father. His mother still believed the truth may be painful, but it is still the truth.

**

2

Where we look further at the story of Respect, and its consequences ~ we identify the loneliness of heroes in a world of 'them and us' ~ we uncover the secret ambitions of States, and suppression.

There were other forces at work. Reactions to protests, to counter-cultures, went deep and far. After the fifties, when governments went public early on about their issues with disaffected youth, or any other people who rocked their boat, many of them decided to follow the example of those who were rebelling. They went Underground in setting up ever bigger snooping and sweeping up operations. As the states became more convinced their citizens needed more rules and regulations to ensure they were docile, more and more people were paid and trained to keep surveillance. There were parallel worlds of doers and watchers. There were also plenty of people around who had been trained, served, and left the states' service, with plenty of ideas of their own to practise, and the skills to do it.

***

The beginning of 1968 was an interesting time for fifteen year olds in British schools, even if they didn't know exactly what was coming. The government was losing tax revenue on skirts. Only skirts of what was then measured as twenty four inches from waist to hem were taxable. The fashionable length that winter was between thirteen and twenty inches. The press might have noted that things had been looking up for some time, outside the tax office. In a geography class the short round teacher kept the class riveted, waiting for the moment he would make the innocent but magical pronouncement, "Watch the board while we go through it". Some school exercise books would be slowly filling with drawings of cwms, corries and cirques, as Tom Glob the class-described teacher drooled and dribbled the boys through the stultifying way the ice age had left its mark on what they otherwise called England. When someone at the front wasn't trying to set fire to the master's tired black gown, someone at the back was rapping a desk with a ruler and chanting "Ho, Ho, Ho Chi Minh", trying to encourage other class members to join in, even though they had no idea who or what Chi Minh was. The chanter had other exotic names in his repertoire as well. Che was common. Regis Debray was charmed into a classroom rhyme. Here was the source of a fountain of revolutionary material, picked up from an elder brother already at university. Whether dialectical materialism meant much to the group mattered less than its power as a pair of words in another chant. Most of the teachers wouldn't have got it either. "Glob" was discovering that the world of teaching was changing, and that the authority he felt he had as a natural part of his vocation was being eroded by dangerously restive children. He walked out, gown singed, heading for the debatable safety of the staff room.

The joy of rebellion, the privilege of youth, was fuelled by material that had never been so widely available before, and contained a spectrum of frissons, depending on whether the items were considered to be in poor taste, outrageous, dangerous, criminal, or treasonable. Copies of the *International Times* and *Oz* were traded and passed around like contraband. Che Guevara's *Guerilla Warfare* circulated, a paperback dog-eared from those learning how to survive in the jungle, a mere footstep of the imagination away from the urban environment the lads lived in. It was closely followed by *The Virgin Soldiers* and *Nymphomaniac.* Sensory stimulants were overwhelming, from concoctions of drugs to new music, television to the wonder of space travel, new doors to perception backed up by gurus and visionaries, Maharishis and McLuhans, Laings and Learys, Levy-Strausses and Lennons. There was something happening in the air, something going on out there, which you were just a couple of years too young to have been in on at the beginning of it all. As a junior it had all been about The War, the stories, the movies, the so-called excitement you'd missed. And now there was something about the new war, Vietnam, and you weren't sure whose side you were supposed to be on, or why. The only difference was that when you saw the news today, you felt maybe the deaths were more real, they meant something closer to you now, not like the rat-tat-tat of your comic stuff killings from the junior school playground. On all sides there were different worlds beckoning if you chose to look. Many chose not to. There were those who'd already decided they wanted to go and read chemistry at a safe university, others who couldn't wait to leave and get into hairdressing, others who wanted to stay focused on stealing scooters and being close to the mythical temptations of the football kop. It was a typical group.

***

Danny Mullan was not a conformist. He hated school. He was a conduit

124

to the exotic. He was bored in class, had no time for bullying teachers. He was a free bird. He appealed to his mates because he seemed to have more freedom outside school than many others. He had his own keys to the house when he was nine or ten. He knew where the food was and how to put it together. He was generous when there was stuff around. There was always a sense of adventure because each year there was a new house, or apartment, new places to explore while you stayed in the same old place. He could watch whatever he wanted on the TV, listen to whatever sounds were around, come and go as he pleased. Sure he had a brother, but he'd already gone to university. That was good as well, because at the end of terms, at least through the first year, he'd come back with great new sounds you weren't likely to hear locally, and books with impressive titles and numbers of pages, like *The Social Origins of Dictatorship and Democracy*, written by people with exotic names like Barrington Moore Jnr, or books that hinted at dark radicalism. He had filaments connecting you to a world *OUT THERE.*

He was confident about that place, and he devoured what came to him from beyond the boundaries of his current exile. He would sing The Doors' *Five to One* loudly at bus stops, leaving old ladies to shudder and wonder who the young hooligan was, and what his intentions might be. He was thinking lyrics, writing songs, he was Jim Morrison in the wings, songs about revolution and eastern peace, soaking up material from the seats of higher learning, fuelled by the economics and politics of the stories of his elder brother, and his own imagination. Raids on the local bookshop liberated fresh texts for his hunger, from the *I-Ching* to Jung's *Man and His Symbols*, Penguin Specials, art books opening new doors, Picasso one week, Braque the next. It was a world that was barely at the school gates where he entered, most days, bored and distracted by the unconnected teachings and the conservative staff. Shoplifting was just another way to get a buzz. When most people were trying a Gauloise or a Player's for that experimental fit of coughing, he'd already mastered the three-skin roll-up and talked of Lebanese Black like it was something out of the tuck shop. Roaches and rolling boards, he could advise on grip and breathing, blow-backs and pipes, weights and prices, sources and scams. The little deals meant he was able to buy things when he didn't feel like stealing them, so more albums came, more exotica. He even turned up at the church youth club when the drugs squad was giving an illustrated talk about the evils of reefers, to make sure he hadn't missed any tricks and to pick up tips on new rolling techniques and materials. Many of the boys treated him with caution – they weren't at all sure about the juju stuff he was into, or they just had no idea who he really was, or who Che was, or Daniel Cohn-Bendit, who might just as well have been the chief thug at the nearby Catholic school, or the big cheese at the town's football kop. But for those close to him, he was the source, the link to the Star Gate, the way out of the repression, the ticket to ride.

His apparent freedom came from his father almost never being around. He was always chasing some new nearly deal, some second-hand car dodge. His smoking drinking mother hid behind her addictions when she wasn't working to provide for the family in ways that Dad never did, his money never quite making it home. Danny had learned to cook by improvisation, driven by hunger when his parents repeatedly failed to make it home. He experimented with bizarre combinations of leftovers and tins until the hunger subsided. The frequent house moves followed one of two patterns. Cash was scarce so downsizing to an apartment was the only option. Creditors were becoming impatient and it was always timely to do a runner. One month's cash up front on the new place, two months in arrears, another cash fix and a promise of regularity, three months past payment, a default, and then another runner. It was a different kind of road movie. He was always going to get the Triumph Bonneville or the Norton Commando and ride out of it all, but he could never get it together enough before what was there disappeared in the next set of smaller deals.

The brother began to show up less often. Tales had it he sat an exam and wrote the entire paper over the same line, over and over. He'd found another world he liked and had gone there. It was Planet Acid. He'd tuned in and turned on but he never did find the original station again. He wasn't on *Receive* again, ever, for most people. He really was in the centre of his own cyclone, but he wouldn't be coming back to write about it – not legibly anyway. Danny was in another kind of world. In some ways it was just as imaginary, but the younger brother never disappeared into infinity. He always researched his journeys. He never worked on anything legitimate at school. His attention deficit was huge, his application minute, his consideration for the pieces of paper, the certifications that might have got him to the next place, non-existent. He got out of the system as quickly as he could, and tried to define his own space elsewhere. But for those few who had rubbed against his mind, those who had given him time, space, attention, ears, smiles, he was very loyal. He knew few understood him, and for those that did he would always have time, be it his own form of time.

Danny Mullan was basically a survivor from a crashed family, borrowing the ideals and trappings of his brother and his mates because somehow, somewhere in all those thoughts and costumes were the keys that would let him out of the door and into the world where he felt they would recognise how he belonged. Unlike young Brando, who was a rebel without a cause, Danny had plenty to back up his eagerness to live out the movie through his own version of the great question, what are you rebelling against?

Whaddya got?

He didn't realise that without focus, rebellion tended to dilute. He tried to pour his anti- cocktails into too many glasses. He was rebelling against a society smitten with bureaucracy, managed by people who still went home at night and smoked pipes in front of electrically glowing fires, wearing cardigans their wives had bought them for Christmas. He had tried squats, learning only how to loathe the constantly hassling police who were trying to keep dirty hippies and other outmoded groups out of society's eyes and way, out of their about to be gentrified houses. He had been passionate about punk until he realised it was yet another snake in the music industry's hair – a Medusa of strategized rebellion.

At one point he was even offered a job by the very system he loathed, the all-inclusive Civil Service. He found it easy work, his particular role, and for a short time was even enthused about it. He walked out when a union representative took him to one side and told him that if he didn't start slowing down, his work rate would be noticed by management, and it would be embarrassing for the others.

He drifted for a while, and then found a passion for food and drink. He came second in some regional contest for creative cooking, and then coupled his recently broadcast skills with knowledge about wine he'd picked up from books and drinking it, getting a job with a rising group of independent drink retailers. It suited his nomadic nature, a throwback to the childhood days of having to keep moving on, and he changed cities regularly, the job, and the retailers' expansion, allowing him to grow with them. Word got passed back to his former schoolmates, those still in contact, that he'd actually managed to find a girl who wanted to be with him, that he'd even married, and, yes, they now had a daughter, which confused several of them, having rationalised their way into believing he was actually gay, a condition that suited their versions of the stories they had heard. He remained contrary, lively, sardonic, but always appeared to be still on the trail of some elusive missing piece of life.

Then came that November. He had joined the thousands of people looking to complete their daily commute home, heading for the entrances to stations across London, and the cramped, uptight rides out to homes in the more affordable parts of the city. King's Cross had always been one of the most crowded of these commuter hubs, with people pouring out of The Tube and heading for over-ground trains, others swapping buses or taxis for underground connections, people passing each other in long transit tunnels, some looking to switch routes on ways out of the city, others looking to switch routes on ways in, for that night's entertainment or work. Some giant with a very large stick would have uncovered a huge ants' nest of bustle and pre-programmed purpose around and beneath the old railway station. He might also have spotted the smouldering underneath one of the wooden escalators.

The Underground had been going in some places for over 100 years. Numerous projects were in place to try and upgrade or modernise the service without closing the entire system down. People were used to disruption, and had formed numerous ways of coping with it. Despite their being a ban on smoking on the trains and platforms, tired, squashed and squeezed smokers would leave a packed train and seek solace in a cigarette as soon as they reached the escalators and smelled the potential surface air coming down to meet them. The rapid smokers, coming or going, would toss their butts onto the steps. On this day, one of them wasn't extinguished, and as the escalator rolled out of site, the cigarette dropped and fell into an old storeroom area, meeting dry paper and dust that had been collecting for a long time. Coupled with the air being pushed around the labyrinth by trains and people in a hurry, the flicker of flame had found the fuel it needed to grow. Very quickly, the fire sought an escape path through the old wooden escalator, and on.

The unusual and unexpected are great routine breakers, and as smoke began to curl and then billow in the walkways, people began to react instinctively, picking up pace, heading anywhere that was what they thought was away from the source of the growing problem, except the way the tunnels were designed helped the fire gain a hold more rapidly.

Danny was one of the first to notice the danger. The keen sense of smell that had made it easier for him to build his knowledge and understanding of wines had alerted him to the unusual aroma of burning, before it hit the noses of many others. He began to shout 'Fire'. At first, a number just looked at him and thought he was one of those loonies who hung around the Tube to stay warm on November nights, and they moved around him, trying to avoid catching some undefined germ or disease. Then the smell grew stronger, and the panicked herd instinct kicked in. People started to run, to push, to swear, to help themselves, to take off in different directions, well before any authorities were aware of what was going on. Danny stopped. He knew what it was like if you weren't the leader of the pack in a crisis. He had seen people in some of the squats he'd stayed in, when there was trouble, unable to move, or even be aware of what the danger was around them, drunk or drugged or just too depressed or tired to stir. He had shaken and pulled them, shouted at them, hit them to get them moving, away from attackers, or out of a building that was just about to collapse, in the dark, empty tins and discarded food wrappers lying around, smouldering embers from old fireplaces that had surrendered their heat, leaving people caught up in dirty sleeping bags, their legs wrapped around the nylon in poor attempts to keep the cold outside.

It was the same here. Unlike the others, he stayed where he was, and braced himself against those trying to rush and push past him, people now picking up on the word 'Fire' and beginning to shout it themselves among the screams and other shouts. He moved towards the blackening smoke in the tunnels, and picked up a can of coke from the floor, still miraculously standing on the edge of the floor, half full. He pulled his shirt out of his trousers and poured the coke over it, before pulling it tight over his nose and mouth. He headed into the smoke and called out to see if anyone was there. He heard voices, some frail, some scared, some confused, and he began to collect those who hadn't had the strength to go with the first wave of runaways, half- coaxing, half-ordering them to their feet, and into a space between two intersecting tunnels that wasn't yet full of smoke and darkness. Some were too frightened to speak, others were losing the plot big time, but he managed to get about twenty together, still commanding their blind loyalty to him, before deciding it was finally time to get the fuck out of there.

As a regular commuter, he had tried every combination of routes to get to his train with the least fuss and distance. He knew the station layout intimately. He began to lead his band of strays along, imploring them to hold on to each other in the fading light. He hit the trisection, and pulled his people through. With about five of the party left to come through, the fire decide it needed a taste of flesh. Meeting the cold fresh air, it suddenly threw itself along the tunnel they had been coming down, and the searing heat and pain floored at least five of the stragglers. It was too hot to get near them, and the smoke following the fire burst was too choking and blinding to let anyone go back. Danny collected the remainder of his party and herded them along to the last

129

staircase before the surface beckoned.

By now the emergency services had been made aware of the situation, and they began to appear, taking over the collection and leading to safety of those near the surface, trying to ascertain what was going on deeper down, and what they could do about it. Danny's team were led into the November night, coughing and crying, choking, taken away from the entrances and exits to the waiting ambulance crews. Of his original party, he had saved fifteen of the twenty. In the overall event, twenty seven people lost their lives, and many more suffered from inhalation injuries. Dan drifted away from them, lost in his own thoughts, oblivious to the questions and invitations from firemen and paramedics. He found a bar, and sat down in his smoked and singed clothes, no problem to the bar staff who were now beginning to re-tell updated versions of the emerging story to others in the traumatised hostelry.

**

Danny couldn't forget. He never sought the front pages as a hero. People tried to track him down, but he had never given them a name, and the Underground system wasn't monitored then in the same ways as it was later, linked to all kinds of other databases and systems. He couldn't let go of the people he thought he'd left behind, left to the hungry fire, and he didn't seek out any professional to share his guilt with. As he got quieter, he turned to one of the things he knew well, the wine, and began a lengthening relationship with the grape, refusing the temptations of the store he managed, rationalising his attempts to run away from his memories as merely tastings, sampling product for the customers. Sales began to slip, more imbalances between stocks and sales began to occur, and there had been some complaints that his way of treating customers was becoming aggressive. The overlords made some comments, made some suggestions, after all, it wouldn't be the first time a drinks business had staff problems related to booze. Objectives were set, warnings issued, improvements were not made. He was fired after the sixth transgression.

Danny went to the grave with the grape, his wife and child leaving him for more peaceful pastures, never quite understanding how they'd lost him. His employers soared on, reporting increased sales, profits, and the highest customer satisfaction ratings in the high street. They didn't need or want non-conforming Dannys.

Danny had run out of generosity. The world around him could

fathom no reason for respect.

***

For Lech Nowak school was just somewhere you had to fill in time. Outside the gates the uniform was transformed, the flares looked wider, the jacket darker, the scarf replacing the tie, a wide brimmed floppy hat covering the rebellious hair, an ankle length coat completing the look of being out of there. He chose his friends carefully, one or two from school, but only after close inspection, and if they earned the pass from a hidden rite of passage. No, most of his major friends were older, they did things. They'd been to places. They owned record shops. They organised gigs with cool bands who would be big one week after they'd played the venue, Man. He was with Those Who Know. He was never without a to-die-for girlfriend, unattainable for the rest. They always found him mature and witty and would do anything to help him refine their beauty. He was a radical in a different kind of way. He was prepared to use what was available out there to support his ends, which were just within the bounds of legal, well almost. He was an irritant to conservative established society, not a major threat. So he was always busy organising action groups, getting magazines and newsletters and petitions going. He was always the one who had found the next new bar you had to be seen in before everybody else found out, and then it was already time to move on, to the next new place to eat, the next new album from the next new band. He was the intellectual working both ends of the system. He was tangential to warring groups, the one who wasn't always available, keeping time to cultivate his own charisma, the granting of his presence as a favour in life's whirligig.

Both his parents were lifers in the civil service, a world of comfortable conformity. His breakout was from a harbour whose boats had never rocked. They were straight. They lived their suburban lives civilly, with their cautious investments and their metronomic moves towards the state pensions they had worked for without question. They were grateful for what they had, for what their parents hadn't had, and they weren't going to jeopardise that. Lech used the dull stable background as a wash on which to paint his own wild canvas. He was always ten years ahead of himself. He was self-confident, energetic, experimental, gregarious. Most of his male contemporaries couldn't stand his coquettishness, he was so far out of their league. He was into everything, and if he saw he'd missed out on a tiny piece of something, he'd throw himself into having that too. So he flipped from group to group, a chameleon, a cuckoo, a craven thief of ideas he would sign off

131

as his own. He was into all things public – especially self-promotion, but he extended that into all known and available media of the day. In each week he would play the role of writer, broadcaster, concert promoter, salesman, cause champion. The only thing he wouldn't share was the girlfriends everyone else coveted. He dropped them when they became normal, wanting normal things, like more of his time, or his respect, or his attention, and they would reject all offers of comfort from other suitors for months. He was in a hurry. Time was moving fast. His hair had noticed and was receding rapidly to reflect the speed he was running through life. In a moment of weakness he married a girl, bought a house, got divorced, and left the country, all before others had finished college. You weren't sure where the rush was destined to go, but clearly he saw something about getting there first that the others didn't. In fact, then there was no destination, just a never-ending drive that kept him pumping out the stuff, the words, the thoughts, the sounds. When it came to needing a beacon, you could always count on Lech to be the one who'd put out the most light and the most noise, exactly where you wanted it.

Lech resurfaced in the UK after two years of country-hopping. He decided to slow down the pace for a season and earn a little pin-money along the way. Time to learn a little more about the language he used every day, and was planning to use to build his future empire.

The summer of '75 was only beaten by the summer of '76, when the temperature rarely fell below twenty eight degrees, a heat prod pushing Londoners into new behaviour, squatting in fountains, even more irrational aggression, late-night parties and bets on ice-cream and lager running out, how much vendors on Oxford Street would be getting away with as they sold their 'refreshments' to innocent tourists. It wasn't quite Lebanon, but it could have been. For some time an area radiating out from Marble Arch, to Queens Gate in the West, Marylebone in the North, Knightsbridge in the South, and Baker Street in the East, had become the centre of the new summer residence of a variety of Arabs and their supporters. Properties had been bought up and estate agents had been among the first to benefit from the boom. Restaurants selling Middle Eastern food, cake and sweet shops, casinos, clothes and jewellery shops of the styles that drew Arabic glances, pavement cafes, car accessory shops selling customised wheels, all appeared along and close to the Edgware Road. Stories grew and spread about the behaviour of the new guests, crowding the local car parks with brightly coloured Bentleys and loud Lamborghinis, using apartments once and abandoning them, forgetting them, gifts to all kinds in their thousand, cash, Rolexes, small tokens of appreciation for the army of servants and sycophants, security guards, concierges, waiters, shop assistants and chancers who flocked in. For a short while there was a budding tolerance from the locals, eager to display the sophistication their new oil-wealth brought them, eager to demonstrate loyalty and interest in the free-spenders. Then greed triumphed.

The Arabs who cared began to spot it and move on to new pastures, in Monaco and Marbella, where they could more readily create their own exclusion zones, looking for the next set of willing parasites to serve their needs and myths. Some things lasted longer than others. The new banks, the new private hospitals, the massive swelling of the accounts in Wimpole and Harley Street, the relationships with private clubs and a core of hotel managers, cheaters, fixers, and friends. Aside from the wave of hedonism, there was also a small amount of cultural activity, art acquisition, and the odd piece of kow-towing to the new neighbourhood, like having children learn some English while their mothers shopped, and their fathers spent the afternoons in the lowlights of the casinos dotted around the area.

In one of the language teaching establishments, close to Baker Street, a converted house managed by a suave Italian and run by a dour Scot, offered small classes and private tuition, from the most elementary 'hellos' to the 'why do you say football crowd and not football mass?' scenarios, from prepositional verbs to the monster of the gerund, all the joys of grammar supporting the luxurious English language. Students were mixed. Groups of Italians filled morning classes, always being banned from endlessly lapsing into Italian, learning nothing. There were pedantic learners, stoical older middle European bankers on corporate time refining their business English, reluctant Asian girls who refused to speak, sitting out their time, waiting for the end of summer when they would return to wherever they had come from, to be married off, never to be seen again. There were Iranians, the children of wealthy friends of the Shah, many already speaking English well. It was these who made teaching rewarding.

Lech got in quickly. It had happened benignly through the word of a friend still at university who had known the Scot as a former teacher in his quality London School, and who had also known he had left Dulwich to chase down a higher salary and better material prospects in the burgeoning business of taking the English Word around the world, an ironic 'open sesame' to international wealth, and opportunity. In those days the idea of qualifications for Teaching English as a Foreign

133

Language existed in the worlds of British Councils, but in the private teaching sector, as long as you were at least one chapter ahead of the class, anyone could teach the lingo. Far more important was the cachet of the London address, the smart building, and the piece of paper issued at the end of the programme, for which quite substantial sums of money were exchanged in fees to allegedly demonstrate competence. Some of the teachers had been doing bona fide work for years, around the world, and, licensed or not, appeared to be good, but in the high summer season a good level of English comprehension was enough, and you were launched into a class with teaching notes and a hand-shake. It was good money, but tiring for some after eight or nine hours a day, sometimes with no real break. Lech had the energy and the enthusiasm. You learned a lot, quickly, not only about your own language, but about others' tongues, about the way people learn, about characters, psychology, motivation and reward, judging, assessment, personal preferences, irritations. It was a good learning ground. Some classes flew by, others were stodgy and glum, some people really wanted to learn, others were just time-fillers waiting to get out and play again at whatever it was that got them going. Yet there were always the special ones, however hard you tried, the ones you liked just that bit more, where there was a stronger interaction. It was just about minds connecting, male or female, a mutual enjoyment of time or company, coming to terms with different cultures and expectations, sense of being and space. There was no way other kinds of relationships with class members were sanctioned, but if people were adult and open there was little that could be done after hours to prevent liaisons with mutually interested partners. This was how Lech developed a strong link with two members of particular Iranian families, who loved the English Teacher. There was a trigger that made him more determined to enjoy the friendship.

In one of the classes with two of the brightest and eldest of the Iranian families, a class of some sixteen to twenty advanced students, a tall, slim, fit male sat at the back. He was probably around twenty five or six years old, alert, attentive, but never one to volunteer answers. He was always the listener, watching and seeming to laugh along with the rest. After a couple of weeks, he lingered at the end of a class and said it would be very interesting for his English if he could maybe spend a little time, socially, with Lech, and use his time in a real context to work on his language. Lech said that was OK, and they could do that over the coming days, the student working slowly on him and eventually saying maybe it would be a good idea if at first he just went round to Lech's place for a drink and then took it from there. He said that was fine, he had the time.

They found themselves together in the apartment Lech shared with another university friend, part of a large house his parents owned in St John's Wood, not that far from the language school. Sitting down in the kitchen, the social centre of the place, the hot evening sun continued to burn its way through the westerly facing windows, and to the background of the topically named *Heatwave* album, a conversation took place. Lech drank white wine, the student drank water, emphasising now he was from Israel. His English, when he spoke outside the classroom, was significantly more fluent than the other class members. Lech had a few open-ended questions but got generalised answers in return. The Israeli asked a few questions of his own, about what Lech thought about the new Arab scene in London, about who he knew, about teaching, about the others in the class. It was a reasonable evening, more like a relaxed extended one-to-one tuition session, and they parted amicably, no indication on either part that they would pick another date sometime soon to continue their dialogue.

Lech asked the Scot about the Israeli the next day, but got little in return. The Scot was really only interested in the fees, not the character backgrounds. Then the Israeli left, as elusive as his arrival. The fit, fluent, water-drinking student disappeared. Lech thought about his questions, his style, his approach, his nature. It just didn't add up that at his age, with his level of fluency, he needed to be in that class at that school to study English. And the nature of his questions, always probing. No, he was something else. Lech realised that the Israeli, whatever his real name was, was there to check out the Iranians and their teachers. He was there to see what they did, what they said, what they thought. He was there to see how their teacher reacted, what he also said and did, what, if any, political or cultural sides or positions he took. Getting closer to Lech was simply an extension of getting to know more about the Iranians through the teacher. Someone was clearly prepared to spread resources far enough to have one of its operatives planted in the language school when two of Iran's rich families were letting their children perfect their languages, to keep an eye and an ear on what was going on. This was an expensive piece of coverage. What was it worth? The realisation that the Israeli was there to spy on him and his new friends was the only reasonable deduction from the behaviour, and the disappearance meant he'd either learned all he needed to know, or it was a waste of time pursuing that piece of surveillance further. Two things Lech knew. One, he was now a file note in some Israeli database, linked to the Iranians, and secondly, he was more determined than ever to continue his friendship with the lively students. He didn't refer to the Israeli again.

***

In the late 70's he came across an interesting piece of news, first mentioned in a short piece in England's *Sunday Times,* in the days when Harold Evans the editor was still able to fund some quality investigative journalism. It was about a mysterious boat and its strange passages in European waters, its shy crew and their unexplained cargo. Lech got into the story deeply, and speculated on its implications. He figured a scenario years before a more revealing confirmation of what was going on was printed by the English newspaper. He had continued his friendship with the Iranians he had met in London, and decided to share some of his thoughts with them. He figured their cousins in the Ruling Family might find the insights interesting. Just as he finished his storytelling, the summer crisis of 1979 snatched all the headlines, as the Shah was deposed, and life changed significantly for Iranians.

Lech guessed that the wandering boat was carrying material that could be used in connection with nuclear power, and its creation. If this was true, then unless the African-registered vessel was delivering things to the few official nuclear-weapon states, which it wasn't, then something very worrying was going on. He figured the boat was officially smuggling material to Israel, which would have all kinds of implications for the region. It wasn't until 1986, when John Crossman showed his photographs to *The Sunday Times,* that the story of Israel's nuclear programme at Dimona came into the public domain. Mossad's tradecraft was revealed when they arranged the kidnap in Italy of the former Dimona technician and whistle-blower, whose original name was Mordechi Vanunu, and Israel's secret was now a global headline.

But Mossad didn't always reveal its methods. In the panic and chaos of the changes in Iran, people were willing to trade all kinds of things to stay alive, to survive, to escape, and the insight into the purpose of the shadowy boat sounded like it would have significant value in the current circumstances. The cousin who had heard Lech's story was desperate to help her family, and decided to share her secret with one of her uncles in Security; maybe he could ensure none of the family came to any harm. He did what came naturally to a man in his position, a position where he had carefully tended safe alternatives, and in return for some overdue gifts of thanks, passed what he heard on to the

136

Israelis.

The convenience of Cordova Street in Vancouver, is its location as a hub for transport to many other parts of the city and its surrounds, 24 hours a day. No-one noticed the three travellers and their back-packs, looking like they'd been on the road for a few months, probably crossing up from Seattle most recently. They were looking over a much folded map, and after appearing to decide together on a direction, moved quietly on and deeper into Gastown. Where there were travellers, cheap accommodation, and all kinds of paraphernalia shops, there would also be drugs, and people who weren't quite managing them as well as others. Gastown was a place then where caution was a good word to keep in mind. The place also attracted all kinds of young people with the latest news and views on the arts, on music, on leading thinkers' views about politics, life, war, peace and most other subjects. Lech loved it as a source for a number of his on-air stories and articles, ever since he'd found the city, loved it and moved there.

Friday afternoon he was down there, smoking a joint, and trading stories about the state of the music scene. Towards six he made his farewells and got up to head on over to the station where he would be putting out a new bands show later in the evening, and where he always listened closely to new tracks, so his quiet commentary could always contain little insights that would keep listeners close to his guru-like broadcast. Coming out of the back of the building, through the public part of the record shop, he stepped out onto the street and turned left, beginning his usual route to the radio station. After fifty metres, he began to walk under the scaffolding of a building someone was trying to resurrect with an eye on a healthy return some time in the far future.

The girl in maybe her early 20s, max, seemed to suddenly lurch forward and left, like she was about to fall over or feint, the sign of a druggie who'd either just tanked up, or just begun to run on empty. She stumbled towards Lech, mumbling, and his natural reaction was to try and hold her up and stop her from sliding to the ground and damaging herself further. He also could never resist the proximity of a beautiful girl. In his preoccupation he didn't notice the other two, the males, until they had also reached the girl. If anyone had seen them, it would have looked like three guys trying to handle a female junkie who'd run into a problem, not an uncommon sight in that area then. The bigger frame of the action disguised the second male's move well, and, pulling Lech's sleeve up his forearm, while the first guy seemed somehow suddenly to have control over Lech's other limbs, pushed the needle and then its contents deep into Lech.

They held him down while the cocktail kicked in, minimising movement, but ensuring anybody in the vicinity would be side-stepping to avoid getting involved and close, but ready with a rehearsed excuse just in case. Lech responded quickly, and soon passed out. They pulled him up against the base of the scaffolded building, waited until they felt sure he wouldn't be fighting the overdose for long, and then they acted out the slow withdrawal of confused addicts abandoning their lost friend on Drug Street.

They moved on up the street like three dependants, all the way to the bus station, where, in the crowds, they drifted apart and began to resume the body language of normal, drug-free people. They silently parted ways, knowing that after two days, their separate exit routed would bring them back together again in Seattle. The newspapers this time would speak of the DJ's death by overdose, and beneath the headline would speculate on the mysterious absence of any previous signs of an addiction or leaning towards heroin.

On this occasion, Mossad's tradecraft remained a secret, and the Dimona development would continue to enjoy its private development out of the public's eye for another seven years. In Israel, the force celebrated the value of the lengths and depths its files went to in protecting the country's interests, another year's budget increase guaranteed, and which the language student from London was now directing. In this place, there was little respect for freedom of ideas that crossed the state lines.

***

Jules had thought about it. At school you could avoid it, but he couldn't completely hide from it – there was the parental pull on him. The early days there had meant the sports days, the marching round in Yellow House to the RAF signature tune, played by people in blue on their shiny instruments, a creeping feeling of pride without comprehension. Then there were, later, the volunteers, the CCF, the flying cadets, those who stood looking serious at remembrance days, whose musicians tried bleakly to capture the lost through their broken versions of *The Last Post*, paper poppies twitching as the notes scurried around the tune. These people dressed up, they stayed behind, they went away, but you never quite knew what they did. You saw the recruitment literature, always thought the RAF would be the one, the serious one with the real kit, and you wondered secretly if you'd make it, the selection, the trip to Cranwell, the wings, even though another part of you hated it all. It was a way of being connected to a glorious past and a dangerous present, protecting people for the future. But it was also tied in with the questions about discipline and rules, authority, fear and excitement, passing and failure. It was also a puzzle wrapped up in the much wider one about what was really going on not only out there, in the world beyond where real decisions had to be made and paths chosen, where few those seemed to know how or what to do, but also in your father's weird closed mind. Those slats in the fence from school yard to life outside got wider as the consciousness of what might really be out there grew. There were forays into the pages of the big newspapers you thought were different kinds of gateways to the world, and which all your adult acquaintances were wary of. They took their inspiration and titillation from the *News of the World*, and couldn't see the point of the price of *The Sunday Times*, with its long copy stories and its share prices, making you then want to be an arms dealer one week and an economist the next, the first because it had to do with extravagant lifestyles, the second because it sounded important, clever, involved.

London existed in two forms, the London you went to on the school trips, where you played endless private jokes the teachers couldn't penetrate, and the parallel place driven by images from magazines and TV programmes, the fictions of aspirant escapism, a diet of James Bond and the Avengers, *Melody Maker* and the *NME*. What you wanted to be came from *The Sunday Times*, but you still looked at the News of the Screws when your parents had finished nibbling at the naughty bits, the molestations and the exposures, the spankings and the sex, the hypocrisy of the outraged editorial moralists and disgusteds of the Home Counties.

There were all the voices around, the teachers and their selfish pressures for you to excel in their poxy subjects, the peer groups, the other pressure points, shop assistants, barmen, waiters, concierges, an array of still-uniformed representatives of rules you could only grasp obtusely, and whose invisible nets you got caught up in, determined to cut your way out so you could escape to another invisible freedom.

So you watched, everywhere, and listened. You saw groups form and dissolve, collide and react in pubescent chemical configurations, as everyone fought for definitions of themselves. You were happy with tangents, touching circles that were isolated from others. A bit like Lech, only without the girls. Some friends were in the Mods circle, and others with the Greasers. Some were in the library, some on the sports field, some were swots and some were subversive, like mad chanting Danny. School was where you tested the tolerance of the new acquisitions you'd made, the letting through the barriers of new knowledge, names, touchstones. The Cohn-Bendit you'd heard chanted, and Ali, Cream and Hendrix, Braques and Burton, rebels and changers, names that brought ignorance or anger out of those you shared them with.

It was testing time. It was years since you realised lying worked, that it sometimes made life less painful, that it helped you construct different versions of reality, and avoid consequences. It wasn't difficult to hold conflicting views, to suss out positions with committed friends, to challenge, to sift, to create a secret set of comparative worlds. You could be in the Peace Pledge Union on the one hand, collecting letters signed by Benjamin Britten, and going to agit-prop meetings in between, seeing what the student movements felt like. You could challenge the Methodists with Mao and watch them get jumpy and defensive. You could ask no end of people about dialectics and get no material answers. Having had a brother of the revolution liberate your copy of *The Little Red Book* from the local capitalist bookstore gave it more cachet. Is there anything you want me to nick for you today? And they'd come out with something pretty and large you could experiment with, Jung or Carrier, Picasso or even just a recent Penguin special. Pro-war or pro-peace.

It depended on who you were with. You were supposed to be grateful your parents hadn't emigrated to New Zealand, because they had the draft there and you could be in Vietnam in two years. There was a pull from both sides – the desire to be a witness, like the photographer Don McCullin fuelling a future misery, or a Californian burning flags, a diverting need to be connected to it all somehow. When it wasn't in the news you were with Burton and O'Toole, the Welsh Beckett fighting off the irascible Irishman playing Henry II, or pretending to understand Godard, trying to relate his latest screen offering *Alphaville* to your local grey and white town. What choices there were. The gloomy Alec Leamas, Burton again, *The Spy Who Came In From The Cold,* or the intriguing Harry Palmer with Michael Caine, the inconsistent Pink Floyd or the luscious Jefferson Airplane, the fried rice and soy sauce Friday night food, or the new fruity yoghurt (no, yoghurt wasn't it).

Journeys had to be made to everywhere, through astrology, through philosophy, through meditation, and some tickets came with a higher price than others. When it wasn't a mental map that was being charted or followed, there was a physical one to play with. If you weren't making discoveries of your own there were plenty around trying to

140

persuade you to let them reveal you to yourself, some furtive, some not. There were all those who wanted to talk and more, those who were just not interested, those on other planes, who were frightened, or who wouldn't reciprocate, or who wanted to maybe, you know, try, but were too, you know, shy to come forward, or make a move. After bottle-spinning and blind dates, coffee bar encounters and dark pub corner tables, late night walks and parties all over town in new houses, linked by living experiments in all forms of contaminants, punctuated by police requests to turn down noise, parents throwing out house wreckers, post-party analyses about girls and the benefits of the soon coming revolution, the problem with trying to get Janice to dance, the length of the latest live album drum solo, the move from cider to barley wine, another exotic brand of cigarettes, the switch from Sobranie to Passing Clouds, Disque Bleu to Stuyvesant 100's in the soft gold pack, the Marshall versus Orange amplifier challenge, there was still the old old problem, what to do about the other side of the fence.

There were escape routes. If nothing else, he knew he wanted to escape. The newspapers and books and records and stories from outside represented a fresh place to belong to, even though he had no idea what they might be like in reality. Jules didn't like chemistry, or biology. He liked arguments, debates, the new, the different, the foreign, anything his father loathed and had tried to ban him from liking. His father, who had never fulfilled his quest for fame and had taken solace in sulking and soaks, and whose only words were delivered in short sharp venomous bursts, just couldn't figure why his son didn't show him the respect he felt by rights he deserved, he was entitled to. He turned the turmoil deeper against the world, against the insolence of the challenger who, unlike his mother, had not remained in silent conformity at the altar of the almighty male, the breadwinner, the rule maker. The differences weren't merely generational, they were about fundamental ideas, creeds, ethics, sinews, rights to breathing, to living, forms of imprisonment, the nature of freedom. The son had demonstrated the cardinal sin of his father's world – lack of respect. It was the stake which defined and drove the schism in their lives. Yet both deserved it in different forms. Fredo's came too late for him to appreciate it, but he had after all served, even if his style of service hadn't endeared him to all.

Jules would earn it and lose it in a different way altogether.

***

141

J's Invisible Diary. Entry.

Since most people have seen nothing but change since they were born, yet have no direct experience to compare their way against others, it is an extraordinary surge, this drive to wanting more change, knowing you just want things to be different, because they are wrong the way they are.

You've already had everything better than we did, moaned the parents. You're selfish, accuse those who have only known sacrifices. They don't understand that the new generation is against something simply because it can be. It is theirs to be against. Down with war. We want peace. And love. Love for most of them is still boasting about non-existent conquests, fantasies and awkward fumblings, secrets in warm moist spaces, surprises. But the rebellion is bigger than sex. You don't have to know about sex to get on with the business of being iconoclastic. You can play music really loudly, everywhere, wear clothes that cause people to swoon, say things in language cohorts on the other side of the world, chant mantras, read those little red books, wear untreated afghan coats, smoke dope, listen to Captain Beefheart or Stockhausen, it's all about what's in your Head. Build a better prison, push out the walls, and just remember to make the most of it, because no-one here gets out alive. And just in case you are wearing a disguise, you always have to be ready to answer a question with another disguise. Hey, what's your position? The old get old and the young get stronger. Climb on through to the other side.

The need for rebellion remains constant, only the names and dates and places change.

The lessons of rebellion are easily learned. Just standing there practising got you a clip around the ear or a detention. No, it is necessary to do something to get attention, media interest especially, if you can do it without being caught, saving precious time for the next gesture, not blowing it all in a climactic *If....* Graffiti on walls is fine as long as you don't leave your hands covered in spray paint, as did the early protesters. Setting fire to something, even now, is not as controllable as you'd like. But it can arouse interest outside the narrow confines of the school gates. There are checks and balances that can be achieved. And there are always others who either crave the publicity or who are prepared to be bit-players in the production. Those who will lie down in the path of politicians, or stay out of classes, even if they think the protest is just to have a go at a teacher they despise, or because they think the protest might help them get better food, or not be stopped from smoking, or let their hair grow over their collars. Getting things closed down is good. It helps get people outside, so they can see glimpses of what could be out there for them. Sit-ins broaden the mind. We shall overcome. Remember how Abbie Hoffman protested by burning money. It was visual. It attracted cameras.

"Ultimately, you have to take a stand with your life".

Or get someone to stand in for you. We're looking at armies in taffeta uniforms whose weapons turn to ashes, whose wounds are signs, lesions in minds. The Messiah was going mass media – ElecChristity. Capitalists continue to rob people of freedom. Liberation will only come through action. Through more change. Change change change.

What is great about protesting is that if your audience has doubts, if they can't see the opposition for what it is, you can still appeal to their other fears and superstitions to get attention, the fear of the dark, the fear of being sent out at night down a dark alley to the shop to get some treat you'd forgotten or couldn't be arsed to get earlier in the day. The fear of going upstairs, the lights off, things in cupboards that make noises, under the stairs, that only you know about. And for all those witches and monsters and made-up creations, you can bring onto centre stage the other real but invisible threats – the secret police, the watchers, the monitors, the big brothers. And this world will stir up a response, fear in some, but in others the desire to stand up against the hidden significant danger, the behind the scenes manipulators who are trying to shape lives for their own spurious ends.

People in positions of boring authority, like politicians, are not to be trusted. What goes around comes around.

***

3

We continue our quest to understand Respect in corporations ~ we confirm its increasing rarity in today's so-called society ~ we feature the growing numbers of those who don't come close to getting the respect they deserve.

It's exactly the same with the people from the corporations. They are told they are not wanted, and are cut off from the benefit streams. Then they are told they will get a great reference, but if they ever divulge they were made redundant the company will make sure they never get a job around this town again, and any future pension of option rights will be jeopardised. Meanwhile they will be able to review the news stories about how their ex-employer continues to soar and keep shareholders happy. Books about excellence in corporations will continue to be written, and concepts of excellence revised. So-called human resources departments will continue to threaten uninformed staff that the company's deep pockets will ensure victory against any about to be considered legal threats concerning such crazy notions as unfair dismissal.

***

Nathan had left home every weekday morning at six, his usual time over the last eight years. He would be taking the 06.30 commuter train to Grand Central, rocking down the coastal line that began at New Haven. He would make the walk briskly from 42nd Street to his office in Times Square, his twice daily fix of exercise and steamy air. He'd man the phones and the machines, making trades on streaming numbers, encircling the world. He'd keep up with the emerging jargon and the jokes about disasters, the sardonic survival techniques of those wired to the clues behind tiny shifts that sometimes signalled significant gains. Every year there'd be other kinds of movements – headcounts tagged market fluctuations and fortunes. People would file out with little cardboard boxes, their laptops and phones confiscated by their erstwhile employers, and within thirty minutes they'd be in Starbucks plotting what to do next. The flood of locked-up accessories, hard-drives and sim-cards replaced, would appear at auctions or at dealers within days, followed by fire-sales of late-used cars with aspirational marques, and occasionally boats and planes, apartments and houses, as income steams dried up, and the hocked up symbols and badges of success turned to tarnished medals of remembrance. He'd kept it all going, and his wife and three kids, still the same from the start, had carried on swimming in the heated comfort zones of country club pools and summer houses, never belittled by missing out on each years' must-have toys and fashions, fees and subscriptions, anniversaries and parties, paid, paid, paid. There were lots of other bodies left lying out in the cold.

He'd spent most of his time working in an area of operations that had been a regular cash provider to the corporation, but to some eyes it was looking dull and tired these days. Newer forms of rapid enrichment, like CDOs, had become all the rage, and his corner of the floor was being passed over by the new Masters of the Universe. That's why he got the call.

Truth is, he was told, your stuff isn't what we really want to do anymore. Not sustainable. It doesn't turn anyone on, doesn't grab new investors' imaginations, and at the strategic level it's just been invited to join the dodo.

He was despatched with a fuck you bonus and stock options he would have no ability to influence. There you go Nathan, enjoy tomorrow's world, you sure have earned a break. The words echoed around his head as he passed on Starbucks, and took the train home, saying nothing.

The next day, and the day after that, and the day after, he'd let the non-stop train go, and took the slower service, getting off two stations down the line. This time he did set up in a coffee-shop, a regular Starbuccaneer, new lap-top and mobile, miming doing deals and monitoring the body language of lookalikes. He did in fact try a few deals, tried to hook up with buddies and colleagues, soon discovering he was a dead duck, with many none too keen to associate with the recently departed. At home the family kept their ignorant remorseless pressure on his depleting funds and hidden growing anxiety. He would smell the stench of corporate corpses growing, pulling him towards their frigid perfumed proximity.

He'd fixed it so when he was home emails kept buzzing in from auto-updating sites, and the phone kept saying *Talk* as he subscribed to a number of concierge services that would say anything you liked as long as you paid their rates. It looked like business as usual. People who lived locally were still happy to take drinks off him at the local watering holes, and only one co-traveller wondered why he wasn't on the 06.30 anymore. Shifting markets, he said, no need for that start.

Where the work is right now, nobody's up, nobody's trading, but this means the early bird still gets the worm, even if arriving at the desk after sun-up looks like a part-time day. There were no letters, no snail-mail to accidentally reveal what was really going on, simply the auto-office replies acknowledging receipt of the CV or call or email, which never moved forward to a real meeting, a real response, a real call. He wasn't even yesterday's man. He was fossilized on a digital planet, a carbon-dated dinosaur who once roamed the earth as the king of long-term returns, looked on by economic historians as a once fashionable but ultimately non-survivable species.

Increasingly, he couldn't talk to the family who thought the Fountain of Fortune was forever. He couldn't stand the creeping loss of self-esteem, the loss of face. In three months the reminders would start to come in, the virus of polite correspondence about unfortunate and understandable forgetfulness in meeting debt obligations. The language would grow monstrous consequent to a negative response. On Tuesday, 14 February, he was at the station just as his old faithful fast train approached. As it got to the end of the platform it was till decelerating from around 45 mph as it timed its long rake of coaches to fit the platform perfectly. It was so easy to step out and not make the driver's day. He closed his life's trading account several points down, and any number of inconvenienced workers cursed the jumper. Why didn't the drones just fade away?

That night at the Valentine's Day Ball, people pushed wives and mistresses, lovers and friends around the dance floor at the Plaza, turning itself into the stage for the corporate event. Krug and Crystal vied for podium places as the most drunk bubbles, and massed orthodontics smiled their successful way beneath the chandeliers. A thousand rising wannabees sized each other up. On the dance floor, like everywhere else, it was about the survival of the fittest. People like Nathan were so totally over. There was nothing to remember, so nothing to forget. Today there was no midnight bell, no Cinderella sentiment, same as every other day. In the cold north, his wife stared blankly at the unsigned Valentine's Day card, as the police tried to piece together the last days of the lost romantic's life.

***

Ulrich sat in the wine bar, tracing equations in the condensation from the glasses on the table top, indicating the two of them were now past their second bottle, and into the stuff the sommelier had decided required balloon glasses big enough to have interested the Montgolfier brothers. One of them, the one picking up the tab, was still in the money, the other was out.

Down and out in Paris and London. Rafa was still liked by some of the senior veterans in the organisation, which is why he was sitting under the chandelier and letting the Petrus slide down. That was the subject really. It wasn't about friends, or competence, or profit for partners, or any of those things. It was politics and ageism. Ulrich had lost little energy, had no enthusiasm, and had increased his skills. But there were touches of grey creeping into the edges of his strong hair, betraying his thirty-five year-old looks for his real forty three.

Myths got mixed up with the ice of reality. The myth was that at thirty six you were collectively considered over the top unless you were at the top, in a group of about seven. The reality was that despite the not-insubstantial benefits package, you could be replaced tomorrow by a dozen newcomers, with even more expendable energy, and the company would still have change, especially when most of the arrivistes were disposable annually, and were the first to go when markets got depressed. There would always be one or two 'chosen ones' in each intake who could do no wrong, and for the rest, there were plenty looking for scapegoats. You didn't have to have done anything wrong, you merely had to appear in the sights, after which your name would keep flashing like the world's most annoying banner ads, until you were extinguished or unsubscribed to. You might as well have kept upping the cocaine, none of it mattered if it was Time to Go, an Islamic irony in a capitalist universe. "TTG dude". So if you hadn't pre-fixed your next assignment, and a cosy signing-on bonus, you were well tainted. Loser. What you needed was a takeover with a few friendlies in it to help you weed out the Bad Ones and keep you on as the Head of the New Team, at least until you had got a hand on the next deal.

At this stage the head hunters didn't want to know – too old, too expensive, wrong profile, wrong experience, just plain wrong in fact. Wrong. Wrong. Wrong. In the olden days there were still ways out, nods and winks, like the FILTH option, and for those too young to know, it meant Failed In London, Try Hong Kong. Sniggers and smiles but there was still a chance. The whiff of maturity and wisdom outside the boardroom was the scent of death the sharks always picked up. Mixing analogies with the third bottle going down, it was better to be shot as you bagged over the trenches, pistol in hand, frozen as a youthful memory, an undying rockstar.

147

So what had changed at the fabulous offices then? Another year of ups and downs, a new set of heroes, a brushing up of the clichés about pressure and performance, the need to tighten up, the challenges of the next four quarters, and a summary of all the broken promises that again wouldn't be kept except for the very few who had a claim on special spoils, and Holiday Greetings to you and your Families, whatever your persuasion. One or two had secured different short-term futures or even been hired in, and reputations were moulded about Lucky Jim or Unlucky Juan, Clever Cecilia or Doldrums Daniel, oh and not forgetting non-sexual harassment Miranda and her unambiguously managed assets.

Ulrich went back to the office. Rafa returned to the apartment, now his alone. Since he'd been spending more time there, and the corporate weekend junkets had gone, he no longer had the aura of the gold-bar safety stash, and his girlfriend had gone, seeking solace in a different form of futures, a more known-known, who could massage a lifestyle without any embarrassing moments at Manolo's. She had been with him for, oh, weeks, until he stopped many of the cards and clubs and memberships, moulting a huge entourage of personal trainers and new-agers whose ways he could barely pronounce, let alone understand. The trophies were getting tarnished. His lamp had somehow been vacated by its genie, and nothing was responding to his Open Sesames right now.

Dismissal was the price of success. Get a grip. Others slid from peak to penury in months, having lived over-compensatory lives to counter the stress of the front-line. Some took refuge in drugs, others finessed affairs with alcohol, marrying their mistresses until death us do part, honouring and obeying a brand that would still be unfaithful years later, after you'd gone, sirens to the tired and corporately oppressed. Some hung on as mentors, life coaches, willing all, with tales of transformation and happiness to tell, never quite finding the escape velocity from their mostly lost world, pretending they were happy with Gravity's Rainbow. Maybe it would change, the cycle of things, and suddenly he would join others, surfing on a wave of recruitment, or whatever the latest jargon for hiring would have become – new-sizing, competitive hedging, silver-plating. Whatever, there'd be a transient phrase to suit the attraction of the affordable, experienced, re-usable. And for every half-smug old wonder, there'd be fifty mega-qualified wannabees ready to do anything for the price of a cheesy night in The Four Seasons, Lonelyville. Easy to see the way of the world when you were sitting on the up-slope of the demand-curve. No-one could be bothered sifting through the rocks on the downside for the once high-flying wreckage. Ben Jonson got it right four hundred years ago – "Hello World, and next my gold". It was indeed a world of Foxes. Nature raw in tooth and claw. Red.

OK, so put everything on red. The roulette wheels will continue to spin, and rakes will continue to pull losers' chips back to croupiers and vaults, the dried blood of the addicted optimists. What's the point giving these people money they said – they don't know what to do with it? It's just our way of getting it back, providing a happy conduit for the believers in Lady Luck. Fortunately these folks were dumber than most traders, temporarily on winning streaks. Fair? Of course it's fair. The odds are declared more than on any other market. Unfair is the sort of word the weak use to explain their feebleness. What is there is there for the taking, and if you're smart enough to do that, then you get to keep it. The perspective so far appeared to work, depending of course on where you were sitting. Rafa said goodbye to his 'in' friend when he'd decided he had to get someone pre-armed for tomorrow's session, when he would be putting his chips down a little later than usual. He had stayed on to finish the wine, something he wasn't sure when he'd be tasting again, the balloon pricked. He drifted back into the mood lighting of the loft, lights outside keeping their place in the tall glass towers. He looked around and wondered what it had all been for, falling asleep and dreaming of nothing. Tomorrow he would do the same, only the wine would be different. At this rate, if he dropped a couple of points on Parker and settled for the top of the second division wines, he could keep this up for years, and watch the greyness catch up with others, feeding the hands above that would eventually bite them. He was in The Cooler, he felt like one of the few winners in *The Great Escape*. It was the power of the grape. The Grapes of Wrath. Ecstatic he wasn't.

His former bosses went on to break the bank, and then spend years blaming others for the unforeseeable events that overtook them, having made only the slightly noticeable error of stashing huge amounts of money away in offshore trusts in the preceding months.

***

Lou was 'rationalised' in November, so he wasn't entitled to any extra payments because he hadn't completed a full year of work that year. He got a week's worth of pay for every year served, and then he was out – some said he should have been grateful he'd got such a great contract.

The usual platitudes were delivered by a survivor in human resources. He couldn't afford a lawyer's fee to challenge the kiss-off, and with those vipers on the top floor paying out bigger whacks to protect themselves, he wasn't sure he was going to win a case anyway. So he thought, it's a chance, it's an opportunity, it's the moment to really make a change. He and Jess had talked about it. Now there was the coming together of elements to make this work. Over a bottle of champagne where he kissed the ass of the corporation adios, they chatted about the new life, the place in the mountains they'd fantasised about, not too far off the beaten track, affordable. A change of lifestyle, good for the one-year old, fresh air and spring water, big skies and sun, reduced pollution of the man-made kind, with the summit of the range behind them, and the sea on the other side, Nature, but connected to the present. There were quite good links to places like the ones they'd lived in before, some seasonal variations. It wasn't as if they were moving to some totally remote wilderness. They could be together at last, the office wouldn't be the third thing in the marriage, and anyway, these days you could work from just about anywhere anyway. Why did you need to trudge into some Central Business District every day? It was the quality of the work that counted wasn't it, not just being counted in and out? Wasn't that some kind of old-fashioned notion of overseen work that was fading now?

He mapped out his idea for the business, sitting behind the screen with no onlookers and no diary full of meetings to discuss whether there should be a meeting, no water-cooler bullshit about departmental gossip and golf handicaps, Monday-morning quarterbacks and the failings of overpaid pundits. Bliss. Jess sat there and took it all on board, while he carried on bleeding out his anger at those who had disappeared behind their name-plaqued corner office doors when he thought they would step up to the mark for him.

The very next week he'd got on the plane, conducting the 'recce', the advance party of The New Life on Earth, and he emailed pictures of all the pretty places he thought fitted the bill, each and every one abandoned by locals who had moved to cities in search of stimulation and fun, service and smiles, leaving behind no clues about the temperatures and the winds, the lack of amenities and the legacy of poverty, imposed or self-inflicted. He was in love with The New Dream. From his balcony in the hotel, he concluded he was making progress as he gazed across the vista of the horizon. He'd already got the used car that fitted in with the theme of his script-writing, and a noisy bike that said Freedom all the way through its legendary branding. He was even thinking of ordering some kind of local boat to tempt everyone onto the water and to show the locals he was investing in their craftsmanship. Each day the messages and the calls went home, and Jess's responses got shorter as she tended the child. For someone who was on the wagon he was making a good disguise of it, and by week 12 with a beard and several bars recognising his face, he had drifted into the arms of a local girl looking for a way out, only to regret his actions in the limp mornings after, when he couldn't recall the promises, and woke up to the lingering odour of hurried sex, and pieces of the song, *Love The One You're With*.

His dreams were laced with other kinds of fantasies now. Money was burning fast. If he wasn't being ripped off by the locals who quickly spotted his weaknesses, he was charming the pants off the new lovely with extravagant ephemeral gestures she was happy to take and enjoy. After another month he found the bank he'd left behind wouldn't give him any cash. He tried a couple of cards and found the only one that worked was in his name only. Flailing around on whiskey and frustration, leaving long swearing messages on speed-dial numbers that cut to voicemails, he swaggered round the town, buying food and drinks for anyone he'd ever met, telling them he loved them all in his new life in the hassle-free zone. He didn't drink for most of his next day, because he didn't wake up until four thirty in the afternoon. When he got it together he found he could focus long enough to read what was coming out of his message box on the screen, and he remembered the name of the lawyer that prefaced the letter. In flat, legal terms it described how his wife, Jess, would now not be joining him. It explained how their child would not be joining him, and that funds for the mother and child's joint future had been secured from former joint accounts, together with paragraphs describing orders banning him from approaching his child and former home. He'd been wiped out by his wife. He left a couple more threatening messages on his wife's phone, something to do with killers and kidnap, and went out on the town again to tell his new best friends what life was going to be like round here with the new found Free Man. He invited the new love to join him and several newly acquired life-long friends, and he took them off to what he called the local restaurant and drinkery.

Everyone had a story to tell, and if the pace slowed down, the restaurant owner would produce another round of bottles, knowing there'd be shouts for more, and the wild man would pay tonight, in cash, from the pile of notes he'd tipped into the empty bread basket. Women came under the cosh, and the New Love got tired of her unwanted membership of the hoes and bitches club. She slipped away on one of the waves of laughter, deciding flight was better than fight with the forked-tongue gang of fuelled-up heavies. Steaks were sacrificed, and wine was poured to cool the blood as the net of misogyny trawled deeper. But tonight no-one was asking for the volume to be turned down. It looked and smelled like a cheap club from a dim past, where everyone secretly craved the bigotry of the comedian who would come on stage, and they smirked behind their fear of the foreign and different, all those other countries out there. Wine was reinforced with wine, a force-field of defence. Spirits poured forth again, and did what they do best, falsely keeping spirits up. Slowly, as the night wore on, the supporters began to drift away, the money changed hands, and the last energy was focused on heading off to swaying sloping beds and floors, spinning dreams.

Lou left, lurching towards the iron horse he'd tethered earlier. He fumbled and started up the machine, gunning the engine and shouting Fuck You Jess between twists of the throttle. He skidded off, a defiant wheelie revealing the bald patch on his helmetless head, roaring off towards the stars. Five minutes later he was doing sixty on the dirt-track side road, three minutes from the home of his sleeping New Love. His front fork shuddered and snapped as the wheel vainly fought off the rock a tractor had dislodged earlier. The irresistible force had met the immoveable object. Just as he mouthed the word 'shit', his head struck the ground, absorbing the weight of his drunk hound-dog body, following him faithfully down the long road to Comatose. Way to go, boy. The ones who'd let him go, the Masters of the Universe, didn't even hear about it, and if they had, they would have simply written him off as lacking 'the right stuff'. It's a tough old world out there, dude.

***

Narayan was late into his second marriage with a young kid, the alimony still hurting from the first failure, and a much younger wife who hadn't peaked in wanting to see how far up the materialistic maypole she could still climb. So he'd just about survived the last round of corporate right-sizing when he was invited to join a team that would be driving new kinds of changes through the company and the region. A narrow escape he thought. With his insider's knowledge of the organisation and its turf, he'd be invaluable to the outsider who'd been brought in to be the Change Master. His significantly increased salary seemed to signal his self-appraisal of his worth had been justified. What he hadn't quite worked out was that most of his surviving colleagues were deeply mistrustful of his new role and micro organisation, of his new package, and of what might still become of them. They were unwilling to play along very far, hesitating to share gossip, tips, rumours; reluctant to share information, deliver materials on time, make meetings. They still had old structures and older bosses. They'd seen plenty of radical new approaches in the past. They liked Narayan up to a point, and they could hardly blame him for jumping at the chance to survive, possibly for the sunset period of his career. But some of the trust had gone. He'd sold out to a maverick. Would they have done the same? Some would, others wouldn't. His temporary survival, his safety extension, came with a price. It was a protraction of living and working with a contract he could only see the upside of. It was a Faustian offer, and he refused to countenance what would ultimately be wanted in return for the good times.

He had no shortage of tricks, ways to make the numbers sing, the practised smile of long-term inside knowledge, the loyalty, the always looking out for his boss stance straight out of *The Godfather*, one of the movies he had been enthralled by when he first moved to the USA. He had bought totally into his new saviour, his protector, his new found source of domestic stability. For this, he maintained his smile when the corporate honeymoon was over. The smile covered the scarring of his soul and self-respect as his Chosen One ranted and raved about the inadequacies of his new empire, which had not adapted him as a vital new force in quite the way Narayan had, or he had expected. He maintained the smile when he was mocked and insulted in front of his team members for some failure he hadn't anything to do with. He didn't fight back, he didn't take a swing, a hit, metaphorically or physically. He kept his mouth shut, he rode the storm, he fielded every observers' questions about how could he let his boss do that with the knowing smile and the gesture that said well it's just the way he is and what do you do? He spoke about the need to be empathetic, sympathetic to the guy with the Big Job, the challenge, the real pressures. Platitudes. It was just his way of letting off steam, kind of Latino, *no problemo*. Here he was, being demeaned every day, but since he'd bought the ticket, he was going along for the ride all the way.

When the call came he just went on automatic. He'd jump on the plane, 3,400 miles to the emergency meeting, to the high five, the assembly of others who'd also flown in from other far-flung spots, waiting for the pronouncement, to find there was no new crisis, no agenda, no reason for the gathering other than "Just need my team to be around me", which was all the reason. That was all the compensation Narayan needed, then he could weave tales about the significance of what had to be done, why absences at a moment's notice had to happen. Hell, the boss jumps every time The Big Man says Boo, so the least we can all do is be around to support him. There's plenty around who'd like to see him take a fall, so we're gonna be strong here. Is it strength that keeps you working or weakness? Narayan appeared to be ready to swallow himself to stay in place. It was just possible enough people would remember he had been an OK kinda guy when it all ended.

When it all ended the company was half the size, and he was with the half that had be eaten. His boss, the saving grace, stayed on as a consultant to the operation he had failed to change, finding plenty more problems for other consultants to fix. Gee, it was hard being a genius.

***

We take a closer look at those who are busier taking out than putting back ~ the idea of the refined List is recorded ~ we see how some of the networks are joined up ~ we look at how those who rebel will be regarded ~ we meet Fredo's son, Jules, again ~ we wonder who is the real new enemy?

The ones who were sitting out there on all the thrones, getting it right, in their heads, had all the admirable qualities the leadership books wrote about. They were full of drive, of energy, of force, of purpose, sometimes quiet, sometimes loud. The only thing they inflated more than their self-defined worth as contributors to a largely dumb society, were their appeals for more adequate compensation in driving towards the future against such poor odds. Some respected the people they engaged in pursuit of heroic profitable goals, some put back pieces of what they'd taken out, or as they would put it, had deserved to be given. Others treated people as disposable commodities, there to serve the greater good, gift-wrapped in jargon about inclusivity, corporate social responsibility, sustainability, and all sorts of other 'ity'–bitties that ended up finishing people off for the sake of "building a better world". There were plenty to go round.

***

Sam Danello was fat. He used to quip to death that his body was a temple. It was clear he had never missed an opportunity to worship there, bringing offers up to the oral altar all day. But let no-one else be caught within earshot making sacrilegious references to this holy relic. Danello's Inquisition would soon root out the mockers. Tiresome parasites and other courtiers displaying any level of wit that came close to upstaging the one Fool other than himself he permitted to tell jokes would be rapidly dispatched. He had grown his girth gastronomically with other people's money. Vini-culturally his appreciation of wines bypassed varietals and was based only on the size of prices marked up by voracious restaurants. The king needed to be amused, distracted and protected from the realities washing up on his surrounding shores. He had become institutionalised through first class and private travel to the point where he didn't realise that baggage didn't move itself. He had more houses than he could remember, and hated all of them because they were fundamentally connected to people. There were always too many people in his life, too many wanting his expensive time, his presence, his sanction. He really only liked about five of them out of the six billion alive around him, those he considered not dangerous who thought they knew him. That was why there was only one child, the accident he tolerated. It was, in his mind, his only weakness. It was a useful weakness for the researchers too.

The one who developed a mastery of putting others down shared the same traits as other practitioners, and couldn't ever take at joke at his own expense. He was a petulant twelve year old in a fifty five year old body. No-one could remember when he'd last had a great idea. He was the one who always knew what wasn't right. He was a Shiva, a creative destroyer without the ability to bring things back to life. More a Shredder. He was caught up in old fashioned ways like ox-bows left stranded by meandering rivers, head of a micro-world of views and perspectives that no-one ever challenged, a kingdom of constriction. He had done well.

He didn't notice the protection, the levels of adulation, because he had become so accustomed to it all. That left him free to focus his loathing on those who depended on him for their survival, on those who made contributions to the organisation that sustained him at gargantuan levels. If he was good at anything, he told good stories. He was the Chief Storyteller, a narrator who had honed his series of tales to entertain his varied audiences. They were quick to applaud. But people lately rarely sought him out to discuss real things. He was there to say yes or no, an intuitive response honed out of years of snap judgements. He was the head of his self-proscribed fiefdom with the ruling council that administered all this domination of the organisation's heart and

155

veins. The host body wanted to reject its own blood, deeply aware of the consequences. The arrogant council straddled the world, the excesses of their lifestyle dribbling onto those below and beneath. What a group it was, to know it had always been right, to have grown fat on trivia and the rapid disposal of dissenters. Look at the numbers. They never noticed how the end was getting closer, how the world was finally closing in on them as the years passed, but like the event horizon of a black hole, it was sucking the life out of everyone else as well. People recognised the fading Danello and began to wonder how his interminable presence continued to be justifiable, but if they ever thought it they kept it to themselves. He continued to seek solace in his audiences, in the faithful parasitic worshippers of his idiosyncratic fame. That's how his vision had come to the shape it was in. He had forgotten how to earn anything, how to pay. He didn't notice what services were except through their absence. He still roared "Don't you know who you are talking to?" "Oh, you did that, did you?" in reverent tones, waiting for the tales to be told to the court again, ever more embellished. Danello was the king of the quips they would say. He was the man who couldn't be bothered to understand how the machine which fashioned him worked, as long as the adulation kept coming in. He'd missed it once when he tried to be king of another corporate country, an even bigger fish in a smaller pond. But when the going got tough and the treasury was becoming bare, he managed to return to his rightful kingdom, with expansive tales about how everyone missed him so he had no choice but to return and make the glorious comeback. The prodigal was back in the place where he had spent over almost all of his adult life, back in the familiar sights and sounds, surrounded by the fawners and the handful of special friends. He refused to accept that reverence could fade, that youth had the right to say things and see things in its own way. He clung to the only raft he could, though he couldn't see that is what he was adrift on. He was on his makeshift lifeboat, hundreds of bottles loosely lashed together, containing little messages about everyday things, things he'd sent around the world hoping that people would believe the wisdom captured in the fortune cookie papers enclosed. He was the Better Man. Cleaner than Clean. Tastier than Tasty. Er. Er. There were some things he'd never say. "Let's go to lunch. I'll pay". "Don't worry, I'll take the stairs". There was one, so the story goes, who told him the truth to his face. By the time he had returned to his office in another country he had been fired, an event for which he was finally truly grateful.

But if it wasn't for these lumps loafing around, who else could you

156

turn to for an explanation of all the frustration going around? Where could you spot a planet-sized centre of gravity for selfishness, and hold it in some kind of check? Danello gave a new meaning to the idea of a mass medium. He had been Nathan's Boss. He was on The New List, qualifying under the code of The Index, there to suffer eventually if there was no putting back. Meanwhile, hundreds were let go to maintain the edifice of his temple.

***

Many women had bought into The New World Deal, not just as wives and partners, the easy targets of the practice runs, but as drivers too, Change Masters in tailored ensembles, Number Ones. 'Worked with the Boss' once before, it said on the CV, a while back, but hey, look at what's here now, Mephistopheles working overtime on sending us new Helens of Troy. And you know, once in, the other guys see your strengths straight anyway.

The storyline was clear – You'll transcend the starter set-up. You'll be indispensable within the year. You'll have a direct report to the Main Board, there's no way you'll be tied down to this, what you've now got is a catalyst for your own continuing success. And so, one of the new female team members went about her way building her empire within the wider world. For the Big Boss, everything, for the middle man, something, for the rest, nothing.

Marcella had always tried to steal the show. In any hour, she would try and stretch it to eighty minutes. For any 'no more than ten charts' show she'd have had fifty. For any big cheese she'd have hours, and no time for anyone else. She'd pretend to be friends with some of the team, giving away fabricated snippets of her own life in return for real confidences, jewels she would use to trade. She was after points, trust and loyalty. Confidences for her only existed as weapons for betrayal, like the conspiracies she used to test others' strength and resilience. Did you ever hear tell about how Rita faked an illness to avoid a tough meeting, and then boasted about it afterwards? No you didn't wasn't going to be a satisfactory answer. No, you had to have a secret to trade back, or another piece of a conspiracy, or a doubt that could be fuelled by her and used later, like half-chewed bones still to be savoured, spread around. You were then privileged with some tale about her sexual spontaneity with strangers, or what she used to like to do when there was more time, and that you really should appreciate the adventurousness she once had before the kids came along because, hey,

157

you weren't just looking at the most brilliant team member here. You were looking at someone you wished you'd had a chance to be fractionally like. Oh she's so good, so clever. She was Professional, spreading out and strangling everything to get control, to leave seeds of doubt about those who weren't quite subscribing to her vision, her style, her genius. There was her view, and there was her view. If you were lucky, and senior enough, there was room for a bit of your view too, treated with a touch of flattery, a touch of condescension, all in the same mellifluous tone. Failing to worship was to be cast out. Failing to be friends if it had been decided you needed to be one resulted in fresh attacks to find weak points where new onslaughts could be launched because, well, somewhere between you eventually was going to be your dependency. Disagreements had always got to be your problem, emanating from some sad but eventually detectable weakness which only she could uncover. Discovery meant control, and if you then didn't take her remedial proposals, your lack of gratitude would be broadcast as selfish and uncooperative behaviour. You know, what is it with that individual? This is just called trying to help. Smile. Deep behind the blue eyes was coal. Dead carbon. The only way you could strike up a relationship was with a match.

As usual, there was only one interpretation of the world. Many perspectives, one interpretation. So, like, what people really want is to be a New Yorker. What do you mean haven't you travelled? When the loft was being refreshed in the village we lived on Columbus for three months. Or, women don't want that kind of pantyhose or, women don't want that kind of hair care (the trichologist says). These are all of vital importance to the twenty three year old mama with two kids living on the edge of Sao Paolo, Delhi, and Mogadishu. No, but eventually they will be. They will? Yes, in the same way that everyone will eventually want to able to order a skinny decaf Frappuccino, with a half-fat blueberry muffin on the side. All those heroines pushing the corporate agenda forward. No, that can't be right. They're just not driven by those guy things. No, it's about being true to yourself, to your values. That's what people are buying from here. Your worth. Because you're worth it, as the ads confirm. What do you mean, not a team player? If someone doesn't like being on this team they can leave. It's up to them. As long as they don't try and step out of place they'll get full support. But don't you ever forget who's here for you. Always. If there's ever a problem you can guarantee it'll be used as an opportunity. Men at work may be strong, but there is nothing devious a man can think of that hasn't been thought by a woman first. Corporate women of the world unite. It's a bit that's going to be tough to deliver.

Marcella had all the makings of being on The New List, all the characteristics, and if she kept bringing home the bonuses, she'd be pressing all the buttons, and the lights would start to flash. She had added points to her score by letting Lou go, among hundreds of others.

***

So what? That summed up the CEO and President's attitude in that country operation. He knew everyone in the world of football, because he was a big guy who'd played averagely once. This puffed up prowess appeared to give him great sporting credentials as far as his working life went. When they say 'his working life' they meant to put this in its rightful place. Work was something to be squeezed in between social events, sporting events that enabled him to be witnessed as a spectator with privileged access to the best seats, wherever, and a private life of spectacular shabbiness. Work could be dealt with easily. It only required a personal assistant or two who could be counted on for their loyalty and devotion because they needed the job, a group of workers who could be bellowed at, distant bosses who could be schmoozed benignly, and contacts and prospects who could be reached remotely from hotels, airports, cars, restaurants, marquees and sports arenas. Because you had to be seen to be busy. You had to be seen to be moving. That was the job. Action Man. Managing and nurturing and seeding relationships. Being there for the punters, getting them the tickets they wanted, the seats they demanded, the meals they craved, the wines they would never pay for themselves, the men and women they wanted to play with. Other people were paid to sort out the details, pick up the pieces, do the numbers, apologise to the let down or ignored, the ones he thought were dull or useless or both, the ones who funded his life to the limits. And what was wrong with his life? Nothing, from where he was looking. There were just a few details that bothered some of those who had to share parts of it with him, beginning with the fact that in his country being the boss meant being God. The Manager, The CEO, The President, was IT. There was to be no challenging his decisions, his style, his attitude, his behaviour. The culture said if he'd crossed the line and made it, he deserved it, and anyone else just better get along with that or vote with their feet. The Manager was King of the Pack, Top of the Heap, and if you wanted to be a part of it, part of old Alec Daniels, then you just kept your head down and bit your lip.

159

"There will be no bonuses" he announced as his new car was delivered to the company car park. "Do you like these new hand-made shoes? Lobb in London," he announced to several who were packing their few personal belongings into those little cardboard boxes we had seen before, the badge of just being culled in the latest right-sizing.

"There will be no pay rises after a tough second half. Tell your team they're going to have to work harder, they can't have anyone else. What? You want me to talk to them? Sorry, dinner at The French Laundry with someone who might want to drop $500 million on us. Anyways, who has time for that international shit?"

In a place where existence largely depended on the international 'shit', the manager, who could barely be articulate in his own language, let alone any other, squandered the profits on trying to enhance his reputation with local players. There he goes again. Charm (in a locker room fashion), height, directness, a winning combination. The man said that things could be done quickly and just look at who else is out there. See who you can be introduced to. Alec Daniels was the master manager, the survivor protected by his only boss who would never admit to the mistake of hiring him. Daniels' demise would have to be down to someone else, some other time. In the meanwhile, any problems arising would simply have to lead to the right-sizing of local offices, scenarios which could be easily constructed, handled and clinically cleaned out from the safety of the distance from head office his regional HQ conferred on him.

What he needed outside the operation was another cash-generating machine. He had many calls on his money. There had been some slightly unplanned events in his life. He had already one kid with his first girlfriend. He never married anyone. He said he was only interested in the kids. The first mother knew about the second. Then he'd had to return early from a management conference after his secretary had called him to say his third girlfriend had gone into labour, which mothers one and two were blissfully unaware of. He expected people to get used to the idea of him turning up at events with different 'wives' and a range of kids calling him Dad. It was his way of demonstrating his fecundity, his largesse, his fondness for the future all children represent. Just like with the mothers, he didn't actually like most of his clients either. It would have been a lot easier if they'd just sent the money and not gone through the tiresome business of wanting something in return for it, at least not from him directly. He thought he needed someone to help him be as generous as he wanted to continue to appear to be, the ever-connected man. You could always touch him for a ticket, but the invitations to the real serious stuff always dried up quickly, unless you were in, a dubious privilege.

He was a victim of his own circumstances, and believed the jovial whirlwind he conjured up somehow endeared him to the clients who were looking to scrape the next layer of profit from their weakening businesses. Alec Daniels' enlightened solution to all this consisted of two parts, dinner or an event, coupled with a demand to spend the way out of any trouble. Solutions were something to be bought, preferably at a premium price. He always went down spectacularly badly in budget meetings, if he bothered to show. Fortunately, a number of critical company clients didn't request his presence. Business would always go into power drive in September, when his children would be returned to schools. For three months he could be seen in theory from 7.30am to 8.00pm except for lunch. Demand from inside the organisation wasn't high, most people trying to fix meetings they knew would clash with other of his appointments so he couldn't bully his way into being involved and proposing irrelevant and outrageous suggestions based on whatever titbits he'd heard that week.

December was the month to express his lavish personal thanks to all those clients he'd avoided or been banned from seeing for the rest of the year. Many showed, taking his extravagant hospitality just to spite him, and making mental notes to ensure accounts uncovered any attempt to load his 'thank yous' onto their own books.

January to March was the laid-back period. There was plenty of time to build momentum in the New Year. If you weren't at every football game there was time to recover from seasonal excesses in the Caribbean, and on the ski-slopes.

Easter and May added up to a long run of public holidays and stretched weekends, leaving June and July to tidy things up before the summer vacation season took care of most of his clients' time. If he pulled off twenty three weeks of work a year it was a clincher.

For seven years he had been untouchable. He had watched people thrown onto the streets for his mistakes. He reduced further the burden of boring clients but still took their dollars. Leaving parties were well-attended, most wishing one of them could be his. This would be the best ever attended, like the old Hollywood parades, as people really wanted to make sure he was on his way out the other side, to be encapsulated in the corporate memory as the pain he had always been. But that was yet to come. Even his closest, most dependent PA, who had juggled his diaries and his mistresses and mothers for all that time, couldn't wait to sigh the sigh of resignation that was dormant in her deep Eastern European stoical roots. But she would never go so far as to speak on the subject.

There were at least twelve victims who would judge him guilty of fucking up their lives. Conveniently, for the researchers, the children got him a place on the List.

***

J's Invisible Diary. Entry.

There are always fights. Sometimes they are called wars and other times they are called keeping the peace. The old sayings creep out, war being peace carried out by other means, politics, the cloudy plays on words so there are always alternatives for keeping something clean and protective before the next attack of viral reality. The late part of the last century was particularly creative at furnishing cushions against reality – friendly fire, collateral damage, ethnic cleansing, or mergers and acquisitions, strategic re-positioning, enhancing the customer experience.

A freedom fighter on the wrong side is a terrorist. Someone fighting to have a job is a troublemaker, a stirrer. And rolling through the classical language are people who are still prepared to take on the role of defending the state or the corporation, to take the reality head-on, and follow orders for the sake of some ideally defined greater good, on all sides, for no guarantees. Successions of qualified people holding on to an idea of loyalty and trust continue to deliver what are called solutions to resistant enemies, be they ever more thinly spread across a more diverse stage of conflicts, zones, territories and borders., from Angola to Sierra Leone, Northern Ireland to Nicaragua, Afghanistan to Iraq, and those only the areas that made the news occasionally, to competitive corporations, about to be obsolete products and services, attackers upon the corporate creed.

Soldiers serve, mostly silently, whether they are in battle fatigues or corporate creased suits. They wear the badge of duty, of obligation, and bear the scars beneath their respective uniforms, sworn to secrecy. A few rebels escape and tell their tales beyond the official territories and company histories and reluctantly released official documents, castigated for the betrayal of honour, or some other code.

The majority go out every day to do a job and come back, settling down into a form of lifestyle that blends with the demands of a civilian society. More than a few don't quite make it, and are plagued with memories, traumas, illness, rebelling through violence, drink, drugs, broken relationships, drifting, loneliness, homelessness and other forms of antisocial behaviour which keep people away from them and the truths they harbour.

From time to time a story emerges about a suicide from one who can't take it anymore, one who hasn't been able to get back to what is called normality, but usually a lid is closed quickly on these unfortunate affairs. Even as we begin to account for most of those who serve on behalf of the self-styled moral high ground adopted by their country or International Corporation, there are still those who haven't been able to respond to the pressures of being normal, following traumatic incidents, as defined by others and captured in long documents about dignity in the workplace. They have worked at integration into society and corporate cultures they have defended and promoted. Some have done so with no visible marks of their former life ever showing through. Some have revealed minutely discernible elements, and they manage those in new and more comfortable roles, everything in its place. Yet that still leaves the others who, whatever they try, are still faced with the challenges of places they are sickening of, have been sickened by, and are looking to do something about.

We are not talking about the truly physically disabled, the obviously visibly suffering, who periodically have their stories put on parade and then curtained behind more immediately graspable tales of circulation-boosting celebrity antics. These fuel the indignity of a few, but this anger cannot be portrayed in documentaries. It is in the blood. The anger can only be managed by the uniting of blood in a cause that can allow the anger to seep away justifiably, that will lend meaning to years of unrequited service.

Letting the anger go will have consequences, effects.

It will result in perpetrators also ending up being called terrorists, criminals, serious organised crime syndicates, so law enforcement agencies will have something to bring before their legislation. Non-combatants will be mandated to see that legislation cannot be ignored, that something is being done before the latest tide of evil. People will struggle to define the cause of the effects of a gang, an organisation of the seemingly socially excluded that has become radicalised. But handled correctly, much more effort will have to be expended to appease the frustration of failure on the part of the chasers, to capture even one example behind the action, because whoever is doing what is going on isn't interested in advertising themselves directly, and they will do a great job continuing the traditions established by omerta.

Ordinary terrorists want publicity, not un-attributable action. We are

163

not ordinary.

***

He was little. The ironically Little Big Man. Predictably, he puffed himself up, like a bird seeing off an irritant. He blew up his ego like party balloons, for everyone to see. Douglas Bannon always had a tip, always had a recommendation, and he never took the advice he dished out to others. He and Sam Danello were buddies of a sort, sharing seats on one or two boards of a highly remunerative kind. He was a rusher, busy busy, paranoid, twitchy. For him people were always conspiring, trying to invade his privacy, pry into his affairs. There were always shadowy people trying to screw him out of a deal, out of potential further riches, out of opportunities, out of ideas that were always ahead of their time. But he was the one who always had the numbers, the business, in his head. He'd have to cancel the first three meetings in any day because of the unexpected urgency of another meeting, another deal, another crisis, another opportunity. He started taking appointments as late as a general practitioner. He was the principal director of The Theatre of Phantoms, whose props were tantalisingly titled files, whose phone calls always referred to the indeterminate, the elusive, as if the concrete and material could only be touched through the mysterious ether of the mobile phone.

The past here was carefully constructed, flats brought up from the scenery store of his mind. He would parade and perform in front of them, hints of old victories with a perfumed allure, a frisson of danger thrown in to keep you engaged, curious, wanting the gauze screen to rise so you could try and see more closely how it was he appeared to fly. For someone so obsessive about his history and personal details he went to tiresome lengths to remind his listeners not to be distracted by his size, that his every physical feature was a deadly weapon, that he wouldn't hesitate to use any combination of lip or limb to defend himself, as long as the odds looked deeply stacked against him. He liked a challenge he could control. Like balloons, he would let you keep him for a while, holding a string, but if you slipped, if you let go, the balloon was up and away, and you saw it drifting off against the sky, going who knows where. He was good. He was always after details. He wanted to know what made you tick, what your beliefs were, and he was never short of exotic theories about what life was meant to mean, and what you should do about it. He thought he had interesting ideas, but when they were staged you'd never be sure how long they would

164

run for, how much would be made or lost, how many people would end up laughing or crying, spread the word, come back again. In the narrative you would be engaged but you would never know if something had been a deliberate one-night stand or a flop.

Other businesses, other players and performers, they were always in the wings, always in other ineluctable worlds. They might be just around the corner, just around from the stage door, beyond the lights, in the rain, outside the bar, and if you thought you had discovered the secret that would give you a glimpse of the star you'd be wrong. He'd have gone through the front door, anonymously with the crowd, caught up in their coughs and plaudits, their obliviousness to his hair, the residual streaks of theatrical make-up and its choking perfume. No, you'd never catch Douglas Bannon's star unawares. Where were these characters in his life? The faceless bankers, lawyers, business partners, they were everywhere. Where were the son and the daughter, the wife, whose existence in the first cases was at least claimed, and in the latter acknowledged in a tiresome way every day in the media? Mrs Arianne Bannon was the larger-than-life woman he'd taken on to distract the newshounds from himself. She had been fine for a while, until she got over-used to the money and became its mistress, flaunting its consuming power around the world's luxury goods businesses. He'd even got his ex-army brother to keep an eye on her as Head of Security, making her feel yet more inflated, and him within the family employ where he couldn't just sit around and spend his army pension on cheap beer.

It went on. Where was the characterful mother who was allegedly well-known too? What went on in the big old family house with its burdensome heirlooms, the famous paintings and the provenances?

He couldn't be fazed unless it concerned money. His extraordinary run of near-death experiences, the fishing accident, the car crashes, the incident with the helicopter and the broken rotor-blade were just part of the bio someone would use one day when they came to make the movie. He decided he was clearly close to the fraternity that watched over things, and his view was that possibly outside their interest in the extent to which bones could be repeatedly broken they had decided to keep him alive for a while yet, and he'd better just put up with his reminders of mortality.

It wouldn't be long to the next production, and his role just might change again.

As a creator, of wealth, he considered himself to be a discoverer of rarities. He researched things in old libraries. Things, things, the parts of wholes others couldn't quite grasp. He knew of new ways to succeed in highly specialised areas, the chances of which you knew anything about yourself, or wanted to check out, amounting to almost nothing. He was always going to fix the next something in the future. His discoveries were part of his calling, parts of the big jigsaw puzzle of life he was crafting. He would occasionally place a piece here, or one there, plotting of what the big picture might eventually turn out as, but in the meantime happy to play with the tiny pieces, knowing other possibilities might exist, other connections might be made, and capitalised on, every month and quarter and year.

He was just a businessman, he said. He didn't keep a big office. He drove an old car. He turned up on the fringes of functions, on the backs of meetings. He was in permanent rehearsal. His productions were all perfectly formed in his mind, and the lights never dimmed. He wanted more lights, he wanted to take the calls and the applause, but he'd never really let the audience see what was on his mind. He never wanted the stuff in reality, he didn't need the accolades. His mind was elsewhere, in Connecticut. Last year he banked $650 million.

That represented a big chunk to demonstrate benevolence with, over time. After all, getting it had cost thousands their livelihoods around the world, under the banner of long-term capital growth, investment in your future well-being, and the demise of inefficiencies. He was noted. He had the profile, and potential for future Lists, beyond his unwitting contribution to the first part of the Message.

Bannon and Danello had just been part of the team that signed off Daniel's plan for the next year, waving goodbye to probationary MBAs and about to be retired loyalists with disputable pension contracts. Shareholder value in their associated enterprises had fallen only by a higher percentage than the bonuses their well-controlled compensation committees had awarded them.

***

It didn't begin like that Elizabethan drama - "Hello world, and next my gold". It was a moment more ordinary. Anticipating the sound of the machine that would state it was officially time to contemplate getting up, the levee, the rising ritual, Jules lay there half way between thoughts about the day's agenda and the smile of the two-years in graduate who'd seduced him in his dream. She'd seen him at yesterday's party where he'd been surrounded by snakes, tongues

166

testing gossip, imprints of scandal and scurrilousness on silk-sheened jackets, catching the lights like their owners eyes never could. The innocent opening lines, "Did you see? Did you hear? Were you there?" the set-ups for the public autopsies of the corporate losers, the courtiers whose time was fading, the over-reaching whose waxen wings were being given an extra blast of jealous heat. There were those quoting snippets of success. "Harry, you know the team was 27% up on profit year on year in the last quarter". It was the week before the Season – Happy Holidays everyone.

"You know, Jules, some of us would really like to work with you on the Abilene Project next year."

In the men's room the statistics were traded without interruption, flowing like the data running across the base of a business channel, punctuated only with the sounds of pissing, of zips, of the sighs of big boys letting the Coors steam out. Men scoring points with detail. Do you know the new 911 GT2 RS has 612hp? Yeah, but the Enzo Ferrari has 651. Really? Wow. Everything, every application, every chance to remind the guy in the next stall who knows best. It's all assembled and calculated like baseball stats for all those fanatics locked in the bar-room together for a weekend of sparring and cock comparing.

The party? That had been gruesome. There had been the customary long debate around the boardroom table, the representations from the checkers and the balancers in human resources. We're a dry site, a dry company. We shouldn't be doing anything like this at this seasonal time. It's bound to upset someone. Someone's going to get drunk. Someone's going to get aggressive. Someone's going to get screwed. Oh, sorry, molested, and we'll have a dozen lawyers all over us next week, not to mention the press, TV, the church, the help and self-help groups, and all those who weren't invited anyway. It was eventually decided, in wording that a UN press spokesperson would be proud of, that for those present in the corporate HQ between 5 and 7 on one night only, transport would be available to take the interested to a nearby hotel, where a private room had been graciously donated by the hotel management (and duly noted in the gifts and donations record).

There, a variety of refreshments was provided equally magnanimously (and noted), by dedicated suppliers. More transport would then be available to take guests home so they wouldn't be accidentally run over or caught DUI in their company car. It was a 'Happy Holidays' gathering, and commiserations were extended to all those whose diaries placed them elsewhere at this time. There were no levels of invitation, it was an all-comers and hot-desking type affair, no

167

top-table. Inevitably, people segregated immediately on arrival, and the clusters and cells spread out across the ballroom. Every once in a while someone would splinter off and link up with another cell. Always time to network. From mock caviar to coffee, tofu to tzatziki, Jack Daniels to OJ, most all tastes and styles were covered, except for those who loathed all forms of corporate bonhomie, who hadn't been pressured into coming along, and who could moan about what was or wasn't in it for them the next time they showed up at their work stations with their morbid hang-ups. All this for one glass of champagne if you drank it and the alleged opportunity to say a few words of thanks for the contribution to the company of those present, and another year of triumphant success for the shareholders, who wouldn't need to be sharpening their teeth and claws for the next AGM with the corporation, no sirree. The Danello Seger Daniels triumvirate was triumphant in the company press release.

But Jules Seger, who had led the team that delivered 2/3 of the incremental profit, had been told there was no place for him in the corporation next year. He didn't fit the emerging operating culture, it had been decided. After 30 years of making passage through the often dangerous charted waters of American Corporations, the ex-pat was up against the wall.

He excused himself for a few moments. Needed to make a call then needed to visit Jose, his deputy, briefly. Be right back. And he stepped out of the circle, walking across the ballroom floor towards the large entrance doors, returning the nods to raised glasses as he passed the ones paying homage, the ones making sure he noticed they were there, the ones looking to take the next seat on the board. There was no call to be made, but he took his phone out of his pocket, pressed a couple of buttons and held the piece up to his ear anyway, a signal that said don't disturb me now. It stopped him being touched or excuse-me'd all the way out, along the lobby, and into the small Blue Bar at the other end of the hotel. Maybe Jose would be there, or not. He went into the corner he preferred, where he couldn't be seen directly from the door, and one of his waiter acquaintances, Anton, produced a glass of Condrieu for him to freshen up with. For a moment he wished he was in France, wrapped up against the steel cold that closed around Lyon in winter, tinkering with the truffles in old man Bocuse's cathedral of kitsch, snug in the service of the long-standing crew who had dedicated their lives to keeping Paul's pilgrims happy, fed and watered. But that felt like a parallel life, another person.

He took his eyes away from the lemon light of the wine and glanced over at the mirror behind the bar. And there she was. He didn't know exactly who she was, but he had caught her looking over at him in the ballroom. She was, as the French might have said, enchanting. She too, looked almost French. Must have been the hairstyle, the body, the movement. She was with someone he did think he knew, had talked to, from one of the divisions, and it looked like they'd also decided to take a short time-out from the main distraction. They weren't chasing each other, this couple. Maybe they were talking about some work deal. Whenever the guy looked away, gathering his thoughts, she looked across. Then, once, she just raised her eyebrows, briefly. Was it a hello or a question? All he knew was he liked the look. He didn't want the image destroyed by a voice coming up saying she was in sales and hadn't the department done brilliantly. He wanted to know more, but somehow felt he would have nothing much to say, because she had stilled his tongue. As a widower, he had no calls on his time outside work, and although he also knew life could be difficult getting entwined with other work colleagues, he also knew something they didn't.

She looked like one of the ambitious ones who could pull back the curtains and say step through here, come and see what you've forgotten about. And he would. He would step out into the darkness, give up the retreating light, to see what she had to show him. He could see no cause for alarm from the temptress. He needed the break. He needed to step out from the work commitments. So Jose wasn't there? He'd looked. Who was going to ask him about it? He needed to reflect. He needed to think about the other things the eaters and drinkers didn't know about.

He'd made many of them rich already. If he decided he was going to buy something, they wouldn't do anything about it other than make a show of noise briefly. Unless he was really dumb, the board wouldn't object, and he had plenty of money to pay advisors to support his decisions. There weren't many out there who'd turn down his fees. The shareholders? Apart from the usual ten small shareholder cranks who turned up to ask their predictable questions every year, there were few voices of dissent today. What he worried about was if there was ever going to be any real pressure again. He needed it to live. He needed to spot it in its fancy clothes. It had come before dressed as heavy handed suppliers, planning permissions, workers' rights, environmental friendliness, all of which were dealable. Rational things were easy. What concerned him were only issues that hadn't surfaced before in his world. He needed people out there who were really going to push things he didn't yet have ways to deal with himself, even at this stage of life.

He knew his moves brought benefits to swathes of people, but questions were bubbling up big now. More and more people were talking about some businesses making too much money, making excessive profits. Who were these people? What got them to this point? What were they really going to do after he'd gone?

He didn't need any more money. He needed an outlet for short-term anger, and for energy. He needed the outlet his father had been looking in the wrong place for, for all those years.

He'd given people lots, given communities things they could only dream about before he came along. There's no pleasing some folks. He finished his drink, looked over again at the woman who was now listening to another of her new partner's monologues, this time giving her full eye contact, his spiel practised, so she couldn't break contact. Jules walked out of the bar, his account tabbed by the familiar staff. Back to the main event, his re-entrance immediately picked up by the detectors of the aspirants, tiny gestures of hand and head signalling, was he OK, did whatever it was go well, did he need their action, their input, always the same, caught up in their web of care, their desire for intimacy, to feel the warmth of the blood of their inner circle, to be near the source of the heat of the power these creatures craved? And he nodded, to the left, to the right, finding a friendly fawning face, one of those who thought he was A Chosen One, and he had been. Distract me, he signed, and the protected one broke off from his last piece of tittle tattle, heading over to play the smart one, the trusted jester, until the Boss laughed, and all was resting merrily in the time they used to call Christmas.

When he finally got up to shower, he had decided he was going to do something that was more sustainable than simply showing a ten year straight line profit growth. Although he didn't know it, he was already building up credits that might get him off the List.

***

Sanjit polished his already polished shoes. He put his foot on the chair, a duster taken from the desk drawer, and pursued the ritual so each black toe reflected his pumping white shirt-cuff, reflected the radiance of his energy and success. He did this in front of anyone he considered beneath him, so it happened often. It was his demonstration of position, of attitude, one from a doorstop catalogue of demeaning gestures. You were meant to adore, acknowledge, pass on the word down the line. This action was followed by the simultaneous raising of his right knee above the desk, and the drawing down of his right elbow, lower arm upright, fist clenched, slowly, in a power salute to his own fitness. Satisfied his limbs were fluid and flexible, he pinched his cuffs to ensure they settled two inches below his jacket sleeves, fastened one button on his two button suit, patted his pockets to reassure himself that the cloth only complemented his muscled torso, and announced he was going to see the company's Biggest and Best Customer.

When will you be back?

Who knows? He wants to do the seeing. Stick around.

Around could mean hours. Rujuta had only arrived minutes before for a totally unnecessary session at 0730 that had entailed leaving another continent the night before during the first weekend in months that was allegedly family quality time, to be greeted with the shoe-shine trick. Hey. Show some respect. We all got busy customers. Get in line. You're being paid to wait. This was the serial time-rape she had come to expect. Sanjit was the new messiah. He was the boss, who was The Word. The messiah was full of verve, full of light, full of passion, energy, commitment, and all those things the job ads demand, all those qualities the head hunters want from people who get things done. God, the customer, as is often the case, was less visible, less outspoken, but there in spirit. No, what we had here was the Man In Deed. The intention was sound, even the vision, but one look in the eyes told you that you were staring into the space of the newly converted, the superlatively insightful and gifted, blessed deliverer of the Mission. Here was someone who would have made the Incas welcome the Conquistadores, the noblesse oblige outbid each other for the guillotine, the rich volunteer to pay more taxes. Here was the one who truly loved his own God, and believed he was loved back, the only Son, the one who would work on God's territory without fear, preaching and teaching and walking the walk, the deliverer of the new Mission, the one who would get the fearful and the wretched, the blind and ignorant, the dumb and despicable, out of their conditions and into the new nirvana, quickly. Here was one who, like Hitler's chosen, travelling freely bearing letters with the Fuhrer's signature, the rite of passage, would spread the Word, and bring the children into Heaven.

As with many of those finding a calling, he was initially surprised at the reluctance of the populace to embrace change with equal fervour, and rational appeals were quickly replaced with emotional threats and ferocious, endless displays of crusading ego that were meant to instil fear and consequent submission in their audiences, or to drive groups into catatonic states, which he could also capitalise on.

171

Let's do lunch. We don't need to eat. That had been one of his earlier endearing catchphrases, where the unwary would be taken to the local fitness centre and, unless they had the kit, would sit, or stand, and listen, while he declaimed the vision between the warm-up cycle and the arm-press. Clinking a bottle of energy replacement soda against your water cup was the way of saying welcome to the team. And there were plenty of people who took this as dedication, and for a while followed suit.

Of course there were disciples. But let's look at what devotees meant here. These were people who were either financially or emotionally dependent on their leader. The recently divorced, looking to provide a sustainable future, the eight years to retiring types looking not to rock the boat, one or two who were cleverly slipped into the enclave by wily old masters, cleaning up their own pitch, who had got bored of the slow but medically protected long time servers.

If there appeared to be talent around, then the leader put in the extra time to find flaws. He tried many approaches, many angles of attack, behind the smiles and the suggestions that a closer understanding could only enhance the quality of the relationship, the team, the fulfilment of the Mission. If he couldn't discover some seam, some fault line, some way of mining out a weakness he could then exploit further, other players or trusties were brought on board to find out where weak gaps were in the A team that he might have overlooked. Meanwhile he would simultaneously defend the team against all outsiders, whether they wanted that or not. He would have done equally well as the leader of a small, suicide-minded religious sect, a guru-follower artistic group with a slant on Big Questions and ideals. Sanjit saw all of this as simply getting the best out of the team, as networking, as support, as making justifiable sacrifices to protect the Mission against the threats and evils of the bad, diseased parts of corporation and its executives. Remember that God himself didn't appear to like many of the creatures around Him, and his Chosen One was indulged because he didn't conform, he wasn't dull, he saw the way it should be when all else had their eyes closed. He had feelings, passions, sentiments, spirit, none of the patient, rational, political elements that held the chemistry of the rest in a careful balance. Sanjit was a smart bomb.

Food and drink were of little interest except as fuel, late late late, when everything else had been done. Food was just an irritation, something that could damage the jacket as he leaned towards a bowl and wolfed its contents, talking all the while. God liked the peasant habits which years of urban conditioning had failed to change. He was

172

foxy, the wild animal in the urban forest, living on cunning and wiles. The untamed wore clothes to conceal some of the wildness, but it always showed in other ways. He couldn't drive a car unless it was in the red zone, so much, so much hurry for one who never showed on time for anything unless it involved The Customer. Life was a long running meeting, with players coming and going, a parallel world of people on phones, an agenda ever to be changed, a diary written in sand, a circus where all kinds of freak acts took place, anywhere, anytime. As long as the meeting never stopped, life went on. Look at how to Live the Organisation, look at this dedication, versus other temporary employees who are so unworthy. No-one was prepared to challenge the Chosen One. No-one was prepared to tell the gods the Truth. Not until there was a new God, and in that world, one day, there would be a new God. That was all they knew.

Sanjit's approach was brutally simple. This is how it's gonna be, the vocabulary and accent honed through imitation, impersonation, the nurturing of a chameleonic character that had come through the business school and all its Americanisms. These people know nothing. They only respond to fear. They need to be told what to do. He held most of them in contempt, and told them. Some actually thought he was great, a great wave of honesty, of directness, of iconoclasm, as long as its application applied to others. He's great. What a guy, said those who didn't want God to know the truth. And you know what, as he would say himself, who cares? Sometimes he would stand out, some of that fevered drive would rub off, sometimes there wouldn't even be much in the way of patronisation, or sarcasm, the droning on and on that matched their own sounds, dictators of dreary countries falling in love with themselves every time they addressed their nation. Hey, if you don't want to be with him every day, everywhere, it could almost be fun. Proximity is a great leveller. He was the charmer, the seducer, the caring deep observer of life, continuing to attract people, thrilling to his commitment, his experiences, his devotion, his suffering, his challenges. He turned easily away from previous patterns, trails of dead relationships, disaffected kids, employers who had always let him down. By rights he should be bringing changes to a major nation, in a major historical role, and those who were enthralled with the concept of that continued to play the role of special disciples, loving and caring and childbearing in the way only the smitten can.

Increasingly he would stand on tables and desks, making pronouncements like a Shakespearean tragedian schooled in the declamatory ways of a nineteenth century theatre. Half the audiences were worried more about the potential damage to corporate head office furniture than anything else. The other half were trying to avoid being balled out on some yet to be selected topic. The louder the pronouncements, the deeper parts of the company slipped into the quagmire.

Here are ten things to do. Go do numbers 6-10. And then he does 6-10 faster and moans about 1-5. Why haven't they been done? Where were you? Why buy a dog?

He got himself on the List.

***

J's Invisible Diary. Entry.

They're funny old things, governments. Full of contradictions. They uphold freedom, but only their version of it. Governments have to control, contain, count even though everyone knows, including them, that intervention and smothering help no-one and nothing. But governments see enemies everywhere, especially with all that surveillance they get us to pay for. Transparency is only for insiders. Enemies, and potential enemies, everywhere. Who knows what lies behind the mask of the old lady with the cheap rucksack and the walking stick? Bombs, potentially, all over her. Then there are those who stick a finger up to the speed cameras as they rush by on motorbikes. This can only be interpreted as the crumbling of deference. Deference only comes to the short term rich, and that doesn't extend to their new cars, which, while everyone wants one, doesn't stop them being vandalised in the name of excess. Everyone is as good, or as bad, as everyone else. It's called brash individualism and it must be legislated against with a fence of government-led authoritarianism, they say. That doesn't stop the premier only liking rich people. He leaves someone else to try and steal all their money. It's not about dual standards or hypocrisy. That would suggest conscience. Not, it's just old fashioned schizophrenia. There's always a problem when 'Others' are identified as the culprits – those who want the same things as you but don't want to follow the same paths to get them.

They want impossible amounts of money for no effort. At least the hedge-fund guys used to work a bit. Why can't they have it? As you said, they're just as good as the next person. And they absolutely believe that. They have Faith in themselves. Their beliefs, their convictions, their truth, lie in the mirror. From selfish to selfaith, it defines what you do, who you see, what you dislike, hate, what you

174

choose. You are your own filter, your own corrective lens which affects the way you see the world, the way you assess threats, the way you judge your experiences.

So it's not surprising that when you've decided you can sing and be a star and some dentally enhanced bastard, pointing to the video of your coruscatingly bad performance says you have no talent whatsoever, that your mouth opens and you absolutely cannot believe what you are being told. It's simply not the case. Not the truth. The old fogey just can't recognise your talent. You'll show them. Show them all.

Same with football, basketball, baseball, acting, you cannot stand for nothing. Now the old government thinks differently. It thinks you must stand for the community, and any form of self-expression must be an act of selfishness. You need to be crushed for the sake of the common wealth. Unless you are a leading politician, in which case you must be clearly and easily identifiable as an individual others should aspire to.

You epitomise the acceptable face of the party's value system. And then you want redress. You want your own back for the public humiliation. Vengeance starts to grow. There is a need for it, and it dwarfs other needs. It creates a desire for death, a lust that stultifies other desires and feelings. Using revenge restores mental status and self-respect. Your personal Faith has been rewarded through the sacrifice of revenge, and your God is happy. Yet your God is also wrathful and sensitive, and the need for demonstrations of obeisance will continue to flow. There must be fresh enemies to fuel vengeance's pull and power. There is no need to question how this cycle grows, because it is determined by Faith, by belief. Mortal action against unarmed civilians is always murder, and there is no expiation for the crime. But they are not unarmed civilians. They are armed with power and money and fame. They are armed with protection and ego and sycophancy. They are terrorists. This is Civil War. Civil Terrorism. Of course, new terrorist attacks will bring on ever stronger security and control. Doors will start to close. As Engels said, war will be waged against combatants, those we see as enemies, those we describe as contagious in our society. The collapse in society is reflected in the broken mirror of your own fractured faith and personality. You are both overprotected and overexposed.

You are a tribe of one.

***

His permanently crafted five-day beard was silver and grey now, matching the much reduced hair, which in its blackness had shadowed his face twenty years ago, a backcloth where his eyes cast out a roving light for large-hipped girls from fourteen to forty. Sebastian never minded faces much, it was the figures that pulled the neck muscles around and kept his appetite button permanently on. He had been on the periphery of the sixties students, never brave enough to be on the '68 front-lines, but fighting the revolution through words and feelings, the weapon of choice for the slim depressive waging of his own battle against the dark side. Then he was the poet, the writer. It was only later he dabbled with the philosophy, attempted, like so many others, to fathom Derrida and Lacan, seeking to break out of the confines of text and context with their own freedom of madness. He was almost an intellectual, yet he was always drawn by the light of large denomination bank notes, and sought to satisfy his easy laziness through commercial channels his purist peers wouldn't touch. It was a lucrative compromise, a large space to play in, and his charm and style allowed him still to bridge the crass with the closeted, stay in touch with the two sides of his needs. Of course, to some extent he would privately admit to selling out to the heinous world of exploitation, the world of the hidden persuaders, and to others he remained too rooted in a tenured perspective, an academic never quite grasping the commercial nettle. But he made several stings for himself. He was a survivor in numerous playgrounds.

He pulled off the trick in France of being respected for working in the media, yet in a despised role, for an advertising agency group. His ability in the early days to write pithy copy, and seduce the major clients with his charm and charisma led to his early elevation to roles where he was largely untouched and untouchable, an expensive overhead whose failings, if any, were nothing to do with him, but were manifestly the weakness of others around and beneath him. He was always there to listen to a belligerent client, sooth a frustrated suit, charm a prospect, turn up the volume on his French-English accent when it mattered to English-speaking colleagues or targets abroad, never be seen to destroy, only to endorse, to encourage, to nudge. Dear Sebastian could not be attacked because he had the gist of making his clients feel he was indispensable. The strugglers, the strivers, the ones who vociferously defended their ideas, their styles, their presentations, these could all be sequentially dismissed, disposed of, replaced, as they failed to grasp the true nature of the business, the culture, the tone of voice, the style of operation. Sadly, they would say, only Sebastian

176

could understand, and his tweaks, his touches, became the signature of many masterpieces from his irascible school of dependants and disciples. It was a talent that helped him maintain his Parisian base, enjoy his Breton connections, top up his tan from Guadeloupe and San Maarten to Corsica and Casablanca. It enabled him to accompany clients on international trips where his mistresses could magically appear to ease the stress from his strategically exhausted body. It kept him on fawning first name terms with restaurateurs and their staff, with the press and specialists seeking advice on styles and fashions and techniques in media practices. It kept him busy enough to be away from battle-lines when blame was about to be apportioned, but present for medals and gongs. It worked because he easily read the signs of wants and needs from those around him driven by different goals, short-term objectives, career moves, political plays, aggressive ambitions.

But none of it stopped him being bitten by the Black Dog. He never quite sold out, but he did have to contend with him being a close acquaintance for a great part of his working life. At least he always had an audience. People listened, even if they subsequently ignored what he said. His abandonment came with a degree of grace, and he saw off any number of contenders. The secret was that he never pretended to greater things. He never ordered the purple cloaks. He was someone you felt you could spend time with, and he'd never tell you to your face whether he felt the same way. It was amazing how far a little English could carry a creative Frenchman in that environment, at that time. He was attractive to women in the way only French actors can be. His looks were put together like an accident on a construction site, transparent seduction lines, blatant flirting, persistence and patience that would see off all-comers. There were worse states to be in.

He was a Survivor. He had the respect only certain benign rogues can have. His autumnal days, and his family's future, were assured. The research was robust.

***

The look said 'Watch me.' A star. One that's going to shine so bright you'll need shades to greet him. He didn't have much time for the lowly stuff, the day to day business that kept the company moving. No, he was a man with an objective. The objective itself was sound, ambitious but sound, that's what going over the presentations always came back to, and they would have suited a significantly larger or better connected operation. But Jockum Jessen had seen the future, and for

177

him there was no other way – it was going to work. Here was the man who only wanted the biggest and the best, spare no expenses. If someone had to be triple A, the Gold Standard, the bench mark, the ultimo, it would be JJ. His new enterprise would be admired everywhere, his starting point the base for a global network. He'd done the numbers a hundred times, and they always worked. He talked of the best suppliers, he'd set them up against each other. They came, they saw, he conquered, comparing prices and capacities, keenness and the seniority of teams, the potential willingness of customers to queue up, sign up, and fill up his order books. He was already spending his yet to be granted salary, something that would finally reflect his status on the world stage, recognition he'd so long deserved and hadn't quite found. And there was no shortage of interest. It was a time when technology was the hot zone, when everything was possible, when everything could be done. Was there truly a time when this was not so? Money was easy, the livin' was high, and everyone would naturally want a slice of this new world, early on, at a premium, when it carried cachet and kudos. JJ never thought about the laggards, the wait and sees, the cynical, the cautious, the deal-seekers, the sweepers up of pioneers' mistakes. No, he was on the front line, the new Frontier, and he only needed a few other brave souls to satisfy and subsidise his discovery, and they'd all be rich.

Technically, he sounded quite good to most outsiders. He learnt fast, traded terms and jargon, marketed his vision with gloss and global partners who were keen to get to market with their massively spare communications capacity. He was at least a chapter ahead in the book of most of his students, and of those who weren't familiar with the way technology was going he was on another planet, and one they didn't have the spirit to explore. Oh yes, he had worked in the business before, for months even, but had tired of his bosses' refusal to accept that he was their equal, that he was a man of broad scale, not a drudging detail operative. As it had ever been, from job to job he always reached for the stars, and he always burnt out his fuel before reaching them. He was a director (he was an assistant), he was a manager (he was a co-worker), he was an expert (he'd read about it and talked to ten people who were), he had the contacts who had the contacts (they always said). It was these features that also attracted the dragoons of hucksters, con-men and other smooth-talking crooks. For only a modest starter sum of money this succession of men and their inscrutable assistants would open doors to investor funds at almost no risk or commitment. They would produce clients and customers who were only ever the most senior you would expect to see, or know about, from Arab entrepreneurs to Fortune 500 CEOs. They were always on the verge of completing another dozen or so deals. They never quite got round to showing their credentials from other experiences, but they had bold numbers for their current projects, as defined by the ten lies most often told to venture capitalists. They also never quite had the most up to date business card, but they promised to forward details. Some of them never quite had fresh shirts, the money to buy dinner, pictures of the big house they allegedly lived in in LA, but if you just forwarded them another ten, twenty, thirty thousand dollars, they'd pull in the big one for you, until at the last moment the inevitable glitch would occur, the strategic direction would shift, the investment priorities forced to adjust to meet unexpected developments in China, Texas, Kazakhstan, the dependence on two other partners in an extended chain would collapse, and JJ, frustrated and gullible, would ball them out, telling them to sign up or stop wasting time. They'd scurry away like rats, knowing they'd taken all they could get. It was time to disappear, switch off the flattery, update the potential links, and offer them repackaged to the next crazy adventurer. So this is how they bled the money JJ had acquired from other star gazers, for JJ of course had no money of his own. Never did. He was desperate to get it, didn't mind squandering others', or bankrupting faithful benefactors in the process. He just wanted what he believed was his due. Recognition and idolisation.

He couldn't recognise he was among his own in the frontier town, because he really believed in his dream. He only wanted to do something, to help, to give people better, richer lives, a better experience, a quality they had yet to reach. He was meant to turn dreams into reality. And he only missed it by a millimetre. Others bullshitted their way to a share of the future, some with backers who shied away, others who stayed, using the hucksters in their own way and discarding them at the appropriate moment. He only needed one other to back his dream. But where he came from, he'd cried wolf once too often, and because it was JJ, it guaranteed no back-up, because everything he'd ever done or said before had come to the same thing. Nothing. All his castles collapsed with each tide. He was the wrong man in the wrong place with the right idea. He was stuck in a dream he could never root in reality. There were plenty of people who spotted the chance to cash in on the gap. Those who dangled the piece of string to keep his balloon connected. Just a dollar away from the final connection. But in a world where the price was always a cosy round figure, he always stayed the dollar short. He was the $999 man. The dream disappeared every waking morning. But he went a ways to fulfilling others' dreams, every day. He never did anyone any real harm other than himself.

The research remained robust. He never made a List, never got Indexed. The Message was about helping those who hadn't been given the acknowledgements and respect they deserved. It wasn't about normal losers, it was about those who had been abused for serving everyone other than themselves.

***

J's Invisible Diary. Entry.

Everyone thinks they're doing best. They know. They know better than the last one, the others, the predecessors. Challenging is not possible because challenging infringes rights. We've got rights. You can't say that. You've got no right to say, think, feel that. As the poet would have it - Don't laugh, don't cry, don't walk on the grass, don't drink in the park, and on and on. If you're not getting something done either do it yourself or find someone who'll do what you want without it being a challenge to their ego, self, aura, creed, colour, whatever.

So if no-one can be told, you can only know what you choose to know. That's right. And that makes you as big and strong as the next one, who has the same rights as you. What are you entitled to? Epicurus asked that – food, water, shelter and warmth, plus friendship, freedom, and thought. Well, maybe things were easier in those days, and maybe they weren't. The only problem with this little list, which old Maslow picked up on and made a mint from some time later, is the same thing that Aristotle smartened up to. You know, where's the happiness word in there? If you go chasing money, power, possessions, beauty, fame, you do it because you think it will bring you happiness, and then what?

Just a few words, and then only a few centuries later some guys (for it was still that way) tried to embody it for a new country, and we ended up with the gems of the American Constitution.

Did you walk into your neighbourhood today and try and find out what your rights are, as opposed to your expectations? Freedom can't even be defined anymore. It can be ring-fenced, restricted, caveated and curtailed, but in no way or place can you find any simple expressions of what you should get in return for your word these days. Challenges today apply to the micro not the macro. What do you mean by 'information'? What does 'is' mean? It depends on the context the challenges create. You're entitled to the same rights as those celebrities

180

you identify with. In what context? The President's no better than me. The Boss is no better than me. Jesus may have been better than me but my lawyer says that's bullshit. So you have every right in the world to defend yourself until we take that right away from the very words we use to construct a context. 'Who are you?' is now being replaced with 'What do you mean?'

The clever cast their own meanings and make the most from the masks they mould. Others then try cast-offs. Eventually the mould breaks and it's time to move on again. So if meaning is so fleeting does it matter anymore? Only so long as it can capture enough attention out of enough people to get the one thing everyone wants. Respect and happiness are the bookends of the library shelf full of tomes on how to extract the most value out of others for your own ends, with a smile on your face.

***

Let's pull another one out of the raw data bag. This one's also harmless. A real bullshitter, but he's so generous. Everyone loves him, none more than himself. His home is a Holy Place consecrated for the worship of his Trueship. Never have so many world-famous people been brought together to endorse their gratefulness at the opportunity to meet with the big Leon, presidents and patriarchs, unable to resist the handshake, the possessive arm round the shoulder, the shared laughter caught oh so accidentally off camera by the coincidentally present PR photographer. But it doesn't rest with the eye. No, there also has to be the word. So the words are framed as well, the acknowledgements and the thanks for the big Leon's contribution to business, to fun, to making the world spin round another day. Fame by frame, by association, celebrity through shadows, unfathomable detail, osmotic success. Flags and awards, medals and trinkets, tables, glassware, paintings, all attest to the selfless contribution of the big Leon to the greater good of beings and enterprises, from pleasure seeking to politics, nurturing to nation-building. But a gentleman needs more then mementos. A gentleman needs learning. You will find much potential learning on the spines of the many hard-backed books that line the shelves along the walls not covered with magical signed memorabilia, books whose jackets have never been creased, or whose spines bent, whose knowledge remains pristine and un-fingered in their unturned pages. This is knowledge that can be bought or sold. No need to digest it. It is there for others to stimulate their own sense of understanding, and ultimately to acknowledge the broadmindedness of its guardian, the librarian of mint-condition copies, who has never met a challenge or a question that couldn't be dealt with from a scant reading of a review, or a confident bluster speckled with numbers and dates warranting no further questioning. Eager to have the big picture and the accompanying trivia- it was all there in the volumes, the politicians and parties, battles, financial cycles, transportation, business school bibles, biographies, coffee table books on travel and trinkets. You could, and were expected, to absorb new facts, anywhere around the house, which lent a gloss to many of the fictions which also lived there. Story-telling is not necessarily a harmful thing in itself. It can be entrancing, engaging, and Leon the Narrator often told good tales.

There were narratives that had been honed over years. Variations were added, edited, threaded out to fresh ears, refined, discarded, embellished according to the audience, the time, place, and state of the imaginative narrator himself. He was another in a long line of an oral tradition, whose core tales were themes on which to weave new and exotic patterns, tales which were extrapolated from others, tales which then became mythologised further in the company of others, meeting and comparing versions of all the other tales they'd heard tell. Here was the one who could barely produce a literate letter, yet had no problem telling others he was fluent in written and spoken variants of several languages, guessing he would rarely be challenged by the receiver of this information, either at the time or on other occasions, shrewdly calculated to be highly improbable occasions, so setting in train another facet of the Grand Legend of the Mystical Leon. The shrewdness always left the faint possibility that the claim might be true – the best stories always had their roots in experience of a kind. The plastic polyglot practised his arts every day. It was natural. And like the survivor of the 1001 nights, there was a different story every day, even if it was the same audience, because someone had to direct the narrative, someone had to keep everyone listening, laughing, drinking, eating, sharing, because like the tree that falls in the forest, without listeners Leon would be nothing. He never liked himself enough to think people could like him for what he was, so he hoped they'd like him for what he wasn't, which he went to great lengths to tailor. Magnificently disguised behind an attitude that said he didn't care about anyone. He didn't as long as they accepted his never ending hospitality and his fountain of stories. The best way to put an end to it all would simply be to ignore him, because, alone and confronted with himself, he would have nothing to say.

There is effort, even genius, in forms of charlatanism. Ever aware of opportunities to pick up a story, repackage it, and present it as personal experience. The ability to argue black is white and vice versa at any moment, and with the same person, with no reference to any level of contradiction. The ease that comes from being able to debate anything from memory, with no consequences, as it suited occasions. And why not? Mugs kept coming back for more, or was it just freeloaders prepared to package up their tolerance to obtain fine wines and feasts under the tinsel of friendship? Much of the time the living and the largesse was easy. It came from other people's money. Everything was a business charge. Being invited to drinks or dinner ended up as an expense, usually billed to your own account. There was always someone hanging around, someone whose time Leon didn't care about – a guy in a car, waiting for the next set of directions, a guy in a bar, knowing Leon wouldn't turn up but waiting anyway, someone waiting to hand over a package, cook a meal, meet at a specific place, beat a deadline. There was always a gap between promise and delivery, on size, on time, on quality, on price, on expectation, on reliability, on delivery, gaps which turned out to be your own problem, or which could always be settled somehow with a late cheque or an expensive meal, another promise.

Leon was addicted, to drugs, to fads, to women he couldn't have, but most of all he was addicted to himself, his ever expending girth, the failure of his permanently prematurely ended diets, his last cigarette, his fake tan, his habits which had resisted change for more than thirty years. Trading on his wits, abusing his nerves, he cultivated a disdain for anyone with links to education, to culture he couldn't grasp, to anything he'd never been able to have, easily and directly, himself. This was nothing to do with circumstances and everything to do with attitude. His brother, sister, family members, they'd been achievers, they'd done things, and for the most part, unless it suited a useful narrative, their existence was rarely acknowledged outside a storyline he controlled.

But his past clung to him. He always ate like someone who had never had anyone tell him how to use his mouth. When he was awake he only took in a mixture of oxygen and tobacco smoke. He was surprised you generally didn't drink wine like pints of beer. He was surprised that eating and drinking for three produced residual results over his body, which wasn't obeying his mind. He would diet one hundred per cent for three days and have his tongue tell everyone proudly how much weight he was losing for three weeks, by which time his interest would be 100% on something else.

Some women adored it, from a distance. They liked the rebelliousness, the lavish care laid on them as a pretext to the rarely given ride he craved, the way he listened, for even minutes, and then weaved an elaborate tale about travel and tribulations, emotions and commitment, which was an occasional change from the information and statistically rich dialogue they had from many of the other men around their lives. Everyone loved him like the maverick family member, the loose cannon, the one to help you laugh your way through your own troubled times. But you wouldn't want to take him home to meet the parents now, would you? Which was just as well, since Leon actually loathed women. As far as he was concerned, they were either Madonnas or whores, and both let you down. They were targets, conquests, objects to fuck and leave, toys to play with and abandon. Dangerous toys could not be kept. Women were for changing, to support him, to dress the way he wanted, to service his desires, to follow his way, blindly and silently. Digressions were punishable for long periods. He boasted in the bar about what women had done for him, and never wondered why so many never wanted to go play his way. The only thing worse than women was the Church.

He had forty eight years of fantasy, forty eight rings of protection to cover him from his own fears, his inability to see who he was and what he could do about it. No-one could tell Leon anything, because they couldn't know him. What was there to know? He was so many Leon's, which one were you talking about, which particles could you ever capture, pin down. He was surrounded by himself.

Whatever you thought about him, and the many like him, he still caused little serious harm. There was no way he was on any list. He had never realised respect wasn't something you could buy.

***

184

Part III

Grand Unified Theories

"The enemy is crushed, like the fall of a grindstone upon an egg, by knowledge of his strength and weakness, and by employment of truth and artifice"

"Disguise your movements; await a favourable opportunity; divide or unite according to circumstance"

Sun Tzu, *The Art of War*

How the new religion moves up a gear ~ working in real and cyber-space ~ the tried and tested effectiveness of the team ~ the continuing power of mystery ~ the magic of numbers and the useful bias of statistics ~ tighter targeting and the turning of the screw ~ the lives and timely deaths of those on the finessed List ~ the globalisation of the Message ~ the second level of deception ~ the value of trickle downs ~ how life remains cheap if you don't put richness back into it ~ closing circles ~ refinement.

J's Invisible Diary. Entry.

So there we go. Minting money, as The New York Times put it. If you wanted to get into the club of the top twenty five hedge fund managers in the early part of the 21st century, you personally had to take home $130 million dollars in a year, and the top dude 'made' $1.5 billion. Now that's what you call respect today. Mr S, for let it be he, charged a 5% management fee and took 44% of any gains, arguing you guess that that's not much when you consider what you're still getting for your investment versus a lot of other failing financial vehicles. You'd think someone might be a little embarrassed taking that kind of money for what in many cases were still humdrum returns.

Take Mr Bannon, whose modest performance gave him only $650 million in compensation last year. Is it any surprise these guys don't rush to return calls from journalists asking how they feel about having 363 thousand times more than the average Joe, and what are they going to do with it all anyway? So the predictor who suggested that economic motivation is not about rational desire but a manifestation of the desire for recognition probably got it partly wrong. Money symbolising status. The creators of new wealth, services, technology. They are at the summit of capitalism and liberal democracy. How much recognition does a boy need these days?

Hey, it's a peaceful way to make money they say. Well yes, looking at it from the glowing side of a plasma screen. And you're still going to tell me the investments in countries with less than liberal democracies have nothing but a peaceful impact on the indigenous people? Well of course you are, providing you can always keep to the selective script-writing of politicians who protest that any conflict, any war, any insurgency, can be rationalised if it is part of the process of building democracy, western style. And all those needed commodities, the ones that make the mobile phones work, they don't really come from countries do they, it's all abstracted?

J knew one of the hardest parts was to hold back, to still keep something behind. Not only was it essential for survival, to keep the trackers on the wrong scent, it would be the means of delivering the gift to imagination, his own work of art, the knowing there is something more than meets the eye. Fulfilment requires participation, room to let the mind work on things, not filling in all the spaces.

He hoped his messengers felt the same way, those he believed understood what honour and respect should represent, yet everywhere in life he also knew the power and pull of betrayal, and how, sometimes, that could be a mightier force for carrying messages than simply trying to get on with the Mission. After all, it had happened before.

He realised the only one he could truly trust was himself, the only person he could be certain about was the one he kept in his mind. If ever there was a call to action, a calling, it came from within. This was his Rock, his Holy Place, from which all his voyages emanated, and where all the mental treasures would also be laid to rest. Whatever else happened, the wiring that triggered faith was founded here and the circuit charged. He would carry on.

***

J's Invisible Diary. Entry.

Secrets. The secret. Does it have any allure any more? Yes. And no. Some people want to keep secrets, but they demand openness everywhere. On screens, in magazines. The only ones who worship secrets are the ones who simultaneously spend their lives trying to legislate against privacy, demanding the degradation of personal space, intimacy, the unknown. Everyone is supposed to be transparent, free. Everyone gets further and further away behind the smiles that say sweetness lies here. The goal of knowing everything is total isolation. Nothing is relative anymore.

Time for the next phase of the Message to go forth and multiply, to let the Gospels get finessed, let them take on more power. So that more people will now be able to get a grip on content and intent, it will be necessary to help them understand that those on the List are behaving in a criminal way, an immoral way, not one yet enshrined in legislation and codes of practice, but one that will become so. To do this means being able to mix some real bad dudes with those who claim they're not, behind political or corporate fences, lawyers' fancy justifications for legitimising their selfish ways. That way, some of the ones who think they're above it all just might start to be regarded as the lowlifes they really are, and then the time for re-balancing things can really begin.

***

There were two kinds of victims. They'd both volunteered. They'd both given. They'd both worked for causes, and in challenging conditions. One had worked for the nation-state, the other had worked for the multinational corporation.

One had been sent out to defend the nations' values in areas and ways that the imposed upon rejected. The other had been sent out to push the corporation's values in as many markets as possible.

The first set of victims either made the ultimate sacrifice, or returned and, these days, was expected to reintegrate into the latest definition of civilised society without reference to the unfortunate military interlude in their life. The second set of victims either made the ultimate salary cheque or were sacrificed in the drive to realise shareholder value, equally expected to hunker down and behave responsibly in society's Eden, where things can only ever stay perfect. Whatever happens, don't try and bite back at the hand.

The armed warriors and the corporate warriors had both gone to war with different weapons, yet neither had been trained for what happened afterwards, when they were relieved of duty, or dispensed with. Sure, they were given phone numbers to access counselling, re-training for jobs, but not by anyone who'd actually been where they were. They hadn't lived through the after effects. What they'd done was observe, count, monitor, appraise, check, reassure, submit data, reports, assessments, allocate resources, fill in time.

***

As the preparations for the next phase of stirring things up developed, the statistics changed favourably. Now over 80% of the world's assets were sitting in the hands of 10% of the people. That was still around 700 million, so there'd be plenty left to go for. Within that number were a very few who gave conspicuously to good causes, while too many of the rest were out blinging each other to death – an all too true

189

consequence some would discover. Meanwhile, outside the Blingosphere, more groups in society continued to be abused, fired, not given real chances, and the whole idea of social mobility that was once chimed was now being suppressed in societies where privileged social networking was the only space to be in, if you were invited. A global digital caste system was being created. The occasional sports star or other celebrities could be let in temporarily, or even for longer if they still had the money, if they hadn't blown it all, which was often. Just wanna be famous was the rallying cry of the otherwise dispossessed.

On the corporate battlefields, more and more people were being removed by cliché. Thousands were 'leaving to spend more time with their families' or 'to pursue other interests', or simply being told by text message that they were being 'let go'. Corporate soldiers were being taken out of their theatres of action and left to fend for themselves, their so-called compensation packages being surgically amputated by human resource departments in hock to management self-savers. The other soldiers returned from their theatres and, true to all previous engagements, enjoyed the conspicuous long term absence of support to help them recover from their often traumatising experiences on behalf of their host nation, and to an unworkable reintegration into the societies whose wishes they had tried to make come true. In different bars, houses, alleyways, woods and streets, disaffected hostages to others' fortunes drank, drugged, argued and fought their demons as the otherwise employed pretended to ignore them. Fair weather friends disappeared, citing 'changed circumstances' for why they couldn't meet, or return phone calls, or make referrals, and the System saw a steadily rising group of dependents arise, victims of a vicious circle of recruitment and rejection in pursuit of hypocritical public goals, masquerading the accrual of taxes and distractions for political survival, and other forms of protection at the end of failed terms. The corporate rejects often had more means to disguise their condition for longer than the corporals, and mutual respect stayed in the back seat. If you were given five million notes of whatever to shut up and go away, how many would hand it back and say thanks but that's really not necessary. There's no question mark because there's almost no chance that would happen, and if word got out, media hounds would rush to reveal fresh foolish blood as a tiny circulation booster.

The more cautious, or the more aware, tried harder to retain some degree of anonymity. Others thought it best to demonstrate their self-awarded superiority through extreme ostentation. It might be the impractical pride of having a yacht too big to fit into most harbours, or to throw away the once-used, diamond studded snow board after a weekend in Courchevel. Whatever the place and time, the showstoppers were still at play, and a small army of stokers remained on call to fuel their fired-up thirsts.

As another 1000 workers somewhere bit the dust, a compensation committee would yet again inflate a CEO's package. As the cynical would note in old language – it was ever thus. There was always a string of statisticians ready to draw up graphic comparisons citing ancient kings, caliphs and princes, merchants and other rulers. Ah, in today's money that palace would have cost two hundred million, and that collection would have been worth over half a billion. In reality, there was nothing to compare the scale of today's players with the past. It was the irrelevance of scale as real measure of value that allowed the latest lot to accumulate so much. One per cent to most still at first appears to be such a small figure, so little to take, they chorus. One per cent of a trillion is still a big number for one person to have and to hold. Fractions and percentages are such adept statistical masks, allowing their owners and advocates to hide behind a veil of modesty and faintly embarrassed surprise. The model worked just fine. Nothing illegal about it. Maybe something morally irritating, but that's a matter of subjectivity. Selling rubbish, and then selling people the idea that rubbish wouldn't ever really stink – hey, where's the problem if people want to believe that? Where's the conflict of interest if you then sell them something that says, well, if it ever starts to smell a bit, here's something that will perfume the odour, and make us money too. There's no corruption here, it's all clear in the manifestos and the prospectuses. It's all about how you define the deal, and who's doing the dealing. Anyways, people have choices. They don't have to buy this stuff, do they? And if you can do a better deal than the next guy, isn't that what it all comes down to, whether you're dealing diamonds or family, arms or rights? In this infinite progression onwards and upwards, harmonising with the illogical hopes of ordinary homeowners and shareholders, sleeping the same dreams of ever-rising profits and security, until the certificated houses of cards and paper all fall down, it's all go, until the politely termed 'period of correction' comes in. That's what's required here. A correction. Not some cheap Robin Hood trick of robbing the rich to help the poor, some crazy re-distribution of wealth. No, it was time to show that for quite a few, money doesn't make you happy was going to become a form of reality they hadn't really planned for.

* * *

J's Invisible Diary. Entry.

Target-wise, for the next phase, some areas initially look more attractive than others. The Hamptons, or Knightsbridge, Marbella or Monaco. These might have made it to an early mental start list. There is both opportunity and barrier in these kinds of choices. The opportunity is that they are known, static, and can be studied. The downside is that the predictable places are increasingly swarming with guards and other claimed protectors, on the ground, underground, in the air. Incomes aren't yet being noticeably dented by this kind of cover. Potential targets that have moved, or about to be on the move, are sometimes going to be easier to access, more interesting as a challenge, but also more unpredictable, especially those who actually listened to their advisors about avoiding regular patterns and repetition. It would mostly have to come down to some combination, both for effectiveness and for stimulation.

The basic idea is to force an increase in cover after the next phase, and drive threat awareness levels to the highest states. This will cost more and more, utilising more people, which is precisely where mistakes will creep in. The allegedly protected, many of them, will begin to find the new levels of intrusiveness irksome, to say the least. For others it will mean continuing to spend with abandon. They will end up in their homes under a graded form of house arrest. This appeals. Some of the more extravagant, or wealthy, will start to demand the kind of security that leaders of states have come to expect. Sweeps of destinations days before trips, and beyond their departure, cavalcades, exclusion zones, triggering more frustration with ordinary hapless citizens going about their daily drone business. Others will turn into Howard Hughes clones, closeted in their secret spaces and minds, another form of sentence handed down to those who had twisted views about a sense of entitlement. Don't you know who we are, would migrate to an anonymous silence. Don't stand out. Don't be conspicuous. Don't flash the cash. In the Don't World, the protectors, the warders, will get richer, and the world of the super-rich will get more and more secret, a parallel world, invisible. No celebrity profiles except for the Z-listers, and the paparazzi encouraged to stay well outside this exclusion zone, except very occasionally, when perhaps one or two, by invitation, would be allowed to be falsely embedded to witness events. Surprise parties, weekends whose destinations will be changed just as the flight plan is about to be filed, and for those who ever found out, the quiet surprise that last weekend a gang had met in Baja California, or Baku, and not on any well-trodden circuit venues. There will still be plenty around to splash the cocaine-coated notes around, the nouveau naïve riche, the merely careless, the couldn't care less, but the picture will slowly alter.

As with traditional war and state-sponsored conflicts, there is a reminder of the insight of Daniel Mannix, his role in the church aside, who said "the wealthy classes would be very glad to send the last man, but they have no notion of giving the last shilling, or even the first." Capitalists exploit wars, but few pay for them. You know that these people have a remarkable facility for passing these obligations on. It reminds you also of the catalysts. Remember Alexander Helphand, or Israel Parvus, or other variations of his name. An exception, a supporter of Bolshevism and a war profiteer at the same time. Why do anything yourself when, if you identify the right characters and their motives you can get them to do almost everything for you themselves? After a while, when the momentum has been established, and the methodology demonstrably successful, others will take up the refined role, the disciples. Risks will still emerge. Not everyone will support the cause, and the media will again stir up a twister over blood and morals, turning round itself to cite outrage as it sucks in more to capture events as it comes across them, revealing gory details and exaggerating conditions to suit its own path, 'in the public interest'. Even if those pursuing the action try to harness information about emerging trends, there will be others who will take the Message forward, believing in what they considered to be a just cause, the rightful way, or whatever other kind of vocabulary could be conjured up to tart up the moral hazards.

***

Oleg Romano didn't believe in the word luck. Luck comes to those who make it, and if you make it you don't need it. Being in the right time at the right place with the right people was all about planning and preparation. Luck was how losers talked through their idiocy. Born in Odessa, the son of an Italian soldier and a Ukrainian Jewess from an émigré German family, they had managed to save each other from both the clutches of ambitious Germans in the Second World War, and cathartic Russians afterwards. He had grown up both as a belonger and an outsider in the post-war survivors' port that was left after the serial raping by vengeance seekers and patriots. Within the culture, he grew

193

up knowing that the purpose of children was to work, and work hard for their slap-happy parents and family. This was the secret to being a good child – familiarity with graft and beatings, and learning to be silently grateful for it all. It was in these early years that he quickly learned to grasp the power of evasive action, either through physical disappearing acts, or through well-constructed lies. He learned how to blame others for all his own negative actions. He learned how words could be powerfully rallied to destroy people without leaving scars. He learned to laugh off taunts and insults, smile with cold eyes, wait for the time when he could return a compliment, level someone with a scathing sentence, even before he knew how to back that up with other people's violence and weapons.

When he was fifteen he was tired of the State, education was about dead souls and unworkable rules, a language of strings and knots tying your mind up in constriction. He had had a dream, and his mother's ribs revealed its coming to life in half-starved ways. He wasn't going to die of malnutrition in his country of birth. His father had finally gone local, succumbing to dubiously derived vodka, retreating into the shadows of memories of the war, and he took himself back regularly to the winters of '43 and '44. He knew his mother would soon follow, her heart exhausted by devotion to her failing husband, and she had neither the will nor the strength to carry on alone. She elected to disappear and decline, and nothing Oleg could do could bring her back. She too was lost, caught up in her husband's expanding fate, and her love for her son shrank behind the drawn dark curtains, no compensations to ease her pain. She decided Oleg was strong enough to move on alone, and told him so, when she revealed she now belonged somewhere else, and never wanted to be in a position or place where she could be used to distract her son from his destiny. In death she set him free, and at the same time locked him into another kind of world, one of intense selfish protection where he vowed never to get into a situation where he could feel desolate again, so hopelessly dependent on an immature and unreasoned love for someone so close. No, to be strong meant only one thing, to depend on oneself. Families were too weak, full of weak ones who were propped up by the wasted energies of the strong.

The borders with Ukraine's neighbours were more porous than the authorities would have the tempted believe. Oleg was able to slip himself through other areas by stealth and stamina, and found himself in Turkey. With his parents' mixed features on his face and skin he found it easy to get attention when he wanted it, and easy to blend into other mixed races too as it suited. Belgrade was no Odessa, but it had

194

been a superb training ground for gang-based crime groups, who, after practicing on their amoral home turf, were well equipped to Go West and take over the soft amateurs in the countries that were willing to pay good money for their goods and services. Oleg had found his ability to pick up languages, and his lack of fear, his collectedness, were soon recognized by certain brothers in crime. He found himself being encouraged to develop other skills, like in the freeing up of new high-end motor cars from their owners, smuggling contraband, particularly cigarettes and software, and then the daintily tasty form of people trafficking that other jurisdictions called under-age prostitution. He was leading pretty young girls into nasty, brutal and short lives in squalid city centres where rabid male losers were willing to throw away their money on victims without redress. It was, from an investors point of view, a deliciously interesting prospect – high cash flow, high yields, low to no maintenance costs, minimum overheads, virtually no litigation, and no wearisome audits. It was like the liquor and fags business, with occasional free gifts.

Oleg could hardly believe the naiveté of the girls, who bought into the princess-making stories, or of their mothers or fathers, who also bought into a dream they either could never deliver, or turned a blind eye to. It was like a pyramid game. Money would come in to the old folks for one, maybe two months, and that would be it. They didn't know, or didn't want to know, where their daughters really were any more, what they were really doing, how they were, or where they might end up. The daughters themselves were now working to a maximum level that still kept them attractive to most punters, drugs and lodgings deducted from their inflated fees, their deteriorating bodies being moved as 'fresh in today' across twenty or so cities, before they were finally discarded. Oleg had long ago heard about those hedge fund managers doing what the Americans called 2 and 20's – charging a 2% management of funds fee, and taking 20 % of the profits. He could keep the administration charges down to less than 1% point of sales, and his take of profits was more like 90%, the difference being taken up through the boring issue of things like transportation costs, the occasional border bribe, or little rewards to those privileged enough to be his tenanted landlords and ladies, hosting services in his ever-growing legitimate property empire. Traffic was two way. Worn out girls were shipped back east. Oleg hadn't been brought up on Russian soil not knowing about where and when to dispose of bodies with no future interpersonal potential. It hadn't been an easy ride.

He discovered early on that life was much less respected in Eastern

195

Europe. He learned about loyalty and initiations, things borrowed from other societies, many as old as the mountains to the north. Relationships were continuously tested, and lapses rarely tolerated. As in many cases, blood triumphed and defined trust and faith. He countered his unclear blood-lines with ferocious demonstrations of support, and became first a trusted one, a courier and runner, and then a consigliore of sorts, ready to settle others old scores with vicious finality. Since the only people he had ever loved in any way that was meaningful to him were his now dead parents, he got on with life untouched by the pain of outsiders. People were just entities. They had uses, they played roles, they were there to serve ends they could not conceive of. He smirked at the idea someone older had once shared with him about the Yankies' idea of democracy. It was all, "There, there, nice doggie, nice doggie, there, there", until you could find a big enough rock. Oleg was the good cop, Mr Nice Guy, as he saw it, but others might not quite tally with his ways of motivating those he needed to carry out his desires, or what became his terminal commands. There were plenty out there who would kill someone with no finesse for $200, or a couple of cases of vodka, and they weren't worried about witnesses or cameras. Life was for now – who cared about five years away. These were guys who would steal a scooter, ride up to someone in the street who looked vaguely like the photocopy of the old photograph of the target, and after the driver revved the engine to catch the person in surprise, would leave it to the pillion rider to raise the gun and drop them. They were off before anyone could capture the moment, and subsequently nobody saw anything anyway. After all, there were always idiots in the street making loud noises with weak-engined machines. If you stopped every time you heard someone gunning an engine you'd never get anywhere. Besides, in many countries, gunfire was not an entirely unfamiliar sound. Gunfire was used for celebrations, for funerals, for making a point, even for punctuation. Killing people was just a by-product of the noise you could generate in other countries. A street killing was almost part of the weekly timetable, you might stay away, but plenty of people didn't, thinking the dead one in the street was no better than the killer. Everyone had it coming. It was a parallel universe, and as long as you weren't in any uncommonly close parameters of trajectories, you would still be walking safely down the street, whistling, like the bullets meant for others today.

By the time Oleg had made his major move westwards and got as far as Hamburg, he was significantly covered by layers of lawyers, accountants, and well-suited aids, all paid to legitimize his business interests under the banner of a multi-country on-line job search and placement operation, with a high proportion of temporary offers. Its complex database was designed to keep him abreast of all personnel and moves in his benign contributions to society's well-being. Fees, commissions and wages paid out of off-shore handling operators played only a small part in the rest of the legitimate, tax-paying operation doing admirable work in tired democracies and fledgling states. Oleg was a Man for Our Times.

Cash was quickly turned into property, and each placement company quickly found itself without rent to pay, and a growing portfolio of buildings to manage under its expanding remit as well. He was a secret spider overlooking an enormous web. Managing the trafficking of the girls was just one function under the 'temporary job seekers' sections of his empire. Like in many such areas of work, turnover was high. It was convenient that there were always plenty of reasons why young women didn't turn up to the cleaning job or the filing job after a few days – illness, a drink problem, attitude, home problems, men problems, girl problems, getting up problems – all too petty for police forces and authorities to pursue. If taxes were paid, social security contributions made, forms filled in, the state was quietly satisfied. Who wants scandals that decrease tourist numbers and business and get the morally twitchy up in arms all over the press and TV? People disappear all the time – they have accidents, fallings out, divorces. They get fed up and want to see if the grass is greener on the other side. They run away from home, from jobs, from husbands and wives. What's a few more in a statistical universe of hundreds of millions.

Sure, the loss of Irena or Anoushka will mean something, it won't be entirely insignificant, but in the grand scheme of things a few dead fruit flies count for not a lot. That's not the way to see progress. Progress is hedonistic. Hedonism is fuelled by cash. Oleg wanted digital statements of pleasure given, by money that literally stank, but which didn't talk back at you if you did something it didn't agree with. Money was like a pet, loyal, even if you didn't care for it much. You cared for what it represented. What it represented was the means to keep people at bay, to have privacy, not to have to watch all the co-mingling over-heated sweaty summer people having what they called relationships up close and personal near you.

Things these days needed to be held at a distance – space was required. The people should not be seen, or get too close to the court, where they might form the wrong ideas about the new Tsar and his empire built on fake orgasms and cheap perfume. He believed his growing fortune was helping him wash his hands of the primeval conditions in which he began to accumulate it, and bury all the bones that were his foundation. He had plenty of acolytes, and still owned 91% of the business. He would still hold meetings in penthouses and roof-top offices, on private jets and boats, where he would review his world and discuss plans and personnel like any other regular quoted company his enterprise wasn't.

Like those CEOs and Presidents, he like to keep a few things to himself, his own uncontested choices, and whatever the security advisors now said, he wanted his own choice of communication device, without all the bullshit warnings about eavesdroppers and hackers. He told them all to go away, find a way, just fix life, keep him fucking secured and no hassle – the usual frustration of the impatient in power, the paranoid avoider, denier of truths, who ended up more isolated as their close counselors chose not to pass unpalatable truths on to him. That was why he wouldn't let go of the iPhone.

He wasn't a wireless addict. He didn't spend all his time monitoring incoming news – that was for others to manage, but he did occasionally send messages and mails to others, when he chose. Like an old cowboy, he kept his piece by his side at night. He enjoyed contacting people when it was most inconvenient for them, on the other side of the world, waking them up with some partner, fucking up some party, because he could.

The message went out – Meet Friday 2200. The recipient knew this meant he would have to arrange a suite during Holy Day. There was a list of venues. Oleg would arrive as the guest of a weekending friend, on his private jet, the mandatory oligarch accessory. He would be escorted swiftly to the venue, and a detailed but rapid summary of the business would have to be conducted. Most of the business would be coming from the newer, more fashionable enterprises, but every so often Oleg wanted to use his imagination to think what it would have been like only twenty years ago, when the Intercontinental Hotel was a sure sign of luxury, its restaurants and bars serving everything from Cornish pasties to Persian elegance to a global clientele of dealers and chancers. The then sky-high bar had run one of the better meet and greet operations for high rollers and high fleecers, and female Russian accents were the precursor to the uptake of the whole language as the city's third to appear on signs and shop doors. Oleg had been asked to supply talent for the hungry, feeding off the tolerance of the self-selecting host nation. Transportation and administration was provided, all he had to do was supply the raw material, and count the generous returns, with his own tame audit to ensure the value of his contribution was appreciated. This was a newer venture, beyond the seasoned activity of Europe. Oleg wondered whether to convert some of the cash here into property, and then decided it wasn't for him – too many ties to people he didn't believe he could run so easily. No, it would remain pocket money for little indulgences now and then.

The only problem with small business jets was that, unlike those that were the size of commercial airliners that hooked up to air-conditioned tubes to disgorge their passengers, you had the brief indignity of being blasted by hot desert air as you stepped from the aircraft and down to the waiting limousine. It was time they ferried VIPs to an air-conditioned hangar, something he noted to be passed on to one of his frequent flyer friends in the future. At 9pm it was still searing, and he remembered to avoid touching any exposed metal surfaces, whose heat gave the same pain as frozen metal in a Russian winter. Opposites, and none of them attractive. The re-built Rolls Royce, with its bullet proof hide and its truck sized temperature control unit restored his level of cool within two minutes, and the ease of immigration from the friendly local operatives made the entry to the city more appealing. He thought back to pictures he had seen of a forlorn runway stamped on the almost colourless desert floor, and a small cluster of buildings that had marked the destination in the fifties. Even ten years ago, the whole city worth visiting had not extended beyond ten miles of the airport, and now the focus was marked by the skyscrapers, signposts for swathes of easily distracted hedonists who rarely complained and were often one-trip wonders – an ideal forgetful clientele. The girls were turned around often, trailed back to Russia like the other commodities crammed into fat Antonovs flying fridges and plasma TVs to distant grey markets, where upcoming professionals were predictably trying to out consume each other with brand names and impossible price tags, the privileges of gizmo addicted citizens of the new world.

Dinner would be in the traditional Persian restaurant where the rice was perfection, the lamb tasted of fresh hillsides, and the tomatoes flushed with concentration, a feast of nature enabled by yet more fleets of aircraft, busy transposing food from one side of the globe to the other.

The one in charge of securing the penthouse where the official business would take place had used his network to disgorge some honey-mooning non-entities from Northern Europe, and he had ensured any of the duty manager's embarrassment would be swiftly extinguished. He had established the procedure for meeting Oleg's demands at short notice, and things were running smoothly. He was the controller of a concierge service for a tiny group of not-to-be-messed-with entrepreneurs. Because his skills were in a tight circle of providing specific kinds of satisfaction, he had worked out that whatever was needed by a particular Big One that day or week, and for the entourage, then it was largely a set of variations that needed to be produced for a few others. He knew most of the clients were infrequent visitors, and he took the risk that there were likely to be few conflicts of interest in spreading his services across a wider client base, few of whom would ever have heard of each other, and were unlikely to meet. He congratulated himself on his deduction that his own cleverness had prevailed, and how he would be getting seven to ten times the money for much the same service. In ten years, he would be needing his own dedicated concierge, and he would be running similar operations in other places, where his clientele would continue to be demanding, but, he confided to himself, perhaps marginally less dangerous. His naïve optimism blinded him from the reality that his real enemy took on an entirely different form.

Being acquainted with so many services to the upper echelons of the business jetting global nomads attracted its own form of discreet attention. The Arab hosts were well practiced in cultivating their devoted watchers and listeners wherever substantial amounts of money were present. Beyond the official investigatory channels, there were plenty gaining supplementary benefits from passing on what they allegedly knew, or had seen or heard. For many, they thought this form of demonstrating loyalty to their hosts would enhance their chances of continuing to extract a living from the nation they were guests of. Some were eager to demonstrate their commitment with frequent enthusiasm, albeit from behind metaphorically closed windows and doors.

Collective intelligence assessment had noted that our little Indian career builder was connected tangentially to a series of intriguing customers, and although they didn't know each other, the Indian might have useful snippets of information that would be useful for the overseeing powers, looking to construct bigger pictures and connections. He may not know the true value of his information, but sometimes even simple things like the arrival and departure times of his occasional benefactors could provide specially shaped pieces in the multiplicity of jigsaws being put together on the screens of observing agencies.

It was most fortunate that the Indian had selected a handset and service provider that made eavesdropping a simple matter. His phone had been giving up tit-bits to the listeners for some time now, which was how they came to know Oleg was about to drop in on the Pleasure Zone. Use a spider to catch a fly.

The penthouse was perfect. It was one of four on the hotel's top floor, with a dedicated elevator service, and suitably discouraging access codes. The other three penthouses were occupied, one of them taken by another guest through a similar path of expediency the Indian provided. The other two penthouse occupants were busy elsewhere, and just in case they were tempted to return early, distractions had been planned to detain them for long enough to leave the roof lobby area empty for other matters to be handled.

As usual, the business part of the trip was coming to a rapid conclusion. Still enjoying the memories of the Persian meal, Oleg had looked at the numbers on the encrypted laptop, and after one or two of his customarily penetrating questions designed principally to remind the presenter never to try to fuck him over, he pronounced himself almost satisfied with the way his little leisure earner was coming along.

The guards in the security detail got ready to escort Oleg on to his next stop, as the guest of another weekending oligarch who had decided it was time for Oleg to share some of his rare brandy-based hospitality on his locally moored motor yacht. One opened the penthouse door, and two others checked the lobby outside, moving over towards the elevator to summon it. As it neared the floor, Oleg appeared behind the second guard, and they began to move towards the elevator's open doors

Then the door to the third penthouse opened, and in less than three and a half seconds, three darts had entered the neck of the two guards and Oleg. The one presenting the numbers had stayed behind in the penthouse to shut down the machine and breathe a sigh of relief that the spreadsheets had passed Oleg's scrutiny. The two guards, now lying on the carpet, would be out for around ten minutes, long enough, and would wake up with virtually no recognition or evidence of an ambush, and an almost impossible task should anyone try to identify what had surprised them toxicologically. The guards' darts were swiftly retrieved. The dart in Oleg had contained a different cocktail that would still be working when they brought him round, unable to speak, and with his muscles failing to respond to any messages from his brain, but not killing him there and then.

Oleg was toppled into the laundry basket that had been left in the third penthouse earlier, and the guest visitors wheeled this into the nearby service elevator, pressing for the journey down to level -2 in the service area. No-one commented on the trolley joining the others in the back of the laundry van, almost ready to go again on one of its four times a day runs aimed at keeping guests pampered sand perfumed at all times. The penthouse principal guest walked casually out of the service bay and round to the front of the hotel, where he joined a dozen people ambling through the entrance looking for further late evening entertainment. His silent assistant drove the van on its customary path away from the hotel, and only after five minutes did he take a left turn to another smaller hotel, where he drew up in its service bay area. He got out, leaving the ignition key in the vehicle, and he disappeared effortlessly into the night.

Three others appeared two minutes later, opened the rear doors of the van, and found the laundry trolley from the penthouse immediately. They extracted the limp occupant, who was beginning to reach a level of consciousness where all was not quite what it seemed.

The men were Caucasian. They wire-tied him to a steel topped table that looked like it acted as the reception area for meat deliveries. One of them grabbed his hair, and forced his head in the direction of the screen of a large laptop that the second man had switched on. It looked like some kind of picture show, the ones you could easily configure on any number of social networking sites. It was a series of portraits, pictures of girls, captioned names, their ages maybe from 12 to 22. He knew what they were, but he knew no-one, none of them, and he knew what this meant.

The third man, the Ukrainian, said the number, 2,116, and whispered, "For the girls, you see:

The first and second men produced surgical knives, and sequentially began to cut off parts of his body, beginning with his fingers, then on to his wrists, lower arms, and down to his toes, feet and on upwards as he saw in immobility the desecration of his body. His entirety was dropped into a series of plastic zip bags, and the lot was tipped back into the trolley, the van, the steel table and its surrounds washed off with the service spray, scrubbed and disinfected, restored to its pristine state. The third man drove off in the van, out and along to the boats along the edge of the old town. The trolley was trundled onto the deck of the old slow cargo vessel, piled with cartons of white goods destined for the northern shores, too cheap to be flown by planes. Five of the large cartons were opened, and bags placed in the drums of washing machines. The trolley then found itself sinking in the creek, and the boat set sail into the dark warm waters. No one was going to be enjoying the fruits of Oleg's laundering any time soon.

Headline: *"Job Centres in Sex Scandal"*

Cue: *"Woman in Chains"*

***

There was nothing unusual about the flight. The jumpers had boarded, the pre-flight safety checks had gone smoothly, the team briefed. After a month of changeable weather, it and other conditions had harmonised. Favourable winds, cloud conditions, visibility, air pressure, temperatures, and schedules congratulated each other on the success of their conspiracy. The wait had been long but worth it. Good to go. The pilot requested taxi and then take-off clearances, and soon he was throttling up and rolling along the grass runway, lifting off towards the South West and the early evening sun on the May Sunday. The group had an impressive number of jumps logged, and some had even more special experiences from their time in the Army. The slow-turning engine donated considerable energy to turning avgas into noise, and the plane groaned its heavy way skywards, not taxing the lazy altimeter. The climb took longer than it could have, if only to spare a few of the late tea-timers below from the ever-so slowly diminishing noise of the engine, voluntary noise-limitation guidelines, which would never satisfy the groundlings, who spent much time trying to close down the long-lasting Parachute Club at the local airport, a much coveted greenfield site, that voracious developers had spent years trying to get their hands on. Old aircraft paraphernalia propped up the club bar in historic defiance, and the infernal sounds lived on. Maybe a gliding club with a line launcher would have been just about tolerable, but the tradition continued, drowning out the purr of German engines from expensive saloon cars and drive-on lawn-mowers, whose sounds were vehemently defended by their owners in turn. It was an earthbound society in Southern England.

There were six of them. The drop was to be from 12000 feet, by which time the aircraft was almost background noise, and only those with binoculars would see the cluster of jumpers as they left the big side door, the plane flying its brief section of straight and level flight before the exit sequence began. The idea was to have a short free fall down to three thousand feet, and then to enjoy a close team glide back down to the little markers in the landing zones at the airfield, where the one furthest from the spots would be buying the drinks. The first jumper confidently contained his descent to let the others catch up, and

203

the fifth jumper soon made it to the now enclosing circle and their controlled ballet, just like the display teams at other aerodromes and fields around the country.

The sixth jumper left thirty seconds after the fifth, when eyes were on the earlier descendants, and he pulled the rip-cord after only four seconds of positioning and downfall. His canopy was translucent, and had all the performance characteristics of the advanced design of flying wing that it was. As the others formed up below, he began a meticulously controlled glide descent. The host aircraft continued for five miles in the opposite direction, and then began its return to the airfield, another exercise almost complete, and a log-book and radio record showing clearly that five jumpers had set out, and five had returned safely, all but one in the centre of the spots on the grass. The sixth was now cruising south westerly, using the favourable winds at different levels to shape the flight path, his direction, speed, and rate of descent being captured on his oversized wrist watch. This was definitely not the most dangerous or difficult of jumps, simply one that required great control and precision. He knew he was well inside his limits, with a long collection of HALO and LALO sorties behind him. On exercises and assignments, he had infiltrated facilities and countries from well outside exclusion zones, crossing borders from many starting points miles and altitudes away, with breathing equipment and flying techniques that allowed him to deceive even the rare enemies that might have conceived of his stealthy approaches. This was the good part. Exfiltration was usually the harder part, when the consequences of his largely invisible presence had been noticed. So far he had lived to not tell the tales.

The transparent helium drone had been over the target site for weeks. Its four noise-suppressed motors, inertial navigation systems and its radio-controlled steering gave it a high degree of manoeuvrability. Its high resolution digital mapping and observation cameras gave a wide range of perspectives to controllers. Sitting both outside controlled airspace, and out of the flight paths of regular club craft below, the drone sat at around eight thousand feet, enjoying its survey of the estate in the East Sussex countryside below it, a most encompassing experience. Around the house were the fields and forest, the small farm, the stables and other outbuildings that made the property an estate agent's dream, and the rolling setting exuded a feeling of peaceful security, comfortable privacy, and a studied timelessness. Hedgerows, bushes and copses, together with parts of walls, gave the perimeters of the estate a feeling of relaxed tranquillity, and they played their parts well in helping conceal the state of the art deterrents to intruders, who would discover some antisocial approaches to their welfare if they tried to penetrate the grounds. It was also clear from the eyes in the sky that camouflaged armed patrols toyed in the bucolic landscape, and occasionally tested the patience of motion sensors and CCTV cameras, controlled from a base point discretely placed near the big house, where the comings and goings of changing shifts could be monitored. For casual passers-by and rubber-neckers, the house simply looked like the kind of place many people would dream about owning. The invisible security was there to help the occupants feel free and unmolested without the disturbing visibility of searchlights and watchtowers, a countrified fortress, a digital prison.

The airborne cameras had been monitoring events, and for the ardent observer, it was becoming clear that security was doing what it usually does. First, it was reinforcing the statistic that there's no such thing as 100% security, second, that in so many cases, security weaknesses or lapses were down to human behaviour. Things were looking encouraging. After this adventure, security policies would be revised. Right now, things weren't looking up, and that was just fine. Two more encouraging things emerged. The first was that there was a helipad. The second was that the owner of the house appeared to have a soft spot for BMX bikes, and liked to ride round his grounds as a way of relaxing, or thinking, and keeping fit. Trails had been created through and around the woods.

Because Ethan was a creature of control, he clicked on the bike-mounted monitor as he pushed away, and took patterns of routes, hoping to knock off milliseconds as he continued his pursuit of perfection in all things, the ultra-light, ultra-strong bespoke bike a part of his means of crossing tough personally set boundaries. Within the estates perimeter, someone was switching the motion sensors on and off as he traversed sections and the race against time was being won. Timing was all. If Ethan was at home and there was only a small window of notice, he would emerge around six in the afternoon, bike and gear readied, and set off for an hour's pursuit of his own goals. His security detail didn't ride with him – it was always a solo performance, but they could see him on CCTV most of the time, just not for a few seconds when he would disappear behind some old copse well within the grounds, and then the pedal-pushing fiend would re-emerge. As usual, and once routinized, the human monitors reduced the frequency of their checking. The drone had mapped his preferred courses, and one route took him behind the main house, just inside a copse, some forty metres from the helipad. No-one was going to tell Ethan to vary his route here. Several ex-security chiefs had tried the simple approach, diplomacy, deference, and advice, discovering it paid no dividends. No, security at home needed to be seriously discreet, a veil. It was their job to make it happen, not his job to be obeisant to it – that wasn't the price to pay for being successful in trading precious metals.

The jumper landed at 6.20pm, on the helipad, and Ethan was on the far side of the circuit, no human eyes on this part of the grounds. He wasn't an incoming helicopter. He had gathered in the wing as the sun turned redder, and made it to the copse in less than fifteen seconds, no motion sensors here as they freaked under rotor blades, and other sensors near the house and fences would pick up signals first. In another twenty paces he was by the tyre-grooved track, on a gentle incline. From his vantage point he was able to relay the wing and its lines on the other side of the copse, repositioning it for its next role. If he was seen at this stage he would simply act out his rehearsed performance about a training flight and losing control, a story the school would back up.

He took two packages from his flying suit pockets. One contained the eighty metre coil of razor-wire, like a tape measure, the other the telescopic baton. The trip wire he then set across two potential pathways, around the trees, and unless Ethan stopped altogether, for some reason he had never done before, he was going to be breathing hard as he stood on the pedals to attack the incline, head bobbing up and down as he pushed on the higher gear he had set himself this time, beating the stopwatch, pushing almost half-way round the course. The next CCTV log was twenty five seconds away, even if it was being precisely monitored. The wire was matt black, no sun could betray it. Ethan came panting towards it, and the front tyre snagged, twisting the wheel and the frame round, and knocking the bike over to one side. He was still in the grip of one attached bike shoe, laying half under the frame, wondering what was happening, the breath knocked out of him.

Jumper six moved forward and hit Ethan on the back of the neck, just below where the helmet offered any form of protection. For good measure, he then broke Ethan's neck and heard the satisfaction of death clicking in. It was suddenly silent after the swift efficiency. The baton was re-telescoped and re-pocketed, the wire recoiled and returned to its rightful place. It would take a little while for people to decide it wasn't an accident.

As with other missions, getting out was often the tougher part of the challenge, the least controllable. But today was just, today was benign.

Studies had shown clearly the prevailing winds and speeds over the hillsides. He returned to the wing, harnessed up and let the air take up the weight with practised hands. He was away above the hillside in the wake of the copse just as the cyclist would have begun to be expected. He was building speed and height away from the house, and within a minute looked like another ridge-rider on a late Sunday afternoon. Before the alarms were really raised, he was in sight of other riders in the glorious conditions. Soon enough he would land near their take-off site, and be offered a lift to a local village for the debrief and the tantalising post-flight quencher.

For Ethan, the markets were going to close several points down in the Asian markets that Monday, time zones away, minus one trading legend. There would be quiet commiserations in parts of the arms-trading community. The well-connected Israeli would cause headaches for those with merchandise in various stages of distribution along his secret supply chains, both despatchers and receivers. Some folks might just live a little longer after the response for their own particular call for alms.

Headline: *"Mystery trader dead in BMX bike Crash"*
Cue: *"It's All Over Now"*

***

J's Invisible Diary. Entry

Only the little people pay taxes, old Ma Helmsley said as she defended herself in court. For that naïve truth she was sent down for tax evasion. Such innocent times. So little money. We had to wait for the Bernie Madoff man to come along before we got into a seriously noticeable amount of money disappearing, like $65 billion by one dude. You'd think that was quite a bit to hide or lose, unless you were running a US-type war, but he seemed to have done as good a job of that as he had from extracting it from punters in the first place. Being wasteful with others' money and lives was par for the course. Even as recently as The First World War you saw observers' anger coming through clearly as the super-rich made the point. Bernie could have made the List, but he got shopped to the police first.

They, the super-rich, do not talk to ordinary people, by and large. They talk to people as pig-headed, blind, and greedy as themselves: industrialists, politicians, bankers and economists who lie about production capabilities and fiscal soundness; to army group and army commanders and their chiefs of staff who lie about ground gained and

207

enemy killed and the state or morale of their men; to navy admirals who almost a century ago guaranteed that not one American soldier would land in France to participate in the First World War.

Life is cheap. Blood diamonds. Blood money. Blood currencies. From greenbacks to red-backs, the colour of money looks the same to the colour blind everywhere, a full grey market. You can count the philanthropic exceptions on the fingers of not too many hands. That leaves a lot of ungenerous hoarders behind.

Every man shall do his duty. His duty is to die. Some deal. We all end up dead anyway. Maybe some should feel just a teeny bit more scared than others that it's going to come earlier than they planned for themselves. But they still have options. This wouldn't soon be put down to Allah's will, so forget about it and get on with being a full-time hedonist in the meantime.

The new headlines will come thick and fast if the spectacular route is opted for too early. Take out a big chunk of the Bilderberg Group, or the Sun Valley Idaho fest, or Davos, souks of superiority and self-congratulation. There are even more around offering protection for these people, people apparently ready to take one for the bank president and the hedge fund manager. No point. These folks will just go into more secret squirrel mode and move their venues around, leaking their views after they'd disassembled – not much of a barrier to a determined force, but dull – why set the bar so high? The better course is the trickle down. Trickles are patient but can lead to mighty yields downstream. Trickledown. Someone in the CIA has probably already logged that as a project, only viewable to those with an access clearance level of 10 cubed and above. Do we care?

It's the thing to think you're living in a shit time full of unreasonable hassle and needless violence. But take a look at all the other times. We think we're in the middle of a firestorm because we are so locked into our own egos we can't be arsed to look at any kinds of comparison. We top that by thinking some people can improve matters through extant forms and processes. The world moving forward through Health and Safety. Way to go.

The second concentrated period of Message delivery is on. We will still need to see if we need another decoy, another website, to stir the chasers into life.

***

Sunday afternoon. The Breakers at Palm Beach. The day had started late for him. A champagne brunch inside, well out of the way of the Beach Club and the pool full of kids. It was a day for little treats – a leisurely drift through the news, the quiet efficiency of the old-school service, none of the dark or other monotone minimalism of the Schrager-inspired haunts further south that gadget addicts flocked to. In the distance, in the long high-ceilinged lobby, arrivers and leavers stood in well-attended lines, those who hadn't used the automated concierge services, and they passed on their comments as the unflappable staff treated each guest as if that kind of request had never been made before, and would be dealt with tact and imagination and immediacy. Sometimes a little daydream hurt nobody. The ocean sat out there in its place, only occasionally daring to leave a tiny salt spray on the uniforms of the seaters and greeters outside. Manicured lawns held out for semi-conscious approval as the limos drew up and slipped away. Flags took care too not to draw so much attention to themselves today. He even thought of wandering down three or four blocks to the small restaurant and shops, changing his mind when he remembered he was bound to be stopped by a patrol car. No-one but trouble walked around here, and he wanted no cause for any form of suspicion or recollection at all. Even his drinks drew no regards, as usual. Mount Gay rum and coke – easy, Cuba Libre man was back in the fine old US of A. From around 4pm, a short way to the south, the background noise increased. Not too much, but about every five minutes the air was punctuated with the noise of turbo-fans grinding their executive jet owners asses into the skies for return flights to business centres, and back to the delicious tedium of generating cash. Gulfstreams clamoured for take-off slots in their abundant anonymity from a distance, and weekend shore-line homes turned themselves back over to weekly abandoned wives and lawn trimmers. The Fort Lauderdale Executive Airport was peaking with amended flight plans and clearances, as the Eastern Seaboard got cluttered with contrails and pilots requesting preferred flight levels above the heavy commercial traffic.

The day before he'd been at a cocktail party held by a widowed hostess who, like her compatriots, tried regularly to outshine each other with demonstrations of the residual buying power of their former husbands' efforts, dresses and jewellery clashing to be seen as bottles and glasses popped and chinked their percussions behind the false laughter and tired jokes about money and happiness and well-being. Briefly he was cornered by a woman who didn't quite look the part, but said anyway she was a regular on the widow's cocktail circuit, because that was where the new arrivals and new rich won spurs, and got the intros and name drops to the exclusive clubs and sects and sets of shakers they simply had to join to belong, and to have any hope of credibility and the appearance of establishment in the hallowed upper atmosphere. She commented that she hadn't seen him at these events before, sizing him up. He said he was there as the friend of a guest, and generally preferred to spend his time on the West Coast, before switching the questioning back on to her, asking what she did to enjoy the company of the others around here. She said she was an aviation services ambassador, for which he read salesperson. She said she was only really interested in talking to people who wanted her company's planes, so we were talking here about those whose net liquid worth after property and such was around $100 million. Good luck. He raised his glass, tilting it in her direction as a sign she might be talking to such a one, but she'd have to try harder, and moved on.

Most of the older ones were well marinated by six thirty, or pretending to be, several were being pampered by their staff and assistants by seven, and several others had quietly withdrawn, returning to the deals they had yet to finalise. It was the same old deal-ful life at this time of year, only 30 degrees warmer. A few documents needed to be signed, some discreetly, others under spotlights of publicity, to show the keepers of the keys they were flocking correctly to get voted in to the do-gooders society. Some were there with their own money, some with only slightly dwindling inheritances, old names whose legacies had been remarkably well-managed, and the rest were there with other people's money, all pacing round and round and checking each other out through friends and spies and advisors, great and small, in the court of Palm Beach.

There was one guy who thought he was going to make it to the Top Dog slot in a major corporation. But he came second. He had to leave. At that level, there was still plenty of corporate clubbing going on, so, apart from the issue of pride, he wasn't going to have to wait too long for an access all areas pass to be offered him by someone. It came. He left a world of financial services and highly-engineered products and joined on invitation a company that was geared towards helping ordinary folks spruce up their homes, paint their fences and rooms, shore up the garage and in quaint ways help them keep up with the Joneses. If the company had got depressed and wanted to kill itself for personal reasons it couldn't have found a better person to provide the pills. Within a year of his arrival the stores were haemorrhaging sales and staff, with products un-stacked on bare shelves, and loyal customers wondering what was happening to their household friend.

After two years, the company's stock had shrunk by 90% from its high before the Prince of the Future had shown up. The compensation committee, even with Danello and Bannon sitting there, was embarrassed. They didn't want to fess up to having made an error of judgement. Besides, they supported each other's appointments across a network of enterprises, and weren't about to fall over easily after years of mutual protection. But someone from Chicago finally spelled out that this time it would be worse for all of them if they didn't unite to act against one of them. Chains and weakest links. With arcane language and even more expensive third party help they were able to craft a staged exit strategy regretfully announcing the resignation of the CEO in the interests of investors. To ease the pain of this personal blush-making turn of events they decide it would be germane to let the individual out of this 'situation' with a $450 million severance payment, and a few toys. He resurfaced again a couple of years later. Meanwhile he had joined some of the members of the charitable coastal society, being careful to minimise his personal contributions and maximise his future revenue potential. Until today.

Since 9/11 Homeland Security had gone from zero to some 2000 agencies and enterprises all claiming to be contributing to the government's war on terror, whether it was being waged by infidels or inhabitants. Its scale was a reassuring sign that turf wars and scoop disputes would be taking up time, energy and budgets that could otherwise have been used to collect and collate data eventually leading to action, but that would be just too easy. So if you were a clean skin to start with, you had a much better chance of working with the system than against it, than if you were flagging the beginner's profile of a terrorist suspect. While some WASPy mother and her eight year old daughter were being patted down at a small provincial airport, you could get on with the real business of tackling issues in an unmolested way.

However beautiful the design, however good and appealing the overall concept, all aircraft have their own kinds of glitches. Some get fixed through later generations, some just characterise the version, and pilots and support teams build up their knowledge as they go along, like understanding a partner's foibles. It could be trimming issues, indicator mis-readings, any number of part combinations that conjured up unexpected challenges to operations in certain conditions. The astronaut summed it up when he said it was kind of interesting to be sitting on top of a Saturn rocket comprising three million separate parts, all of which had been tendered out to the lowest bidder, as the US ran its mission to allow Richard Nixon's signature to sit on a plaque on the Moon first.

Then some planes just got unlucky, and that was useful, like the Lear 35. Neat, efficient, numerous. Cuba Libre man knew the type, how it worked in detail, and where its surprising defects might come into play. He also knew that The Big Man had never grown out of responding to flattery and gifts. They were never bribes to him, simply open demonstrations of thanks or gratitude for the opportunity he gave people of having the privilege of being near him momentarily. There were no issues of self-esteem here. He had gone to the GA terminal about thirty minutes before take-off. He always took the chance to see if he could have some face time with potential new helpers and door-openers for his personal strategy. He tried to get to know many of the others on the weekend private shuttle runs. Some would talk, some declined. At one point, between smiles and small talk, one of the receptionists approached him with suitably deferential body language, and handed him a personalised embossed envelope. He excused himself and opened it, seeing it was from the company he had just gone sports fishing with. Apart from the boat, which he simply had to use as the fastest and best equipped in the fleet, he had the best support crew, and they enjoyed his tips. They knew he'd be back, that was good for other business, especially when the season got tight. The note basically said the cold north might be a little more enjoyable if he had a hamper to remind him why he should stay south more often. He smiled briefly and nodded to the receptionist. Sweet lobsters, swordfish, and a magnum of Krug he'd no doubt paid for anyway were on their way to be scanned and placed on the waiting plane.

The baggage and cargo handler escorted the gift, and they put it and its dry ice packaging in the baggage hold, ensuring its freshness in Manhattan later that evening. Payload and passenger were signed off, the flight plan sanctioned, and at 4.32 they were cleared for take-off and the climb out to the ocean, turning north east. After six minutes the control tower got the call saying the flight was moving out of local airspace, and the tower gave the radio frequencies and clearance to pass over to the next controller, saying its quick goodbye to the call-sign.

Time passed and then the aircraft was not responding to messages. Its flight path altitude was shifting slowly upwards from its filed plan. Homeland Security meant that shortly after, two F-16's were scrambled to go check. They intercepted the Lear 35 and reported no visible external damage to the airframe. They also reported no response to radio or visual signals. They did note a larger amount of frosting at the fuselage windows than normal at this altitude. The plane flew on,

212

gradually rising as its fuel burnt off and the craft grew lighter. Eventually, and after creeping just above its conventional working ceiling height, it was running on empty, and its spiral descent began. There was no need to take the plane out. It wasn't headed for any homestead. It crashed into the sea, and no unlucky sailor caught a boat full of jet either.

The crash investigation would eventually reveal a major cabin depressurisation malfunction, causing rapid hypoxia and the inability of the crew or passengers to do anything other than slip rapidly into oblivion, closely followed by the plane. It would be years before anyone figured the deleterious effect of dry ice on oxygen in the Lear 35's systems, starvation followed by rapid failure. No-one was going to remember anything about hampers and personalised messages. No-one knew there had definitely been something fishy going on.

Headline: *"Business Giant Killed in Ghost Jet Crash"*
Cue: *"Eight Miles High"*

***

J's Invisible Diary. Entry.

The latest phase runs have gone well. Most of the targets have disappeared without too many tears, without much in the way of lingering false sentimental memories and drawn- out practiced morbidity. No-one yet has drawn any palpable links to the deeds, the victims, or the variations in their demise, except perhaps their link to money – lots of it. No-one has sent out messages or threats or claims. That will all come along later after the second pilot part of the main long-running show, after what is starting to look like it may after all need a little teaser. It leaves almost all the inquisitive on the side of the law safely asleep in their predictable worlds.

It is only to be expected in today's world that a few people with envious onlookers will disappear from time to time, the perpetrators never being brought before the courts, a parallel world best left alone, apparent sins dealt with in an outsourced closed circle, if the events weren't simply accidents in the first place. There are so many conspiracy theorists around now, it actually makes it easier to do bizarre things and then have some crazies blame the government, or aliens, for what's going down. Most of the time it's now the private security operators who are starting to make some money from even closer protection assignments, with increasing physical security around houses and places of work, and on transportation. Anyone standing up and saying a pattern is emerging, and a driving force is behind it, at this stage, has about an equal chance of being deemed credible as those who said Osama bin Laden was going to be trouble back in the early 90's. It's just like other human patterns, people settling on the familiar as comfortable, and avoiding the improbable because it is less easy to predict.

Just like in the financial markets, no-one wants to know about power law distribution curves. No-one is getting compensated for throwing that cat amongst the Bell-curve pigeons, well, except for folks like Nassim Taleb. This is the conception of a new form of asymmetric warfare, or home-grown rebellion, where border patrols are irrelevant, because the force already exists within the domain. In most places where action is required, weapons and other means available for the tasks are already around in abundant innocence. There are only two visionaries here, driven by dollar lust, who recognise this as a potential opportunity for further enrichment. Like those entrepreneurs who built private security empires to support such programs as the 2003 invasion of Iraq, there looks to be a chance to make a home-grown killing, as it were. If you could get away with a private third force, that wasn't the police or army-based law enforcement operation, and have only an ill-defined and unprecedented relationship with the legal executive, there will be a big short term opportunity to clean up under the banner of 'supporting democracy at home'. If you could do that abroad, why not at home?

When will the governments tire of spending public money protecting rich folks, when they could pay for it themselves, through a well-resourced private operation, leaving constrained government funds to cover other, more widespread and socially inclusive crime-fighting demands, protecting regular citizens from themselves? Well, well, an elite force protecting the super-rich from their own pockets would appeal to no end of politicians looking to win elections, standing up and demonstrating how this could be a great way to free up tax payers money to protect ordinary folks from day to day threats.

By the time the lawyers and legislators catch up with it, enough money will have been amassed for the instigators to slip away and produce another loop-holed variation that will take even more years to tackle. Pure investment. Take the money out before the bubble is pricked, and leave others to worry when the bubble gum bursts on their faces.

*** *

Money-made power is like security – when you look closely at how it is put together there are always little flaws that can be exploited if you wait. Here is one who was in the job-swap club, to-ing and fro-ing from private to public sectors, spreading the word, ensuring light regulation would enable a clean sweep on profits when he returned to the private sector and its esoteric money-making schemes. He cast his private sector colleagues and performance in a favourable light whenever he met them as the states' counsellor. On the other end of the seesaw he was also able to exploit conditions that enable him to do things few others could. At one time, when he had made a move as a particularly influential private head honcho to an even more one in the government, he had been told that he wouldn't be able to retain his shares in his former operation – a conflict of interest. This was an irritating inconvenience. Mitigated to an extent by those who wanted him in government he won the day and was allowed to be exempt from any tax on gains as he relinquished the shares, a little gesture of goodwill welcoming the incoming genius. Then, after struggling through on the federal package, he was able to return to the private fold and make hay under the sunshine opportunities he had unlocked in his other position of power. It was a benign virtuous circle, and no-one was going to dissect him with any challenges. There was too much in the harvest for anyone to say they were being starved of opportunity.

But Big Men sometimes have an itch. This one occasionally wanted to play the Regular Guy, the little big man. Here was the one who responded to allegations of collective corporate greed back in his private domain by increasing bonuses after a ruinous episode of financial hubris, and boasting to the media about it. At the same time he cut corporate contributions to charitable causes by more than thirty per cent. What's the problem? He had come from a lowly background and in his terms had come good. No-one was going to win preaching to him about elitism. He said that making people lean made them tougher, and more determined to get up and out and on to the top, like he had. Whatever the corporate accusations he, The Man, carried on like he had done for years, showing he was still connected to his roots.

He would have the limo stop at the edge of the park, and for ten minutes, while his security guys kicked blades of grass and gazed around the clouds, he would watch the kids playing basketball on the fenced-in courts, all limbs and hoods and newly-coined words, kings of a space they didn't move far from. Then he'd say 'Now', and someone would produce two or three new balls from the car, and he'd throw

215

them into the court. In the early days the cool kids would ignore this son of a, not wanting anything to do with the rich mother, but the balls would always be taken up after he'd gone. Now, now he'd done time on their terms, he'd get a nod from one of the pack's top dogs, or a languid high five, and the rest of the hierarchy followed on, incorporating the bit of theatre into its daily rituals and its unspoken un-captured choreography. Now he even went into the court, but never did anything really dumb, like try to look the part, or feedback some of the words and phrases he'd heard. He knew he could never belong truly again, but he got off on thinking he was making a contribution to their potential, and he secretly liked being the crazy motherfucker they called him – a cool acknowledgement he was a fringe part of their golden circle. He thought it was so much less bullshit then getting the thanks of the museum parasites and wannabees forever seeking his contributions for some new piece of must-have artwork for the collections, oh and of course for the people.

Like so many times, the security men didn't like these moments when he was playing The Patroniser of the People. But since they didn't want their employer to lose the lucrative contract either, they worked at coming to terms with it, and the longer it went on, the more the creeping familiarity made them less concerned than the first time they ever responded to his desire to be the world's richest ball-boy. The familiar became the probable, and the improbable receded in their minds, fading away. Victory, off the field, comes to those who watch and wait. There would be an easing of vigilance because the threat level appeared to have shrunk. Building the profile of this guy's activities had paid off, as usual.

There was no point trying him at the apartment. If he died there it would be explained away as a heart attack with complications. At many events he was too closely surrounded, and not all of them deserved to go down. Unusually, he also appeared to have little taste for female exotica, and so his end, as it were, wouldn't come that way. It would be his purely selfish act of charity that would provide the ironic opening and the basis for his tragic denouement.

Over a couple of weeks two new kids had appeared on the block. They were treated to the usual rituals of suspicion by the semi-established crew, and then the slow initiation. Being able to show they could play good ball didn't slow this down. They were also able to use variations of fuck as a universal set of constants in the sub-languages being traded around the court. The new guys quickly became a part of the scene, no further questions. If anyone had listened closely they

216

might have heard Columbia or someplace south of Mexico in their voices, but no-one bothered to find out where they really came from, or where they lived. Like the others, they came and went, slinking in and out in hoods and trainers, signs and grunts and private phrases the codes of acceptance and the trades of respect. The taller kid, around fifteen and already over 6' seemed like a seasoned player, with an eye for trouble and a low flashpoint, not negative qualities round here.

He was being shown and promised enough dollars to keep it mostly in check for a while longer. He also knew he was going to be going away again soon.

It was a typical seasonal day. Grey, overcast, wet leaves drying out slowly in the park, and the court in session with its usual suspects, a few playing a game, making cool calls or making tricks, some leaning against the fence, smoking, or rehearsing menacing stares. Cyclists and joggers unconsciously upped their pace as they passed the court, sensing their presence was not entirely welcomed. The players liked that. Then cometh The Man, and his entourage in their own uniform, short hair and reflective shades even in the grey, with the tell-tale little curly wires going from behind their ears to somewhere inside their shirts. Jerks. But no-one got near them. He was now in the court, and had thrown the first of the three new balls up in the air. In customary thanks but no thanks fashion, it bounced twice and rolled across the ground, where it would be ignored for about five minutes now, as the main action of the game went on. At some point, while no-one seemed to be looking, the ball was suddenly the main event, and it had been taken up by the players now. It had become the new form of the pattern. The tall Latino moved up the side-line, looking as if he was waiting for a wide pass before making an attack on the basket. As he stepped along, he got closer to The Man, who was watching the ball being bounced on the other side of the court. The Latino pulled the stiletto from inside his jacket in a swift well-rehearsed move, and before anyone else saw anything, he had pushed it through the Big Giver's throat. As he began to spurt and stagger, the main thrust of the game closed in on the side-line, and a crowd of players swamped the scene. It was only then that the security guys noticed all was not strictly cool, and they started yelling Back Off. Move Away. Get Down. They pulled their preferred weapons from their cheap jackets, but no way were they going to shooting randomly in the park with all the kids around. They started to fall away, in all directions, they couldn't be contained. They were not scared of guns in the hands of these men. One of the security guys got to The Man, now on the ground, and a practised war zone eye saw there

217

was going to be no need to rush to save the dying client on the ground. The two other ear-pieced dudes tried to rally the remaining kids around, but it was difficult, and collectively and silently they reckoned they weren't going to be coming to any harm at the hands of private security guards on Manhattan soil. Maybe a different matter in their original homes, but not here. Only truly postal guys started firing off guns in NYC if they weren't wearing uniforms.

With the bluster and the adrenalin, the one cooler than the rest had dematerialised. He had backed unhurriedly through one of the entrances, walked slowly towards the bushes, and then turned, walking normally across the park, hood down, heading towards the Plaza hotel and the Apple Store on 5th Avenue, where he reckoned a new iPod touch wouldn't be denting his pay-off for this hit. Easy. Back where he'd started building his reputation when he was nine, he thought little of taking out targets for a fistful of dollars. Life was cheap. Death could be postponed for a little longer. He would be home via Miami in a couple of days. No-one in the basketball court knew who he was, except he had said his name was Vengador, the Spanish for Avenger, for a laugh.

The media had it down as a drug attack, a crazed angry illegal trying to rob one of New York's finest for the price of a fix, which had been heroically refused by the Big Man, who was only trying to help just such losers and victims in the community, a place he'd escaped from himself, only now he hadn't others would comment on the deteriorating state of the city, now that attacks in Central Park had returned to daylight hours.

The wife, the widow, was strong in her mournfulness. She had made him buy the coveted address and the apartment it came with on Park Avenue. Her experienced eye had judged it, and found it wanting. She had to devote time and energy over two years, together with $19 million dollars bringing it up to some form of respectability. She had pushed for them to buy their way into the Modern and Contemporary Art Market, vying with the other bankers and the lawyers and the hedge-fund managers for the adulation of gawpers staggered at the Shock of the New Prices auction houses were getting on behalf of the new generation of global wealthy badge-wearers. Giacometti now joined Picasso, Hirst joined Monet in the pantheon of phenomenally priced art. Sharks for sharks. She would put on her brave newly assisted face, and be strong, in New York and Palm Beach, for the sake of her husband's name, and their joint reputation. New invitations would be arriving soon. Such tragedy and sorrow.

218

Headline: *"Banker Stabbed in Central Park"*
Cue: *"Can't Buy Me Love"*

***

It was cold outside. It was dark. He'd already driven for three hours and wanted to be there. The French auto-route had an encrustation of traffic cones, its two northbound lanes keeping traffic huddled in the glow of brake lights, stop, start, the November damp promising a freezing fog. Six forty five. Finally, Valence took its place at the top of the road signs, and the car followed its hirer's signals. Toll paid, the window re-sealed from the cold, there was just the small point of following the Satnav's recommended exit from the busy roundabout, and looking for signs of familiarity from the first visit ten years ago. There were few people on the streets walking. The navigation system had continued to insist on him going straight ahead, about three hundred metres. He did, and there it was. The restaurant and Hotel Pic. Somebody appeared from inside before he had turned the ignition off, looking to ease his entrance, taking care of bags and keys, welcoming the stranger from the cold and the wet. This was a good sign, none of the aloofness that comes with the word, "full".

Do you want a place for dinner as well?

Yes. Dinner and a good room.

Well, we hope so, monsieur.

The greeting ritual went smoothly, the presentation of the room, the agreement about a time for dinner, and the registration. No problem.

Finally in the room, he removed his clothes, put on the generous bath-robe, unpacked the essentials and fresh clothes for dinner, took a beer, set a bath, and sighed peacefully. The long road was forgotten.

There were three steep wooden steps that led up from the tiled bathroom floor to the edge of the deep bath, and nothing to hold on to. Reception probably kept an eye on arrivals – the old or injured would only worsen their circumstances by attempting to conquer this piece of design, and in many countries inspectors would have condemned the feature, wagging fingers and filling in forms to protect the innocent from this aesthetic danger. The next step would be to have another set of checkers and tickers make pronouncements on the wall coverings, the paint, the bedcovers, the furniture, and the artworks. The intrusion of the ignorant masquerading as Protectors was becoming more and more pervasive. People shouldn't be allowed to trust their own judgements anymore. That yellow is just too powerful for the tranquillity a traveller needs. Eventually the shade of green of the trees' leaves outside would be pronounced inappropriate or otherwise disturbing and, failing modification, the trees would have to be destroyed, so removing the shady courtyard beyond the bedroom window. It's not enough that you pay a fortune to stay in a room you know will fight your sense of decorum as only those rooms do whose owners occupy the upper echelons of restaurant star-systems. No – you need help. It's been decided that here too there has to be someone to watch over you. The presence of all-pervading care would continue to announce itself in markers and signs all the way from the room to the restaurant – fire-exits, cautions in elevators, steps in public passageways with highlighted edges, notices about the impossibility of smoking, warnings about the chef's use of local natural ingredients, items themselves simply waiting to pounce on innocent guests' allergies and their ambulance-chasing litigators. It was all for your own good.

There was a time when you sat down at a table such as this and savoured every moment. The invitation to take an aperitif, the presentation of the menus, the perusal of the wine-list, the expectation aroused by the amuse bouche, and then the commanding of the dishes themselves, a prolonged comparison with the memories of your imagination and all those other comparative treats from dinners past. But today, other things trickle in, voices and questions, doubts and criticisms, and while you gaze down on fleeting miniature masterpieces of scallops, of truffles and aspic, diced and patterned vegetables and spices, someone spoils it all with a Sunday magazine comparison. Do you realise you could take five people from Venice to London and back for the price of that? And then there is the other side. The ones who go on about how they sipped Fijian bottled water in Reykjavik, while the mussels joined them after their flight from New Zealand, and the Madagascan vanilla flavoured the fish sauce. Meanwhile the Condrieu tastes better here for its lack of travel, and you don't have to hear endlessly about the reviewers' omniscience about anything from Socrates to Sybaritics. Looking around revealed the table of celebrants, another birthday party, the anniversary couple, the restaurant critic, alone, trying to be serious, the business couple negotiating their way towards a post-prandial deal. Some German, mostly French, no Americans. There was a flurry of waiterly activity, the coming and going of savours, culminating in the half-expected surprise of the special birthday cake and its enormous sparkler, cascading over a twist of chocolate – the chef's delight, a reflection of the professional passing on of the gift of information from reception to the kitchen. Here were people who understood the purpose of pleasure, the last bastion of the role of service, so far from the stiff defenders of other establishments where you were chastised for not sharing their degree of formal severe worship of the offerings sent down from the maestro's mountain. If ambrosia was meant to be treated so miserably, then best to stay away from so-called heavenly delights and stick to the sauces of the devil.

The stars here were the dishes themselves, not the other things in the room. There were worse ways of spending an evening alone. Early tomorrow the drive to Geneva would begin. Happy birthday, Michael.

***

For some, it was about the internal combustion engine. Well, alright, it was about shaped metals and leather, performance statistics, rarity. And the industry for which automobiles were originally purposed bred a sub-industry of auto-statics, or very occasional runners. Cars were talked up, worshipped for who had driven them, or sat in them, what records they had set, anything that added value to them that simply wasn't in another example, a clone with no provenance. The sub industry split into a further two parts. There was the concourse finish section, which took old cars and restored them to a level greater than when they had first been born, and then there was the fake industry, where a whole new car was built around one dubiously original part, given the credentials of a different or destroyed one, like a car witness protection program, and then sold to a customer as the original of the breed, or type or example, at a premium price. Forgeries in steel and other substances were a major business.

Just like any other markets where there were fluctuations of cash available, like with guitars that had once been played by someone once, a car that had once been owned and not even driven or even sat in by the owner, maybe because at the time they didn't have a driving licence, or were living somewhere else, which became a legend in its own right, and kept being sold, on and on, transferring some bizarre kudos onto its new owner. John Lennon's Ferrari, James Bond's Aston Martin DB5, a real car driven by a fictional hero, commanding millions. Or the Enzo Ferrari, which if you had one, you weren't supposed to drive. But that was just one level. There were others who collected one marque, or versions of one model, or whole ranges from Hispano Suizas to Hummers, keeping them on heated floors in temperature controlled garages, like so many Egyptian sarcophagi, waiting for the adoration of future generations, sculptures from a

221

petroleum past. Look what's here, as the lights came on in underground caverns, and over a hundred cars in discrete spaces showed off their curves and preserved skins, the private real-sized toy collections of drivers and devotees, building their fleets with care, while city showrooms came and went, surfing on fashions and cyclical markets. At one time Florida held a wondrous bundle of pre-owned cars and restored splendours, many of them coming to market through drug busts and confiscations, with blind eyes being turned to aftermarkets by judges and cops, letting the money fuel the growth and interest, good for the state economy. For others, the focus was simpler. Pick a marque. Any marque, and let's turn to the family resemblances of Rolls Royce and Bentley. Excellent choices, with well-recorded idiosyncrasies, log books, warehoused unique spare parts, and well-known owners.

Prices varied dramatically for special or little-used examples, and sometimes there were spectacular one-off opportunities open to those close to the action. The replacement of the Hong Kong Peninsula hotel fleet after a flood, or The Sultan of Brunei's younger brother being relieved of his six hundred vehicles, waiting to be taken up by dealers and collectors, keen to keep their own dynasty alive and profitably kicking. Performance and reliability were irrelevant compared to prestige, the comfort of unique leathers and wood trims. Cars whose owners grew rapidly tired of the canary yellow or brite-white versions were ready to have them shipped off at the end of a holiday to others in other markets, where two-tone finishes were considered cool, or where bullet-proofed versions were treated with even more souped-up engines capable of giving the driver and his passengers a useful level of protection and potential escape velocity. It turned out to be convenient that Antonio had a penchant for the big saloons. Those he collected sat in garages in the cities he spent most time in, plus an assortment across his several homes. His two personal drivers were always ready to fly in advance to meet him, pick up one of the machines from the full time technicians who fostered them, and that meant careful planning to keep ahead of his often changing schedule. Madrid or Geneva, there would always be a car and its designate driver there. The ageing cars turned up ticking over nicely, warm creatures, like fireside hunting dogs. One of the drivers lived in London, and as part of the package that made unsocial demands of him, he got to drive any of the cars there as his when he wasn't travelling for The One. He considered there were more onerous duties in the world than this. As a buyer of new versions of the car, Antonio also had access to several dealers, as well as the sourcing

222

and assembly factories, and knew a number of people who had given substantial parts of their lives to the cars and owners like him. He too was a living legend among builders, sellers, re-modellers, service and after care personnel, the whole lineage. Some were sitting on a fortune of spare parts, like whole left hand or right hand drive conversion kits for earlier models, with leathers and woods and lacquers kept pristine. It was still tough trading in the prestige business, and reputations were fiercely built and protected. Tips were passed on to loyal drivers, and perpetual mechanical or electrical niggles that came with the breed were shared around the family, the nagging warning light that indicated nothing but the sensitivity of the light itself, the use of essential and varied oils for the smooth running of suspensions and other systems absent on most cars, the general loving maintenance of foibles that kept the thoroughbreds apart.

Specialists always had further contributions to make, from designing interiors to sourcing materials, from dyes to finishes, from fuel pumps to air-conditioning systems, turbo chargers to exhausts, from cushioning to protection. There were many secrets behind the exterior of these creatures.

And it came to pass, that one such beast of the field was due some care and attention. A preferred creature, she served her master faithfully on trips in and around Geneva, never going too far, always blending in with the quiet celebration of affluence the Swiss enjoyed – subtle colours, quiet speed, little noise. As Antonio was still away in Asia for days, the coddled car could be safely removed and restored without any irritation from its owner. It was time to bring the interior back to life, a professional restoration, tweak the power and the still remarkable torque. The car had barely done 10,000 kilometres in ten years, so was barely run in, and was cleaner under the bonnet than in the ebony trimmed and Cohiba infused cabin. Antonio, The One, did not like light woods, and despite the weight, had bought or fitted all his cars and planes with dark hardwoods, each offering a kind of seamless transition as he moved from air to car to club to home. All were members of the herd of this particular Dark Horse. The joy of the cars was that they could be built to absorb all kinds of undesirable interference. Unwanted looks or sounds. Onslaughts from bullets to ram-raids, these modified carriages would take good care of their occupants up to a not totally unreasonable level of aggression in relatively civilised environments. To keep this level of service also required specialists, and that required input from people in places that were slightly less fortified than the cars themselves. That was the opportunity. The cars protected you from the outside. Cars were cocooned in heat and covers and protective polishes, like they were in the master's own facilities, but apart from that, to a professional not interested in stealing a vehicle, they were kept in commercial garages for the restoration work. Major deterrent doors rolled down and clicked shut at night, keeping the cars from being rolled into trucks and spirited away to some waiting crime host who could afford a new one but got a cheap thrill from boasting to his friends how he'd freed the beast from some legitimate capitalist worthy.

The weak point was not the workshop, but the sales and service operation, the front of house show, and the come-and-worship set-up of the conversion-to-sales operation. As with many dealers, there was a loose link between sales and service, with shared facilities for the two separate waiting areas. There was also a crew of assistants who combined talents – in service it was the efficient professionals who justified their bills through technical blind-siding, and in sales it was people who manage to combine obsequiousness with unavailability, depending on how they read the prospects' real buying power, or whether they really knew their established customers and their preferences. From the service reception area Michael could see several cars in different states of undress and repair, a couple waiting to be delivered or collected, one or two up on ramps, a couple being virtually rebuilt, and several being spruced up for sale, and almost ready to be turned over to the stage show in the sales area. He was able to wander into the service area unmolested, as he had surmised, and found it easy to get into the back of the dusty late '70s saloon in its tired combination of banana and caramel exterior, and a faded white leather interior. The vehicle had clearly not received a lot of attention or interest lately. It helped that the car was jacked up and against the side-wall, so no-one was suddenly going to want to move it. It wasn't in any through passage area, and next to it were a pair of almost wedged-in Bentley Turbos, not immediate priorities, but they would find supporters with tight budgets and a lot of enthusiasm, usually failing to appreciate fully how much these badges of respect could cost if anything serious went wrong, outside their majorly low service interval of six thousand miles. The workshop and sales office closed at six pm. Computers were put into hibernation, and the operation was wound down for the night, the intruder alarms coming into play as the garage doors clicked and locked shut. That's what they were – intruder alarms. If you were already inside you weren't a problem they were looking for.

He waited for what he considered was long enough for the staff not to bother returning for something they might have forgotten, deciding it could wait until tomorrow, and he extricated himself from the neglected car. CCTV cameras were also pointing towards the garage doors and the reception area, leaving the workshop free to move around in. The target car was in the middle of the activity zone, being worked on, but not yet ready for the final sprucing up and polishing act. In being transformed, it was immobile, and so, unlocked. Pieces of leather and wood, trims, were dotted around the floor, and the interior, as the car's Club Room was being re-decorated. The beauty of this model was the way the air-conditioning controls for the rear of the compartment were configured. Not content with overall temperature control, each rear seat passenger could adjust airflow and temperature to suit their preferred micro-climate. He knew as he looked down that all he had to do was what he had done before, practicing on a similar model. From inside his breathable fashionable jacket he took out the small multi-tool that would allow him access to what he needed. Behind the airflow nozzles he was able to insert and fix the two flexible cylinders. Each had two in-built micro-dust triggers, and they were as powerful as any other receiver in this car. Since he also knew this vehicle had not been bullet-proofed or fitted with jamming devices to deter any eavesdroppers, he was sure any signal put out would be well received. Triggers that only responded to a signal meant that low constant power or unreliable batteries were not required to maintain a connection between the signaller and the device. This little operation took no more than thirty minutes. That was it until the morning, and since he was in some of the world's most comfortable snooze zones, he made himself at home back in the banana boat, and set himself the vibrate alarm for twenty minutes before the first guy would turn up to open the garage with typical punctiliousness, curling up on the plastic seat covers which he would dispose of in the morning as he passed the general waste bin.

Once the doors were open, and the operation was gearing up for another day of care and pampering, he watched the team settle down into its routine, greeting one or two customers with cars being dropped off for servicing, and then he waited for the lull before any prospects showed, a time for the staff to hit the first coffee before getting down to the serious stuff. After 10am, with a couple of people in the showroom, and the mechanics with their heads down inside or under the cars, he stepped smoothly out of the car he had bedded down in, and walked slowly and naturally towards the reception area and the exit. If confronted he would feign innocence about not being aware he had crossed some invisible line, and he was just really interested in one of the Turbos and wanted a closer look before bothering anyone for further details. He looked like he could afford a new car, so there would be no suspicion about his intentions, just another prospect who had to get near to the beloved creatures, a pull they had seen many many times. He also had a back-up story about buying something for a colleague and enthusiast who had just secured a major contract for his business. No-one got to see this performance, and he exited the showroom unattended. The cameras were only keen to see people coming in, not leaving, so all they saw was his back. Who would have thought anyone would have wanted to spend a night in the garage? Anyone remotely caught up in the closing sequence would have phoned or triggered an alarm to be released. It wasn't logical to cover that option. It was assumed the premises were empty when the doors closed. All that left was more waiting time.

Michael got the message two weeks later. Antonio was in town, and he was being driven around in the re-launched cherished possession. Michael ended his overnight meditative rest in the lakeside village of Yvoire, another traveller taking pictures of the romanticised place, with its restaurants full of lake perch and higher altitude wines, and headed back along Lac Leman and across into Geneva.

Antonio didn't like entertaining in his apartments when he was on business. He didn't want people looking at his antiques and artworks – they were for his personal pleasure alone. So he took to dining out, often greeting people for cocktails at the Hotel Kempinski. The staff knew him well enough to discreetly cordon off an area for him when he was there, and a seamless service measured up to the generous tips that had never failed to materialise in his presence. Michael watched the activity from his place near the bar, nursing a glass of house champagne and reading a spread of half-day old international newspapers, two mobile phones in front of him on the table, currently muted but twinkling the silent passing on of messages and news. He looked like a regular global corporate traveller away from home, passing through.

The habits kicked in again. At 7.45pm, Antonio would close proceedings, or make his departure plans plain, and he would pass through the lobby and into the back seat of his purring cat, the driver closing the door and returning to the driving seat to go God knows where. Third time lucky, he thought. It was Thursday, a sporadically wet unmemorable Spring day and evening, lights reflecting off the lake and pavements alike, the throb of the fountain and its wind-blown spray. He got up sufficiently slowly and behind Antonio for no-one to notice anything out of the ordinary. He had paid for the drink and looked to be heading out to a rendezvous of his own. Just before he left the hotel lobby, he turned the cap of what looked like his Mont Blanc fountain pen, and the signal to the car was sent. The dust stirred, and the micro-machines came to life, coolly setting about their business. Three minutes and six blocks later, the cylinders pushed out their compressed gas, and within another forty seconds Antonio was on his way to a different kind of rendezvous altogether. It was too late to raise a smile on the faces of the hundreds of thousands of destitutes whose money he had taken in property scams across Spain, Portugal, Florida, Dubai, and lately, Thailand, the endless promises of returns on investments, and unbelievable mortgages that were just that.

Michael took a cab, asked for a restaurant, and dialled up a piece of music from one of his phones, through his state-of-the-art ear-pieces. He knew someone who would enjoy the irony.

Headline: *"Property Tycoon Dies in Street"*

Cue: *"Classical Gas"*.

***

After four days of snow, and very low visibility, the ski resort was iced over for Christmas like some scene-opener in an old Disney movie, or a set of sculptures at an extravagant party. Somehow the bad weather suddenly decided to take a vacation too, and the morning of Christmas Eve greeted the people with clean blue skies and crisp air, the clouds pulled back like curtains clipped to the distant mountain tops. For once the snow ploughs had rested, few lights criss-crossing the pistes through the night, and those opening shutters with weary eyes were surprised by the sunlight's brightness and the glare of the snow. It was time to wait until the early risers rushing to the lifts to get the early snow had gone, when the queues would become more tolerable. It was a leisurely breakfast, coffee and fresh croissants, maybe just a slosh of cognac in the second cup, and then one for the morning. After that came the performance that went into putting on this season's must-be-seen-in ski-wear, the colours, the goggles, the boots, and later the bindings and the customised skis, waiting in the hands of the ski escorts a short snow-mobile ride away from the eight-bedroomed chalet, just far enough away to miss the noise from most of the après-ski revellers, yet visible enough to be coveted by the very same as they looked up and around the resort. It was a day for a full set of runs, morning and afternoon, followed by the torch-lit descent into the village, which Torsten would watch, and the de rigueur visit from Santa to brighten the children's eyes yet further.

Torsten always went with three others. In this case, in the mountains, the escorts were life-long skiers, and trained in close protection as well. The local authorities would not countenance closing ski-lifts for the paranoid mighty, so they had to take their chances with the hoi-polloi, cushioned from contact by the bulk of the bodyguards. Torsten was no great skier, but the carefully selected routes made the evening stories of his exploits seem full of controlled risk and derring-do, a stage-managed performance, and no video evidence. The escorts tried to make him feel good, but he wouldn't admit he knew he was never going to get really good at this pursuit. He was even happier on water, on decks, on waves, with a different kind of crew, and a different kind of wetness in your face, two or maybe three weeks a year, max. But the time had come around again, and he had to be seen here, the ritual credibility rating being maintained, like it had for the last four years. By January 3rd, he'd be in St Barts, and the cold would be forgotten. That was the plan.

Towards the end of the morning he'd made it down through a third set of spread out woods, and as he slowed, winded, he saw the black Range Rover pulling off the mountain road to escort him back to the village up the hill, and the pre-booked table at the restaurant, the Montrachet acceptably cool, and the just flown-in caviar waiting to be spread on blinis and slipped down with sour cream. Ski-snacks.

In the afternoon the helicopter took him further up the mountains, and in the gentle slopes of an indentation close to the summit of the range, he skied on virgin snow. The helicopter was able to pick him up again, and he descended with the pilot after a little mountain-top cruising. The security escorts had been cleared to have some fun and make their off-piste descent back to the chalet. Torsten was soon out of his afternoon kit and into the layers of après-ski after the sauna and shower, all spruced up and after-shaved by five thirty. Other family members and guests went through their own little rituals, each with stories to tell, and with their own security shadows handing over to the next detail. Some of the closer family guests were offered the service too, but most declined, happy with the hospitality and believing they were far too dull to warrant any adverse attention at the resort. As in previous years, the young ones were getting excited about the torchlight parade, and they left in good time to get a ride up the mountain. Others walked to get good spots on the slopes to watch the descent, capturing it on phones and cameras, while the Christmas moon began its ascent from behind the mountains, and the snow drifted off to sleep. Torsten knew he would be seeing clips and stills from the parade from every which way, and as long as he was there at the end, near where Santa would show, to hug the torch bearers, there was time now for another tradition. This was the one where he slipped into the bustling cocktail bar, catching Henri's eye, and nodded it was time. Within fifteen minutes, the glass mountain had been built, and three dozen bottles of Crystal had been disgorged into the glasses. They were handed out to everyone in the bar, an unacknowledged little gift from the anonymous smart donor. That's what Christmas is for, isn't it? He put out to no-one in particular.

Since 6pm, in an apartment opposite the clock tower, facing the town square and the spot where Santa would appear, he had been patiently waiting. The apartment had been patiently reserved months before, for two weeks, and was still virtually pristine. It would be at least two more days before anyone turned up to give it the little wipe over and the fresh linen. From under the gable, the window opened beautifully, and the sound of the piped Christmas music drifted in from the village PA system. Because the building followed the square, its slab sides presented three faces, and the narrowest, with only two windows width, belonged to the apartment, so window watchers elsewhere in the building wouldn't be able to see him. In the square, most eyes were looking at where the torch parade would descend, or at where Santa would show, or at the now rising moon in the south east.

Alain blended in with the shadows. He had elected to give a quiet performance, and had practised his role in safe havens for some time, working on angles and timing, air pressure and weights, and any number of other variables from weather visibility to temperatures. He was ready. Not nervous, this was like the end of a season, a friendly game on a winning champion side, familiarity and relief tinged with a touch of sadness as he anticipated the post-adrenalin drain.

Torsten stepped out of the bar, and, reunited with his fresh team of escorts, walked up the gentle slope towards the end of the torch parade and the beginning of the Santa spectacle, where the fireworks would kick off later.

The joy of repetition and muscle meant Torsten was able to secure his customary vantage point, and he knew that in ten minutes he would be greeting excited skiers full of tales about their torch-lit adventure. All was in place. At 6.30pm the carillon sounded its sensual half-hour chimes and song. Two seconds after the first chime Alain pulled the trigger on the crossbow, and the specially crafted needle dart left the instrument at 400 feet per second, taking next to no time to make its journey across the square and into the forehead of Torsten, just below

229

the conveniently situated branding on the hat he was wearing. The escorts had no chance, and all they saw that made them aware of any trouble was the slowly collapsing Torsten beside them. It could have been a heart attack in the first milliseconds. No bangs, no echoes, no mass panic. He was caught on the way down, now enshrouded by the escorts, and onlookers barely noticed in all the other action. One called in for assistance. A couple thought the guy had fainted, drunk or ill perhaps.

He had withdrawn the titanium crossbow and closed the window almost before Torsten had begun to fall. In less than a minute he had dismantled the machine, and it now looked like a kind of executive desk toy or puzzle, a set of parts that didn't immediately suggest anything with a recognisable structure could be configured from it. The pieces easily fitted into the several pockets of his dark grey and silver snowboarding jacket, and within a further two minutes he had descended from the apartment, down through the car park, and out and onto the skateboard he had left outside a bar. He looked like anyone else off to a Christmas gathering somewhere, which he was. He sang the *William Tell* overture in his head, and quipped at how Torsten had taken his final bow on the stage of corporate greed. Miners may moan. Even with a dead wife, he had learned nothing. It was time for him to be extracted.

Headline: *"Mining Magnate in Ski Resort Tragedy"*
Cue: *"Silent Night"*

***

In some places, those who take things up early thrive, mastering new things, new adopters, and they make off with the spoils of their bravery and vision before things get too familiar and every day. In other places, what they call the laggards take on things after they've spent ages watching others do it first, sorted out the glitches, paid for the pioneering and the innovation and the risk and the cachet. Now these latecomers just wanted the tried and tested version, not the expensive thing the idiots bought first, with suitable sets of bells and whistles, at a fraction of the launch price. Luddites didn't even try, rejecting the last best thing, befuddled by change and its pace, or just tired of it all. Stop the world. We didn't get where we are today by adapting that kind of thing. In between extremes, and not all along the way, people still rejected change for good, hanging on to their smaller prejudices and perspectives and tired clichés about better the devil you know. Why would anyone ever want such and such, and it won't work anyway? So the tide of technology meets its curtailers and King Canutes on the shore. Why would you ever want to walk along a street with daft things in your ears playing stupid music? Why wouldn't you want to just look good in your suit and tie and hat and the admiring glances of others?

Cut to a generation given a mobile phone number at birth, like a lifelong national insurance or social security number, without the stigma, where you were never far away from a cloud of digital data, and electronic DNA holding you up to the scrutiny of the great and not so good, the Beholders, depending on where you were coming from. Fingerprints were really short on detail compared to digitally available forensic filing and archiving and mapping you out. That was where Milos had had the vision. There were digital fortresses all around, in deserts and under mountains, in loosely connected cells away from highly targeted centres, in open and closed societies, storing storing storing. He decided to set up something else, a niche for a particular type of publicity-shy client. He established a discreet bank, an identity bank, like a Swiss bank, with all its numbered anonymity, only exclusively off-shore. It was a place, or places, where you could store things, personal information, ideas, algorthythms, formulae, so that when you were cloned or otherwise scammed or had your identity stolen, you had the means to prove your identity and ownership and retrieve yourself and your ideas, without any staff needing to know any details about you. Levels of encryption and access made sensitive government agencies look naïve. It interested the legitimate and paranoid, but also those who desired less public scrutiny, like drugs and arms traders, traffickers and money launderers. Even if you could have got your hands on data, it would take as long as a flight to the stars to decipher it, which wouldn't be troubling any human being during their lifetime. In the beginning Milos set up the facility through one or two friends around the Mediterranean, who liked the idea of a form of digital identity insurance outside of governments. He was proud of the idea, and the level of back-up, but careful not to boast about impregnability and permanence, knowing how that could cost lives as well as business – arrogance attracting unwanted challenges. It was a personalised distant cousin of the businesses his father and uncle had set up some twenty years before, anticipating the need for digital data of any sort to be stored and accessed around the world. They had seen an opportunity to do something lucrative in out of the way locations, and as long as the infrastructure could be set up, their sites consistently enjoyed high yields, and they found themselves welcomed into small

231

communities where the anonymous buildings or entrances to hidden structures brought jobs and revenue and a future to otherwise dying groups, places that had formerly attracted interest as areas to extract ores and minerals, or to grow olives and vines, or flowers. The little premium business flourished. The fatherly brothers had done well, and played a reasonable game. No-one was going to punish you for the legitimate creation of wealth and happiness, until you passed the point on the graph where the unjustifiable greed alarm co-ordinates kicked in. It could even be tempered, as surmised, by significant contributions to others' well-being. The brothers were good givers, perhaps following their favourite diaspora a little too closely at times, but you can't have everything. Milos, on the other hand, had enjoyed a little too much largesse, and although he was ostensibly the lynch pin of the new operation, there was significant input and oversight from others. A typical Milos week was forming. He'd jet to one of the offshore islands to go clubbing and sample the latest batch of cocaine, playing women like decks of cards, sometimes tossing them away violently, a process usually eased with money and subsequent soft-talking. For role models it looked like Milos was focussing on the sons of Saddam Hussein or Moamar Gaddafi, swanning around and being big, knowing he was living on his father's and uncle's name, pushing for advantage all the time. His father thought he knew his son and could lessen the macho elements over time as he matured in the business, but sadly there was little that could be done to rewire the psychopathic elements of the offspring's brain.

***

To enliven the variations of the Message, and to give the interpreters occasional benign alternatives to analyse, it was decided to add some additional criteria to the mix. Those who had not yet entirely sinned could simply be given grace, a warning about the dangers of stepping outside the new desired parameters of behaviour. Premature death in some cases might have seemed a little, well, pagan. What was needed was a form of early warning system, a kind of yellow card, a metaphorical sin bin, so in future, softer messages could initially be sent out from digital pulpits, and fire and brimstone didn't have to be the first thing you met after crossing the line. A suitable form of caution was selected.

Inevitably, in Mylos' world, which had little space for other contenders in the field of Greatest Of All Time, this precise form of conceit contained the seeds of its own destruction. Inspiration was self-derived. Like old circus posters, the Incredible, the Indestructible, the Unbeatable, were all claims that pulled in the crowds. For a few, knowing how it was all put together, how the magic really worked, what was the heart of Milos' matter, was the power of the draw. Beating your head against doors wasn't going to open them any time soon. Toying with high levels of encryption was too tedious. No. There would have to be some other form of Trojan, and that was where J re-entered the frame.

***

J had spent years building ways to keep people and objects out of things. He had moved from physical barriers, walls, fences, missile systems, to less visible barriers, codes, keys, firewalls, and had a labyrinthine mind full of labyrinthine solutions for a wide range of problems and organisations. Being such a constructor meant he also had the power to be a great destroyer, since he was the sole key-holder of many systems. Like construction engineers building in the explosives to bring down their own sky-high creations, he was an artist who saw the potency of latent destruction within creation.

When looking at challenges, he looked at motives. He looked at whether people were asking the right questions. 'How do you break this?' was maybe a less useful question than 'How do you break what made this?' The first sight of a tank, the wholeness of its noisy monstrous lumbering on a broken landscape may have induced fear initially, but closer inspection by the brave and inquisitive revealed flaws in detail, like the vulnerability of its exhausts or track, which could be exploited to bring the beats to a burning death or standstill, simmering in their immobility. J would not place bombs in things himself. It was not his nature. But having the means to collapse structures in previously unseen ways, he would share his findings. He sat in the tradition of those who, in things like the Manhattan Project, discovered themselves waking up one day with a great advancement in science, and the simultaneous awareness of their new role as the Destroyers of things.

***

Milos' idea and its early manifestation were neat. The encryption levels were formidable, as a cynic might pronounce. Core servers sat in well-protected cages, far from the crowds, and data centres looked the part – they were hidden, disguised, un-enticing for most. Yet they still left footprints, thermal ones. Earlier centres swallowed great gobs of power, and electrical equipment turned it into unwanted heat. The physics was undeniable. Heat needed outlets, and hot gear needed cooling. Input. Output. This was the weak part in this chain. Research showed the suppliers of support machinery to keep the queen bees being hosted at workable temperatures. Fire suppressants, continuity and back-up systems, monitors and checks, all were there.

It was relatively simple. Forget the identity data holding servers. Hack into the service systems of the air-conditioning supplier, who supplied units to all manner of businesses and locations. Business resilience, whatever the claims, was not going to be 100% anytime soon, as the data centres learned how to grow. Entry was going to be by one of these back doors. Cool. Or the opposite in fact. The air-con systems were designed to control the heating and cooling system up and down according to external temperatures and demand on the data centres' products themselves. The untouched, un-hackable data hearts were going to carry on running, hotter and hotter, as the cooling systems and their inter-related alarms were sequentially indisposed. No fires were started, so no chemical extinguishers were triggered, but slowly, key machines began to get sluggish and crashed. Most were picked up by back-up across other facilities, in time, but one or two weren't. Key calls and electronic requests were made during the fragile period, the aim being to establish if any significant data or identities had been compromised. The system was definitely down for a crucial time, and who's counting in these situations – any down time is bad time?

The subtle leaking of the flaw and the evidence to support it soon made its way around the burgeoning competitive business, and there was a flurry of client cancellations, withdrawals, threats of lawsuits and worse, as the search for more reliable partners began. A little damage had been done. Assurances would have to be made, costing money. It was a warning tap, a new form of reputation management, and Milos had discovered there was no ultimate defence shield. Fortunately, he benefitted from his father's and uncle's benevolence, and a suggestion he found a better way to play the game. He had better turn down the God aspect of his behaviour, and put something of what he'd taken out back, like his family had. This time he didn't wake up dead, but he remained on the List for now, being monitored.

***

It took months for Kashif to come anywhere near an idea that linked all the recently departed to the website that had gone out and then disappeared. There were so many crazy sites and crazy notions out there, threatening all kinds of actions on envied rich Westerners, that it was almost impossible to get anyone to accept the notion that, beyond a short burst of coincidental criminal activity, there might be something more strategic and unifying behind the deaths of the women. It was considered too far-fetched that even those determined to level the decadent West would have decided that taking out a few conspicuously consuming Princesses would have any impact on behaviour and attitudes. Why go down such a convoluted path to make a moral point? Wouldn't it just have been easier to bomb the catwalks at fashion shows? The mostly males around Kashif thought he was away with the fairies, as they did about many, if not all of the PR Group's so-called insights, even when they turned out to be well-founded. No, the Establishment wanted something that met their expectations, disaffected Middle Eastern types madly martyring themselves for the sake of Islam.

Kashif didn't let go of his theories. Like before, it was what *wasn't* there where clues revealed themselves. For him, the very absence of trails, the absolute lack of capture or conviction of the perpetrators, suggested the hand of co-ordination. He was about to think the women were in fact a decoy for something else when they stopped disappearing.

As the men began to be toppled, it was another in the PR Group who was tasked with seeing if there were any links between the deaths, and in the early absence of even a crazy website to explain the actions, it was harder still to fathom a cause that harmonised the action. The only link remained a mystery – that no-one was being caught for what was happening.

There would also be a further protective element in the finally refined enterprise. This would be to demonstrate that patience would bring its own reward. The refined message would spread differently this time. There was no point in thinking the wrong people had been targeted or left out, or that the perpetrators had now exhausted their avenues of approach. But perhaps the Message was still too subtle to cause any seismic shifts in behaviour. It was the old problem that faced advertisers for government messages, like the Don't Drink and Drive campaigns – they never worked because viewers always thought the

235

messages applied to others, not them. Why should you rich folk get taken out of the equation – it's only the Bad Uns that get hit. Furthermore, it was time to move beyond the original geographical centres, and take it global. The ultimate kick-off, with a couple of twists, would be fine.

***

Cheng Lee grew up hearing only half-exaggerated tales about his up and down hero, the man across the water, the legendary Constructor, Donald Trump. He'd learned about how the man honed his craft under his father's wing, how he learned to do deals and cultivate big chances, how he reflected his approach to life with the partial resurrection of Atlantic City, how he fell from fortune and grace, only to rise again, like his many branded towers, leaving a high-rise legacy and a string of wives across the States. Once upon a time it was only in America where someone so unscrupulous could be elected to be the role model on a nationwide TV show encouraging young entrepreneurs to out-do each other publicly to claw to the top. It was like putting the Borgias in charge of the Vice Squad. Here was a rhino claiming acute personal sensitivity, a stone and glass sculpture of the times. Cheng Lee was charmed. He had animal cunning and, if you believed in that kind of thing, luck, the stars all aligned, the signs and symbols supporting his meteoric rise from backstage to the microphone, from shantyville to gold-tapped penthouses, the new Emperor of Building. He too had intuited a shift in the atmosphere, a turning away from a part of the past, and the seeding of desire for a towering personal future. China, and Shanghai particularly, took into its embrace the corrupting influence of foreign treasure seekers, and had woken up again to stretch its new underworld muscles to create a more fulfilling future on a much wider stage. There was no way this version was simply a clone of imported models. There was still a heavy-handed approach to kick-starting the New Machine, and many in government tried to exercise major controls over the country's new fitness regime. But it was becoming clearer that those who knew best how to manage this would be getting top-billing on both the domestic and world stages.

Cheng Lee was also fortunate enough to have made the acquaintance of others who knew a thing or two about power and corruption, tactics and strategy. *The Art of War*, *The Prince*, *The 48 Laws of Power*, and other books had all been studied by the hungry young fortune seeker, and their insights matched his natural abilities to

236

detect power and weakness in those around him. He began in what Westerners might call a little Artful Dodger way, running errands for low-level guys on sites where health and safety was till an unrealised concept. He learned from old hands, scarred faces and the brows of those who had fallen or been partly crushed, those who knew their way round scaffolding and concrete, those who could always find the right tool or the right material at the right time, for a small, shall we say, consideration, in cash or kind. He learned where to show, at what time, to secure the favoured little jobs. He knew who to turn to, who to avoid, logging all the faces and names in his naturally prodigious memory banks. He was wiry and strong, fleet-footed, and could almost sense impending accidents, saving older workers from collapsing materials or swinging booms. When he'd gained trustee status with some of them they both recognised other gifts. He could write, he was very quick with mental arithmetic, and soon he was negotiating deals. He was able to secure little commissions, leaving his customers with more money in their pockets than if they'd tried to bargain themselves. He never shared how much he was making, or how many he was making it with, but his energy meant he always seemed to be around for those who wanted something, and he began to see the potential of the weakness of their dependency. Others with similar skills began to notice him. A pattern became regular and predictable. Approaches usually followed two styles. The first was from the less brave, and was always a variation of a threat. Don't mess with us. We know what you're trying to do. Stay off our patch. We know where you live.

The other approach was more cocky.

Hey little one, we've been observing you. You're good. How about you join us and we'll double the money and take care of you?

Sure, he knew they'd double the money once and then take an increasing cut on every deal so he'd be left like some slave rowing some fat cat's boat to oblivion. Then they'd try and get him onto addictions – little gambling scams, drugs, booze, and after they'd bled him he'd be joining the others as some part of a new building foundation, a 'pillar of society'. He'd heard all about it. Life was still cheap.

Time passed, and he found himself getting invited to some of the worker's games after they'd downed tools – a little drink here, a sporting ring there, a dingy basement gambling den over there, and he got to feel his way round the Underground. He noted the weaknesses of all those around, spotted their tells in games, logged the cowards and the bullies, the show-offs and the spies, the shirkers and the grafters, and he produced a mental mosaic of the society of little secrets, no files that could be stolen or traded, and his exclusively alone. The realisation evolved naturally. He began to find ways to increase others' need for him. He did this by securing better terms for them, or ensuring little confidences could be grown. All this was delivered in a style that suited the sharers and the cautious as well as the poor negotiators and losers. There were no brutal physical threats unbecoming of the wiry Negotiator. Then he did what others found so hard to do. It looked like he extended his generosity. He gave a little more commission, the odd extra bonus, the odd favour that had nothing to do with the job in hand. Time generated those who decided it was time to offer their services to him, carefully trying to avoid accusations of switched loyalties or betrayal. There were consequences for every action. Cheng Lee was going to be a Controller in an otherwise inconsequential world. He was moving from a fringe to a centre of sorts, the benign little dealer with the confident smile and the deep knowledge about everybody's business – good and up to no good. Nothing stuck to him but money and favours. Every wrong could be tacked on to someone else, some other debtor, some other momentarily out of favour human blotter who would soak up wrongs in a trade for some hoped-for future status. As had been noted by other observers, psychopaths often had many followers.

Cheng Lee's rise to a position of influence had taken less than three years, and at twenty his was a name that was travelling beyond the boundaries of the construction business and his old tiny wooden home in the shadow of the tall cranes and fresh towers of Babel. He was beginning to really enjoy what the journalists would quip was a soaring success.

By the time he was twenty eight he had one of the fastest growing construction conglomerates in the country, and was being looked upon as a future powerhouse in China's renaissance. There were few wanting to buy or rent prestigious office and residential space that didn't have his name on their lips. Anyone who could demonstrate a connection to him enjoyed the limelight that cachet threw, an almost tradable social currency.

He had done nothing but learn to be seamless. His ability to fathom people and circumstances led to further insights. The building business was just a micro version of the wider world. Whenever Cheng Lee stepped into a new arena, for want of funds or the leverage of friendship, from banking to waste disposal, from beer to water management, everyone and everything felt the same. He had a universal formula, and the benign and corrupt corresponded with it, anchored to him with equal assuredness about their well-being in his hands.

Small projects turned quickly into bigger ones. Cheng Lee could always find a way to get materials on time when others couldn't. Fuel was always there, containers weren't delayed, concrete poured evenly, potential tenants lined up to secure deals at premium rates that became a benchmark for sound investment decisions and prestige value. In the almost shadow-less parallel world, legions of suppliers and 'passage-makers' grew richer in a collective management of corrupt practitioners, and whistle-blowers were discouraged from temptation.

The beauty of construction was the variety of ways in which waste could be disposed. There was almost a virtuous circle of re-cycleability. People wanted roads in a hurry. Keeping them on acceptable inclines as they wound through the hills meant taking lessons from the great old railway builders of the world, not altogether inexperienced in the persuasive arts of corruption either. Banked curves and embankments saved the time and hassle of bridge-building. Damming rivers and ignoring their dependent communities was a fair price for the inevitability of progress. Quality control was a factor designed to guarantee a product just beyond the end of Cheng Lee's time on earth. There was no desire to leave Pyramidic memories scattered over the country. It was a – erm – lifetime guarantee that he offered.

Reputation was built in two ways – the display of award-winning structures, and the whispering world of wee-founded but unproven fears, where nothing ever led back directly to Cheng Lee, except the lingering presence of his smile, hovering in his Chinese Wonderland.

A site-master had been told by one of his expert concrete supervisors that he was concerned about the viscosity and the drying time of the latest batch of product. Here was someone who didn't know about tables and calculations and formulae. He knew by sight and smell and experience when something was sound or not, like the old explosives maker in the arsenal who knew by feel when a plastic mix was ripened to its full eventual potential. A name was passed on to Cheng Lee. He didn't say anything. If he ever nodded 'no', nothing consequent happened.

Two weeks later, in Pu-Dong district, Wu Xuang was drinking in the Cloud 9 bar, and buying whiskies for his friends. It had been a good couple of months, a big contract secured with The Man, and it seemed to have no end. He was supplying the guy with an endless thirst for concrete, a man in a hurry, who was building things faster than people could conceive. Bills were being paid on time, the dream of the house to escape to was coming along well. Who would notice the marginal change in the mix, the odd saving moving swiftly and silently from bill to varied bank balances every time a fresh load was delivered.

So how come you get to have the contract on that one Wu Xuang?

By being the Master.

The whisky turned up the volume on the bravado, so it took more than one go before the ringing phone reached his ears. He took the call and turned pale.

Got to go – now. There's something that has to be done at home. Sorry.

He tabled a large pile of notes to keep his friends and the barman happy, and left to the cry of someone saying "Old Master? Old Masturbator more like", wrapped up in laughter, a memory he would soon lose.

When he got close to the apartment he was stopped by the police, who told him he could go no further.

What's going on? This is home.

You can't go any further. There's been a fire and it's still not safe to go near.

Where? Which apartment?

Don't know. Somewhere on the sixth floor.

His floor.

At this point a fire fighter turned up and gave a slow negative nod to the policeman.

What does that mean?

It means the fire is out, but there are at least two dead in there.

His heart and mind raced. Two dead, in or near the apartment. My son? My wife? Another pair?

The policeman saw the growing look of panic and told the man he should give him his name and mobile number, and go find a place, or people, to go to for a while. Any news and he'd let him know, but it was going to be a long night.

He did what he was told, and went off palely into the night, his mind whirling with the unknown, anticipation. He walked the streets, who knows where, and people intuitively moved around him and away from his troubles.

Four hours later, the phone rang again. It was the police officer, asking where he was, and telling him to meet him in thirty minutes. That was all.

He played the words over and over, in a muddled way – two dead, his apartment, a fire, rapid combustion, lethal smoke, death by choking in sleep, contained from other apartments thanks to a call from someone with a good eye and an even better nose.

He took the news on board in silence, and nodded, half comprehendingly, at its deliverer. He signed some forms, nodded no when asked if he needed to talk to someone else, and returned to the now lightening streets where a pale sunrise matched his drained cheeks. He wandered aimlessly again. The phone rang an hour later.

Wu Xuang?

Yes?

It's Xiuxiu.

He thought the phone was playing tricks, that it had somehow sent him a voicemail from another place. He'd never believed the dead could speak.

What? How? What's going on?

Fear and relief took him equally.

You must come, now.

He heard the voice give him a meeting point off the Huyu Expressway.

Then the phone went silent.

He was totally confused. His wife's voice. Alive? How could that be?

Now working only on automatic, he set off to where she had said. When he arrived at the rendezvous he stood looking around, no sign of his wife. After five minutes, his phone rang again.

A voice came out of nowhere.

Want to see Xiuxiu?

Yes, yes, of course. Where is she? What's happening?

All in good time.

A van pulled up, as anonymous as white vans can be, and a voice emanated from the window.

Get in the front.

He did. They set off. One mile. Three miles, and then turned off the paved road onto a surface being prepared for becoming another connecting highway. The van stopped.

See that? Over there. Look to your left, about three hundred yards.

In the dim distance he could just about see something, someone, lying on the ground. Someone alone.

That's your wife.

What about my son? What about what the police said, and the apartment?

So many questions from someone so used to taking instructions. Oh yes, the policeman was right. There were two bodies in the apartment. One was some kid we got from the hospital after a road crash – cheap road kill for us, nice earner in organs though. Oh, and the other was your son. Wanna see the snaps?

Wu Xuang was shocked, silent, angry, frightened, thrown, unable to handle the flood of messages and experiences reality was supposed to be unable to throw his way.

We took your whore of a wife after we made her light the little house-warming fire. You know, women who live with scum thieves ought to get laid by the more deserving.

The speaker pressed to send an instant message. Moments later the giant road layer rolled forward and its small team of carers quickly had the beast ready for its modern day form of carpet-laying. Wu Xuang looked on in speechless horror as the machine approached the bundle on the floor. He screamed.

Two minutes later the machine had covered ten metres of road.

There you go. We told you she'd get laid.

Wu Xuang almost fainted. He feared now only for himself. He wouldn't have to do that for long.

Don't worry, you're next. In some countries it is apparently the done thing to lie next to your wife in death. A suitable fitting for a living liar. Next time you are thinking of failing to appreciate the largesse of your employer, think again.

At this point two of the men from the van threw tape to each other and swiftly bound the cheat from ankle to neck. They made sure not to cover his head, and taped his eyelids open. Taking him out on the uncovered road they lay him down and placed his hands on the ground. One of them produced a staple gun and pinned him to the hard surface. The machine moved forward again.

Watch how you go.

The last thing he consciously saw were his lower legs being mangled in the machine.

Back in the bars, the tales would be woven and told about lost friends, and how it didn't pay to mess with Cheng Lee.

Cheng Lee hated contract abusers, and if anyone ever tried to raise the issue with him he would simply say that it was time to move on. Such matters are all laid to rest now.

Cheng Lee was also efficient at retaining privacy outside work – at least, where he didn't want it to show. Consistent with all things, he managed a tight operation. Conspicuous consumption was one part of a carefully controlled strategy. Mean and lean at home, he looked in China like someone who had never forgotten his humble origins, and practised an honourable minimalism around the city; encouraging others to accept this was a worthy show.

Offshore was a different story, and he manipulated the desires of the media to keep his exposure abroad to temptations to high levels of legally-backed protection. China was rising, for sure, but Cheng Lee wanted to make sure he could hedge his growing fortune. He began to accumulate holdings in other parts of the world, investment portfolios including property, companies, and of course, people, admirers, other investors, all attracted to the light of his money, and many to his now international charm. He began to acquire things to play with, but not too many. For him the idea of a mega yacht was dumb when he could borrow or hire one from someone about to be dispossessed for a song. More than half the big ships out there were available at any time if the right deal came along, and there were plenty still willing to drop another $20 million or so for that extra metre that would briefly make them the owner of the world's longest private yacht. There was no point commissioning some flash piece of kit only to have it come in late, unworkable, and tied to months of litigation – that was what he tried to prevent every day at work. No, he could take a tried and tested brute recently liberated from someone now languishing in a gaol on charges of grand theft, fraud and deception, and be a temporary hero for saving some classic vessel from abandonment.

Women he also classified as accoutrements. From fifteen to twenty one no girl or woman had given him the time of day. They thought he was either too shy or too cocky, too inaccessible or too open, too smart or too dumb, and he quickly tired of their rejections, turning himself towards other things where he got results. When the money began to make bulges in his pockets, money's own pheromones began to work, and several different kinds of the female species began to make their presence felt. Cheng Lee recognised this for what it was, and he began to enjoy himself under the canopy of this knowing protection, allowing him not to reveal too much of himself, and presenting him with keys to doors he had never been granted before. This made him even more acutely aware of the shortcomings of many of his fellow human beings, and he increasingly began to treat many of them as disposable. Some really believed they loved him, but they weren't even close. One day he would find someone, somewhere, who didn't know about all the trappings, and they might begin to see the real thing. Meanwhile, he was going to enjoy the frivolities of the show, and if there was no Great

One out there – well, he'd managed alone so far.

One of his ambitions was to continue to develop Australia as a suitably invested in resource for his needs. Apart from the natural features, what he termed its pleasure zones also presented attractive alternatives to much of his home country's offerings. To support his adventures, he had had someone acquire a substantial property almost at the end of Sydney's Northern Beaches. Rejecting Vaucluse as overcrowded and over self-aware, a developer had been encouraged to part with one of his creations on a north-facing hillside. Neighbours were sufficiently far away to be less irritating than in a number of other areas along that stretch of coastline. Having secured the property with the kind of bonus that wouldn't be seeing the developer complaining any time soon, the house was soon demolished, and a new bespoke design replaced it from new, deeper foundations through to the terraced rooftops. Blending in with the surrounding flora, and offering uninterrupted views to The Heads, it offered more protection than most from the sometimes blistering afternoon sun. Another bonus of this location was the almost permanent absence of other foreign-based owners. These were largely members of a global tribe of rich speculative collectors with strings of houses in the trophy room they called Earth. Their places were trinkets to mention at cocktail parties across the world – oh yes, almost forgot about that place – such a quaint spot don't you think? Any drive-by folks would look up at the barely discernible steel and glass above the road, missing much of the naturally camouflaged hideaway breathing in the salt from the rolling sea below, as if it were watching the learning surfers nonchalantly, their boards scratching the waves like tiny cat claws hanging on to the ever-sliding ocean top.

Cheng Lee would take himself there for occasional long weekends, and he kept the house very much to himself. A specialist team of builders had been sworn to secrecy about its design, interior, contents and features. This was not the place for crowded house parties and drop-by neighbours. It was a place for relaxation and reflection. For entertaining he preferred to secure a private space at the nearby Jonah's hotel. His tips and general behaviour guaranteed appropriate discretion from the staff, and it left his eyrie free for his own meanderings.

Any paparazzi trying to capture him at home in uncompromising positions would not have been able to acquire images through the anti-intrusion glass. They would fail to pick up conversations through the scramblers and bafflers, and so they would have to remain content with the occasional picture of him with a girl somewhere in or around the cliff-top hotel, a space where he was happy to feed them titbits for their tittle-tattle habits. He would always leave the girls at the hotel, and take the short trip home in a black Ferrari, the car slipping through the electronic security gates and up into the temperature-controlled garage to join its cossetted neighbours in their spotless stables.

That was where the opportunity revealed itself.

One of the great advantages of a Ferrari, but not necessarily from a driver's point of view, is that in many models, rear visibility is limited. Additionally, most drivers would not be checking their rear-view mirrors in their own drive, unless they had been trained to do so. No, most would be looking to see how they could slide smoothly into the garage ahead whose doors were already opening in anticipation. The intrusion detection system wasn't going to pick up anything close to the car's rear spoiler, offering a low-slung aerodynamic plate to hold on to.

Lachlan had waited patiently, the place having been reconnoitred over months. After 11pm, there were only one or two residents going home, or the occasional guests returning to the hotel, and observation had revealed that the nearest regularly at-home resident was an early-to-bed habitué. Other owners were away eating of the fruits and flesh of the world. He had managed to find the ideal spot to wait for the Ferrari to arrive. This was so much easier than lying in wet trenches under bushes for days, watching the comings and goings of likely urban fighters still caught up in long-running religious feuds dominating acts over territorial rights and principles of governance. Here it wasn't cold, there was the right amount of low light, no groups of surprised hostile locals, and an automated security system – so no warm bodies to handle. Since black remained a fashionable colour, he had only had to add a pair of gloves and a hat to blend in with the darkness, and he had all he needed to seize the moment from his hideaway across from the gates of the Chinese palace. He had practised the move, with exact copies of the cars in Cheng Lee's garage, many times. He knew how the camber of the road affected movements, the shape of inclines, clearances and tolerances involved, the right amount of unnoticeable pressure to apply. He could do the move with his eyes closed, time after time. The skateboard was an adapted version, with electric power and globular wheels minimising the chance for skids or tilts, and the whole unit was steered and powered by a tiny tracker taped to his left index finger, which could be manipulated by the thumb. He felt at one on the blackboard, black on black, like a snake hunting at night in a tarmac jungle.

As the Ferrari slowed up to the exterior gate, he launched himself, the power of the board bringing him swiftly up to rear of the car, where his right hand, in its heat-protected glove, was able to grab the spoiler. He rode in the car's wake, up the drive and on into the now opening garage, a quiet caravan being towed in harmonised black, which no cameras were trained on, and for which no motion sensors had been primed. He was in.

Cheng Lee had no dull bodyguards to remind him, boringly, to click the remote in his pocket to secure the garage door from the house as he slipped into the interior corridors. Who still would be here, after all? Skater man knew one of security's biggest problems was the frailty and arrogance of its human component. Poor habits and little or no training were great gifts to security men who always patiently explained why there was no such thing as 100% security. For a man with few worries about insurance bills, it was surprising but also convenient for the professional that the garage lights doused themselves once the house door had simply been closed from the other side. There were no worries about inadvertent light exposure. It had been worked out that once you were the host, and inside the house, the whole interior system was off – only the perimeter was activated, as the owner had grown tired of alarms being triggered through windows being accidentally left open, or where birds had accidentally flown into windows, sending signals to a distantly-based security monitoring service whose people, on minimum wages, weren't highly motivated to check out subtleties. Once the outer wall had been breached, the entire inner world remained free to roam in. there was at least a half hour of time to play with.

Cheng Lee was usefully regular in his habits. After two days he would leave and go back to China. There would always be the sequence when he would call up the voice-activated plasma screen to see what messages were coming from his other worlds. Then he'd go for the sounds – video he found too intrusive. The music would be some Genius playlist, just enough to stop him getting irritated. Then it would be something interesting, an old cognac or an extravagant glass of Petrus. He would walk across the expansive main rooms, glancing at the sea or the stars, and he would briefly replay moments of his games with the latest plaything, varying on whether they were going to claim love or conquest afterwards to their eager gossipy friends.

Over on the other side of the house, the new entrant had gone into the large en-suite area to the master bedroom. Cheng Lee would at some point decide to wash away the skin and the perfume of the already fading memories of the playmate. This would involve a fifteen minute routine in the wet room, jets blasting the detritus from his body before soothing to massage mode, and finally the overlarge overhead shower would be commanded to rain its cleanliness over Cheng Lee's head and face and mouth as he restored himself to what he considered to be a pristine state. The uninvited visitor knew the pattern because he had seen videos of Cheng Lee's behaviour recorded in other similar places at other times – hotel penthouses with easily set up viewing facilities. There were benefits to working with obsessives – consistency being one of them. He worked quickly. He finished his main task, and moved, cat-like, to one of the unused guest rooms.

Cheng Lee followed his routine. His growing sense of superiority told him he could ignore warnings, ignore advice about varying actions, reducing predictability, making it harder for people to spot and exploit weaknesses. Hey, nothing could touch him now.

He stepped into the shower, the treble thermostatically controlled temperature warming the pellets of water coming out of the side nozzles at precisely the pressure he preferred. After five minutes of this powerful massage, he pressed the lever, the only manual part of the program he had to control, and the head shower began its warm caressing drizzle. He loved the Australian sense of civilised tropicality. He let the water drift onto his neck and down his back as the side nozzles now reduced their intensity. After two more minutes he pursued his normal ritual, and tilted his head up and back to swallow the little waterfall on his face, his forehead, his mouth.

It was about a minute before he felt the constraining sensation. He began to splutter, to cough and try to spit the water out, but his muscles were somehow unwilling to play. They were giving in, and Cheng Lee fell to the floor, his eyes fading out of focus on the still pouring showerhead. His last perspective was on the black tiles of the wet room floor as his body succumbed to the final spasms of its relatively short life.

The visitor had placed a thin layer of sheathing around the inside rim of the showerhead. He knew that when the water temperature reached the 32 degrees Cheng Lee preferred towards the end of the head-wetting session, the sheath would dissolve. That left only the cyanide to filter through the head and down onto the unsuspecting face and mouth of the rich Asian. The battle of Jericho was about to be over, and the Chinese walls were tumbling down. For the $2 billion dollars Cheng Lee had put together in the construction of his life, at least 400 hundred had not died accidentally as part of his Foundation. Its growth had been fuelled lately through deals with a number of Americans, including Bannon and Daniels, who were keen to see what China could do to enhance their portfolios further.

Lachlan moved to check the effectiveness of the little rain shower, left the now normal shower running, and made his way back to the garage. Still in his fashionable black gear, he started up the Ferrari with one touch, the skateboard now keeping him company on the passenger seat, and set off, the in-car device opening both the garage doors and the front gates of the house. He set off into the night at a civilised and sober pace, and drove the car to Bayview. He left it on the edge of the public car park, without CCTV here, by the trees, roof down, knowing that it would be stolen or vandalized by the morning, and walked to the dinghy he had tied up at six that evening. By 2am he was sleeping on the old wooden-topped river cruiser, another weekender dreaming about peace of Pittwater. He was truly Sound asleep.

Headline: *"Chinese Construction Mogul in Bizarre Bathroom Incident"*

Cue: *"Waterfalls"*

***

Luke had left school as soon as he could. In fact he'd left earlier, simply because he spent as much time as possible avoiding being near it, and truancy coupled with suspensions added up to a lot of time 'not there'. His parents were several countries away, so it was difficult to summon them to an office and tell them about their wayward son's effect on the establishment. In any case, the head had decided it was better to enjoy the continuing revenue than to make public the issue of the flitting student. He was simply bored. He didn't like the lessons, the timetable, the buildings, the location, or anything else connected with what he regarded as its academic stodginess, and most of his energies were devoted to schemes for raising money quickly, and getting the hell out of the provincial backwater. He belonged, he decided, to another world, and it would belong to him. The lure of margin and profit was almost instinctive, and he never failed to get excited when people were prepared to give him money for something they could have got themselves, if only they could be bothered. So many couldn't be bothered, and if they wanted something, they also wanted it now, because if they didn't have it, they would lose cool points.

He also found the same applied to people when it came to looking for a place to live in. He hadn't had to go through any rites of passage about finding somewhere, sharing accommodation, fighting over who stole the food from the fridge, who hadn't paid their share of the utility bills, and all those other 'in denial' phases people went through when a place wasn't entirely theirs. He had already made enough money on concert tickets, parties, software, and merchandising deals to have bought his own loft apartment by the time he was seventeen, all legit, and he had trust money coming to him in another year. For a kid who 'amounted to nothing' in all those tedious school appraisals, not that they were so politically incorrect these days, he had left the swots and the conformists well behind, looking to snail their way through college and into some dull profession or other in four or five years' time. His peers were impressed with his living space, those few who got invited into the sanctuary. Anyone who is doing this well can probably help others, they decided. Instead of sitting in a squalid old place under the aegis of some life-long uncaring absentee landlord, Luke had started buying into new apartment blocks in city centres, near university faculties, close to the action. He vetted tenants, and they felt good about being chosen, and on what looked like unbelievable deals. They found themselves living in undreamt of accommodation. There was only one condition. Anyone trashing one of his places was out – immediately. No second or subsequent chances. There were enough consequent losers around, back in what you might describe as more traditional types of accommodation, to testify to the truth and application of Luke's word on this subject. Unlike many who had had similar ideas about buying up cheap places in cheaper cities and towns, he hadn't then let any type move in and wreck his investments. He bought new, off-plan, and secured deals with builders constrained by economic pressures. Cash was king. When he moved in on a territory, it didn't drive people away. Prices rose, new enterprises appeared, and when nearby properties slipped, Luke's portfolio held its own.

Now even some of the naysayers were beginning to want his time, his attention, offering services or advice he didn't want, trying to become business partners, or preferred suppliers, anything to pick up a percentage of the rocket man's burgeoning fortune. After seven years of growth and expansion he was getting no new levels of satisfaction from the model. Being bored was easily the worst thing he ever had to face up to. After racing cars, learning to fly a plane, then a helicopter, buying into racing yachts, and a further spread of divertissements, the fundamental driver of his business had gone into neutral. He had mastered the art of getting people to pay for what he wanted them to buy, and to sell him what he wanted to pay them. The trick, in this guise, had lost its lustre.

One night, sitting in that year's movers and shakers club, watching some acquaintances take the strain out of three or four magnums of champagne as he sipped his preferred hyped-up premium tonic water, he saw someone who produced a flutter in his recently flat-lined emotional heart trace. Sitting at a table some five or so metres away, holding a flute of something bright blue, maybe a Cote D'Opale cocktail, and sharing some private comment with her girlfriend, he decided it was time to expand his circle of acquaintances.

Being that kind of club, he messaged reception, who relayed his request to the lady. She looked over, looked back at her phone, pressed send, and, five minutes later, she and her friend and joined Luke's party, beginning the slow process of catch up on the vintage champagne. He didn't overdo the attention, and apart from the occasional look from her, sizing up the stranger, she appeared to be enjoying the anonymous hospitality of the tonic-drinking guy with the deep pockets and the drunkenly grateful partygoers. A couple of them started slurring their way into telling her who he was, but ended up just sliding away as the bubbles continued to pour, and music filled in all the remaining aural spaces. Genevieve and Luke didn't connect that night. He left another message with the concierge services, and left the club around 2.30, leaving those still just about functioning behind to close the early morning proceedings without him, as usual.

A different kind of fortune appeared to be smiling on him. Genevieve made a response to his second message, and from that point they were in contact without intermediaries. They met the following week at a recently opened raved-about restaurant, another international launch in the city for the proprietor, his latest attempt to build starred bridges across other boundaries, where each encounter revealed subtle differences in tastes and expectations, and signature dishes were modified or dropped from the honeymoon period menus. Reservations were not a problem for Luke, and he sat at a table others would clamour for for months, by which time the place would either be one of his regular haunts or it would, like a signature dish, have been quietly dropped for a return to a previously liked place, or yet another new venture.

For two who had only met through the briefest of messages, sly eye contact, and one evening's questionable proximity, the unveiling of each other's interests was progressing well. Genevieve appeared pretty and principled. She knew the significance her looks carried, and the shortage of people who could get beyond that to herself. Luke liked the buzz behind the beauty and enjoyed the evening where there was a dialogue, a conversation, not just a trading of credentials or clichés.

Both found the encounter worth repeating, and elected to go for a third encounter of the close kind, or at least the testing of it, in another week, when they would both be back in that city, and free again.

Beneath the surface, once they had both passed the little social checks of looking for common ground, they started in on other questions, the ones about careers, travel, the future, all those little mental minefields set out to lure the unwary or protect your personal space. They teased and pushed and laughed, agreeing about some things and parking others for later, maybe never. Genevieve turned out to be a carer, an ardent supporter of looking after things, and had plenty to say about the Earth, climate change, and human behaviour in its many manifestations of selfishness. He talked about the way people were as he saw them, about their views and demands on shelter and warmth, protection and care, only he didn't quite paint the picture in the colours he really saw things in – he was just lucky to be able to help people. Their level of harmony was enough to find them sharing a bed, but there their tastes diverged, and the fledgling relationship withered rapidly, unable to fly. It was too early for a protracted platonic friendship. Yet something else had been seeded.

Genevieve had spoken of her favourite places to buy food, the ones that billed themselves as selling better quality products, better for you. Luke wasn't slow in noticing that in many places such food also carried a price premium, and smallholders or growers with walls of certificates and awards testifying to the quality and provenance of their produce were enjoying the rewards. She had talked about local sourcing, about food presentation, about processed products, munching her way through the line-caught fish and the artisanal cheese.

Luke let her enthusiasm for this wash over him, and it triggered another response. Back in his chosen quietness, he began to search markets for things he had previously ignored. Now he wasn't looking at city centre apartments with cool address codes. He was out there in green fields, scouring the countryside for small holdings and farms. He saw how he could assemble a network of independent operations focused on supplying local produce to local aspirational users, in stylish restaurants, at expensive markets, in shops that found it un-embarrassing to charge more for 'natural' things, because their shoppers had money to burn and attitudes to appease. The city man became the gentleman farmer, then the city boutique shop owner, along with a few others looking for somewhere to put their bonuses for a rainy day. Just like with the apartments, he saw himself as an Enabler, the man who helped those with dreams and soil-based talent to bring

251

their view of the world to the fore, but with fewer feudal overlord overtones present. Occasionally he would let the tenants he had bought out re-bid for their land and operation, then watch them struggle to pay commercial rates as interest rates soared, or fuel costs rose, or crops failed through poor experimentation or legislation, nature's disasters, or other forms of bad luck or decision-making. He was always there to buy back his investments, make a second profitable killing, and re-tame failed tenants to welcome his renewed support. If he wasn't so publicity shy, someone might have wanted to make a celebratory documentary about him.

He now had a team of people managing his city and country portfolios, the glass and green team as he billed them, and he occasionally took a break from having them count his revenue, going off in search of whatever was supposed to be the latest from of fun he hadn't already tried and got bored of.

He had read about the new generation of mini-submarines that were different from military models, offering unbelievable amounts of transparent glass to look through. He was on a trip where he had hired an observation platform and a piloting team, off the coast of Baja, California, where he met Kallila. She was on vacation – diving. They were both staying in one of the latest villa hotels that had begun to dribble further down the coastline, offering escapes from metro life for only the average annual wage of one of the local service staff per night.

This time there were no extremes, not of attitudes, of pursuits, of perspectives, and both found in each other what they wanted at that moment in their lives. She was the bored executive in the media company, looking for space and freshness. He was looking to spend time with someone who wasn't trying to be his new best business friend. His still faraway parents gave him their faraway blessing, hers had long since split and gone their separate ways. Within two years there was a surprising Mr and Mrs, a strangely conformist result for both of them, and onlookers were even more surprised when the twins arrived.

Luke's businesses continued to grow, and as he monitored his attention curve, he was soon back at the business equivalent of the seven year itch. He still remembered the insight Genevieve had given him, like some temptress presented by a modern Mephistopheles, but he had not convertible temptation. The local produce for local markets idea was serendipitous, but he was sure there was still something bigger out there.

When the two year old family took one of the longest gulets they could find to charter of the Turkish coastal waters out of Kas, an early summer break before the sun ground everyone down, he was introduced to one or two of the more entrepreneurial locals in their weekend villas and on their own modern boats, the latest speed merchants from Istanbul shipyards, built to appeal to those who could afford the Western Mediterranean vessels, but who didn't feel they needed to spend either the cash, or take the cachet, of brandishing those brand names. These were people who could upgrade each and every year if they chose, adding another deck or another few metres as the new season's profits poured in. The gulet was a modern version of the traditional gesture they forgave the foreigner for, and most of them had one somewhere, even if they couldn't remember the last time they used it, or even where it might be any more.

There was talk about super-marinas, building an enviable haven between Montenegro and the Suez Canal for superyachts, a place where locals could also hang out, where owners wouldn't always have to travel so far to be on their boats for the often very short time they could spare, and for which they gave their permanent crews even less time to prepare, there was talk like building a world-class restaurant, a new kind of El Bulli, pulling in more desirables from far and wide, by boat, helicopter, or Russian seaplane, hoping to bask in the glaze of exotically designed and combined dishes, and maybe even buy a bespoke villa nearby soon after.

The point was, one of them said after pouring out more wine from his own vineyards, we can grow what we want here in Turkey, and more than that, the soil has never been screwed up by companies and scientists messing with ways to get bigger yields, or different strains. People always want something different, and now they want something untainted, like we've always had, and they're willing to pay more for it. So there's going to be people after our land. There's also going to be lazy ones trying to sell it, looking to banking the cash and heading off to wherever for some R&R, after burning their faces off toiling with vegetables for years.

Luke took all on board and began new researches with customary thoroughness. It wasn't long before he had a new team buying jigsaw pieces of land from some eager sellers, and then letting other locals do what they had been doing best for years and years – tend the land, but this time on his terms. Whether it was apartment seekers, artisanal traders, post graduates or recent peasants, they were all able to get something from Luke they hadn't been able to get before, and so was he. Luke was now very international, yet managed to keep a lid on his

253

portfolio, and its accounting. As he grew older he also began to be less patient with those who hesitated before accepting his offers. Now he was trading in places where it was often less clear what the law and land rights were, and he decided he could raise the threat levels to encourage the undecided.

He maintained a distance from the on-the-ground negotiations with many now. He worked instead to ensure he knew precisely what his people were doing in pursuit of his goals, and he let them get on with things in ways the local recipients of his largesse would understand. This meant accepting that techniques of persuasion might go further than other jurisdictions would sanction. There was a healthy smattering of bribes, deals, gifts and tokens that would smooth the way to new ownership, helping drown the sorrows of those who felt they might have been dispossessed, or the intermediaries in government agencies and political parties, those who believed they held some sway, or were entitled to different levels of respect as they blocked and then opened doors to new ownership. Haggling might be too kind an expression for the sort of leverage that was being applied to prise a piece of land out of the hands of incumbents and into the clutches of newly titled and deeded documents confirming ownership by legitimate parties. Where ownership trails had been difficult to establish, patience was extended, but produce was still cultivated and grown, and profits still divided between growers and distributors and any other links in the logistical chains between begetters and consumers. So now Luke was in the distribution business as well. Excited by the latest diversion, he decided he liked it enough to keep extending his footprint on the world. The next step was to find and acquire quality land in quite challenged parts of the world, where he began to learn about different again levels of security and protection that were far different from those he had grown up with in old Anglo-Saxon climes. So far, being a landlord, farmer, investor and international entrepreneur had kept him away from nasty predators. He had pushed premium products at premium prices to eager markets and more eager users. He was like a drug dealer in greens and reds, and he stayed ahead on most of the deals. But in Africa things started to change.

There were too many cunning warlords with fingers in many pies, looking to fuel trouble in what they considered to be justifiable ways to enjoy opulent living. Someone coming along and trying to make their own money out of recently claimed inheritances needed to either pay for the privilege or surrender the business. Surrendering the business benefited nobody in the long run, because skills to extract the best from the soil were lost, and Western markets would boycott 'blood vegetables', or mercenary crops, such was their moral fickleness. No, it was much better to broker deals protecting the crops and profits, but taking slightly less than before, and giving significantly more to the locals than they had expected, until greed forced some other temporary solutions to be called into play. He began to have locals negotiate contracts on 'trust' with factions that came and went, ensuring the business kept moving, keeping a few rebels leaders in khaki and weapons, cocaine and whisky, until the next claimants surfaced, hungry to feed the next cause.

In his dealings with the Africans, he noticed something else. It wasn't now just a few entrepreneurs like him making moves along with the established multinationals. There were more and more sovereign state representatives turning up and making their preferences felt in the towns and regions, sizing up the situation.

Luke realised there was another opportunity emerging. He went on a further round of acquisition sprees, buying people out in places no-one wanted to be any longer. In Australia some stuck to their pasts and their ways of life, others gave in to the promise of a different and easier lifestyle away from the frontline of hardship, and the perennial stress of failure or unaffordable challenge. Luke acquired land and the businesses on them. Once again, in places where the law was not all-seeing, he extended the nature and harshness of threats to the un-compliant. Now he told prospective sellers that if they didn't close a deal on his terms, and soon, their land would be mysteriously subject to damage, and their growing capability would be seriously impaired. Of course, only he would be able to restore the land to its former abundant glory. Most went along with the ultimate threat against the land itself, and found their own rationales for letting go.

In places where the law allegedly had a more embracing vision, he waited, wearing down prospects with trickle deals that would tear apart families. If people still didn't co-operate, he left them in their own stubbornness to starve or go broke. The accumulation rolled on. He wasn't buying land for conversion to housing or manufacturing or tourism. He was buying land for its potential as food provider for what was becoming a hungrier world. It was this period that became the focus of his attention on food security.

This was what future-gazing governments were really interested in. Those that had still growing populations, or had little land that was truly suitable for all their food needs were looking to a time when they couldn't guarantee safe-trading for their essential basic materials. This was not about organic treats or purely untainted soils and their fruitfulness. It was about the sovereign survival of states, their wealth and independence and well-being. Luke saw opportunities to approach these expansionist growers and help them meet their needs without the world at large waking up in the morning and collectively asking what was going on.

State representatives who were good at knowing what their bosses' strategies were, but less good at doing deals on the ground, welcomed his style. They were shy of businessmen, and they hid it behind a flowery dislike of them, their greed, their penchant for public display, and all other evils they patently practised themselves, but behind the convenient mask of state affairs and style. Luke understood what they needed and how they needed to present themselves. He also knew they had to be careful. Some markets were easier than others. In Australia, the government seemed to be compliant with Asians picking up their natural assets, and although there was supposed to be some form of audit about land being sold to non-Australians, this didn't appear to have resulted in robust counter action. With his ability to cover his tracks, and the way he was generally welcomed as an asset himself in the need for 'sustainability', he had much to enable him to disguise his activity and motives. Some states would pay very well, for the land, for the produce, or both. In the meantime Luke was one of the most effective go-betweens they could have. No-one was too keen to know exactly how much money was going out or coming in, products were delivering an excess of profits, and no one was counting properly. The future seemed fair. The future looked bright. Luke and Kallila and the twins were growing off the fat of the land. In thirty years, when the struggle for resources got hotter, it would be time to judge whether he had returned any of his fortune to those beyond his immediate family.

He was added to the file … J listened to another old song, and savoured the irony of Tears for Fears' *"Sowing the seeds of love"* coming out of the sound system, and he made the mental leap towards what his next indulgent track would be, another old favourite, if it came to pass that a headline would soon be required.

Cue: *"Your time is gonna come,"* rockily crooned by the sweetly monikered Robert Plant.

***

J's Invisible Diary. Entry.

They sit there on the sides. No-one knows if they are on the same side fighting a common enemy, or on opposite sides fighting each other. One group, one team, is in a camouflage that holds them together, the other is in a uniform of chinos and button-downs, tassled loafers and digital weaponry. They both stay there, uneasy in their domains, tired, in the unspoken presence of others who will make their dreams troublesome. Sometimes they go all night, leave and holiday cancelled, constant vigilance, re-writes of scenes, real and imaginary problems, until some boss says stand down, or start again, in their presence, or remotely from some treat-filled feather nest. And you are all supposed to take succour from the translations of aphorisms – family is stronger – value is in the collective – value is in membership.

The night before Christmas, waiting for action and a result, the Ho Ho Ho of Santa Claus, and the different bringer of light, the Ho Ho Ho Chi Minh Trail.

Officers and MBAs alike look to head their identical warriors to something, somewhere, battle or pitch, and their approaches are equally rooted in the past, leading from the wrong front, endless practice learning obedience reluctantly.

The leaders sit there building sets of images, for winning and losing, for bluffing and saving face. Ultimately no-one pulls you out of the mess and pins a medal or a bonus on you – you all get blown to bits in the balls-ups, lying in heaps, and others come in to do their bit of mine-sweeping, the re-writes of what was never to be. There are only objectives here, not tangible entities.

***

We serve and die for images, and every image is diffracted, differently seen. The winners hold it together for a while, smiles of shared victories, and the losers quit, leave, going their separate ways, with separate memories, separate stories, weaving tapestries about what might have happened, and the Bosses sign off on official stories. No-one means the sounds they utter.

They have to sell the cars fast, the hocked up signs of keepy-uppy, badges of corporate campaigns won on the fields of white boards and plasma screens.

Meanwhile, the wives of those carrying machine guns for laser pointers had six weeks to leave their homes if they suddenly found themselves without a partner to share the brunt of living. And every time, the winners sought subtler shades to cover unfortunate lapses, colouring over the dark aspects of life and death, inventing new euphemisms for bad actions, and eventually no-one wanted to spend time with the losers, the ones who suddenly had no campaigns, no far-off destinations, and more time than enough to spend with their family and friends. The victors go on, searching for yet more victories, garlanded glories, and tranches of armed and corporate warriors toy over empty glasses, reliving the battles they never won. It is always the victors who protest that one should simply get on with life and its hurry, where the losers now have no pressure to catch the next express to nowhere – sitting in life's sidings, shunted into the despair of a slow motion other reality, the deniable space of the used and consumed.

Barracks and board rooms hang on to the laughter of the brave and the bold before the battles, and shrink from the odour of those deemed losers.

"The temperature outside is 103 degrees and the ground fire is light to moderate."

Some laugh in the tents, others by the water cooler, and the more they labour for the fulfilment of The Great Dream, the more they resent the higher-ups.

So who has a grasp on the reality of the casualties? Statistical offices push out data like the number of times rock stars fuck each night, or the chances of being struck by a full moon. Numbers don't care whose side they're on – they don't get souls. They simply serve, like those they're tagged to.

So the ones who know they're on the ground, the witnesses, don't get rolled up into one great objective judging crowd. For every two enemy dead it's four back in the office, and for every two friends killed it's one – don't think for one minute's silence there are only those killed whose official statistics record it. Remember, it took fifty years for the Russians to even begin to accept suggestions there might have been a few more victims of the thing we call the Second World War, and as for the unscarred after skirmishes like the demise of Enron, it's mere handfuls of losers, they still claim.

There are those still ordering take-aways, producing mess meals, fuelling their long nights and tension. And when it is all over people wander into hotels, shacks or high status places, and take out their frustrations on tired flesh, cooked and sizzled in pretended recovery, whores all to others' victorious claims. And for those not left behind, it's business as usual, the continuing forgery of a shiny polished reality, a mirrored façade.

Both groups pledge allegiance to flags of convenience, flags of a corporate kind, capital statues to star-spangled empires and stock-quoted fiefdoms, ravenous states addicted to production, and averse to dross.

***

J's Invisible Dairy – Entry

They couldn't vote if they were under twenty one. They could be drafted earlier, and then wouldn't be allowed off the boat onto the enemy land until the midnight bell chimed their eighteenth birthday. *Dulce et decorum est pro patria mori.*

By next year there will be the makings of some more quality conspiracy theories. Was the creator of confusion a fanatic from a strange country, an alien, a local with grievances, combinations and numbers of these, some dark international body, behaving like a virus? Maybe something worse, neither an inside nor an outsider, something hard to define that is free to roam and difficult to detect.

What will all those people be thinking who have generated large amounts of money, the 'dictatorship of the rich'?

Reasonable interest on loans isn't usury. It was old John Calvin who sowed the seeds that making a buck or many out of loans wasn't going to be a sin any more – at least in the West. Muslims, who didn't rate Monsieur Calvin too greatly, held off on this for years. Variations ensued. Profit is OK, just not interest, so choose your words carefully. Make sure you don't catch your capital being used in what the Koranic custodians would deem to be a predatory way.

Funny stuff, faith, those beliefs, those convictions. They make you do strange stuff, draw chalk lines round who you are meant to see and spend time with, and fuel your little head with bigotries and misconceptions. You really think you are making choices over in the Western world, but all things are filtered first through the beliefs that sit at the entrance to your mind, consciously or otherwise. You only ever interpret, you don't see the world in its primal language. You call this filtering experience and you use it to reinforce your beliefs, garlanding faith. Finding others who appear to share this creates comradeship that can be corrupted by those with an allegedly deeper knowledge, corporate fanatics and robed faith healers. Killing enemies to protect this virtuous circle is considered a just cause. This in turn creates both powerful feelings and then the love of power itself, the demon of man, as that chirpy Nietzsche noted.

Both soldiers and corporate citizens get unwittingly closer as the years go by. Hours or simply a few days after killing enemies in

259

territories of competing corporate entities, both could be sitting down to food and beer and wine with friends and relatives in nonchalant suburbias, with disconnected parents making small talk about the next set of career opportunities.

When it all goes wrong the shadow of war and love appears, and the stage gets new scenery, new props, as vengeance struts across the boards. Vengeance becomes a primary driver, a principle force, a fresh destroyer. Something to sate the continuing lust that felt so rewarding when the battles were raging on. Helping some with the avenging might dowse some of those still inflated passions, helping to restore status and respect. Others simply have to respond to its pull, slaves to vengeful demands that ironically promote the idea that killing is a cool way to assuage painful feelings or disrespect.

This is easier to handle than being encouraged to kill enemies by your host company or nation that prohibits it in polite media-muffled societies claiming only to want riches through peaceful recognised correctness, that laughs at how anyone could take seriously the straight-faced line delivered in the movie – "Terminate with extreme prejudice".

People then start to rationalise all their actions, and go on to legalise them. They turn themselves into visions they see in the mirror, angels of light and grace, with no rules other than their own, no inhibitions about demonstrations of faith, no limitations on defence, and attack becoming once again a form of protection. There are no objections to killing people or putting enterprises or even nations out of business if it all happens within a moral framework endorsed by so-called leaders. The idea of killing off human beings is generally interpreted to define them as members of your own tribe. Members of other tribes are sub-human. Frederick the Great thought a nation was worthless if it didn't set everything upon its honour. *The Secret Agent* was there to destroy faith in legality over a hundred years ago – there to do just that, shatter frameworks, becoming a new moral agent, a long tradition continuing through shifting ideals. Generating capital for corporations became the unspoken mantra for military operations after World War One. Pledging allegiance to a flag was merely cosmetic fluff. You were now pledging allegiance to some production outfit like Dow Chemicals.

The original creator of the Assassins understood this, how reinforcing beliefs delivers dignity and honour to its ideological believers. Conspiracies are splendid places to hide conspiracies.

***

You don't remember the man who went away. You only remember the one who comes home.

It was interesting to see someone had bleated about the Army and its perceived decline, saying it just wasn't considered a desirable career for many ambitious young men any more, and recruiting was still based on outmoded notions like patriotism. Feelings about nationhood change. New soldiers visiting Bergen-Belsen were surprised at the numbers of coaches of German tourists looking neither moved nor sorry, simply curious, and wondering why they still had to put up with constant reminders of a past they couldn't influence, and which they would like to see let go. Not everyone wants state-sanctioned killers to protect the very peace people crave, and a number see no justification in violent means to ends in any circumstances.

No-one felt sorry for the battalion of Lowland Scots born of the Great Depression, sailing on a boat called *The Empire Pride*, and being posted on landing to the toughest fighting in the Asian theatre of the Second World War, with few surviving. Why would you fight for a nation you despised against a nation you didn't understand?

It made sense to Pathans to ask for rifle racks to stow their beloved Lee-Enfield rifles when they went to work, and to ask to be paid daily, because you never knew what tomorrow would bring. Two hundred years ago you could be in a battle of major proportions, like Waterloo, and have no idea what you were really a part of. War today, in the field or in offices, is regarded as a variant of a live mass multiplayer online game.

People playing paintball duck and crouch when they run across exposed areas, thinking they are safer, because generations of extras have done that on the cinema screen before their eyes, directed by those who have never seen real action. The old officer advised it was useless – what counted was one's turn of speed in such scenarios.

You only had to fly from Saigon to Paris with the Air France flight that did a stopover in Nice to see the student kids of affluent families avoiding the draft, chilling in their old folks' Provence second-homes to see how the majorly defended South Vietnam was seedy and FUBAR before the Americans started to 'help'. It's only Americans who feel guilty about that war.

Meanwhile the tolerance of friendly 'boil dissenters in the bag' dictators continues from the heartland of democracy. Why have one set of standards when you can have double standards? The best way to deal with this kind of society is to use the same Messianic belief systems to rock the boat of contemporary non-values. It helps to leave the home-based to pick friends whose behaviour couldn't ever be endorsed on your barbecue patio.

The joy of fighting the all-American Book of Law and its infinite capability for adaptation to immediate self-serving needs is that new attacks, and forms of attack, could generate even stronger security measures (i.e. 'protection'), closing more doors and hindering the exchange of ideas and goods and the free flow of innocent citizens.

Like T.E. Lawrence, it becomes necessary to become a man of the shadows, an armed idealist, committing what some might consider atrocities in the service of an idea of one's own. Time to recall Regis Debray who said you shouldn't have to ask if an idea is right or not. The point is about whether it makes an effect because all serious power rests on the imaginary. Absolutely.

***

J remembered the second conversation he had had over dinner with his female friend, the part where she said she would tell him what to do with his book.

What's that?

If you really want to get attention you should kill the powerful guys' sons.

What do you mean?

Kill the sons. The ones who might become the carriers of the Power, the ones the fathers really care about, the ones who get protected these days from the messy details about war and blood and physical harm, or boardroom battles and disgruntled workers, closures and shortfalls. They know nothing, but think they can have everything

J thought about the ones whose lives are protected by the electric fences of humungous wealth, conspicuous security, the ones who are monitored and cosseted and know only that life waits for their command, whose only dealings with dirt come in distilled management summaries when the performance of their trust companies tell the Boys they've put on an extra ten billion or so this season. Maybe the next season there can be an extra ten metres on the boat to piss off Larry or Paul in life's pursuit of conspicuous Bigness.

But the plan to use the Mohawk strategy was even better.

***

Part IV

Tomorrow and Tomorrow
and Tomorrow

"The place selected for attack must be kept secret. If the enemy know not where he will be attacked, he must prepare in every quarter, and so everywhere be weak"

Sun Tzu, *The Art of War*

***

Where the long-term strategy for the Message is truly seeded ~ questions of identity remain a mystery ~ dedicated teams continue to execute the grand plan ~ time is less of an issue than principle ~ the idea of the Levellers is outlined ~ that way Respect lies ~ the Followers path is made explicit.

Sitting behind the rain-lashed windows in the bar, you could see the island pulling the mist across its face, a veil against the winds which would come and blow its disguise away in a couple of hours. He had been there before, at the same table in the bay window, sometimes drinking beer, sometimes wine, a choice decided by heat, thirst and suggestion. Today called for the darkness and length of beer, something to make the rain seem less cold and the time pass more measuredly. People had looked out of this window, from this perspective, for over a hundred years. Some of them had watched the light dance on the horizon, drawing the islands nearer and then playing them out again as the sun rolled slowly over. Others watched clouds tease the land while the sea played like a bored dog, occasionally jumping at a rock, or turning restlessly over and over. There was tenderness, and there were tantrums. In his head were snatches of Norman French songs, and local island pieces, snippets of thought – a poet is the creator of the nation around him. He gives them a world to picture. Exiled Victor Hugo would have respected that it was here all that time ago that he had made the decision, when he decided the gesture should be made, the gesture requiring discovery, interpretation, refinement, the gesture that became the Message.

His own Message remained disembodied with no connection to its progenitor. Versions of it had caused a little stir. It would eventually be seen by some for what it was, a slow spreading out, like light. The whole point had been just that. Something had to be done, and no-one had looked like they were doing much.

Connections generated signifiers, and sometimes wrong impressions, reasons to allocate an action to a person, a movement, a cause, a madness, to hedge against the nature of the thing itself, which was, after all, a point of purification, a correction.

It wasn't possible to change the world with thinking unless you could turn the thoughts into action. The challenge was to see if the action could finally be disconnected from the source, from its initial cause, and if the action alone could engender new meaning.

266

Other people passed in and out of the bar. Some looked for a regular perch, their regular drink, their regular chatter about the weather and the way news circled and covered the inertia. Others shook the rain from their hoods, brushed the water from their shoulders, wiped their glasses, squinted at menus, tried to warm up behind whiskies, soups, and local specials assembled by migrant workers unable to spell or pronounce the dishes, hoping for other opportunities to spring them forward and away from the damp green prison they had been seconded to. Two regulars laughed at an old jibe about an absent friend, and called up another round loudly. A maudlin television presented a washed-out version of a German weather report, the volume muffled, the picture struggling, waiting for someone to lean on the satellite TV hand-held controller and restore order with the return of the football channel playing endless repeats of old matches.

The pictures on the wall kept their counsel, a silent parade of the public house's past, from old riggers nestling up to the quayside, through the time of occupation, frames holding in suspense the sound of metal heels clicking on cobblestones, liberation, aeroplanes, those serving the nation, the names of pilots and other crew, local and foreign, signed in flourishes across fading photographs, the remains of visits, of long drinking sessions when other reminiscences were being recreated.

Bar staff resented interruptions from their Slavic banter as customers attempted to negotiate fresh rounds of drinks, and occasionally food, from the other side of the bar, the barrier. The staff didn't realise how connected they were to the place from their diverse pasts. Their ancestors had fought people who had been sent to the island for rest and recuperation, for misdemeanours, for the whims of disgruntled officers taking a moody dislike to disruptive faces or disobeying mouths – people sent to work hard doing something for nothing, or next to it, just like them. The links were often well hidden, the memories not sparked two or three generations along, lessons consigned to the recesses in granite walls and corridors, libraries of breaths and murmurs from a fading past.

He knew there would be more action. He knew there would eventually be attention, and then the slow deterioration after the initial impact, the triumph of post-rationalisation, the processing of the affected, wounded, touched, disaffected, the eventual normalisation of it all, through naming, through repetition, through time, the amalgamation of truth and legend, fact and fantasy, the signals of time and place, eventualised, more commercial versions of the Roswell

Incident, the Kennedy Assassination, the Moon Landings, the Day That…

Another drink? The temporary landlord asked as the bar fell into its late afternoon lull and the East Europeans dwindled until the night shift kicked off. He nodded, passed four of the local currency notes across the bar, and waited to sip his way through another pint of possibilities.

He'd only ever met passers-by here – the regulars he'd always noted and kept away from. For company there were other places to go where he'd find the right faces, acknowledge the greetings, and get on with the gossip, just like nothing had ever really gone on in the outside world, which was why it was such a perfect location.

***

J's Invisible Diary. Entry.

A life in the ordinary

The thing is, see, you have to make sure people know there is nothing special about those folks claiming they are top of the heap because they've managed to rip off others, or used them without respect to get there. There have to be ways to remind them about what they really stood for before they suppressed thoughts behind charades of celebrity, behind masquerading perfumes like the aroma of money, behind houses whose doors conceal basic behaviours, like those of everybody else. Whether you are running the cottage store or the country you still need to share, you still occasionally hanker after things you did before you got so big you weren't supposed to do them anymore. Well, not publicly. So you have to get people to realise again that folks really are no different, no better, and if they chase all the signs they think badge them as superior, then they'd better watch out, because if they start to believe in the outward signs they'll lose touch with themselves. And that's the crime.

If you lose touch with yourself you have no right to touch others.

Look at jealous old Nixon sneaking out of his office to go bowling in the executive building at the White House, trying to settle old scores, knocking down pins, letting the photographer know he was just a rooted guy down at the alley, him and the ball, relaxing. Look at Old LBJ taking an electric shave at the ranch, the unassuming grasp of the white heat of technology, an ordinary Joe keeping trim. Look at that little race to the helicopter with the daughter, the scooping up of the presidential pup, the walk around the grounds when you've just gone to war. And always someone, some invisible self, there to capture the

268

moment on camera, a life lived through pictures, with captions, Hey, he's just an ordinary little feller, a regular guy, really. Look, see for yourselves. And they were, but not in the way they meant.

***

Hey, you're the tops today. Look at that face. You know you really should do extra well today. The inner voice is checking itself. Reminding you of the dialogue you permit before launching the public you on the world, the variations on the scripts that say you always knew you deserved this, the little congratulations to remind you how good it feels to be there, in that position, as you check your looks again, for lines, for contours, tiny blemishes that the re-touchers themselves wouldn't even spot. My how good that smile's looking today, the one that keeps front pages company, the one that says the world's OK with me, what's with you, that keeps the other photos in the files, the ones the cameras snapped in your unguarded moments, lapses like when you stumbled on the aircraft steps. The ones they keep so they can crop tight and then blow up the details, the one that makes you look like the rabbit in the headlights that will be used to crown some story where you're not so sure, where the editors can go – look, a chink, formed from the links of words and pictures from totally separate contexts, brought together to make a dent in your personal and publicists' armour, wherever there's a call, when it starts to go downhill, when the desire for anonymity is outweighed by the demands of the crowds to see the star extinguished, the talisman broken, the one-time leader toppled.

But for you it's better to be forgiven than forgotten. What's the point in having made it this far if you can't keep reminding people why you so much deserved it in the first place, in a modern manner of speaking? Did that make sense, face?

You didn't get where you are today by reading self-help books. You made it by being the basis for them. And you can enjoy it too, for just a while, until the pyramid collapses and every fool is broken again, back to helping themselves to the nothing that's left when the hucksters have moved on to the next best thing, the next new thing.

The new fashion, the new film, the new sound, the new diet, the new holy grail, the new extra-terrestrials, the new stock, the new investment scheme, the new colour, the new destination, the new attitude, the new partner, the new reason why, the new threat, the feeling of newness every day in the calendar of the future, the race towards immortality everyone has to be ready for, giving it all our best look. And snippets of song come past and we all remember the world of tomorrow, remember the lyrics when we'd all be driving flying cars and have holiday homes on Mars.

The world seemed more innocent when there was only one enemy to notice, commies in other countries, unions at work, students on the streets, the other side at the game. But now threats could come from anywhere, the neighbour, the colleague, and no display signs. The enemy could be your family, giving great old names a chance to be noticed again, the resurrection of Borgias in the time it takes to eat a bagel, especially if you're a Taurean, born in the year of the pig, not yet fully actualised, or whatever this week's self-attainment flavour happens to be.

***

J remembered that time in Montreal. He'd met another leader, a Big Chief, only this time it was the real chief of an indigenous tribe. This one actually cared about his people, and had worked hard to get them out of a state dependency, which had so clearly fuelled others' descents into alcoholism, drugs and uncivil inertia. He had used their land proudly and conjoined Original Americans to technology, building digital pathways to a broader world. In only a few years, with micropayments and commissions on all kinds of transactions, the whole host of services had added up to quite a respectable pile, and he had freed all but the most addicted from their state of reservation, from their fetid fossilizing and their abandonment of hope. It was during one of their dinners, in the city, where he heard why the chief had done what he had done, and what drove him on.

In our tribe we believe we are judged by the seventh generation after us, so all we do is directed towards our progeny, towards our future, and if we do it well, we will be well remembered, and live on peacefully, expecting others to follow our example.

That was the moment. It was one of the missing insights. One of those little twists that changes destinies. He knew that 95% of his targets didn't care a hoot about generations down the line. Many of them only rose to the tops of their poles in their own short lifetime, racing away from humble parents or poor immigrant backgrounds, inventing their lives on the run, like some Soap stars with ever-more fanciful plotlines, and an interplay of characters with boundless capacities for birth, incest, and celebration, now under the tagline 'it

270

was all a dream'. These fulfillers of dreams felt they all commissioned the producers, writers, stories and casts themselves, and all destiny within their shining domain was down to them alone. If all serve you, it makes life so much easier to manage. You don't need to worry about subtleties and hierarchies. Those who don't know Who You Are have a whole host of their own troubles to manage.

At the heart of the matter was the fundamental indifference of these people to long-distance suffering, out of sight, out of mind, out of memory. Plastic poppies and flickering racing old footage of mud and horses, men in heavy coats, churned up landscapes, the overdubbing of hooves and artillery shells, the scenes of bodies piled up, living skeletons squatting by their side with shaved heads and hollow eyes. Lines of people thrown out of sky-high offices, clutching small cardboard boxes, clinging to the stapler that they thought held them on to a corporate life, the continuing pretence of normality, riding the train to nowhere after the doors had closed, too proud to share the troubles with those who depend on you, the shame of losing status granted by a faceless global corporation, yet one you had come to depend on.

In each case it took only two generations for the memories to mean little, to have any significance outside historical statistics, the league tables of the greatest killers known to man, from Alexander to Khan, Stalin to Mao, Hitler to Pol Pot, Slave Trading Companies, chemical companies, arms manufacturers, tobacco corporations, numbers assembled like American football figures, details about everything adding up to nothing. But just for a brief time – Warhol's fifteen minutes of fame, a day's worth of headlines, a weekend's worth of news analysis, pundits, letters, phone-ins, blogs, podcasts and general airwave stimulation – there would be attention, an after effect on a few, and that was all you were expected to count on any more. When one or two minutes' silence for remembrance were as common as the commonest things remembered, all you could do was try for a bigger headline, before the wonders of the next news story, the next disaster, the next distant diversion briefly took their place in the talent parade before your mind and its fleeting applause. So many people dead, for freedom, so some American songster can pronounce she likes most of the places she's been to but has never really wanted to go to Japan because she doesn't like eating fish and she knows they are popular out there in Africa, isn't that the same area anyways?

People were divided into those who craved wealth and fame and those who crusaded for causes, the second often leading on from the first. There was a time when singers entertained, and sang of love, of sadness, parting, joy, in all colours and flavours. Then it became necessary to sing about issues, to protest about anything from drugs to politics, war to sexual liberation, the smothering of large Big Bad military-industrial complexes, the ones who were so willing to advance huge fees to the performers who continued to castigate the very forms of capitalism they were the principal practitioners of, singing with an acoustic guitar under a solo spotlight – of the reasons why they didn't want a dead end job, jetting away in a private plane afterwards, the sea-shell echo of the applause of sixty thousand people mixing in with the racking up of turbo fans, another night on the road, the turbulence and displacement of the merchandised tour. When they tired of that, they watched TV and spotted something on the news they momentarily cared about, in Africa or South America, anywhere but home, and got caught up in causes – feeding the world, making poverty history, kicking ass at the courts of Davos, G8 summits, being embraced in photo-calls by presidents and popes, passing on their profundities in chat shows. There's no excuse.

Meanwhile the folks on the ground haven't a clue who these cause leaders are, and all they know is that there's the same old chance there ever was of money or aid or respect reaching them – none. And after the causes there's the great return to rock's roots, topical references to ailments or accidents, the studied anger and reflections that have been honed in the mirrors of the Eden Rock, the cash-only rock stars.

There were those who used books for centuries to support their version of the righteousness of causes. The Bible, The Koran, other codexes. The fights on their behalves continued to dominate the league tables of conflicts. J had been tempted to use the traditions straightforwardly as a springboard for action, and had succumbed to the temptation initially. One of the first creative sessions had led him to the view that it could be very useful to borrow signatures and identities from radical groups to craft particular responses to the plan. Still remember the early killings, allegedly from disgruntled Islamists? Taking out a number of women was one way of making a point to the West that there was no respect for the interpretations and teachings of the Qur'an.

The Koran, as some others call it, holds that men are the managers of the affairs of women ... for that God has preferred one of them over the other, and for that they expended of their property. Righteous women are therefore obedient, guarding the secret for God's guarding. And those you fear may be rebellious admonish, banish them to their couches, and beat them.

That was, for a brief flickering moment, one way of bringing some fundamentalist attitudes into the heartland of the West, and giving a new zest to the fundamentalist bashers. Who would expect to go and give the Taleban another kicking for their unequal ways? Anything other than face up to the real Homeland challenges, that had less to do with equality in a relationship than with a fuck-you attitude to everyone and everything, and that if a solution couldn't be obtained at a price, it wasn't worth considering. More than that though, it was a great way to test the robustness of his teams, and their loyalty, their honour. He knew plenty of people in the messy businesses who would feed off scenarios like this, but in the end he decided it would be too much of a distraction. You see, the problem wasn't really about them, it was about us.

***

J's Invisible Diary. Entry.

The ever hungry media and the addicted celebrity seekers feed each other's habits. There are still A-list folks simply lining up to get photographed in disaster areas, and, as one journalist put it, authenticate the existence of calamity. You have to keep your image and your existence afloat on top of the flood waters of disaster. All those artists are out there struggling to articulate what the more sober press has already covered in the front lines. This is triumphalism and the massively misplaced assumption that the ego's success in one area qualifies them as automatic experts in others. They'll be sending B & C list types out to minor disasters soon, as long as their smaller chartered craft can get in. So the stars' points of view radiate beyond their status, and we judge power and influence as triggers to action, to donations of time and sprinkles of stardust, until they turn to some other front and polish another facet of their character. And so patriotism gets eroded, national energies mired by local politics, cocking things up, arriving later and later like the legendary cavalry, blaming all around, while the beacons of brighter stars stand in the firmament, saying here's what needs to happen *NOW*, and flouncing off expecting there to be a sea of roadies to re-fix the stage on which they have just performed. All of this goes to help in the collusion of the dismissal of your country's heritage, a place too embarrassingly awful to be talked about in our selective sharing world.

But as Santayana said, a country without a memory is a country of madmen. Worse, memories, if there are traces of them at all, are being further manipulated. Soon it will be considered a crime to volunteer to

273

serve, unless it's corporately. What's different is that Christianity has shifted its ground. In the old days it was closer to Islam, but what remains today is no willingness to celebrate glory, to depict heroes as martyrs. Today's Christians try and say their faith is something other than successful violence for a cause. And it has nothing to say about the armies working for those other bodies that aren't nation-states but behave like them in so many ways – the corporations.

***

So you have to work hard – celebrity as hero only works if you keep a distance. The celebrity spies and their ironically covert cameras are dangerous iconoclasts. If you descend from the level of icon to that of mere entertainer you are criticised first and ostracised second, you trivialise your position, your exalted place. When you show yourself, or are revealed, as simply ordinary or human, your worshippers and adorers become angry over the loss, the relegation of their part in the extraordinary, the fantasy of being close to the star, of being one with it, of being it themselves. War heroes were once like that.

"There is little doubt among military commanders that the soldier who has the willingness to die and is not preoccupied with living, more than with doing his task of killing, is the best soldier – and if we survived, it was as madmen, never able to adapt to the peacetime world."

"Submergence of self for the good of the group eases the acceptance of death. It also achieves protective anonymity and the individual loses his sense of individual responsibility. That shift often creates a startling change in values and behaviour."

"We count for nothing. They use us to keep good things for themselves"

***

So, just like for all the others, the ones who came back, J held on to the best surprises. Until last. Serving your country or your company wasn't something people wanted to hear about after the millennium. The word serve was out of fashion. It left a nasty taste in the Pinot Noir, drew tense silences in expense account restaurants, provided dinner party debates on morals and values as long as the indecency of it all was kept at an acceptable distance. You went where? Messing with those poor people? You worked for who? That was all they gave you? You were

274

better off before.

What you became if you were temporarily or permanently finished was a fresh kind of internal enemy, best not seen, best ignored. If you were seen at all again, it was because you were re-called to clean up someone else's mess, to keep shovelling up the ashes when pockets of civilisation flamed up and reminded people of the fragility of their attempts to keep the beast at bay, or when some failing organisation needed some cheap temporary help. There were always signs, shelves of magazines, newspapers, reminding people every day of the statistics of success, the annual round of stories about squillion dollar dinners, the nerve-ending chase to having a seventh house in the Hamptons, the pursuit of luxuries you either couldn't display or which disappeared in a cloud of bouquets. It was a time when people would wait months for what they thought was a privilege, buying the exclusive gig for the twelve year old, continuing to drive demand.

People would queue up at nights to get their hands on things that were hyped for months, the midnight release of the game, the mobile device, so they could flash it around for hours before the media saturated it and you could buy a barely used model online. Others were so desperate to show their kids they were on top of it all they'd spend thousands to get and deliver the latest must-have piece to the altar of their child. How important it was for the little boys and the little girls to be cocooned from competition and protected from the potential labelling of 'loser' by being caught without gadget.

Meanwhile millions died around the world unable to reach the next level of any kind of playing, as they were still hard-wired into the basic game – survival. But J knew. There was no point being idealistic about any of this. Jesus. Even the Pope gets to feature in the style magazines wearing designer shades and upmarket watches, as if the House of God was some kind of couturier place where a misplaced sense of fashion would send you to the other place, a Sunday street market of cast-offs, the congregations of searchers looking for bargains that had taken the place of cold churches and colder services, another kind of business altogether, whose concept of delivery had somehow not quite hit its customer targets. And as another Krug or Crystal was sprayed around a city, 75cls of soft-porn bubbles covering other guilt, whether they liked it or not, someone was spraying larger volumes of blood around a differently stinking room in a booby-trapped house in the Middle East where, minutes before, another freedom fighter had been forewarned about the imminent visit of some dedicated group that was a supposed to be liberating the nation of conspirers.

But what was there to work out here? It was always like that. That was the point, the theme, the purpose. You were there to make sure the condensation on the champagne bottle could never be mistaken for the cold sweat of fear that kept bankers worried in untrustworthy havens, another bunch of rebels rooted out from their profane former temples.

The third part of the Message was ready. The Index was vibrant, the Lists were primed, the monitoring and research running accurately and secretly. People out there were being given the chance to put something back. Doing that would get them taken off the Lists, until they rescinded. The methods of displaying dissatisfaction had been tested, and not found to be wanting. Chasers and investigators were still trying to figure out links, find just one perpetrator, one piece of evidence, tangible, that would unravel the deep action.

In a short while, the succeeding generations of sons would be selected and taken out, no seventh generation to revere the selfish wealth amassers. It would all be too late then to go back – impossible even, so the time to think about the future, the blood-line, was now.

That way respect lies.

He laughed. Yes, J laughed when he thought about the old days. Just a little fantasy, about when the tyrants and animals that were the cream of the navy, when they were lavished with titles and rewards for their lately legitimised piracy, their thieving for the realm, their protecting of the states' interests. It was a laugh that the children of Captains of Industry, with their lands and their treats, had used to shape their bloodlines into new forms of symbol, signing their superiority over the ordinary land-bound folk around them. Go sail and kill a few Spaniards, cartooned to dusky fearful excesses, bring home a large amount of theoretically tradable booty. Even better, fight off a bunch of clods in poor boats, officially, on behalf of His or Her Royal Whatever, and get made. Make sure it's romanticised en route, you don't want blood contaminating the look of the diamonds. But there you are, the dashing and derring-do of mercenaries, all cool until you get caught, when the world slips into denial.

Deniability. The Deniability Corporation. Another world for first-world nation states. First World. What kind of arrogance is that? First at what? Global fuck-ups?

Cue: *"Respect"*

***

That was the beginning. The rest Follows.

www.ingramcontent.com/pod-product-compliance
Lightning Source LLC
Chambersburg PA
CBHW021005260626
47169CB00006B/1953